Stuart trained as a teacher and has recently retired after 37 years in school. His family keep him very busy, travelling the country, supporting their many activities. He still loves sport and his Napoleonic passion started when he was taken to see the film *Waterloo*!

Dedication

For Mum and Dad, who inspired a love of stories.

Stuart Fox

A DANGEROUS HOUR FOR ENGLAND

AUSTIN MACAULEY PUBLISHERS™

LONDON • CAMBRIDGE • NEW YORK • SHARJAH

A CIP catalogue record for this title is available from the British Library.

ISBN 9781788239189 (Paperback)
ISBN 9781788239196 (E-Book)

www.austinmacauley.com

First Published (2018)
Austin Macauley Publishers Ltd™
25 Canada Square
Canary Wharf
London
E14 5LQ

Chapter 1

The warmth of the sun still spread its blanket across the land as the sky flamed orange and red behind the low hills across the valley. As carefully as Fin trod, it seemed that the sound of the beech nuts crunching underfoot would sound the alarm to the game-keeper, who he knew would be patrolling this coppice to ensnare any would-be poacher. In fact, it was a surprise that he hadn't seen 'Old Spiky', so called because of the short wiry bristles that seemed to protrude from every possible part of his head; he was so regular in his rounds and determined to protect the birds for the shooting party that had been arranged for the next day when many of the most important personages of the county would descend upon the Hall at the invitation of Lord and Lady de Lacy.

Fin had taken the precaution of unstringing his bow and carefully keeping the bowstring folded inside a leather pouch in his pocket. Grandfather had taught him well not to get caught in tree branches as you ventured into places where you ought not to be. The weapon may have been outdated and replaced by flintlocks but it was still accurate, and it could release more arrows, many more than a musket could fire bullets in a minute. But most of all, it was silent.

There was a trace of woodsmoke in the air. Fin had taken care to be down-wind of any likely prey and knew that the only dwelling that could have provided this aroma, that he loved so well, was the Smith's cottage and workplace. Fin thought it strange that in the village there was one family that needed no introduction: the Smiths, the whole family, were the people to go to, for all metal work! Whether a horseshoe, a cartwheel rim or even some elaborate gates for the Great House, Will was your man, ably assisted by his wife, Jane. George, who was old as Fin but as strong as an ox, and huge! Most of all, Fin knew the smithy so well because of Betsy, beautiful Betsy, the terror of all the boys in the village; face of an angel, hair the colour of ripened wheat and, in spite of living in a smithy, the most delicate hands that were forever getting into mischief! Fin had often wondered how long the family had been workers of metal or for that matter whether you had to do what your name said. It was the same for the Shearers, the Dyers or the Tanners, you just knew what they did to earn a living. So what had happened to him and his family? He was a Ross, what did a Ross do?

Fin was jolted from his amusement by a rustling in the branches, a little way ahead and almost on the edge of the coppice. He couldn't see anything, and he was worried that his scent had drifted to alert someone, or something, of his presence. He carefully edged forward, stepping as lightly as possible, then froze as the branches tossed in the air, raining hazel nuts to the floor. It had been a good summer and although he shouldn't be here for his intended purpose, he also knew that all of the village would be allowed to scavenge and glean the hazel and chestnuts that would be in plentiful supply. Lord de Lacy had tried to look after the people; he just didn't want his sport spoiled, or that of his guests. Fin edged further forward. He used a track that was seldom used, except for the animals that made their home here. He felt it strange that in times of increased risk the senses seemed to develop extra power: the drifting woodsmoke from the Smiths had to be at least half a mile away, the rustling had been at least forty paces, two cricket pitches (the game Fin loved), away when he had first heard it. What was causing it? As the shower of nuts settled, Fin could see two horses, loosely tied by their reins to the lower branches of a large beech tree. There was no sign of the riders and Fin closed the gap stealthily. One horse, a beautiful chestnut coat with a mane and tail as black as the tar he had used to waterproof his father's coracle, he knew well. It was from the Great House, Master Robert had taken it when he left for his regiment, so he must be back, but where was he? However, the second horse was more unusual, a stunning grey with a dappled pattern on its hind quarters, with all four legs having the appearance of black socks or stockings from hoof to knee, but it was the saddle furniture that intrigued Fin. He had never seen anything like it but he had heard about them; it was a ladies' saddle to avoid the rider having to ride astride the horse. The seat was obvious but there was only one stirrup, for the left foot Fin guessed as it was on the left flank of the horse, and then an unusual upward facing leather padded stirrup shape at the front of the saddle. Fin was intrigued with the shape – he would have loved to have tried it out for the fun of it – but, more importantly, he had to assess how much risk he had put himself against, by coming tonight. His grandfather had always told him that he was far too nosey and he should keep out of other people's business. He knew he would have told him to leave the coppice and return home, but Fin just had to know more. Who had Master Robert brought here, and where were they now?

The horses were happy where they were, grazing where they could find the sweet new shoots of the little grass that survived the shade of the interlocking branches of the beech trees forming the boundary with the adjoining field packed with wheat chest high and ready for harvest. Fin decided that he could afford to explore a little further. He stayed off the main path, but he knew that he was headed for the bird pen. Ducking the lowest branch of the hazel, he could hear faint voices. He was close enough to the bird pen to see that a protective net had been placed around the wattle fence and across the top: it appeared that a fisherman had cast from the sky and captured a catch, the like of which Reverend Green taught about in church. But these were birds not fish!

Why couldn't he see the owners of the voices? Fin decided that he could skirt the pen and search from the far side, more risky as he could disturb the birds, but he had to know. He had only gone a quarter of the perimeter when a flash of crimson caught his eye. As he studied it closely, he could see that it was the crumpled jacket of an infantry officer. The contrast between the pea-green cuffs and the jacket sleeve was stark – you could never be a poacher in that, Fin smiled to himself. Next to the jacket was a corn-flower blue bonnet, a striking feather faintly fluttering against its fastening, under a ribbon, a much darker blue, perched like a protecting hen sheltering its chicks. One more step to the left… there they were! Master Robert had his back to Fin and the little he could see of the lady – and there was no doubt that this was a lady – captured his heart. Betsy was beautiful but this lady was dazzling. The careful hair setting of ringlets, the specially fitted riding clothes that complimented the blue of the bonnet, down to the gloved fingers protruding over Master Robert's shoulders – this was unlike any woman Fin had ever seen. He stood transfixed but uncomfortable that he was intruding at a time that he shouldn't be watching. The fingers disappeared from the shoulders but her eyes never left Master Robert's face. Those eyes sparkled but also showed that they were in control and not Master Robert. Fin could hear her voice but not make out the words. It didn't sound like the language he knew but he could plainly hear Master Robert say, "But why?" The only reply was her gloved finger to his lips and "Shh", followed by further whisperings. Whatever she had said or done had an immediate effect and Master Robert reached out for the tree trunk as if he was about to fall. Fin decided it was time that he should be gone so he retreated with the image of the most gorgeous creature imprinted on his heart.

He left the coppice empty-handed. *A night wasted? No,* Fin thought to himself. He had discovered a beautiful lady and she had taken a power over him. Perhaps he would never see her again, but as he gazed at a leaf imperceptibly moving along the current of the brook that edged the southern edge of the village, he was alerted to a noise of horses, and as he turned, he saw two riders silhouetted against the dusk cantering towards the manor, one man, one woman.

"I see'd you Fin."

Fin twisted to see 'Old Spiky' not more than five paces from him. Where had he come from?

"I see'd you and I foll'ed you. I know who you saw and what you saw but as you took nothing, I let you be. But I'm warning you that if you take what 'in't yo'rs, then ther'll be 'ell to pay. And I don't mean just them birds, Fin. I see'd the way you were looking. You'd best be out of it and back home. You shouldn't ha' been there. We see'd things that are best forgotten, best forgotten." With that, he turned and was gone. How he could be there one moment and then disappear, Fin did not know, but 'Old Spiky' was famous for it, and Fin would love to be able to do the same!

Fin trudged back home wondering what 'Old Spiky' had meant. As he lifted the latch to the weather-beaten door, he heard his father, "Any luck Fin?"

"Not tonight Dad. Got interrupted."

Fin's dad twisted his head. "Who by? Old Spiky?"

"No, not sure who it was. Most likely people from the big house riding. Mind you Dad, there's going to be great heaps of hazel and chestnuts – the branches are creaking under the weight."

"That's true, and tomorrow there'll be a great harvesting of birds! We're up sunrise and have to get ready to beat the birds out onto the lower meadow so that his Lordship and his friends can have some fun... never know, we might even be given something for helping!"

Chapter 2

Breakfast had been a chunk of bread torn from the loaf dipped in the remains of a stew Fin's mother had cooked yesterday, but it had also been a hot cup of tea sweetened with honey collected by Fin himself from the hives near the smithy. He loved his tea as did his father; they had tried stewing leaves from the local trees, but it wasn't the same and made Fin feel sick. He had been told that it came from India when the army had driven out the French but for a young man who had rarely been away from his own village, it meant very little: he knew it was a very long way over the seas but he had only ever been in his family's coracle, the strange oval craft that was light enough to carry and allowed them to fish on the larger river.

Mist covered the river meadows – Fin and his father drew their coats tighter round them as they made their way to the coppice. The bark of a fox alerted them to a weary hunter returning home looking bedraggled – perhaps it had tried to jump the brook but slipped? Fin was used to the rhythms of the year and knew autumn would soon be here: the first signs of leaves turning to the flaming colours before being pulled from their branches by stiff breezes, had already started. The fox glanced their way without stopping and disappeared through the hedge that Fin and his father had helped create by splitting branches and laying them entwined. It may have created a solid boundary for the livestock, but it was not a problem for the nocturnal scavenger.

Within eighty paces they emerged from the shrouded valley and the only visible sign of their village was the broken tower of St Stephen's church, once the focal point for every Sunday and every big celebration in the year, but long since derelict, which was the reason that Fin, with every other member of the village, had to walk a mile or so to the church of St Cuthberga in Wimborne instead. The incline was not great but now they were out of the mist, they soon became warm in the early sun and opened their jackets. Walking straight along the ride – no need for hiding this morning – they were

11

soon in sight of the bird pens. Fin noticed that part of the netting had been withdrawn and there was a section of the pen without birds.

"Morning Tom, morning master Fin." Old Spiky had done it again, appearing at their side as if an invisible door had opened. "Had trouble sleeping, Master Fin?" he asked with a wink and a nudge into Fin's ribs with his elbow. "The others are all yonder by the great chestnut tree. Well, all except you two and master George – he's nipped back to bring back some old pots and pans before Will gets to mendin' 'em."

The sound of muffled clanking announced the return of George Smith, carrying a large sack over his shoulder. "You daft bugger," scolded Old Spiky, "we don't want the birds flying yet."

George slowed his pace and put his free hand up in apology. "You young'uns are daft as a brush." Old Spiky muttered as he made his way around the bird pens and off towards the others.

Fin knew that the meeting place was a minute away and duly followed, allowing his father to lead the way and hoping to meet George on the other side of the pens. As he passed the simple hut that Old Spiky used to store the few simple tools that he needed in the coppice, as well as ropes and nets, Fin noticed a glinting amongst the husks of fallen hazel nuts. He quickly glanced round to see if anyone was watching, bent low without breaking stride and picked up a small ring, so tiny that he knew it would not have fitted any of his fingers. Perhaps it was because it was early but it took a few steps before Fin realised that it was the exact spot that he had seen Master Robert and the lady the night before. "What you got ther'?" called George as they closed the gap between.

"Nothing, just picking a hazel nut to chew on."

"Don't you be daft, Fin, you'll get stomach cramps and then you'll have the –"

Fin interrupted before George could be more explicit. "Just to chew then spit out, don't you remember what Old Spiky told us, when he was in the wars and had nothing to drink? They tried a pebble in the mouth, so I thought I'd try a nut."

"Don't you go believing everything he says, and if you be wanting a drink... here."

George held a canteen, a simple wooden drum as wide as the span of a hand, held by two metal rims which had a metal ring to take the rope that allowed George to sling it over his shoulder. He had pulled the wooden stopper covered with leather for a better seal. Fin tipped the drum and allowed the liquid to fill his mouth, instantly spitting it back out. George was bent double laughing. Fin's father turned to see what the commotion was.

"Sorry dad, I think George is trying to poison me." His father took the drum and smelled it.

"Where d'you get this George, and does your father know?"

"Well, not exactly does he know, but he was given a barrel as payment for some work he did."

"I'm guessing this came ashore without the Excise men knowing, knowing George and Will. Best keep it well hidden. Don't you be giving this to anyone today or there'll be trouble. Now come on, we've work to do."

Old Spiky was at the centre of a wide semi-circle giving instructions; every family in the village had someone there, familiar faces. "Now young George has brought some pots and pans to bang so that the birds will fly up for the shooters. They'll 'ave dogs with 'em so no chasin' after any that fall. We stay in line and makes our way through this section of the coppice down through the meado' towards the ha-ha – that's that ditch in front of his Lordship's fancy garden. They have set up shooting points and the Militia are stationed to reload the guns for our guests – we don't want anyone having an accident, do we?"

The group smiled at the thought of having someone doing a simple task for them. "We will go slow and easy and the signal to start will be some sort of explosive rocket that one of the guests is demonstrating to his Lordship. Don't see the point of rockets in daylight. I did see rockets at the County Fayre once, but tha' was at the end of the day and they made pretty patterns in the night sky. So, Fin…" Fin paid more attention, "You go down that ride there and when you see the signal, come back to me 'ere. The rest of you will start stretchin' yourselves out down this path on the right and Dick Tanner, you go to the edge of the coppice at the end of the line."

Fin made his made way along the broad path indicated for him, his mouth still stinging and his stomach gurgling from whatever the liquid had been in George's drum. Brandy, he guessed from what his father had said but he had never tasted it before, only had beer or apple cider and he wished he could get rid of the taste. It was about half a mile to the edge of the coppice by this path and Fin made himself comfortable leaning against one of the boundary beeches gazing towards the splendour that was his Lordship's country house. Easily the grandest home that Fin had ever seen, he had never set foot inside, but he had been to the stables and one of them was almost as big as his home! The meadow stretched down the same slight incline that he had walked with his father earlier; the traces of mist holding tight to the brook had gone and in the distance he could see small figures in red coats spread across the lip of the ha-ha. Fin counted along and saw eight pairs of men working at a stake. He had seen these shooting parties before: each guest would shoot from different points along the line to make it as fair as possible. It wouldn't be good for a guest to have no birds to shoot, would it? Fin noted that a different group, this time in blue jackets, were setting up to one side of the men in red and a good distance back. It was difficult to see from here but it looked like a large tripod set up and Fin was intrigued to know what it was.

Fin shifted position and his leg caught against something, the ring in his pocket. He took it out and examined it more closely. It was very small for his fingers, but it had to be owned by the lady from last night. It was smooth, but embedded in the golden metal were five tiny sparkles. Fin had never seen anything so delicate: the rings he had seen were simple bands of metal or large hoops for carts and horse harnesses. A sudden squealing and swooshing made Fin cower down and then a huge almighty explosion erupted in the morning sky. Birds flustered, sheep bleated and ran, and Fin slowly emerged to see the remains of a dirty smear fading against the blue sky, drifting slowly on the same breeze that had helped shift the mist. So that must have been the signal. Why had he been sent here – surely the whole of the village would have heard it? Fin wondered if the whole of the county would have heard it. Glancing back toward the house, Fin noticed a few men in red coats had slipped into the ha-ha ditch and others were trying to get them to clamber up the wall. The guests were making their way towards their stations and Fin must go to his.

Chapter 3

"What on earth was tha'?" George asked as Fin came to his point in the line, ten paces away.

"Some damn fool's idea of a signal, scared the life out of me."

"Ready to drive?" Old Spiky shouted down the line and then took a pace glancing both ways to ensure everyone had taken note. The canopy grown over the spring and summer meant that the brambles were not as thick as on the edge but there were still growls and shouts as a beater got caught with a tear to his breeches or smock. As planned, the birds scuttled ahead and it wasn't too long before they emerged into the meadow. The grass fluttered in the growing breeze as the warmth of the sun had taken effect but amid the rich green, appeared brilliant blues, yellows, reds and pure whites of the flowers so frequently collected by Fin and his friends, in the hope of gaining favour with the girls of the village. Soon they would be decorating the tables and garlanding the barn as they celebrated harvest.

"Slowly on," Old Spiky was in command of the line and he had purposely held back to allow the ends to extend forward and shape like the horns of cattle that grazed by the river. Fin noticed that the birds hopped forward but didn't fly and wondered how the Lord's guests would get any sport from this and more worryingly, would any of them be daft enough to shoot level and risk hitting the drivers? They were still three fields away from the shooting party and Fin heard the popping of guns, not at any birds he knew.

Must be someone teaching a novice – that's all we need, he thought.

It was a bit like a family stroll to church, not too much of a rush and everyone keeping their own thoughts without conversation. The occasional bang of sticks on metal drove birds into the air but it wasn't until they had reached the latest of Fin and his father's hedge boundaries that Old Spiky asked for the halt. Everyone was called to get through the gate and it was comical to note birds roosting peacefully amongst the branches. "Knock those birds off as you come along – no good them staying here. Take the same positions for the last drive."

Old Spiky chivvied the laggards into position with the cheery news, "Don't worry, lads – we've got to go back and do this again after the first shoot! Now make some noise and get these birds flying. We'll be in range soon enough."

A cacophony of sounds drove the birds into the air and a number of bangs met them. Fin's father called across, "Only a rifle will hit at this range, musket won't be any use till we're half way across." Fin glanced ahead and could see the red-coated figures handing guns to some of the shooting party, but more importantly he noted the smaller figure of a woman with a gun in hand raise it to her shoulder and shoot, handing the weapon to the red-coat and taking the next without taking her eyes off the field and prospective targets. The wiser birds, as far as Fin thought, had flown to the limits of the line of drivers but most simply went headlong towards the shooting party. By the time the line had crossed the field and were at the foot of the slope of the sheep pasture that ended at the ha-ha, dogs had collected and returned over two dozen birds, when suddenly the same swoosh and squealing noise from earlier in the morning erupted, with a fine line of smoke heading straight towards the drivers. Fin had seen this from the edge of the coppice but at less than one hundred paces, it was a terrifying sight and sound. All of the drivers ducked or lay flat as the same explosion from earlier left the dirty smudge in the sky.

As he rose to his feet, Fin glanced towards George and then his father to check they were still all right. "Be the work of the devil that." It was Old Spiky appearing from nowhere again. "Anyone would think they'd be trying to kill somebody." Clear laughter from the shooting party could be heard and the shooters pointed towards the drivers getting to their feet. "Thought they would wave a flag to end the shoot, not another one of them rockets!" grumbled Old Spiky glaring towards the House.

Two riders appeared cantering towards the drivers, the same two riders Fin had seen the night before, different clothes, but the same horses and the same riders. Old Spiky called the line together and emphasised "Mind your manners now, Master Robert is coming our way." He turned and took off his woollen bonnet. Fin thought it was the first time he had ever seen Old Spiky without his head covered and he smiled at the way the grey bristles matched those on his chin! Almost as if he could tell, Old Spiky turned and, to Fin it seemed like he spoke directly to him, repeated, "Mind your manners, hats off." As if on parade, all raised their hands and took off their head gear. The two riders were within hailing distance now. Fin still thought her to be the most captivating woman he had ever seen, when Old Spiky welcomed them. "Good mornin', Master Robert and your Ladyship. I 'ope you were successful with the shoot?" his voice intoned, inviting a reply. Master Robert drew his mount to a walk and replied;

"Many thanks to you all, we have had a splendid shoot. I bagged three but Lady Ellen got four!" Old Spiky turned his head, winked and nodded so the group cheered.

"You are all too kind, you drove so many my way that I couldn't have missed, it was like shooting at the proverbial barn door!" Master Robert burst into fits of laughter rocking in his saddle and the drovers joined in.

"Well my good men," Fin hated it when Sir Robert spoke to them like this; he had done so since he was old enough to ride and it grated against Fin's independent streak. "Father, his Lordship (*As if we didn't know it,* thought Fin) has said that there is no need for another shoot today: We have had enough sport and some, don't you know, could spend all day and wouldn't hit a thing! So you can all go back to your own work." With that he turned his horse and started to walk away.

Lady Ellen was close to Fin but George was between him and the horse. Fin levered George aside causing him to growl, "What you doing Fin?" but Fin was staring at Lady Ellen while fumbling in his pocket. The commotion made her turn her head and Fin took his chance. There were a few steps between her and the rest of the men, none of whom had replaced their hats, except Old Spiky, and Master Robert was already ten paces away. Fin summoned up his courage. He had never spoken to a real Lady, he found it hard enough to talk to girls in the village. "Your ladyship, I found this in the coppice, I thought it might be yours?" He held the ring in the palm of his hand reaching up towards. She was even more stunning than he had imagined last night.

"Where did you say you found this?" she took the ring examining it with gloved fingers.

"In the coppice, your ladyship. I saw you last night, and this morning when I saw it, I thought it had to be yours."

"So you saw me last night, did you? With, Sir Robert?"

Fin blushed and lowered his hand quickly as if he had touched the hot kettle on the fire. "You were there? I lost it when I removed my gloves, we both searched but couldn't find it. This is wonderful,"

17

and without halting turned her head towards Sir Robert, "Robert, come back. This young man has found what I lost."

Sir Robert reined in his horse, turned his head and seeing Fin so close to lady Ellen spun the horse and rode straight back, clods of earth flying as he came to a halt.

"What's the meaning of this Ross, get away from Lady Ellen – you do not speak to a Lady unless asked to." The horse almost pushed Fin over but he regained his feet, slowly backing away towards the other drovers.

"No Robert, he has done me a great service, he has found the ring my father gave me, I thought it lost."

Sir Robert was not listening, "What were you doing in the coppice last night, poaching I daresay."

Fin protested, "No Master Robert, I didn't take anything."

"Only because you saw us, or perhaps you were spying on me."

"No, no I wasn't spying."

"He were with me preparing the birds for the shoot Master Robert." It was Old Spiky.

Master Robert turned in the saddle, "I don't believe you, and why have you got your hat on in our presence and the presence of Lady Ellen?" Old Spiky slowly raised his hand, his eyes never leaving those of Sir Robert.

"Beg pardon, your Ladyship."

"Now Ross, I am going back to get the Militia and have you arrested. You were trespassing last night and if not poaching, you were spying, Sam Wood (Old Spiky's real name) is trying to cover for you. You men, keep him here!" Sir Robert turned his horse and ordered "Come Ellen!" riding back towards the House.

Lady Ellen did not follow. "Ross, is that your name?" she was looking directly at Fin, "I am most grateful. You have found something that was irreplaceable, but you have also angered Sir Robert, who is being most pompous as many young gentlemen seem to be. I am in your debt and would like you to take this. If I can repay you, I will, but now I must return to the House." She expertly spun her horse shouting over her shoulder, "If I were you, I would disappear – you will have good head start against these Militia!" And Fin did, shoving the small card into his jacket pocket as he ran with all of the drovers back towards the coppice.

Chapter 4

Running up the incline through the long meadow grass wasn't as easy as Fin needed. He knew that time was going to be vital and every step he could gain upon the Militia now would serve him well later in the day. An advantage of being outside and occupied in manual labouring was that it had made most of the men from the village reasonably fit and they reached the screen provided by the beech boundary to the coppice well grouped.

"Fin!" It was his father's voice and he stopped and turned. "Whatever Master Robert has got against you, this is no place for you now." They both continued to walk through the trees, straight along the main ride that would bring them to the main junction of rides. "You can't be coming home either." Fin stopped and his father put a reassuring hand on his shoulder. "Look son, you have to get away from here. Master Robert won't let it drop – you know him well enough. The first place they look for you will be our home. You must get to the river, take the coracle we hid at Cowgate where the cattle ford. I'll send you some things and then you must head down river to the coast."

George butted in, "I'll bring 'em to you Fin."

"No George, they know what friends you are; best you take a stroll in the other direction, you never know, they might just follow you."

"Right Mister Ross, I'll take a bag up to Badbury Rings to make it look like I'm going to help him get away." George gave Fin a hug, his eyes glistening. "Take care of yourself." He turned and was gone, taking the right fork for the shortest way to the smithy.

By the time they had reached the far side of the coppice the plan had been made, Fin clasped his father more tightly than he had ever done. "Sorry dad."

"Don't be daft son. Don't forget, when you get there, ask for Tom, just Tom, no captain or anything. He'll get you busy!" Splitting apart, Fin watched his father for a brief moment as he took the beaten track towards home. Fin had hoped he would turn for one

19

final glimpse but he didn't. What Fin would have seen were streams of tears making a course through the wrinkles of a weather-beaten face, dripping through the black stubble of an unshaven face and onto his working smock. He was not flinching to wipe them in case he alarmed his son. Master Robert had a lot to answer for.

Fin raced as fast as he could towards the old mill. Before he could see the three-storey building, he could hear the paddles churning as the power of the water forced the wheel round, generating the energy needed to drive the cogs that would turn the grindstones and make the flour for the community. As he turned the bend, he clung into the shade of the overhanging branches of the ancient oak trees. They had been cleared from the mill to provide a courtyard for the wagons to load and unload, a big enough rectangle to allow carts with two draught horses to turn with ease, but on this side of the road, before the slope started to rise towards the village, there was plenty of cover. Fin knew the family of millers but the last thing he could do was to allow him-self to be seen. Slipping from tree to tree, checking each time that no one had come out of the mill, Fin managed to evade detection and move downstream. The creaking of the wheel axle grated on his teeth and he knew there would be someone given the job of greasing it, a smelly and onerous task, as bad as mixing the daub for the wattle in the wall of his house; you had the stench with you for days, it made him reach just thinking of it!

Listening as intently as he could, now that he was out of earshot of the mill, Fin scanned the road in both directions. His father never left the coracle in the same place twice – you never knew who might have wanted to use it as well– but for the last ten days it had been carefully covered in the osier beds, an area that was used in the same way as the coppice to harvest hazel, but this time in wetland areas for willow. The willow would never grow too tall but tethered to get maximum height in the shortest growing period, the branches had been used in many village workshops. He had also seen some willow left to grow specifically for his beloved cricket, carved bats were much sought after, but he didn't know when he would next play. It was too early for the osier beds to be harvested so Fin was confident that he would not meet anyone there; nevertheless, he walked in a crouch below the line of the hedge to ensure that his silhouette was not visible. Reaching the end of the track, he took great care in lifting the wattle panel that barred entry into the beds. Keeping to the edge, he made his way along the hedge line to a place that looked a mass of entwined hawthorn, alder, birch, willow and hazel branches, with a few brambles and ivy for good measure, but this was the exact spot where he and his father had created one of their hiding places for their boats. The other coracle – two always best for fishing with a net strung between whilst the oarsmen controlled the boat one handed – was across the river in a similar hedge.

Based upon a small wattle panel, they had trained the branches to grow through the gaps that they had deliberately left but, by taking his knife and cutting away some troublesome ivy and weeds at ground level, Fin was able to lift the panel to retrieve his means of escape. *Not now,* he thought, *I must hide myself and wait till dusk, no point being seen on the river.* He didn't need to look around, he knew where he would go: the massive willow that had been left to grow on the bank of the river and whose branches reached the surface as a mother tickling a baby. He had hidden there before and he knew that if he climbed well into the branches, no passer-by would spot him. He just had to sit and wait.

The sun had slipped behind the distant hills but the moon was not illuminating the meadows yet, Fin hoped it would stay that way. He didn't know what time it was but he knew he would only travel at night, down the Stour and onto Christchurch where he would try to find Tom. He had never met him before, but his father had, and Fin knew that there were questions better left unasked, so trusted this man to be someone to help him.

A faint scurrying sound drew his attention to the willow reeds below. Something or someone was searching through the wispy saplings. Screwing his eyes to make the most of the little light left in the day he was sure he could see a cloaked figure, a small figure peering about the beds. Carefully, taking the knife from its sheath on his belt, he started to ease himself out of the branches. His legs felt a bit numb from the long wait sitting in the branches but he was soon on the ground and creeping to the far end of the beds. The figure was coming back towards him so he crouched at the side of the tree entirely in the darkest shadow. As the figure crept forward to just a large stride in front of him, he pounced, knocking them to the ground and landing heavily on top of the small body. "Get off Fin you daft thing – we got no time for cuddlin' with you needin' to escape." It was Betsy, George's sister, "It's a good job I'm used to rough and tumble with George or you may 'ave 'urt me!" Fin felt a broad smile fill his face and could see Betsy grinning from ear to ear whilst dusting herself down. "Just look at this cloak. Mother won't be pleased with you, but she ain't the only one, is she? What did you do Fin, somethin' wicked I guess – it 'as to be to 'ave the Militia after you."

"Betsy, I've no time for explanations and you have to get home. Thanks for coming but we both have to be gone."

"Here you are, it's not much, a bit of bread, cheese and a drink wrapped up in some old clothes George doesn't wear. You make sure you come back Fin, come back." Then she turned and in the same crouch made her way back up to the entrance.

Fin made his way back to the hiding place, lifted the screen enough to slide the boat out, looped his arm under the seat and up onto his shoulder, making sure he had his bundle and paddle in the other hand, and retraced his steps to the great willow, this time lowering himself down the bank to stand, shin-deep, in the river. Swinging the boat onto the surface of the water, he silently dropped his bundle, steadied the edges with as wide a grip as possible, placed one boot into the foot of the boat then, with a motion that pushed him into the gentle current, lifted himself onto the seat keeping low to steady himself before daring to make his first tentative paddle stroke.

Chapter 5

Fin had taken to paddling the coracle with ease. His grandfather had taught him the figure of eight pattern, catching the water with the broad paddle just ahead of the hazel woven lip dipping to the surface of the river as pressure on the paddle increased. Fin had also helped make this boat. He knew each hazel and willow branch had been carefully selected, he had helped stretch the cow hide across the completed frame, and he had held his breath as he brushed each glutinous stroke of tar to waterproof the boat. They were the only family with such a craft in the village (probably the only one in the county), hence the need for a safe hiding place. His grandfather had been the instructor for building and for rowing; he had learned from his time when he had spent time in the Welsh Borders as a shepherd. But grandfather had died five winters since, and it was for his son, Fin's father and then Fin himself to continue the tradition. Excellent for fishing – it rippled the surface so little – and everyone knew it was the Ross family out on the river, so, Fin was extra cautious as he started his escape.

He had listened to his father and wasn't going to try to get to Christchurch in one night, even though he thought that he could, but he would paddle till the first glimmer of the lightening sky in the east and find a safe hideout. He was sure that, heading east along the Stour River, he would easily notice the day awakening.

The first obstacle that he would need to overcome was Wimborne. He knew the outline of the Minster, the church of St Cuthberga, the towers taller than the surrounding oak trees, and he was pleased that he could take the wide meander to avoid the town centre. He could see a bright glow in windows that surprised him how much light spread from such a small source. Only once did he see the comical dance of a hovering light, alarming at first but soon explained – a lantern held on a pole as a late-night reveller was making his way across the fields back towards his own village.

He had navigated his way through the quicker flowing parts of the river, avoided those white water warnings of a stone or larger below the surface ready to tip him out. For the most part he stayed close into the bank, the occasional willow causing him to duck low and miss the tangling branches. He smiled as he glided past two men pulling in a net, the sort of net that you could leave in the river tethered to a branch or a stake, a net with two legs like breeches but with no space to put your legs through. He knew the owner of the large house on the hill would not be happy to have these night fishermen here but he also knew that the two men would not welcome him knowing that they had been there. Fin watched as they emptied the catch of three fish, knocked each one with a wooden cudgel and threw them onto the bank before replacing the trap and scrambling back onto the bank. They were oblivious to their silent observer and Fin resumed a slow and rhythmical paddle-stroke propelling him further away from home.

He hadn't noticed the lightening of the sky, too intent was he to avoid anyone seeing him steering his way as close to the bank as he could, but it was the disturbed heron taking flight that made him look up and realise that he must find a place for the day. He had cleared several wide meanders and stopped paddling to take in the opportunities of each bank. The current was strong enough that he needn't pull any further, simply guiding the boat with the paddle as a rudder. He wanted to clear the bridge at Long Ham before finding his safe haven and allowed the boat to steer into the mid-stream. As he closed on the structure, Fin was greatly impressed by the arches with their pointed cutwaters diverting water and any debris though the arches; he steered away from the bank as larger tree branches, even tree trunks, were known to block the river. Not a person came into view, no alarms were sounded and Fin resumed his stroke to reach the next bend. Two streams, one from each bank joined the main course of the river giving extra impetus to the craft and, after successfully negotiating a slalom of rocks, he allowed the boat to drift into the eastern bank. Slowly pulling himself past the sheer earth bank rising above, he spotted the place he wanted and with two more powerful strokes, he had nestled against rushes the height of a man.

Tentatively, he put one foot into the shallow water and lifted himself out stretching his back before grounding the other foot. Careful not to break the reeds and rushes – Fin did not want anyone to know of his landing, he lifted the lightweight craft and created his best impression of a swan's nest by taking any loose rushes, reeds and leaves to cover the boat. He then made his way to the river bank and pulled himself up. He had never been here before but he had been in a place like it, Badbury Rings.

This was Dudsbury Rings and overgrown as it was, no longer inhabited, it was ideal for Fin's purpose. He knew that the banks looming above would have been cut out of the landscape by hand and that the large gap he had landed in would not have been there, but neglect and changes to the way people lived had made this once secure fortress into a redundant target for nature's recapture. Fin was impressed by the ditch and bank earthworks, and with trees and bushes having been left to grow, he soon found a well concealed spot. Looking up through the trees, even with the first light of dawn chasing the night away, he could recognise the stars of the Plough and Orion. So much hard work on the land and the great hunter close together, how appropriate it was that he should be the labourer being tracked down, but not caught yet!

Fin found the best cover within the branches of the trees growing on the outermost ring overlooking the river, allowed himself a chunk of bread torn from the quarter loaf that Betsy had brought, half of the cheese and a mouthful of the watery beer from the small flask and surprised himself by how tired he felt. Although his father had wrapped the file and flint with the bread and cheese to allow him to create the spark for a fire, he daren't give away his hiding place. He was convinced that a red coated soldier would appear at any moment – if only he knew that they had followed George on the way to Badbury Rings and wasted their time searching there, then perhaps he would have slept more peacefully but he soon drifted into a fitful sleep, waking some hours later, aware that it was still light in spite of the thick cover of branches above him. The ground was a lattice of shadows as the rays of the sun cast their pattern through the branches. Fin noticed a magical leaf, suspended in mid-air, dancing on an unseen thread from a spider's web. His stomach rumbled and he quickly finished the bread and cheese realising that he would be of little use without the energy to get down the river. The only sign of life was a squirrel darting across branches and then down tree trunks scurrying to hide a store of nuts for winter. Fin wondered how the creature ever found them again, there seemed no way of marking each treasure hidden. Eventually Fin dared to move, crawling out of his hide-away and unfolding like a hibernating creature emerging in spring, shaking his arms and legs to get the blood pumping through. He stood in the shade of a large oak, certain that no one could spot him from the landward side inspecting the river up and down stream. There wasn't far to go but he knew there was another bridge, a ford and a mill which he must successfully pass.

Carefully wading into the reeds, he rescued his swan's nest boat and pushed on to the reeds' edge. If anything, the night was even darker than the one before and glancing up he saw a shooting star. "Make a wish," that's what his mother would say, but what should he wish for? He wanted to be safely away, but he would rather be safely home. He knew that was not going to be possible. He chuckled that he might wish to be with Lady Ellen, but that wasn't going to happen either, so he wished to be safely away and avoid the Militia and Master Robert. Launching out into the current, Fin skilfully guided himself to the far bank and in no time, he could see lights glinting as high as a treetop. This had to be the mill, four stories high; it wouldn't be working now but the miller and family lived there and perhaps they were preparing for the morning, or was it that it was being used as a look-out post? Whatever made Fin stop he wasn't aware of, but he slowly reversed the figure of eight and glided across to the far bank. There was something wrong, too much light in the mill – no one wasted that many candles or lamps. He grabbed a clump of reeds and rushes, half closing his eyes to hopefully get a better view, but it was no use – he was at least a furlong away and the night so dark that he could not make out any person, or they were being clever enough to not show their outline against the brightness. Half way between him and the mill, a narrow channel had been cut to avoid the mill race; if he took this it would give less space to manoeuvre but the banks would hide him totally and then it would only be the ford to negotiate. Perhaps because of his nervousness, caused by fear of capture, Fin took the smaller channel holding his breath as he came to the ford. His coracle drew so little water he had no difficulty in crossing the well-used path and was soon in the main flow of the current again. Vigorously pulling on the paddle Fin sped away from his perceived captors – as it turned out he had nothing to fear but there had been a gathering for the miller and his family to celebrate the birth of a son, a future miller, with reckless expense to illuminate the darkness for the party!

The last obstacle was the bridge at Iford, still under construction on the eastern end, crossing islands in the river in three stages with alternating large and small arches. Fin had decided that he would shoot through the western arches, stone and sturdy, steering well clear of the workings at the eastern end where redbrick arches with stone parapets had been created over the last two years to enable the increased traffic to pass safely. The war on the continent may not have reached these shores with battles, but so many changes to life had taken place that Fin was sure that things would never return to as they were when he was a young child. Fin knew that once he had passed through the arch, he had to pull hard for the ferry, the only way to cross the river without making the detour for the bridge. Fin's father knew the ferryman, Patrick Clark, and was certain that he would hide the boat; he had plenty of different craft that he used depending on who was crossing. The sound of voices ahead alerted Fin to the approaching bridge but the closer he got the clearer he could hear the slurred voices of men singing. Raucous laughing announced that two of the group had decided to relieve themselves over the parapet and into the river. *Perhaps not that route,* thought Fin.

At this point the river had been split into channels by islands, submerged in winter but substantial in summer, and he therefore navigated to the opposite side of the island and, although more central than planned, cleared the bridge and set about finding the ferry at the 'quomps', a marshy quagmire area that had a dry path to link with the town. Fin had no idea of the time but the short jetty easily pointed to where he had to land. Silently coming alongside the wooden pilings, Fin lifted himself up but before he had done the same to his boat, a sharp voice pierced the chill of the air: "Who's out there? I warn you, I'm armed!"

"Sorry Mister Clarke, my father said to come to you once I arrived."

"Mister Clark is it now?" the top half of a battered door opened. "Mister Clark is it? I hin't bi'n called that for a while. Who's yo'r father?"

"Jack Ross, Mister Clark."

"Don't be Misterin' me, I'm Pat or Paddy to everyone that knows me and I know Jack so you know me too. What you be doin' 'ere at this time, in a bad way is you?"

"Something like that. I have to get into town and ask for Tom – my father says he will help me."

"Yes 'e may well but take care. It's Fin, in't it? I remember Jack bringing you down when you were a nipper. You be careful – don't know who you can trust. You can't stay out there. Got that coracle have you? I can look after that for you no problem. Prop it up round the back then get in 'ere. Chill's comin' in from the sea and I was right cosy till you disturbed me." Fin did as he was instructed and found the safety of Pat's small cottage reassuring. At least he had got down the river safely!

Chapter 6

Pat's cottage may only have been two rooms but Fin had enjoyed a short sleep and was woken with a mug of scalding tea that tasted strange but most welcoming. "It's wha' I add to the leaves tha' gives the taste. Not bad, eh?"

"Best I've had today, Pat."

Pat took a step and then turned back, "Tha's a good'un: 'Best you 'ad today, best you 'ad today,' it's only one you 'ad – cheeky rascal. Now 'ow's Jack doin' up river? Never been past that bridge inland, but I could tell you some tales about faraway places." Fin didn't like to interrupt but Pat finally stopped, having told him of the time he went to France to collect some parcels that perhaps he shouldn't. He had the chase of his life to get back safely – "If it weren't the Frenchies hollerin' and shootin' it's the Excise men chasin' and shootin'."

"Father and family are all well Pat, but I upset Master Robert, the son of Lord de Lacy, and he is going to arrest me, got the Militia after me."

"Well, I daresay Tom will 'elp you to 'ave a few adventures." Pat opened the door and the early morning light had been smeared by a fine drizzle. "This'll soak you through as soon as look at you." Pat pulled on a well-worn jacket that reached his knees so that all that could be seen was boots and jacket. He finished it off with a hat that looked like it had been painted with the same tar as the coracle. "That'll do, the rain's only gettin' worse today – look at 'em clouds."

"Thank you Pat, I don't want to cause you any trouble, I'll go."

"Good luck lad. Remember: be careful who you trust."

Pulling his coat close around him and putting on the sweat stained and battered hat he had worn all summer to protect him from the sun – another item he found wrapped in the bundle – Fin set off along the path, like a causeway across the quomps. He soon reached a more substantial road and turned east towards the quayside that was clearly visible a short distance ahead. Numerous boats had moored to different quays and were in the process of unloading a catch of crab, lobster and fish from a successful night at sea. Skirting the boxes already piled on the cobbles, he searched for one particular boat. His father had told him that Tom would most likely be in Christchurch, but other than that, he would have to use his wits to find him. "You lookin' for work son?" The most weather-beaten face, even more than Pat the Ferryman's, was looking up at Fin, obviously the reward for many years at sea.

"No, well I'm looking for Tom."

"Tom won't be down 'ere. Best you look in the Ship" and without stopping, the old mariner nodded towards the town. Fin started to walk away but stopped and thought he should reply:

"Thanks." But the sullen look he received in return made him shiver, sending water trickling down his spine. Should he have spoken to this man? Pat had said he should be careful of who he could trust. Fin quickly walked towards the buildings that announced the town centre.

It wasn't market day but there was a bustle of people and as he passed the imposing church building that had once been part of the priory, he was tempted to venture inside to see if there really was a miraculous beam. His grandfather was a great story teller and, when Fin had been small enough to sit on his knee listening to every last word, told of a time when the craftsmen were building the church for the priory; the carpenters had cut, shaped and planed many beams to be lifted into the roof but when they hoisted this beam, it was discovered to be too short. In those days the town of Twynham had been set aside for this magnificent priory but this beam would be the ruin of them, it cost so much. One carpenter – he had arrived alone, worked alone, ate alone and went who knows where each night, alone – stayed behind when all others had gone home. Next morning the same beam had fitted perfectly! How had it happened? The mysterious carpenter became known as none other than Jesus, visiting and working as the carpenter, and so the people called it Christ's Church – so impressed were the people that Jesus had come to their home that they called the town Christchurch and so it has been known ever since. Well, that's the story grandfather told. 'The miraculous beam.'

Fin had stopped and was staring up at the roof of this most impressive building, probably the biggest church he had ever seen, and became aware that people were looking at him. He quickly put his head down, eyes to the ground and strode purposefully into the town. Walking up the main street he quickly found the Ship, a beautifully painted sign swinging gently in the rain-soaked breeze, but rather than blunder in, Fin thought he should make up some sort of story and continued up the road.

By the time he had reached the end he was facing a junction of five roads, in the centre of which was a post with a sign hammered into it. **Bear Baiting at the Trinity Fair.** Fin had no idea when the Trinity Fair was. He knew that he had just celebrated the feast of Saint Cuthberga in Wimborne and he knew that his village would still celebrate the feast of Saint Stephen the day after Christmas, in spite of the church being derelict, but Trinity feast day was unfamiliar. He had heard of dogs being set on bears as a sport but had never seen it himself. He had heard of a large pit with a bear, fighting free against dogs, when at least the animal had a chance, but being tied to a post and attacked didn't seem fair and, judging by the poster, it seemed that the bear would be tied to the post.

His thoughts were interrupted by the rhythmic sound of feet, or rather boots, hitting the ground in unison. Staring along the more westward of the roads, to his horror he could see a group of red coated men marching towards him. These weren't Militia, they were wearing the same contrasting green facings that he had seen on Master Robert's coat and in front was a large man wearing a broad red sash tied at his right hip with a large elaborate bow, twirling a straw hat on the end of his sword and making the red, white and blue ribbons tied around the brim flutter, in spite of the drizzle, whilst a young lad, twelve or thirteen perhaps, kept the rhythm on a drum with one stick whilst holding the drum still, with the other hand.

A hand on Fin's shoulder made him turn ready to defend himself, knocking the arm away. "Best you not stay here son, unless you want to be joining the King's army. Come with me." Fin hesitated, glanced at the approaching soldiers, a recruiting party no doubt, and then back at the stranger. "No heed to me, it's up to you son." Fin followed the stranger as he headed back down the street and then slipped into an alleyway that led to a yard used for deliveries judging by the wagon with three barrels still loaded. Two men appeared from what must have been the stables and shouted across to the man ahead of Fin: "Nobby, who's that? Give us a hand with these, just arrived and we got to get them out of sight for Ted, before any snoopers come looking." Pointing a thumb at Fin, "Can we trust him?" The man who had been called Nobby turned and clapped his massive hand on Fin's shoulder again. "Like a lamb to the slaughter this boy was, standing up at Bargate with the soldiers coming – Sergeant Masters is doing his usual."

"Right, listen son, help us unload these three barrels and put them in a safe place for Ted and we will keep you hidden from S'a'rnt Masters."

Fin did as he was told, he had become used to doing as he was told, he had no idea about what the barrels held, but he could guess they had been brought in by smugglers. He was used to working hard and lifting the barrel was an easy task. He followed his unlikely friend known as Nobby and the other two men back into the stable past a large horse, presumably the one that had pulled the wagon, in need of a good rub down and brushing, and down a flight of stairs, turning back on themselves directly below the horse evidenced by the distinct aroma of dung and urine that had seeped through the cracks between the boards. Candles held by spikes head high lit the pathway and Fin became aware of a greater noise above him. Muffled voices, the occasional cursing and laughter, banging on wood and then he was stopped. Ahead of him, two of the men were lifting what appeared to be a huge rock that revealed a storage space for further barrels. "Quick son, we h'int got all day." Fin pushed forward and noticed that what he had thought of as a rock was in fact a clever screen that was disguised as a rock, just as he and his father had disguised their hiding place in the hedge. Replacing the screen, the men led Fin back down the tunnel, extinguishing the candles with finger and thumb and coming back up into the stable.

"You dealt with 'orses boy?" It was a question directed by the same man, the leader Fin assumed.

"Yes, I have helped out in the stables for Lord de Lacy." As soon as he had said it, he knew that he shouldn't have. The three men turned as one to stare at him.

"You're a fair way from home then son, what's your name?" This time it was Nobby, the man who had got him off the street. Fin felt that there was no point pretending.

"Fin."

"So what you doing here in Christchurch Fin?"

"I'm looking for Tom."

"And how do you know Tom then?"

"My father knows him and sent me here, I had some trouble and had to leave." The third man who had not spoken yet stepped forward and gave Fin a dig in the ribs.

"Got a young girl into trouble did you. She going to have a baby?" and a broad grin spread across a mouth that showed only four teeth.

"No nothing like that. I upset Lord de Lacy's son Master Robert."

"Well, there's plenty of us that have upset some high-ranking good-for-nothing Fin." This time it was Nobby. "You come in here with us. We'll get you some food – I daresay you'll be hungry by now, and then we can try to help you out."

The three men turned and beckoned Fin to follow, which he did. Once in the yard they pushed the wagon to one side, leaving enough space for further deliveries, Fin thought, and then Nobby put that hand on Fin's shoulder again; "Right Fin, I'm Nobby; this is Mick and this toothless wonder is Pugh! If you look after the horse in there, we will get you some food and drink from Ted – he runs the Ship." So that's where they were, the back of the Ship. *Seems bigger than it did from the street,* thought Fin. He turned and returned to the stable, patted the flank of the large horse and started to unbuckle the harness: he was relieved that they had taken the collar off before tethering it to the iron ring above the feeding trough. Fin noticed that there was a small triangular basin full of water, a string bag of hay and a trough of oats ready for the horse, at least they try to look after the animal.

"What's your name fella? I'm Fin and I'm going to make sure you are brushed out of this mud, where have you been tonight – perhaps I shouldn't ask."

"No you shouldn't! You don't need to know what you don't need to know, that's what my dad says. What you don't know won't get you in trouble." Fin turned to see a young woman, about his own age he guessed, holding a tray with a bowl, its contents steaming, a chunk of bread, a spoon, fork and a mug of beer. Fin stared as the young woman knowingly held the tray tight to her figure to accentuate the shape of her breasts. "What you gawping at? Never seen a lady before?" Fin knew he was being teased and watched her bend slowly in front of him revealing more of the cleavage that she was so obviously proud of, and then straightening up arching her back to show her long neck with several curls of fire-red hair glowing against the whiteness of the skin having escaped from the bonnet that she had been forced to wear. "Might see you later." She turned and walked out of the stable closing the lower part of the door but then quickly popped her head back over adding, "If you're lucky!"

Fin smiled to himself and stretched out to start brushing away the dirt. "Come on fella. Let's get you tidy before that soup goes cold."

By the time Fin had finished one side of the horse the soup was cool enough to eat and dipping the bread in, he sat in the straw thinking of the past days. He had food, he might even be meeting a girl later but he had that nagging reminder from Pat the Ferryman, "Be careful who you trust." The soup, a number of fish boiled up he guessed, and bread tasted better than he expected. He had wiped the bowl with the crust but left the mug to get back to work on the horse. "Good as new!" Fin ran his hand down the neck of the horse, its chestnut coat gleaming in the light through the open door, "Yep, ready for wherever you have to go next."

"You haven't drunk your beer." Fin looked up to see the same young woman who had delivered his food but this time without any cap and with the mass of hair cascading over her shoulders. "You've done a good job with Captain." She smoothed her hand over the horse, stepping ever closer towards Fin, "Perhaps you could comb my hair and make it so smooth and shiny?" She was only a pace away from Fin who had nowhere to retreat. She was a little shorter than Fin and in looking down he couldn't fail to notice that she had unlaced the top two fastenings on the bodice of the oak-green dress. "I don't get to meet young gentlemen like you very often. I have them old codgers like Pugh and Nobby putting their grubby hands all over me, squeezing and pinching while I serve them their food. No, I haven't seen no one like you for a while." She closed the gap between and Fin inadvertently brushed against Captain who, being disturbed from eating, leaned back, pushing Fin against the young woman. "Oh, I am glad you want to get to know me but why don't we go over here where there is more room?"

She led Fin to the straw at the back of the stable, the same place that held the trap door to the tunnel. Lifting the mug of beer to her lips she handed it to Fin. "Here you are, you must need that after working so hard." Her eyes roved over his body, widening as she noted the bulge in his breeches. "Leave some for later, put it down in a safe place." Fin was eager at the prospect ahead. He had chased girls in the village, even kissed one or two, but he had never been this close to any girl and he could feel his excitement growing in more ways than one.

"I see'd how you been looking at these" squaring herself to be level with Fin's eyes. "Why don't you pull on that little bow?" and taking Fin's shaking fingers, she let him pull each end of the cord releasing the bodice and enticing Fin with the flimsiest of shifts that was almost transparent. His eyes widened as he could clearly see those secret places that the village girls had kept hidden, the

33

whiteness of her cleavage and the darker colour of her nipples hidden only in part. She reached across him brushing her breasts against his hands as she took the mug. "No rush is there?" and she again tilted the mug to her lips, staring into his eyes. Fin could see her moist lips and she whispered, "Would you like to see some more?" He nodded and she crossed her arms to pull the shift down to her waist. "Here," she guided Fin's hands onto her cool skin. "Let me give you a drink," and as Fin became excited at his first touch of a woman, she lifted the beaker to allow him to gulp down more beer. Fin was transfixed, touching as gently as he could, not daring to move, but as she put down the mug her hands travelled to the buttons on his breeches. "You can't 'ave all the fun, can you? Now what's in here?" She managed to undo buttons that had often been a nuisance to Fin, those times when he had drunk too much and needed to relieve his bladder mighty quick. Was it the cool air or was it her cool hands, Fin was light headed, he was aware of a sweaty feeling spreading across his body. She was bringing her face closer to him. Her hands had moved from his breeches and were stretching around his shoulders. Fin's eyes closed as he felt her lips on his cheek and the faintest of whispers: "Sorry."

Chapter 7

Fin woke to the familiar smells of the stable. A smile crossed his lips as memories of a beautiful girl holding him, touching him came back into mind, rudely shattered by cold water being thrown over him. "Get up the lot of yer, no time to be slouching about here." It was a gruff voice and Fin desperately tried to focus on the owner. A hand hitting his arm and then a body sprawling across his legs announced another person in the stables. These weren't the same stables. There were rows of stalls and penned into this one – Fin tried to count – five, six, no seven men. The man sprawling across Fin retched and emptied his stomach into the straw. It was only now that Fin realised that his coat and breeches were covered in filth: the stables had obviously been occupied by horses until recently and now he, and the other men, stank. "Get out of there now, an 'orse needs that more than you! You will scrub yourselves clean and put on these nice new clothes ready for the doctor's inspection." Fin was confused but slowly got to his feet, his head still pounding. "Gunners! Get this sorry lot out of that stall and get them washed." Rough hands grabbed the seven men and pushed and pulled them out into the daylight.

Fin could hear bells. *Could it be Sunday,* he thought. Where had the days gone? Even in his precarious state he noted that there were eight notes in the bells. Unusual. He loved music but had only heard bells rung at special celebrations. The group bent over a trough meant for watering horses but were set to wash themselves under threat that a Gunner would do it for them if it wasn't good enough. Fin's neighbour whispered, "Too much beer?"

"No I only had one mug, a young woman came to me…"

"Oh no, you fell for the old trick of sending a young girl to you, telling you how she had to put up with old men groping her, but all the while she has a drink that drugged you."

"But she had the same mug."

"No. What you saw was her putting the mug to her lips but she will never have drunk from it."

Fin felt foolish. "What about you then?" he asked.

"My own fault, I like the drink too much."

"Where were you…"

"Where was I nabbed? I was in the Ship Inn and if I'm guessing right, I would say that we are in the new barracks on the west of town."

"We're in the army?" Fin was appalled at the prospect.

"Yes you are, but these barracks are special, because these are for the artillery." Fin tried to take in the enormity of the situation: he had been tricked, they hadn't been helping, she didn't really like him…

"Thomo, they call me Thomo. Really Thomson but never use it." Fin's neighbour held out a hand.

"Oh, sorry, I'm Fin."

"Don't worry Fin, you'll survive."

A dig in the ribs brought Fin's attention back to washing. A Gunner in a blue jacket had poked him with the butt of a musket to encourage more haste. "No time for yabbering. The doctor will be 'ere after church and them bells are the signal that church is starting."

"Roll them dirty clothes up and put them over there, you will get them washed in your own time. Put on these clean shirts, jackets, trousers, socks and boots. Have to have you smart for the doctor."

The file of men, half-naked, took a pile of clothes each and started to get dressed. Fin had never had long trousers before and the white canvas felt strange against his skin. "You will stand at attention, which Gunner Price will demonstrate for you. Look how your heels and knees will be together, your feet will be slightly splayed so that you do not wobble or shake, your arms will be straight by your sides and your shoulders will be square and pushed back to lift your chest forward. Finally, your head will be erect with your chin up." He paced along the line of men. "You are all part of the King's Army now. If you had not drunk too much, if you had not picked a fight with my Gunners, if you had kept your breeches on, you would not be here now, but here is where you are and here is where you will stay. We will learn what it is to stand at attention and the doctor will pass you fit for service; none of you are invalids and you will contribute to the glory of the nation, rid us of that tyrant Bonaparte across the water and, God willing, return heroes into the waiting arms of you loved ones."

Having reached the end of the line he halted, stood at attention himself and roared: "My name is Sergeant Collins. What is it?" A muted response brought a terrifying reaction: the nearest new recruit was hit with the stick that the sergeant carried, hitting him into the next recruit and like nine-pins scattering the whole line. "Get up, and stand to attention. What is my name?" This time all seven shouted as loud as they could, "Sergeant Collins!" "Now that's better, now we are acquainted. I must have your names." He took a book from his pocket, waved Gunner Price dismissed and made his way down the line, stopping at each man, asking: "Name? Age? Where were you born? Are you currently serving in His Majesty's Army with another regiment?"

Having collected all of the details, he gave further instructions: "When the doctor passes you by, you will open your mouth to show your teeth, you will give your name, you will say 'Yes' when asked if you are sound, and if he puts his hand down your trousers and says 'Cough', you will cough!"

One more walk up and down the line was all the time that Sergeant Collins had before the arrival of a carriage with the hood down pulled through the gates. Fin had tried to take in the details of the place he had been put: a two storey red brick building with a slate roof; stables on the ground floor, but they didn't take up all of the floor; there were other rooms upstairs as he could see nine windows on this side, and he assumed the same on the other. The arrival of the carriage was followed by two riders in the same blue uniform as Sergeant Collins, but with far more gold on the shoulders. "Eyes to the front my boys, eyes to the front" Collins hissed, raising his stick as a threat.

The doctor proceeded as Collins had told them, moving from man to man but the whole process was done in a matter of minutes. He signed a book that a Gunner had brought Sergeant Collins with pen and ink and then he was gone. "Now gentlemen, the Officer, Captain Duncan, will come over and address you, acquainting you with the Articles of War that are necessary for you to know and get you all to swear your oath. Now stay at attention, you have done so well so far."

A young gentleman strode purposefully towards the awaiting line of men, his blue coat having longer tails than that of Sergeant Collins revealing a white lining, contrasting against the scarlet lapels unbuttoned at the neck, collar and cuffs. He also wore a bicorne and had a fringed epaulette on his right shoulder denoting his rank, along with the sash tied at the right hip. "Good Morning Sergeant Collins. Not bad for one evening?" The raised intonation indicated that perhaps too few recruits had been gathered.

"Yes Captain, not bad at all."

"Have you the Articles?" Collins handed the book opened at the appropriate pages: "Any Officer, or Soldier, who shall begin…" Fin thought that it sounded like the Church Service, a language seldom used by the hard working labourers of the village but after a constant drone, Captain Duncan emphasised: "And gentlemen I will draw your attention to this Article, listen you all well; 'All Officers and Soldiers, who, having received Pay, or having been duly enlisted in His Majesty's Service, shall be convicted of having deserted the same, shall suffer Death, or other such punishment as by a Court Martial shall be inflicted." Having paused, the captain continued: "You have taken the King's shilling, you are wearing the King's uniform, for which you will pay out of your bounty for enlisting. The doctor has examined you and passed you fit, therefore it leaves me to swear you in. I will read the oath and you will all say 'I swear', sign the book and then, we can get on with the rest of our duties." He paused to let absorb his words before continuing. "We all swear that we will be true to our Sovereign Lord King George, and to serve him honestly and faithfully in Defence of His Person, Crown, and Dignity, against all his Enemies and Opposers whatsoever, and to observe and obey His Majesty's Orders, and the Orders of the Generals and Officers set over us by His Majesty."

"I swear!" Sergeant Collins led the response followed by a collective "I swear" from seven new soldiers.

"Thank you Sergeant," Captain Duncan handed back the Articles of War and turned to walk away when two more riders arrived through the gates, but this time their uniform was far more resplendent with a Tarleton Helmet, crest waving, burnished metal shining, braided jackets of blue with yellow/gold lace and red collar and cuffs.

"Looks like the cavalry have arrived," whispered Dan Evans centre of the line.

"I heard that Evans, and for your information, they is artillery too. But they swan around on horses. Not honest men marching like us." Sergeant Collins had little in common with his counterpart riding with his Captain.

Dismounting expertly and saluting in the best tradition of the army, the new arrival introduced himself: "Good morning Captain. Sorry to have interrupted your parade of new recruits. I am Captain Ramsay of the Royal Horse Artillery and this is Sergeant Webber. Like you, we are always on the look-out for the best recruits and I have brought orders from Woolwich to create new troops of Horse

Artillery. They are damned short of artillery in Portugal, you know, and our commander has asked for more. Have you any new men that can ride?"

Captain Duncan was taken aback, took the orders to check their veracity, looked at Captain Ramsay, looked back at the orders and then turned to Sergeant Collins: "Sergeant, this is most irregular, but do any of our men ride?"

"Sir!" was Collins reply and he eyed the line. "Well, does any of you men ride?" Thomo dug Fin in the ribs and raised his arm.

"Yes Sergeant, we do." Collins strode in front of the two men.

"So we have two gentlemen with us do we?" Then in a coarse whisper, "I doubt if you have ever ridden in your life Thomson, and as for you Ross, I hear you're good for mucking out and brushing shiny in the stables."

"Sergeant." It was Captain Duncan. "Do we have any who can ride?"

"It appears we do… Sir!"

"Very well. Release them to these gentlemen and we can then carry on."

"Listen you two: I know your game. Think it will be easy ridin' horses round, but it won't. Now get over to your new h'officers."

Thomo and Fin strode rather than marched towards Ramsay and Webber. "Can you ride?" asked Ramsay in a quieter tone.

"Oh yes sir, not as fine as you displayed when you came in but we can ride." Fin let Thomo do the talking wondering what he had let himself in for.

"Have you two gentlemen any belongings to collect?" asked Sergeant Webber.

"Just those clothes," Thomo pointed to a row of bundles, flies swarming around them.

"Well if you would be so kind as to get them, we will be on our way, but for the first part you will be walking." "Yes Sergeant," Thomo grabbed Fin by the arm and dashed to collect his old clothes, still wet.

"What do you think Sergeant, will they do?"

"Oh yes Captain Ramsay, they will do just fine… by the time I have licked them into shape."

"Mount up then and let's get going."

As they rode past Captain Duncan, they saluted smartly shouting, "Thank you Captain." There was little love lost between the old foot artillery and the new upstart horse artillery. "Will you two laggards get a move on, we have a way to go if you are to find some horses before nightfall."

Thomo grinned at Fin who was still bemused. "Come on Fin, we won't be foot slogging no more, we'll be riding!"

"But I've only been on a cart horse at harvest."

"You know that, I know that, but you'll get the hang of it!" They left Christchurch at the run.

Chapter 8

They had headed east back through the town and were following the coast. The wind had picked up blowing onshore. Two boats, sloops, with checkerboard sides and carrying plenty of sail on each of their two masts were ploughing up the Channel leaving a distinct white line in the murky waters behind. Fin noticed the boats and, in spite of how hard they were leaning over and leaving a wake, it appeared that he was making greater distance, as they appeared to be ahead of him at first and now over his right shoulder. As the coast pushed a headland south-east into the sea – perhaps this was the reason the boats had had to change course while the road he travelled stayed 'Roman' straight – Fin recognised the hardships endured by the inhabitants of the small cottages, sometimes solitary, sometimes in clumps, hamlet oases in this windswept landscape. Even the trees had grown bent over in the direction of the prevailing south-westerly winds, unable to straighten as so many aged labourers at home suffered after years in the fields.

"Half-way there boys, we can stop for a short rest. Sergeant Webber has a water bottle he will allow you." Ramsay dismounted and stretched himself instinctively as Webber took both sets of reins in one hand, passing his pale blue barrel on a brown leather strap to Ross who gratefully uncorked it, taking a mouthful before handing onto Thomo who did likewise and returned it with thanks to their new Sergeant. The Captain didn't announce that they were moving off: he simply took his reins from his Sergeant and mounted without any fuss, turning his mount full circle and started to walk off, followed by Webber who had not been quite as graceful in mounting, and Fin and Thomo'.

Few people passed them and it wasn't until they could see a town in the distance with what looked like a tented encampment on its outskirts that anyone appeared from the opposite direction. Skirting the town with boat-building yards down to the water's edge and an enticing aroma of food cooking, Captain Ramsay informed the small group: "We're going to drop in on some friends I met at

Woolwich. They're new to the country, won't speak a lot of English but they will have horses for us."

"Foreigners Captain?" Webber queried.

"Yes sergeant. And from what I hear, we won't find a better bunch of fighters in the army. His Majesty isn't just King of England – he has many titles, one of which is Elector of Hanover. These men and their families have escaped the clutches of Napoleon, who also wanted their services, and fled to the protection of their ruler. Infantry, Cavalry, Artillery– Horse Artillery at that!"

The walk slowed as they approached two soldiers guarding a simple barrier across the road that lifted on a counter-weight suspended through an upright over a pulley wheel. It was the first time that Fin had seen soldiers in such dark green uniforms, even darker with black collar and cuffs. They also had different weapons – they weren't muskets, that's for sure. "Goot heeverning sir, yoo must halt heer." Another soldier in the same green was bringing an officer, almost the mirror image of Captain Ramsay, towards the barrier.

"Captain Ramsay, so good to see you. I have collected some horses as you asked, but you will stay the night with us; your two men will be looked after, but have they done something wrong? They are not in the uniform."

"No Captain Kuhlman, they are new recruits. Just joined us, but they have the makings of fine artillerymen."

"Please follow me. Lift the barrier!" An almost effortless touch of the bar saw the road unblocked and Sergeant Webber admiring the ingenuity of these men.

Sergeants were notorious for finding a good meal and drink and Webber soon disappeared amongst the tented village once he had supervised the new recruits in caring for the horses. Dusk had fallen by the time they had finished, the ancient walls more imposing than before. A soldier in a plain blue jacket and grey overalls brought them two plates of food that smelled like no food Fin had been given before. The soldier beckoned to the pair to follow, pointing at himself, "Ludwig, Ludwig" and then pointed at them.

"Oh, it's his name Thomo." Fin pointed at his companion and slowly said, "Thomo" and then "I am Fin." Ludwig found the words difficult to comprehend but did his best to repeat them over and over on their walk back to his tent. As he drew back the door flap, a wave of smoke filled the air and he beckoned again. He had taken his seat on a simple bench leaving space for Fin and Ross.

"Thomo… Fin…" An awkward silence was held before a dozen men were trying to repeat the names of the new arrivals.

Fin looked at Thomo: "We're popular then!"

"I hope we aren't expected to remember their names." The food was flavoured with unfamiliar spices but it was a good meal after a day that had started in such a traumatic fashion.

Ludwig took Fin and Thomo to the sleeping tent giving each a blanket. "Goot Niite Fin, Thomo."

"Thanks Ludwig, great food" and Fin put his thumbs up "Good food." Fin realised that a strange expression had come across Ludwig's face as he looked at his thumbs. "Ludwig," Fin called to attract his attention. "This…" giving thumbs up gesture, "means good, good, well done."

"Ah, goot," and Ludwig copied the sign.

"Not bad for some foreigners, eh Fin?"

"No, best food I've had for a while."

The background of a German song was strangely reassuring to Fin who was puzzling over recent events. He had no idea what was being sung but the mere fact that these men, far from home, were relaxed, helped him come to terms with the momentous change in his life. "I still don't understand why she did it, Thomo, or the rest of them. They were convincing actors, took me in good and proper."

"You're still young Fin, a bit gullible, I'll try and explain; won't change a thing mind. What does your mother do?"

"She makes buttons, mostly from rams' horns, sometimes wood; she has to drill holes through and cover in different cloth for the button maker from Blandford."

"And how much does she get paid for this work?"

"Well, depends on how many she makes, but if she makes six or seven dozen in a day she will get two shillings probably."

"What if you went out chopping wood or shifting heavy bags, flour or corn as like?"

"I have done that and got timed. It was a penny or a penny halfpenny an hour!"

"So if I told you that their trick will have a 'bringers' fee of two pounds, twelve shillings and sixpence… not bad for a few moments work?"

"Is that how they get all recruits?"

"No. For some it's a pretty girl, like you, for me too much drink, but others volunteer to escape something they have done or a broken heart or a magistrate offering the difference between the army and prison or being sent to the other side of the world."

"And what about the money they said we would get?"

"Yes we all get registered with over twenty pounds, but then they have to take off the cost of our necessaries: the clothes we will be given, the shoe brushes, hair brush, clothes brush, the black ball and the knapsack to carry it in, let alone paying for your food and drink... so we won't be seeing much cash in hand."

"So I'm not better off?"

"No Fin. You'll be working just as hard, but this time, you might have the pleasure of being maimed or killed! Goodnight Fin."

"I think we should have been in the recruiting business."

"Too late now. Now try to get some sleep."

Chapter 9

Fin had been impressed by the orderliness with which these foreign soldiers had set out their camp. He understood that they were only on a training exercise heading for Bexhill where their infantry were billeted while they had been in Weymouth with the cavalry. He had woken to another mist shrouded morning and discovered the latrines discreetly screened with canvas sheets down by the sea-wall, another ingenious facet of the camp that allowed the tides to refresh the stinking pit.

After a hearty breakfast of bacon and tea, Fin and Thomo were taken to the temporary stables where they were given the blankets, saddles, straps and bridles for their new mounts. Captain Ramsay had specifically asked for chestnut horses so that his troop would all be the same. Ludwig patted one horse with his right hand, pointing at Fin with his left: "Gretschen, she is goot?" and used his newly learned thumbs up, making Fin smile.

"Gretschen?" the intonation seeming to doubt what he heard.

"Ya, yes, my muther's name," Ludwig beamed, "And Thom-o you haf Jager – hunter."

He was equally pleased and gave a double thumbs up, "Jagger, I like it Ludwig." Fin was pleased that Ludwig stayed to help saddle up, he had seen the grooms at the stables in the big house, he had helped tighten girths and change stirrups, but never for himself. He glanced at Thomo and noticed that he was quite happy on his own. There was more to this man than he let on.

Captain Ramsay was delighted that his two new men were ready. Sergeant Webber was leading both his and the Captain's horse a respectful distance behind allowing Captain Kuhlman to say his goodbyes. Simultaneously the Captains saluted their farewell. Ramsay mounted his horse swiftly followed by Sergeant Webber and a little more gingerly by Fin and Thomo. "Those canvas trousers will rub something awful but we have no others, so we will take it easy." Captain Ramsay was almost apologetic in his comment as he turned his horse, raised his hand in semi salute to Ludwig and walked the path towards the lifting gate. Crossing the edge of the encampment, an imperceptible squeeze of Captain Ramsay's legs brought the horse into a trot, and without any encouragement, Fin's horse had joined in, jolting his back as he sat too stiff, already feeling his inner thighs chaffing.

"Soon get used to it" was Sergeant Webber's encouragement, as well as a broad grin signifying that he knew the pain the recruits would endure.

Fin and Thomo did get used to it but were still sore. He couldn't hear what was being said but he noticed Captain Ramsay and Sergeant Webber in deep conversation, with the Captain taking something that had been neatly folded from inside his jacket, showing his Sergeant and then replacing it. Thomo interrupted Fin's inquisitiveness: "One for sorrow!"

"What did you say Thomo?"

"One for 'sorrow'," this time emphasising the final word. Fin knew instantly that a Magpie had been spotted.

"Bad luck to see just one," Fin twisted in his saddle. "There Thomo, two for mirth, three for a wedding..."

"Who's the lucky lady Fin?" and Thomo burst out laughing drawing unwanted attention from Sergeant Webber.

"Enough energy for us to get going a bit faster, boys?" the final raising of pitch in his voice indicating he wasn't deadly serious, much to Fin's relief who dreaded the jolting to increase on his thighs.

"No sergeant, just saw magpies. Bad luck if you only see one."

"Sounds a lot of nonsense to me..."

But Captain Ramsay butted in. "No Sergeant, when I rode through Lincolnshire earlier this year as part of the recruiting party around Grantham, I saw every local man and woman salute a lone magpie and repeat the rhyme: 'one for sorrow, two for mirth, three for a wedding and four for a death...' don't want to see four do we?"

"What about if you see five or six Captain?"

"Not sure Sergeant but magpies don't often congregate in those sort of numbers." Without turning, the Captain asked Fin, "Know much about birds Ross?"

"I know that that's a Kestrel hovering to our left, must have seen something move in the grass of the meadow. I know those two dots above the hill in the distance are likely to be buzzards using the air warmed by the morning sun and helping them glide, and I've seen magpies, jays, robins, sparrows and the like around the hedgerows at home."

"Well done Ross. Have you a favourite species?" the blank expression indicated to the Captain that Fin wasn't familiar with the word he had used. "Do you especially like to see one sort of bird, its colour or flight…?"

"No doubts Captain. It's the kingfisher – such amazing colours, so quick and what a fisher! I've spent many afternoons watching them catching fish and taking back to the nest; mind you, I never found the nest."

"I think that you will be a very popular man in our troop Ross, you have a lot to help us with." Fin had no idea what he meant but he took it as a compliment and straightened his back that fraction, more proud of the recognition.

Having continued around a bend in the road, the Captain pointed ahead towards an unusually shaped building and a barrier across the road. "This is a turnpike; we won't have to pay but if we had not been in the service of the King, it would have been a penny each, and if we were driving cattle or sheep to market it would have been ten pennies or five pennies respectively. They use the money to keep the surface of the road in good condition: these new Macadamised roads ensure that we can travel whatever the weather and won't get bogged down in ruts or the mire." A sudden shrill note of a horn startled the horses and all four turned to see a coach and four hurtling towards them.

"Step to one side," ordered Sergeant Webber, "and make lively." This was easier said than done for Fin but Thomo guided Gretschen to the side track by side-stepping Jagger. The coach, a deep red colour on the lower half and black upper half with red wheels spinning almost a blur, sped past and the gate had been already opened. Fin was holding on as tight as he could with his legs squeezing but he still noted that there were three people jolting along behind the driver, who was well wrapped up with a thick tan apron across his legs (*Probably leather,* Fin thought), a woollen muffler twisted several times around the neck and a hat, that looked a cross between a top hat and a fur hat, firmly planted down to the eyebrows. At the back was the reason for the shrill blast and as the coach passed the barrier, the man in a splendid black hat with gold ribbon placed a trumpet to his mouth and gave a second blast that cut the air and caused roosting birds to take flight.

Regaining the road, the four riders passed the toll-gate, Captain Ramsay raised his hand in salute of thanks and continued the journey. "Wretched Mail Coaches, think they own the road they do!" Sergeant Webber had not been as impressed as Fin. "Driver has a schedule to keep; he has his timetable; but we have our orders; they must be kept."

"Don't have to be so high and mighty driving us off the road though."

"I daresay when we have our Troop on the road, we would want the same for us?"

"That would be different though, Captain, we would be off to save the country!" the broad grin had spread across the sergeant's face and the captain knew well enough that he was having his leg pulled.

The morning swiftly slipped by as they came off the turnpike, travelled through the thicker woodland, crossed fords and finally stopped at a very welcoming inn named the Jolly Farmer. The host may have been the very man of the title, except he greeted them hobbling out on one good leg and on a wooden stump. "What is it I can be getting you sir?" He spoke directly to Captain Ramsay, "It is an honour to have you with me this fine day." Captain Ramsay was too astute and had served long enough to realise that many a landlord would welcome you with open arms but fleece you for the pleasure of food and drink.

"My men will care for the horses, your ostler can stay where he is." Fin hadn't noticed a burly youth, with hair that seemed to stick out as stalks of corn, approaching and then returning to a stable-yard through the arch which any coach would have taken. "But we will have a piece of your famous game pie and a jug of beer with four beakers." *Captain Ramsay could flatter just as easily*, thought Fin and noticed that Sergeant Webber was noting something with pencil and paper before reaching into his pocket and giving the landlord a sixpence to cover all expenses.

"Always keep a note of expenses boys, have to reimburse when we get to the Quarter-master."

Fin moved uneasily as he knew that he could write very little. Come to that he could read only a very little. He hadn't had a lot of schooling, working out in the fields and woods most days.

"You can dismount now, and stretch your aching legs." Captain Ramsay dismounted, handed his reins to Sergeant Webber as before, and made a leisurely walk towards the entrance. Fin followed Sergeant Webber through the arch and copied him; taking a handful of straw, he rubbed down Gretschen, starting at the neck with slow but firm movements, first on the side he mounted and then on the other, constantly watching his Sergeant. He had a little more difficulty when it came to checking each hoof but having noted that the shoes were fixed firmly and no stones were trapped threatening lameness, he loosened the girth and fetched a bucket of feed from the stables while the horses were able to drink from the trough by the pump. "Give me a hand with the Captain's horse, you two – we'll be eating quicker if you do."

Sergeant Webber was right and, having gone through the back door, they saw their captain studying something he had set out on the table while eating a slice of pie. "You know Sergeant, this pie isn't half bad!" as if surprised that what he had said might be true. "We've skirted Southampton, we're on the edge of Fareham and looking out through the window." They all looked up. "There is the north end of Portsmouth harbour. Don't need to go there either – wouldn't want the navy trying to entice you two away!" He chuckled at his own frivolity but Thomo shifted uneasily, just enough to be noticeable to Sergeant Webber. "Eat up, we can't stop long." *Typical!* thought Fin, *He's been in here while we have been out there with the horses and now we have to get going again!*

The landlord bade them goodbye in the same effusive fashion and they were on their way, horses checked, all fed and watered and the sun warm and pleasant for the continuation of their journey. Fin enjoyed searching the sky for different birds but as he looked up to the crest of the hill in the distance, he noticed something unusual. He fixed his stare to the point so rigidly that it took Sergeant Webber's notice. "What you spotted Ross, another bird?"

"No Sergeant but I don't know what I have seen." He pointed towards the hill-top, "One moment it looks like a tall building and then, the next moment you can see through it."

"See the crest of the hill, about half a mile ahead?" it was Captain Ramsay interrupting, "We'll stop there and I will try to explain what you have seen."

Fin was intrigued by the unknown object, but it did appear to change as he looked. The Captain had reached the crest of the hill, dismounted and tethered his horse to a hawthorn branch protruding from the hedge that marked the boundary to a field of sheep. He was extracting a telescope from his saddle bag as the others dismounted. "We don't need this to see that building on the hill-top; it is a good distance but we can clearly see the shape: a squat wooden structure underneath a rectangular frame which has six paddles, a bit like a picture in a frame. In the building will be two men, old soldiers or sailors invalided out perhaps, who will pull on ropes and turn the paddles vertical like a picture in the frame for all to see, or horizontal and you are left with only the frame to see and hence, Ross, you can see through. These buildings are part of the shutter telegraph and can send and relay a message from Portsmouth to London in fifteen minutes! Just think of that – any alarm of invasion and London will know soon enough and send orders. You know each station can have sixty-three different combinations for letters, words and numbers. There's a book for the code of course. There are two more men in the building with a telescope fixed on the next station in the line, so…" and he paused resting the telescope on the saddle of his horse. "Yes there it is, clear as day, the next station." Fin followed the direction but could not see anything. "Some stations are seven to nine miles apart so you would need a telescope!" mentioned Captain Ramsay. "I believe I am looking at Portsdown station and the one behind is Wickham; as we continue our journey we may see Chalton. Clever system of messaging. I believe the Navy use flags bearing a code of letters, numbers and words as well. I saw a display at Woolwich, did you see it Sergeant?"

"Yes sir, I believe all shutters open was a letter 'A' and all shut was a 'C' but then combinations would need a code book, sir."

"Yes I quite agree. But think about it: fifteen minutes and message in London! If it was a rider it would have to be… what do you think Sergeant fifteen hours?"

"I wouldn't like to be the rider after that sir, I had heard the mail coach set a record of sixteen hours London to Portsmouth – mind you that's changing teams of horses; couldn't do that on one team."

Captain Ramsay took his eye away from the telescope and asked Fin: "Ross. Ever used a telescope before? Take a look at this. You'll be able to see how one telegraph station links to another." Fin steadied the glass on Gretschen's saddle just as he had noted Captain Ramsay on his. "Can you see it? Weather's good enough today to spot that on the hill."

"Yes Captain, I can see the building and the shutters have all been opened."

"Could be nothing but it could be the letter 'A'. Keep watching for a change." After a short wait, Captain Ramsay continued, "If nothing's happened by now, then there's probably no signal at the moment. Now Ross, shift your view to the right where there is a small bay at the top of the harbour – you should be able to spot Portchester Castle. I can see it without the telescope!" He waited again for Fin to focus and was delighted with the surprised expression on Fin's face. "Impressive aren't they? How old do you think these walls are?"

"Don't know Captain, never seen walls like this. I've only ever been round hill forts that were built thousands of years ago. Well that was what my granddad said."

"Have you Ross, where was that?"

"A place called Badbury Rings Captain. Lots of banks and ditches, massive rings and all built by hand tools."

"I'm impressed, Ross. I like to have men who take an interest. You hear this, Webber. Ross here has been back in an Iron Age Fort, earth banks and ditches."

"Sounds like the way we have been trained to build a redoubt."

"Exactly! We can use men like you Ross. What about you Thomson? Take the telescope and have a look. Ever seen walls like this?" Thomo quickly focused the instrument, Ramsay noticed how the slight alteration was made without asking how. Thomson had obviously used one before.

"Not exactly Captain but where I come from was a big dockyard, Chatham, and not far from there was a castle in Rochester. A town wall, town gates at all points of the compass and a really strange keep."

"What made it strange?" asked Sergeant Webber surveying the walls with his own prized telescope, a possession awarded to him during his time in Spain for his efforts in protecting the guns.

"Well, the story goes Sergeant that bad King John attacked the castle and after wasting many attacks and dirty tricks, like catapulting the carcasses of dead horses and the like, he ordered his engineers to dig a tunnel under the outer wall and corner tower. When these engineers judged that they had dug enough, they raided a local farm, stole a herd of pigs and chased 'em down the tunnel. When they lit the fire, the pig fat roasted the beams propping up the tunnel roof and brought the towers down. Mind you, it still didn't work: the defenders locked the interior doors and kept the fight going."

"My word, Sergeant Webber, we have two good men here, engineers and gunners in the making. Right, my story might not impress you half as much but these walls have been here since the times of the Roman invasion, built to last and still strong."

"Don't think that they would stand long against the big guns Captain."

"No Sergeant Webber, siege guns today wouldn't take long. That's where Ross' earthworks could take the impact. Best be getting along. We still have a distance to go, but should be there before dusk and a good meal."

Fin felt more confident riding at a canter and he was amazed how many masts he could see as they passed the whole of Portsmouth harbour. They did see another telegraph station but there was no stopping this time even though it was clear that a message was being transmitted with combinations of shutters opening and closing. They walked their horses through the fords and then cantered where they could but they were still several miles away when Captain Ramsay told them to look ahead to see the imposing sight of an enormous spire stretching into the sky. "It is magnificent, hundreds of years old 'and' the only cathedral spire that can be seen from the sea. It is a way-marker for sailors and landsmen alike. That is Chichester and you might like to explore it one day, but not today. We are going to divert to the north of the city and we will be accepting the hospitality of the Duke of Richmond. It was his doing, or rather the previous Duke, who decided to set up the Horse Artillery at his home – magnificent stables, but you will be sleeping in tents!"

Skirting the outskirts of the city, they had slowed to a walk. Fin noticed several red-coated men with blue facing lapels, collars and cuffs, but he also noticed each one had a sash tied around the waist as well as plenty of silver lace around the shoulders – no simple soldiers these were. Captain Ramsay acknowledged each cluster of men, reinforcing Fin's impression that it was a city of officers.

Winding their way through manicured parkland, a gravel path led them towards the tented village that was going to be home. The first task was to care for the horses. Meeting the rest of the Troop would have to wait. "Thank you Sergeant," Captain Ramsay gratefully handed over the reins, "and well done Ross, Thomson. I know you will be sore, but you will get used to it and I know you will be very important gunners with Sergeant Webber's gun crew." They were led into a spacious stable block where there were more horses than Fin had ever seen.

Sergeant Webber pointed to a vacant stall. "This will be yours. Make sure you take good care for your horses. I'm going to take the Captain's horse to his stall and then deal with mine." Fin and Thomo set about taking the saddles from their horses and then washing and brushing their coats thoroughly. It had already been drummed into them that their horse could save their life one day. So care for it – and so they did!

Chapter 10

Dawn, and it was dawn with the merest hint of a lightening in the deep blue night sky that had brought a restful, if aching and disturbed, sleep. The shrill notes of a bugle had woken the inhabitants of the tent followed by the already familiar tones of Sergeant Webber: "Up and lively lads, plenty to do to get you ready for joining the new troop." Sticking his head through the flap, he asked, "How are you Ross, Thomson? Ready for more riding? Bet your legs are raw! What you need is some best brown paper and cider vinegar; soak the paper in a pot of best cider vinegar; heat it up until simmering and then layer it onto those poorly legs and bind it up tight – no time for that now boys. Get some food, shave and on parade before the next bugle call." With that he was gone and onto the next tent, his voice still audible even through the canvas barriers.

Fin and Thomo only had their old stinking clothes and the canvas jacket and trousers so they opted for the latter – less conspicuous they thought. However, glancing at the six fellow inhabitants, they realised they would stick out like sore thumbs. None of the other men had the canvas clothes but all wore grey overalls with reinforced leather inside legs and around the bottom of each leg to make working and riding that much easier. Fin noticed that the overalls buttoned down the outside of each leg onto a red stripe, and the buttoned flap to make it easier to relieve yourself was also edged in red. All had ankle boots like Fin and Thomo but the overalls fastened under the heel with a strap to hold firmly in place. *If only he had those overalls yesterday*, thought Fin.

"Bob." Fin turned to see an outstretched hand. "Bob Halls, I was in the Militia and persuaded to join this lot," jerking a thumb towards the outside of the tent. "See you two are new, where you from?"

"We got 'volunteered' in Christchurch," taking the hand as welcoming. "I'm Fin Ross."

"And I'm Thomo."

"I expect they'll get you kitted up and ready for riding. Do you ride?"

"We rode here!" responded Thomo, "And have the sores to prove it!" Fin mocked himself standing bow legged replicating the position of his riding, but in all honesty, it hurt a lot. Apart from Bob Halls and Thomo, Fin discovered that he had been sharing with Bill Bennett (a poacher accepting the hospitality of the army rather than prison), John Smith (the youngest son of a merchant trader who did not want to go into the priesthood), Wee Willy Wilkinson (even younger than Fin and enlisted at a country fair), Donald McConnell (a Scottish miner who had a disagreement with some Englishmen and volunteered to escape them), Dai Davies (a Welsh farmer who could not remember how he got there) and 'Tricky Dicky' Dickinson (grew up in London and was 'enlisted' after getting caught in the store room of the new barracks at Woolwich).

The water was more than chilly to wash and his new friends ensured that he had a shave of sorts. Breakfast was quite familiar to Fin: bread, some sort of fat dripping to spread on and the essential hot tea. The sky had brightened and in spite of the first hint of frost, glistening cobwebs strewn across the bushes of the surrounding parkland, Fin felt more positive and less foolish, but still had the nagging thought, *Be careful who you trust.*

Fin and Thomo were soon kitted out in the overalls, shirt and blue forage cap with a yellow band; all other necessities would be issued later, they had been informed. He was surprised that there were only two tents of new recruits but Sergeant Webber put them into two lines of eight and started the process of drill: standing to attention and 'at ease' were mastered relatively quickly. Fin had already experienced some of this in Christchurch, but the commands of 'eyes right' and 'eyes left' confused several of the slower-witted men and boys, not sure which is which. Sergeant Webber remedied this with a sharp crack of his badge of office: official or not, he was never without a long length of gnarled wood that could be used to straighten lines as easily as crack heads. Each new 'gunner', as they would now all be called, who had trouble remembering his left and right, was given a sharp smack so that the recruit had a mark 'left' on his hand! The drill improved but Sergeant Webber reminded them constantly: "This is for team spirit my brave boys; if you can't do this on foot, what hope do we have on horseback!"

There wasn't a great deal of marching, but a morning of constant orders – "Eyes front. At Ease. Atten….tion. Eyes left. Forward march. Halt." – was plenty enough for many of the new boys. As soon as all had taken a drink, Sergeant Webber called the lines to attention, turned them to left face and then proceeded to march them to the stables. Once there, he demonstrated with great care the difference between the curry comb (to get the caked mud off the horse's coat), the stiff brush (to make sure any loose hair and dirt are completely removed), and the soft brush (to make the coat gleam). He warned the unwary of the importance of brushing the shortened tail – the fashion of all British cavalry – from the side so as to avoid being kicked, and he also demonstrated the correct way to lift a hoof to check for stones or other problems with the horse-shoes – which they would report immediately should they find any! Having spent the time demonstrating, he then announced: "Right boys, we will have a little wager." The new gunners looked at each other. "See that firkin at the end of the stalls?" They all glanced towards a small barrel, enticingly placed and already pegged to serve out beer. "The best tent will have it!" A cheer, that made some horses lift their heads, showed Sergeant Webber that he was already instilling the need for pride in their performance. "So once I have allotted each of you your mount, and this will be yours for life, however short that may be – you will set to and have one hour." He deliberately took out his pride and joy. "I will time you on this timepiece that was kindly donated to me by a Frenchie Colonel who no longer had any use for it, him being dead, during the retreat to Corunna with the great Sir John Moore, God bless him, as great a general as you would wish to serve under."

All gunners set to their task with a will to win the prize. Some had more use of the curry comb than others, some had more issues with hooves, but all were determined not to let their tent down. Before the hour was complete, Sergeant Webber returned unexpectedly. "Attention! Come on, come on, out of your stalls. We have an emergency and have been requested to help at the menagerie. Quickly! Collect a rake or pitch-fork and get outside. Line up at the gate as we did this morning, two lines, you know your positions."

Whatever the emergency, the prize would have to wait.

No one had dared ask what a menagerie was, but they soon found out as they marched around the great house, past a glass-walled building and towards a raised earthwork. As they approached, a great squawking and screeching could be heard which got louder as they came through a brick arch tunnel into a clearing that had de Lacy encircling it with layers of seats. "Wow!" whispered Fin to himself, he had never seen anything like it. "This, gentlemen, is what you call an h'amphitheatre, like what they had in Roman times… so I am told," and circling slowly, "and these are the cages that the Duke keeps his collection of creatures from around the world."

Sergeant Webber allowed the group to stare open-mouthed at the array of creatures, the like of which no one had ever seen. Fin noticed a group of bears, like the ones he had seen on the pamphlet in the Bargate, Christchurch. A bird screeched behind him, making him turn to see a creature with a wingspan larger than his outstretched arms, hit the bars of its pen, briefly clasp the bars with talons that would tear anything in its grasp before rebounding back to the perch amongst trees at the back of the enclosure. "Golden Eagle, I was told Ross, some fly free in the north of England and into Scotland apparently."

McConnell interrupted. "I've seen them flying free over the moors back home Sergeant, been known to take a sheep or small deer they have."

"Not surprised having seen those claws!" the Sergeant replied. Howls and shrieks turned heads towards a group of creatures chasing and cavorting after one another.

"What are they Sergeant?" asked Dickinson. "I've seen men chasing after floosies like that, around Whitechapel of a Saturday night!"

Amidst the laughter, Sergeant Webber brought order. "We haven't time to stand gawping at monkeys and the like. We have to go and find one that has escaped, and it is no less than the Duke's pride and joy – a lion, or to be exact, a lioness! Anyone ever seen one? There are travelling shows." No one had. Fin knew about lions from Bible stories of a Sunday morning: Sampson fighting one with his bare hands, Daniel being thrown into the lions' den, but he had never seen a picture of one. "Well it's like a cat – you have all seen a cat I presume, but it's a lot bigger, and the teeth and claws are likely to tear you apart. Ross, Thomson, pick up that net – you will be throwing it over the creature when we have cornered it." Fin and Thomo looked at each other with an expression of 'why us' but diligently picked up the net, far thicker than those Fin had used for fishing. "Right, it escaped through that arch, so that's where we are going. We will spread out and search ten paces apart until we find it. Anyone spotting it will signal by shouting my name, Sergeant Webber. Clear?" Nods from all gunners allowed the Sergeant to lead them through the brick-arched tunnel and into the parkland. Having spread out the required distance with Fin and Thomo slightly behind, ready to go to wherever the signal came from, the lion hunt started!

The first part of the search proved uneventful. Fortunately, the sheep had been moved from that part of the parkland the previous day and there was little sign of any animal having passed through, the ground being baked hard from a good summer with only morning dews giving any moisture, but as they approached the bordering woodland, a shout came from the right end of the line. "Sergeant Webber!" It was Bob Halls, one of gunners that shared Fin's tent. Webber ordered all to halt and be alert, then hurried across to the gunner. "Where is it Halls?"

"Can't see it Sergeant but look at that, and that." Halls was pointing at one large paw-print in a mole hill, as big as the span of your hand and also directing the Sergeant at a gap in the hedge with recently broken twigs and branches.

"Well spotted Halls," and turning to the rest, "We're on the right track, move on."

Squeezing through the hedge into the woodland took time and closed the line, requiring a further pause before the search continued. Visibility was reduced by overhanging branches, still full of the majority of their leaves and none of the party were keen to meet this beast, slowing the pace markedly. Fin recalled his last experience of beating through woodland, pushing the birds towards the shooting party; this time he wasn't sure if he was the hunter or the hunted. By the time they emerged onto a pathway that allowed carts to be brought in for loading logs, most were sporting scratches and cuts, as well as twigs, burrs and leaves being stuck in their hair. "Right, nothing so far, we have to push on. Ready…" But before he had finished his words, Sergeant Webber turned to the right as a gunshot and screams rang out. "Halls, can you see anything?"

"No Sergeant, must be down in the valley."

"Well we will go to the sound of the gun and see what it is. Shouldn't be anyone shooting at this time of the day." Webber led the group to the edge of the wood and on into the meadow that led down to the London Road. It was only a furlong away and there was certainly a commotion. Even at this distance, they could see the horses rearing in front of an inn, the driver using his whip while the guard perched precariously at the back, was attempting to keep his balance desperately attempting to reload.

"Come on men, if that is the Duke's lion down there, he won't be wanting them to kill it!" They headed for the gate, a simple construction of five horizontal bars with one diagonal, but each end had been made more elaborate to appear as shepherds' crooks with the crook resting on the top bar. Fin noted it was metal rather than wood, the Duke trying to impress, he suspected. Turning immediate left, there was uproar ahead, no more than twenty paces away: from an upstairs window a man, with a large white beard covering over half of his face, was shouting for the passengers to stay inside of the coach and not set foot outside. The sign behind the bearded man announcing to travellers that they were at the 'Rose and Crown', a beautifully painted red rose surmounted by a glittering crown on one side but with the same attention to detail; a white rose and crown on the other. The driver was tugging at the reins trying to control the horses whilst lashing at something on the near side of the leading horse of four. The gates to the courtyard had been shut but a dog had appeared from somewhere in the inn and was leaping and barking at the horses. Shrieks of women came from inside of the coach, which had the same colours of black and deep red as Fin had seen on their journey before. Sergeant Webber crossed the road and had approached to within ten paces, calmly turned to the rest of the search party and ordered half to continue around the back of the coach whilst the second half approached the front with him. Fin could now see the lion. The size of a donkey or small pony, it was launching itself onto the hindquarters of the leading nearside horse, which was bucking and lashing, but impeded by its own harness, struggled to make contact with the attacker. Scratches were seeping blood down the leg and belly of the black horse, matching the colours of the coach, whilst the dog, a black and white collie that had belonged to the owner of the inn, leaped repeatedly and bravely at the tormentor. One such attack must have met its mark as the lion stopped leaping at the horse and turned its attention on the dog. The dog hunched down onto its front paws growling and barking defiantly at its adversary, four times its size. The collie was backing away but would then suddenly launch a feint against the lion baring its teeth and snapping but never with a chance of inflicting any real damage. The lion slowly pawed deliberate steps towards the dog, its sleek tan coat glistening, its teeth white as the walls of the inn but still the dog would snap in and out.

"Ross, Thomson, be ready with that net. The rest of you use the blunt ends to corner this beast." Sergeant Webber had retreated as the dog retreated towards them; the horses had calmed but were still skittish and tossed their heads as the unfamiliar figures passed them. The guard had completed reloading and was preparing to fire. "Don't you go shooting that weapon, you'll hit my men, leave it to us!" Fin wasn't the only one to note that they were Sergeant Webber's men, and a sense of pride made them even more determined. The collie took one feint too many and the lion swatted the poor dog with a thumping right paw sending the creature into a hedgerow. Instantaneously the lion had pounced and landed on the stricken dog, holding it in its jaws. "Now! This is our chance. That beast will have to come through us to escape. That hedge has her cornered. Ready with that net!"

The lion backed herself onto her haunches, reluctant to give up her prize but knowing there was danger. A semi-circle of gunners approached with prongs of their rakes and pitch-forks pointed downward, leaving the nervous Fin and Thomo spreading their net as wide as they could and bracing themselves for the impending tussle. "Go on, get nearer," urged their fellow gunners.

"It's all right for you to say that, you're not getting near to those teeth!" muttered Thomo. "Nor those claws – have you seen how big the paws are? Like frying pans they are."

"Enough of your chatter, get closer but be ready. The rest of you tighten in blocking the escape routes – we have to get her into the net." Fin had been in a few scrapes, usually the result of too much beer at summer fairs, but he had never felt the apprehension and fear that he felt now. Sweat trickled down his back. The hair on the back of his neck were standing to attention better than any parade with Sergeant Webber. In spite of gripping the net tightly, he felt his palms slippery. His mouth was dry and he had to consciously force every shuffling inch forward and then he felt the full force of the cornered lion. Fin knew that he had flinched as the lion let out her roar which startled the horses at the inn, but he hadn't realised how hard he would be hit. The net enveloped the beast but neither Fin nor Thomo held their feet. A tumbling tangle of arms and legs hit the hardened surface of the turnpike road knocking the wind out of man and beast. The weight of two men landing on the lion simultaneously made the beast roar again, striking out entangled paws, gaping mouth lashing side to side. Fin could smell the lion, odours emitting from its stomach, and a fang as thick as his thumb smashed into his cheek as the beast tried to writhe its way to escape. Fin shouted, "Don't let go!" wrestling the net to catch as much of the lion as he could. A paw burst through the net, claws scything past Fin's forearm and landing on Thomo's shoulder, shredding his shirt. "Roll on top Fin, roll on top, we can hold it down!" Thomo was desperately trying to wrestle the net to overlap with Fin. The lion had stretched one paw through the net but in doing so, allowed

Fin to tighten his grip, pulling the net up to the shoulder whilst using his feet to force the back legs away, hooking the heel of his boot into the hip and knee joints. Briefly releasing his left hand, he reached across to Thomo and grabbed tight onto his side of the trap, pulling net and Thomo with him and creating a sandwich of men and lion. The snarling and shouting continued as men and beast fought for the upper hand. The net had caught the front paws and got tangled in the jaws, but the strength in the back legs was proving a problem. Fin was desperately kicking his weight into his side of the fight but Thomo was still thrashing against a hind leg that would not give up the fight. "Fin, grab this!" Fin gritted his teeth and buried his head deep into the lion's ribs to gain leverage for his tug of war. He glanced up with only his eyes moving to see Thomo's hand stretching another square of netting over the back of the lion. Fin understood that Thomo was trying to exert as much pressure on the lion to immobilise her and gradually he released his fingers from his hold to grasp Thomo's wrist and heave him further over the back. The additional weight on its haunches was too much for the lion and at last the back legs splayed, allowing Thomo to roll across Fin and take up all slack left in the net.

Sergeant Webber threw a rope to Halls and ordered him to tie the back legs together whilst he did the same at the front. "Well done men! Wilkinson, get a cart from the inn, we have to take this back to the House. You two," addressing his comments to Fin and Thomo, "don't you move – she may be quiet now, but you never know what she might do."

"Don't worry Sergeant, I'm not letting go until those teeth and claws are safely tied!" Thomo was grinning but his arms and back were aching more than his legs had done from their ride.

Finally with a last tie of a knot to muzzle the lion, the Sergeant allowed them to roll away. Getting to their feet, they received numerous pats on the back. "You two are crazy." "You'll be locked away in Bedlem for taking on a lion bare handed!" They didn't know all the names of their fellow gunners, but they were pleased to have the adulation, and more pleased to have survived!

"Sergeant," it was a passenger from the coach, "I say Sergeant. Which regiment are you from?"

"We are the Royal Horse Artillery sir, and proud to be so!"

"Well I can't say much for your dress code, but your men are a credit to you, a credit."

"Thank you sir, came straight from the stables sir, they have just enlisted and not had uniforms issued."

"You have saved us all from a terrible ordeal. Well done, well done!" and with that he turned on his heel and returned to the inn. Stable boys had replaced the team of horses and the coach was about to pull away again, all passengers having had a reviving tot of something, a bit stronger than usual!

"Sergeant, what are we to do with this?" It was Bennett, holding the body of the collie.

"What are you going to do about my dog? Took years to train her it did, and what about th'orse? Mail coaches rely on me for new 'orses and now I got one that is mauled bad. How will I set for next coach?" The innkeeper, the same white bearded fellow who had been shouting from the upper window, had stormed up the side of the road – now that the lion had been tamed.

"I am sure that the Duke will be happy to replace what you have lost." Sergeant Webber did his best to placate the angry owner.

Tenderly taking the dead body of his dog from Gunner Bennett, the innkeeper continued his rant: "Can't just buy new dog. Can't just find another 'orse!"

"As I have said, I am sure that the Duke will make good and support your position. He is a generous man and you will be helped."

"Helped, I need more than help. That beast has near ruined me."

"Sergeant, if I may?" all turned.

"What is it Parkin?"

"I would like to explain to our innkeeper that the Duke will be ready to furnish a comprehensive restitution of that which has been lost, as well as offering him recompense in full atonement for his traumatic experience." The Inn Keeper was not the only one who was slightly bemused by what had just been said.

"Exactly Parkin, will that do sir?" Sergeant Webber had turned back to face the silent owner of the inn.

"Well, when you put it like that, I'm happier." He shuffled his way back to the entrance of the inn, the coach about to pull away.

"Right, load the beast onto the cart, we must get her back to where she belongs… and Parkin, I'm not sure exactly what you said, but well done, got him off our back that did, very clever. Where d'you learn those words?"

"I was training to be a medical man, Sergeant, a surgeon, but got in a bit of trouble for accepting persons that had only too recently been interred following their demise. We did it only to learn more about the workings of the human anatomy."

"You mean that you was a grave-robber!!" Halls had cut Parkin short, much to everyone's amusement.

Loading the lioness onto the back of the cart wasn't as easy as it looked: the dead weight of the trussed big cat was greater than it appeared and, in spite of the ropes, she could still lash out with a kick and those claws were lethal for any unwary gunner. Eventually, Sergeant Webber had the bright idea of getting a strong pole, threading it between the front and back legs and then with men at the front and back, they finally succeeded in the lift. Sergeant Webber had decided that a slightly longer route on the return to the House would be safer and although it added an additional half mile, no one wanted to risk the lioness being bumped out of the cart, trekking over ditches and gaps in the hedgerow as they had crossed in the search.

By the time they had returned, the keepers of the menagerie had lit torches to guide them towards the empty pen, much needed as they came through the gloom of the tunnel entrance to the viewing enclosures. Halls led the horse past the pen and then gently put pressure on the nearside of the horse's jaw to help turn the cart as well as make the horse step back. Fin and Thomo had climbed up over the side panels to be ready to lift the head end of the pole, Parkin and Wilkinson had got the tail end. Until they had walked away from the tail-gate, Fin and Thomo were stuck on the cart, but gradually they edged their way forwards and slipped over the end to plant their feet firmly on the ground. The lioness seemed to have become far more submissive and apart from the occasional growl, resigned herself to her fate. Ducking through the low gate of the pen, the four gunners lowered the beast as gently as they could onto the straw lain over the grass.

"*Now what?*" thought Fin, *It was one thing catching the ferocious animal but how do you let it free?* The same thought must have crossed the minds of the other gunners and they turned their heads towards Sergeant Webber as if he was the fount of all wisdom. He needn't have worried as their answer came in the form of two keepers who had long poles with a wide 'v' shaped prong at one end. "We'll fix these about 'er neck. You must cut the ropes you bound her with, and then get out. She 'in't going be 'appy when she's released, but we have some meat outside that we will have thrown to the back of the pen and that should be enough for her."

Parkin and Wilkinson beat a hasty retreat having played their part, a part that would, no doubt, be exaggerated at numerous retellings over long evenings across tavern tables and around campfires in the future, leaving Fin and Thomo to take the long-bladed knives. The blades were more than knives but shorter than swords and Fin thought the thickness of the blade made them more akin to the tools of a butcher. There was no point in trying to undo the many times tied knots, but they both needed to take care that they did not harm the animal or release one end too soon. They did not want to have a further round of lion wrestling! "If we get the net off her first," Thomo suggested, "it will give better clearance for the blades to cut the leg ropes."

"You'd best cut the muzzle ties first young men." This being directed at Fin, he took a long look at the ropes entangled with the net. Perhaps this might be a good idea to them with the long poles, but he felt very vulnerable again as he started to cut the strands that made up the rope. It took over twenty saws but eventually the knots slipped away allowing the beast to roar in disgust, more as an exercise of stretching pained muscles and jaws than as an attempt to attack, but Fin stepped back and the keepers kept their poles firmly in place. "Let's get the rest of the net off." Thomo had started unravelling the two ends that had crossed during the fight earlier, but Fin could not get any further than freeing the body as the front paws had been tied through the broken squares of the net. For the first time, Fin dared place his hand on the lion, patting her neck softly and whispering: "We'll soon have you out of this mess. Now don't you go escaping again. The locals would have you shot; we were the ones on your side. Now I'm going to cut these paws free and my friend will do your back legs," then raising his voice to allow Thomo and the keepers to hear, "Ready to cut, get that meat ready."

So many knots had been tied that it took several minutes to reach the final bond. A keeper had shown the meat, half a side of cow, and had placed it ten paces ahead of the lioness. She was already salivating and licking her lips as the final cuts were made and the ropes fell free. "Out you go boys, we'll tak'it from 'ere, and thanks for wha' you've done. She means a great deal to the Duke, he'd hate for 'er to be 'armed in any way." Fin and Thomo retreated slowly through the low door, waiting for the keepers to guide their charge towards the meat and then slowly back off, never turning their backs on her though, ducking through one at a time and fastening the gate shut.

"What I want to know is…, how did she get free in the first place? These pens look secure?" It was Sergeant Webber interrogating the keepers.

"Well the Duke likes to show 'er off to guests in this arena and we was guidin' 'er round grass when I slipped and lost my 'old on the fender. She was off like a startled 'are, no stoppin' 'er, through tunnel and away."

"Next time I suggest that you try a leading rein like we use when breaking in a wild horse for riding. If she does try to bolt, you have a strong restraint; if you attach it to a pole staked in the ground, she can't get too far then."

"Good idea Sergeant, we'll have a go next time."

Sergeant Webber turned to the gunners, his face eerily illuminated by the torches placed in the prepared holders around the amphitheatre. "You two," indicating Fin and Thomo, "best get to the medical orderly to get those cuts treated, but then it's back to the stables and finish the task we started earlier. Lion hunt or not, those horses need cleaning, and you all best start again by washing down and brushing from top to toe." An audible groan reverberated in the enclosure, "And don't forget to replace the bedding, oats and water, pile the muck and straw in the courtyard and then you can see about your own feeding."

"And drinking Sergeant, we have that firkin to win!"

"Thank you Halls, yes the beer will still be there!"

Fin and Thomo had very little treatment from the medical orderly. A passing surgeon had been interested to hear the story of the lion hunt but apart from washing the cuts in a mixture of hot water and vinegar, and rubbing a liniment (the same lotion Fin had seen George's dad, the smith, use on horses back in the village), onto the bruise swelling under his right eye, they were ushered out to allow the dinner set up in the marquee to continue.

Even to their untrained eyes, the stables looked a better place than when Fin and Thomo had left to go 'hunting'! Someone had replaced their stalls' bedding straw, oats were in the feeder and fresh water had been put in the basin. "Thanks mates!" Fin called down the stalls causing a few heads to rise above the wooden panelling and glance back through the blackened bars of the upper partitions, allowing a clear view for the length of the stable complex.

"You're back then?" Although Fin couldn't see the owner of the voice, he had already come to know that it was Halls.

"Can't let the other tent have that beer, didn't want to let you down Halls." At this a head did appear, "Now Ross, I'm Bob and only Halls to officers and the like."

"Right Bob, I'm Fin and..."

"And I'm Thomo."

"Thomo Thompson. Unusual name that!" Bob knew that it wasn't his name but took any opportunity to add a bit of light relief.

"Never you mind what it is, it's Thomo… ok?"

"Fine, and you've got some catching up to do!"

Fin and Thomo took their horses outside to wash down rather than create further cleaning in the stables, rubbed the horses dry and then led them back into the respective stalls for further curry combing, stiff and soft brushing. Lanterns, securely fastened in case of fire, were the only illumination for the gunners and it was the voice that announced visitors rather than any sight of approaching officers.

"End of stalls, stand to attention!" Sergeant Webber, unmistakeably. The second figure became more obvious as the pair entered the extent of the illuminated glow in which the first lantern bathed the first stall – Captain Ramsay. He had presumably come from an official engagement as his boots gleamed and even in the dull light of the stable lanterns, the gold tassels drew the eye to the top of each boot. His breeches were immaculately white. A curved sword was sheathed in a polished black and gold scabbard, partly held in place by a sabretache with further gold lace bordering the King's initials on the same blue background slung from a belt, hidden by a red and yellow barrel sash that merged the breeches with the short blue jacket. The abundance of lace, crimson collar and cuffs was half hidden by a Pelisse, a Hussar style jacket, worn over the left shoulder edged in grey fur, lined in the same imposing red of the jacket collar, the loose sleeve gently swaying as he walked. Captain Ramsay had removed his Tarleton, carrying it under his right arm to reveal a well brushed head of chestnut hair parted on the right-hand side and well-groomed side whiskers that reached his jaw, but with no hint of beard or moustache.

"Well done men. I hear congratulations are due, well done! In recognition for the support that you have given the Duke in capturing his lioness, once you have finished here in the stables, you will all receive your share from a firkin, lately sent from the Rose and Crown, set up by your tents. In addition to that which Sergeant Webber so kindly set up as a prize this very morning!" A loud cheer echoed around the enclosed stalls, causing horses to shift their footing. "With men like you, we will go far, won't we Sergeant?"

"A very good start Captain Ramsay, a very good start!"

"Thank you gentlemen. I will leave you now but I am proud that you will be part of our Troop."

Sergeant Webber smartly saluted his Captain and as soon as he had left the stables, ordered the gunners: "At Ease!" He strolled along the stalls inspecting the floor coverings, lifting straw with his cudgel, stepping past nervous gunners to take a closer look at the horses. *Yes,* he thought, *they have worked hard; yes, they have cleaned their horses well, yes they have used the different brushes and it shows a wealth of care for their mounts.* On reaching the end, he turned and rested one hand on the awaiting prize. "You have worked hard but, make no mistake, this will be a sweet dream once we get in the field. No nice stables to come back to. No fresh straw, or oats or water. We'll have to go foraging for it, and always pay for what we take mind you, always pay." It seemed an unusual emphasis but something that needed remembering as soon as possible to avoid further issues in the future. "This has to be the standard that we will mark every day against. You have put everything into these horses, but it can't be once in a month of Sundays but every day for every horse. We have to have every one of you ready for every day and so remember…" – he stepped forward to stand well in the intersecting circles of light from two lanterns – "remember that your horse comes first and then you get fed and watered second." He returned to the firkin and gently tapped the wooden slats causing a dull sound indicating it was full! "The winners of the prize… if only Taylor had brushed that tail a bit more – after all, it is only short being docked an' all…" heads turned with smiles from the opposing tent, "…mind you, on the other 'and, if only Parkin had washed all four hooves as well as he had spoken to the innkeeper, and if anyone can tell me what it meant…" Amidst guffaws of laughter Parkin tried to explain.

"Sergeant, I was trying to persuade the innkeeper to allow us to…"

"I knows what you was about, Parkin, and just because I don't know all your fancy words, I'm still grateful. I bet he's still puzzling over your restititushun and your at-home-ment, but it did the trick and we are here now. So I am judging the competition a draw and we can all go and get our food and have a very good night!"

With cheers ringing around the courtyard, the gunners left slapping each other on the back whist Donald McConnell carried the firkin under one arm, taking care that not a drop would be spilled from the tap.

Chapter 11

The gunners sat round with plates of stew, a mix of potato, carrot, beans and meat from the Duke's kitchen no less, a meal as good as Fin could remember, and there was no shortage of beer! Even with their two tents it meant that they would be well supplied, two firkins offering one hundred and forty-four pints of beer. It was a fortunate late night worker that night, as the later the evening went, the merrier the gathering became and anyone passing by, as were the menagerie keepers, was invited to share the provisions. Fin hadn't noticed before but there were women in camp! Although they seemed to wander from huddle to huddle, he soon recognised an attachment between five of the men in particular: McConnell the strong Scot; Rogers, whose woman had a small child wrapped in a scarf and tied at her back to allow both her hands to be free; Hughes, who seemed only as young as Fin but was obviously infatuated by his lovely blue-eyed blonde partner; Black, who had not just a wife but two children, a boy and girl who toddled safely through the camp-fires, and Hogg whose wife seemed to fuss over him constantly, but there again, she fussed over the food cooking in the kettle pot, she fussed over the refilling of mugs, she fussed over all of the men, women and children like a mother hen keeping her brood safe and supplied.

It was on this night that they discovered that some had more music in them than others! All joined in the songs with varying degrees of accuracy but the keepers found two fiddles, a drum, a whistle cum-recorder and a flute. Fin had long since learned to play a recorder – an instrument passed down through his family, Taylor immediately took up a violin, Black started a rhythm on the drum and Dickinson took the flute. One of the keepers led the music with the second of the violins and dancing was enjoyed by all. The sky was clear, the stars were out and between bursts of music the mugs would be recharged and so the evening wore on. Hughes' woman was actually his wife. They had run away from home to marry. She had a beautiful voice, and Hogg's wife was adept at teaching dances.

The gunners got to know each other around the camp-fires sharing their story of how they got caught but at that moment on that night it seemed that a stroke of luck or fate had bundled the group of strangers into a budding friendship.

"Heh, Fin dearie," it was Black's wife, "Elijah here says you is called Fin Ross, I never heard of a Fin before. Who gave you that for a name?" She prodded the fire with another branch from the awaiting wood pile sending a shower of embers skywards.

"It was my grand-father's idea. He loved the stories from ancient times. Could be because we lived near a very old hill fort of earth banks and ditches to stop invading Romans. There are lots of stories about the way things are and when I was born, there was a mass of hazel nuts, like this harvest. Some believe that hazel nuts give wisdom, and he told me the story of a great chieftain who wanted to be the wisest man in the world, and to do that he had to eat the fish of the sacred salmon from the sacred pool that had eaten from the hazel branches drooping into the water. The chieftain caught the fish and gave it to one of his students to cook but not eat. While cooking the sacred salmon, the student carefully turned the fish but noticed a blister on its skin. He wanted the fish to look its best for his master and so he popped the blister with his thumb, but it was so hot his thumb was burned and so he quickly sucked it to stop burning. He presented the fish to his chief but nothing changed for the great leader. However, his young student became one of the greatest teachers ever – and his name was Finn McCool. So my grand-father thought that, with the hazel harvest being so great, I would be wise and convinced my father and mother to take this name."

"Not so wise as to avoid getting nabbed for the army Fin!" it was Bob Halls laughing.

"Never you mind Fin, I think it's a great name, unusual like, but a great name. Elijah here ain't so religious and I'm Martha. If you need any help with your washing and mending, you bring 'em to me."

"Does that go for all of us Martha?" a chorus of gunners mocked.

"Of course dearies, but you have to pay!"

Another of the women stood and wandered over, it was McConnell's wife. "What about a song Donald? Do you minstrels know 'Over the Hill'?" The keeper struck up a steady drone and Elijah Black beat the drum: Donald McConnell stood to sing, stepping closer to the fire's warmth:

"Our 'prentice Tom may now refuse, To wipe his scoundrel Master's shoes, For now he's free to sing and play, Over the hills and far away. Over the hills and o'er the main, In Flanders, Portugal and Spain. The queen commands and we obey, Over the hills and far away.

"Courage boys, 'tis one to ten, But we return all gentlemen, All gentlemen as well as they, Over the hills and far away. Over the hills and o'er the main, In Flanders, Portugal and Spain. The queen commands and we obey, Over the hills and far away."

Fin picked up the tune and joined in as Donald led the others in further verses and choruses.

Once he had finished singing, Fin asked Donald and Moira how they had come so far south. "Well, as great a land as our Scotland is, there are times when it is best to be elsewhere, you might like to say."

"You were a miner, I hear?" Thomo had re-joined the group around the fire.

"Yes you hear right, I was a miner, all day underground hacking away at coal to bring riches to the foundry owners casting more and more metal for the cannon and cannon balls, muskets and swords, bayonets."

"So what brings you here?" Thomo was persistent.

"Well my wonderful Moira was, you might say, otherwise engaged!"

"Well might you say that, Donald! I was promised to be married to another man I had never met, and if his likeness was anything to go by, a right ancient miserable skinflint he looked."

"So when I met Moira one market day I promised to save her from this arrangement, but the only way to do so was to escape Scotland and come where we wouldn't be found. We are married, legal, so no one can split us asunder!" He moved to pull Moira closer to him, bent his head and kissed her lightly on the lips.

"That's like us Tom," it was the youngest of the women speaking, "We had to run from home before I had to marry Joseph Cooper because my father and his father would always go drinking together and our families spent a lot of time together. Joseph was infatuated..."

"I'm not surprised," interrupted Bob. "We're all madly in love with you Sally!"

69

"Excuse me Mister Halls, I have a husband here who I am madly in love with!" and she sat on Tom's lap flinging her arms around his neck.

"Best you all be getting some sleep!" It was Sergeant Webber making his final rounds of the night before handing over to the night duty officer. "We have a busy day ahead, got to learn to ride these horses properly, army style." He walked over to Fin and Thomo. "You two might want to put this on your legs, I had the brown paper soaked in hot vinegar, lot of riding to be done."

"Thanks Sergeant, and goodnight."

The group slowly dispersed into their tents. Fin was aching, bruised and grateful for the brown paper to ease the soreness of his thighs, but it felt a good ache, an ache that he had earned doing something worthwhile. As he pulled his blanket over his shoulders, he thought of his own romantic adventures: the tricks of the barmaid and the beautiful Lady Ellen – would he ever meet her again?

Chapter 12

A few sore heads greeted the dawn as men stumbled out of tents. Fin was amazed to see Martha already serving scalding hot tea to any who ventured near the fire. "Thanks Martha, you're up early." "With those two to feed, I'm always up early and no reason why I shouldn't make myself useful for the rest of you!" Fin looked across to see her daughter and son arms full of twigs adding to the wood pile.

Few of the other gunners were up and not even Sergeant Webber had appeared so Fin went to sit on an upturned log used for chopping the logs but straightened suddenly as he heard a voice. "Mind where you be sitting Master Ross, don't want that axe doing such a handsome young man a damage!" Fin hadn't noticed Sally Hughes sitting between the tents a shawl trying to cover her modesty as she nursed a baby.

"I'm sorry Mrs Hughes," Fin blushed as fully took in what she was doing and tried not to stare, "I didn't think anyone was here."

"Don't you Mrs Hughes me, I'm Sally or Sal to everyone." she was aware of Fin staring. "Haven't you seen a mother nursing before? This little one has a great appetite, and when he needs his feedin' he needs his feedin'! I'm sure you seen a pair of boobies before, no need to be shy, sit down with you." Fin tentatively retook his seat trying not to stare but not wanting to turn his back on Sally.

"I s'pose you're thinking about where the baby came from?" and without waiting for an answer: "What I said last night was true, we did run away or elope as some people call it. I didn't want to marry Joseph even if he would have had his way with me given the chance. But what I didn't say was that I'd been seeing Thomas in the barn and we got to know each other very well. There was no way that my father would have let Thomas near me. He didn't get on with his family, you see, and if he knew that I was going to have his child…" she raised her head to the sky, "the Lord knows what he would have done. My mother knows but we couldn't stay near so we started walking, got lifts on wagons going to market and ended up in Chichester." she paused to look at the spire of the cathedral appearing above the mist in the valley below. "That's when we, or rather Thomas volunteered," she lowered her voice to a barely audible whisper, "we said we were married last year and had been turned out by our landlord who was knocking down cottages to enclose the land." Fin raised his eyebrows at the risk Sally and Thomas had taken, it made his escape quite ordinary.

"All sorts of reasons bring us together Sally, some volunteer and some are forced, but we have to make the best of it."

"That's funny that is Master Ross."

"It's Fin Sally, please call me Fin."

"Well, my old mum always said the same whenever anything went array, 'there's no use blathering, you've got to make the best of it'. So best we had Fin, best we had."

"See you two getting better acquainted eh!" It was Bob Halls, mug of tea in one hand and chunk of bread in the other. "Don't you let her lead you astray, Fin," He gave Fin a nudge with his elbow as he squeezed beside Fin on the chopping block "Heh Sally you've already got a husband, keep your hands off this young'n." Sally turned and gave the broadest of grins to both gunners.

"Never you mind. Somethin' tells me that Master Ross will be capable of taking care of himself!" She wrapped the baby in its shawl and readjusted her bodice ties very deliberately, knowing that both men were watching intently.

"What you two gawping at?" they hadn't heard Sergeant Webber come across the grass.

"Just admiring the view!" replied Bob but Fin was red as a beetroot, almost choking on a mouthful of tea.

"Good stuff that, is it Ross?" and turning to Martha Black, "Is there enough for an ageing Sergeant in there Martha?"

"You know there's always enough for you Sergeant," and she mockingly dropped her chin and fluttered her eyelashes.

"You're a good'un you are Martha, ta." He took the mug and allowed the warmth to spread though his hands before turning back to the seated gunners. "Bugle will be sounding soon and all of the rest of the sleeping beauties will be up shaved, dressed in working order and ready by the time the hour chimes on the stable clock. We have a lot to do and we will all be riding before lunch."

"Can us ladies come too?"

Without turning, the sergeant replied, "No Martha, you will be staying here with the other women to make sure that the clothes are clean and mended, you have to earn your keep, the army don't like to have women around distracting."

"I bet you like a bit of distracting Sergeant!" Sally was laughing as she stood rocking her baby.

"Never you mind Sal, never you mind. How's young Thomas doin'?"

"He has a great appetite for his food he has."

"Voracious is he?" Arthur Parkin had emerged from the farther tent.

Sally turned to respond, "He isn't a wild animal if that's what you mean mister Parkin." Sally turned back winking at Fin,

"No, no what I meant was…"

Bob interrupted. "She knows what you meant Parky, she's jesting you."

"Oh, I, I didn't realise."

"Never you mind mister Parkin, we all need to learn some of your words don't we sergeant?"

"A good education he has. You have to use the science of war with our guns, I'm sure Parkin here will be a great asset. For one thing, I bet he can read any book you give him and in different languages too!"

"That is true Sergeant Webber. I was taught Latin and Greek at school and recently have been acquiring some knowledge of French and Spanish."

"Well I don't think words will be killin' many Frenchies. It's the guns and swords that work in battle, isn't that right sergeant?" Bob seemed bitter towards Parkin's education, Fin thought.

"Can't get away from the need for weaponry Halls, quite right, but before you get to grips with the Frogs, you have to know where to go and how to get there. For that, you need to be able to read maps – if you have one – talk to locals in whatever language they have, and then read orders or intercepted messages from the enemy." A trumpet sounded. "But we can't be standing here all day." Raising his voice as he poked his head into each tent. "Smells like a latrine in here. Now get up, lively now, time for your day to start. Stables by the time the clock chimes the hour!" With that Sergeant Webber left the camp and headed for the stables. As the others emerged from the tents, rolling the door flaps and brailings to ventilate the interior.

Fin walked over to Parkin. "Don't mind Bob, mister Parkin, I think he's a bit worried when he hears your words that he doesn't understand, he means no harm though. I wish I could read better, I can't do much past writing my name and reading small words."

73

"Perhaps we can help each other out with me teaching you to read better and you can help me with other skills."

"Don't know what I could teach you, mister Parkin, you being so well educated?"

"To start with, call me Arthur, Fin and...you have taught me something already! I loved your story about Fin McCool last night, I never had heard that myth before."

Fin smiled and added, "I've lots of stories from my grand–father, perhaps you might be interested?"

"Always ready to learn more about how our nation has come to be as it is."

In spite of the late night merriment, all gunners were ready, shaved, fed and in two lines outside of the stables before the clock chimed. "Well done gentlemen. A good start yesterday and this morning we will be learning to equip our horses correctly. First things first though, stalls to be mucked out, horses brushed and hooves checked. Fall out!"

The deliberate strokes from yesterday had been replaced with a greater purpose and the stables were ready for inspection in half the time it had taken the day before. Captain Ramsay accompanied Sergeant Webber on his rounds. He had asked for two horses to have their docked tails measured. All horses had to be chestnut in his troop, all horses for riding were fifteen hands and all tails docked, in the cavalry fashion, to an exact length.

Assembled in the stable-yard the gunners could see a wooden contraption that had the look of a carpenter's work block but with the legs having been lengthened and an extra piece of wood added at either end. "This," Sergeant Webber announced, "will be your horse – each of you will have your own." He gestured around the edge of the yard where enough wooden horses stood for each gunner, "and... we will learn how to saddle the horse so that you won't be harming it, or falling off yourself!"

"First;" he took hold of a large blanket, "you will learn to fold your blanket so!" He took the blanket and folded it three times lengthways and three times widthways. "Now I know your horses will fit the blanket as I have done, three folds equally in each direction, but every horse is different and you may have to have four, five or six equal folds if you get something smaller on campaign. Now taking your blanket you will place it high over the withers and slide it backwards to ensure that the horse's hair, that you have lovingly brushed, will all point in the same direction and not cause discomfort when your fat arses are in the saddle!" He

74

demonstrated by taking the blanket well up the additional neck piece of the wooden model before sliding it back to where the saddle would sit.

He next lifted the saddle, inverting it and parading in front of the lines of gunners. "As you can see, there is a wooden frame beneath this rawhide seat. This is called the 'Hungarian' pattern saddle and you must make sure that the nails and staples used to fix the stretched leather over the frame are all secure and flush – you do not want anything protruding into your seat! To mount the saddle, you will first ensure that the girth, this strap made of webbing, and the nearside stirrup are folded over the saddle. If you do not do this correctly, you are liable to have a buckle or stirrup hit you in your face, and as much as some of you might need an improvement to your looks, we cannot waste time with injured gunners. Place the saddle lightly on the blanket – make sure you have it the right way round, the high front goes nearest the neck – and then you will need to reach under the horse to collect the girth strap. Bringing it back under the belly of the horse, and this is why all that brushing is vital – no burrs or hard tufts to rub against – you will tighten the buckles so that you can fit your fingers between the girth and the horse. Take the horse for a short walk round and check again. Horses are clever creatures and will often inflate their lungs so that you think the girth is tight, but when you are riding the saddle becomes loose! It is possible to tighten whilst in the saddle but that is not for us this morning!

So far so good, now for the securing chest straps and crupper." He picked up a 'Y' shaped strap and then lifted the nearside leather flap at the front of the saddle. "Under the flap is a metal bracket that allows you to place this end of the chest strap through and secures it using the buckle and notches as fit for the size of the horse." He moved to the far side still explaining: "The same procedure has to be carried out on this side leaving the longer strap to be passed between the horses front legs, taken under the girth and then fastened with the buckle, again leaving space to have your fingers between the strap and horse. These straps prevent the saddle slipping backwards and this..." stepping to the hindquarters and displaying the crupper, a strap that looked like one long loop but with a flexible guiding loop that would enable the horse's tail to fit through, the loop depending on size of horse, "fixes to two more metal staples under the leather at the rear of the saddle. The same process as the chest strap, tightening as for your horse, fingers between strap and horse and the loop around the tail will prevent the

saddle sliding with you up and over the neck of your mount!"
Sergeant Webber paused to let all he had shown take effect and then
announced: "In front of the wooden horses, you will find blankets
and saddles, with straps attached – this time – so that you can try to
saddle up. It is not a race but we haven't got all day so –
Atten...tion!" all stiffened as taught, still and correct. "Fall out and
saddle up!"

The way a horse was saddled was different around the country
and across occupations, but each gunner had paid close attention and
the greatest difficulty was seemingly the easiest task – that of
putting on the blanket! For some, the folds were so thick the saddle
would sit like a circus performer; for others, the folds were so short
that the blanket covered the 'horse' from neck to tail and dragged
almost to the floor! In time and after repeated folding, the blanket
problem was solved and then the issues over the straps and how tight
took precedence.

Once all were saddled, Sergeant Webber put each to the test.
"Right gentlemen, it looks like a saddle is on each horse but will it
stay? You will hold the raised front and rear of the saddle, put your
left foot into the stirrup and, on command, push up and lift into the
saddle. If... if you have got it right, you will be in the saddle; if not,
you will be on the cobbles. So, ready to mount..." each gunner held
his breath as he grasped the saddle and waited... "boot into the
stirrup...." some had to release one hand to make the stirrup face
the right way and then quickly replace the hand – which Sergeant
Webber kindly ignored – "Prepare to mount by bending your right
knee and... mount!" To the surprise of all gunners, all ended up in
the saddle; a few had slipped slightly askew, but all were in place!

"Now we will do the reverse. Release your right boot, hold the
front of the saddle, swing your right leg and hold the rear..." before
he could finish three gunners slipped to the cobbles with saddles
under the belly of their wooden horse... "release your left boot...
dismount!" Those who had slipped early had recovered their feet
and much to their embarrassment tried to repair the slippage. "Right,
we will take all straps, saddles and blankets off and start again..."
Groans greeted this announcement but he continued, "And we will
continue to do so until I am happy that you will be able to saddle
your horse without fear of injuring it. Now get the saddles off!"

They repeated the process of saddling, mounting, dismounting
five times before Sergeant Webber allowed them to dismount and
stand by their horses. "Now for the bridle and reins!" He collected
the heap of leather. "This is the bridle. These are the two bits that

we will use to control the horse..." holding two metal pieces attached to leather straps "...to get the bits into the mouth hold the bridle in your right hand at the nearside of the horse, gently press against the horse's mouth where there is a gap between the teeth, the horse will open its mouth and you will slide the bits in making sure that they go over the tongue. Next you will need both hands to slide the headpiece up over the ears. Try one at a time..." he demonstrated with the wooden model "...you will need to untangle the forelock and make sure it is over the top of the brow band and then it will be necessary to have the throat lash to fasten the head piece securely. Make sure that you can fit your hand between the strap and neck before checking that the straps have no twists and the nose band and brow band have space for two fingers between strap and horse. Once secure, you will need to loop both reins over the horse's head and back down the neck to the saddle ready for mounting. I warn you that this will not be as simple as the saddling but we will have to get it right: without these reins securely in place, it will be very tricky to control your horse!"

Sergeant Webber was right and many gunners became entangled in a web of leather straps, but eventually and with support from each other, all 'horses' were complete. Having been given time for a short break the gunners took the opportunity to take a drink before being called back to their model horses. "Time to try out your new skills on the real thing! Unsaddle and move to your stalls." Sergeant Webber watched with some trepidation as his new gunners carried the burdens of the saddles and bridles to their respective horses. He strode up and down the stable block inspecting each gunner, stepping in where needed. He was pleased with the saddling but the gunners were struggling with the fitting of bits into the mouths. "Take it slowly and gently press the mouth where there is a gap between the teeth, be ready to lift the headpiece over... Well done Thomson, Taylor, Parkin, Black, Hogg, Bennett, Davies. Now go and help those having trouble."

"It's the two bits Sergeant, I get one in but can't fit both." Gunner Dickinson's honesty drew attention from Sergeant Webber.

"Try both bits in your hand at once and not one at a time," he stepped into the stall to assist, "That's better, see you can do it, now lift the head piece up and over the ears." Dickinson was soon ready and Sergeant Webber was able to order all horses to be led out into the yard.

"I know you have all ridden in a fashion before but we will do it the artillery way. Take the off side rein to the curb bit and place it through the first and second fingers of your left hand, pulling a loop to take up the slack out of the top of your hand by your thumb. The snaffle rein will go from the off side between the second and third fingers with the near side rein between the third and fourth fingers. We ride one handed, in case we need to use our weapons, but if you ever do need to use two hands, make sure that the snaffle stays in the left and switch the curb reins to the first and second fingers of the right hand. We will prepare to mount." Experience had taught him to move on and correct as he needed, too much time confused the more simple gunners. "Left hand reins and front arch of saddle, right hand to the rear of saddle. Left boot into stirrup... Prepare to mount..." All gunners bent their right knee aware that a fifteen-hand horse was a lot higher than their wooden models. "Mount!" Sergeant Webber was able to survey a scene of circling horses with two thirds of the troop mounted, if wobbling in the saddle, but there were still gunners stuck midway between ground and saddle as they lost impetus and balance with the turn of the horse. "You have pulled the nearside reins too far and caused your mount to turn. Let a little rein out, if not, return your foot to the ground and start again!" It was a simple measure, but it proved successful and on second attempt all were mounted.

"Let's go for a walk around the park so you can learn about your new partner. I will not insist on accurate files of pairs but do your best to stay in line." The two files followed their sergeant through the stable yard arch exactly as the clock struck twelve and passed into the parkland, staying to the well-worn paths that countless farm carts laden with harvest yields, shepherds and sheep had used in the past. Once out of sight of prying eyes and taking the troop into an undulation to hide them further, Sergeant Webber proceeded to encourage greater confidence in their riding abilities! All had stayed in the saddle, but that was a far cry from being proficient enough to take on the rigours of a cross-country ride with the obstacles that it may bring. "Without halting you will kick your boots out of the stirrups thus!" and he showed perfectly the release of both feet from the stirrup irons. It wasn't quite as simply concluded by his new gunners but they all achieved this. To the astonishment of the gunners he then moved onto further instructions: "Taking a firm hold of your saddle fore and aft, you will swing your legs back and forth and when confident, bring your right leg over the horse's neck to sit sideways; then your left leg over the tail to face rearward; your right leg over the tail to face sideways and finally your left leg over the neck again to complete your circumnavigation!" At each instruction, Sergeant Webber had carried out the exercise, precisely and slowly for all to see, "Don't worry about your horse, it will only walk slowly on!"

Fin took hold of the saddle and swung his legs back and forward, noticing a numbness between his legs as the swing became more vigorous. In his mind he counted down: three, two, one, lift and he attempted to raise his right leg over the neck of the horse. He realised that, to complete the quarter turn, he would have to let go of the raised front of the saddle. He might have looked ungainly but he managed the first part of the exercise, giving confidence to try to face rearward. This he found simpler as his left leg needn't lift quite so high. Campbell, Smith and Taylor had all slipped to the meadow, still on their feet but frustrated and annoyed at their slip. Fin continued the manoeuvres until he had regained his forward facing position, grinning from ear to ear, pleased as punch that he had circled the saddle. "Well done Ross, Parkin, Hogg; now go the other way!"

The grin left Fin's face as quickly as it had appeared and it was replaced by intense concentration, a furrowing of the brow, eyes half closed and unusually, the tip of his tongue protruding from between his lips. He leaned backwards taking the weight on his right hand at the rear of the saddle and all went well. He noticed that Parky had already completed the second circle as he had arrived facing backwards. As before, taking his leg across the tail of the horse seemed easier and maybe it was his over-confidence, maybe a sweaty palm on his left hand, but as he released his right hand and tried the last leg lift over the neck he slipped ignominiously out of the saddle to land off balance on his left heel before sprawling backwards, much to the merriment of his fellow gunners. "Come on Ross, no time for lying down, back in the saddle... You too, McConnell!" who had not yet completed his first circle.

Once all were back in the saddle Sergeant Webber instructed all to knot the reins and leave them against their horse's neck. "We will walk up the slope, turn to our right and come back down." It all sounded so simple, and Fin realised, as did the others, that control of the horse was essential, and after all, they were only walking, and slowly at that! They all ascended the rise in the meadow, they all squeezed sufficiently to turn their horse to the right – Fin wondered if Gretchen knew how to do this on her own and it was nothing of his riding skill – but it was on the descent that trouble hit. Elijah Black leaned too far back and went straight out of the saddle over his horse's rump, but in so doing trailed a flying right boot that hit the next man, Noah Hogg, squarely in the chest knocking him sideways. In reaction, Noah flung his arms for balance, and anything to grab hold of, which was Arthur Parkin. Parky was easily the best rider but taken by surprise, he could not hold his riding position and both gunners crashed to the ground. At the other end of the line, Fin and Thomo were so close that their legs were touching, but it acted like a brace and Fin felt more secure, which was more than Wilkinson felt as his horse gained the more level ground at the foot of the slope. He lurched forward and slipped over the nearside of the horse; the next man, Bennett, tried to avoid walking over Wilky but this sent his horse sideways into John Smith, who slipped slowly out of the saddle between horses pulling Bennett with him. They could all see the funny side of it, no one was seriously injured and Sergeant Webber simply said: "Shall we try that again gentlemen, and thank the Lord no one can see you lot!"

They did repeat it, and repeat it. Wilky seemed to be having more trouble than most in staying on his horse, but, for a first afternoon, Fin was pleased that he had managed to control his horse and was far more confident.

"Right gentlemen, you can take up your reins, get the fingering correct: first two fingers and loop out the top for the curb rein and third and fourth fingers for the snaffle. No stirrups mind you – let's show that you have learned something this afternoon... And if anyone of you slip out of that saddle, you will have me to answer to!"

Starting at the walk in files of two, the sergeant gently increased the pace to a slow trot as they retraced their path towards the stables. There wasn't anyone to view their improved skills but all had survived and taken their first step to becoming riders. "Ready to dismount... dis...mount!" Sergeant Webber was pleased with the troop. It would have been better to have all as proficient as Parkin but the others would learn: "You know the drill, unsaddle, wash down, clean and brush your horses... do not forget to check the hooves and then you will all clean the saddles rubbing in the concoction in those small tubs to keep the leather supple – it's no use having a strap or rein snap while you are in the middle of a battle!" He dismounted himself and monitored the unsaddling, not having to intervene with any gunner before he left to deal with his own horse.

By the time they had finished replenishing the stalls with fresh hay, straw, oats and water, they were all in need of something to slake their thirst and take the edge off their hunger. They wandered back to their tents but before reaching them they heard the voice of Martha Black: "And if you think you're feedin' in that state, you've another thing coming! Now get cleaned up before you put your grubby hands on this lovely feast what we have cooked for you!"

Chapter 13

Fin got used to the routines of the day: up early to get a mug of tea from Martha before they would all report to the stables to clean each stall, replenish food as well as cleaning and brushing the horses. Every day saw the troop ride out under the supervision of Sergeant Webber, each day saw an improvement in their riding ability; all could turn the circle in the saddle, at a walk as well! They had moved onto trotting, cantering and could gallop together for short distances, but this was where inexperience showed most with the gunners soon strung out. Sergeant Webber would remind them that it's no use the guns getting to the battle if the gunners were not with them! They had started to ride cross country taking small obstacles in their stride and all were confident that they would soon be able to ride with the guns that had arrived in camp. They had watched with envy as the guns were pulled in circles and figures of eight, the drivers hardly moving to get their pairs to turn or to slow down or quicken their pace. All of the gunners wanted to get into using the guns but it would only be when Sergeant Webber judged their ability to be good enough to keep pace with these professional drivers.

After a week of riding, Fin had lost much of the soreness each day in the saddle gave and all of the gunners seemed to have gained a greater swagger as they walked their horses back to camp each evening. Much to all their surprise they had returned early and Sergeant Webber announced that they would commence weapons training as soon as the horses were taken care of. The excitement running through the gunners was almost tangible and the bemused faces told of their disappointment to Sergeant Webber as he arrived with an armful of sawn-off rake handles and a sack of wicker bottle holders. Dumping the pile on the cobbles of the stable yard, he announced: "Right gentlemen, you will each take one piece of handle and one wicker cover; you will then make a hole in the wicker like so – he thrust one end of the pole through the weave of pliant stems and pushed his hand into the opening which would have held the bottle but now covered his fist – and this will be your sword!"

The gunners were not sure whether their sergeant was playing a joke on them all but the look on his face told otherwise and they were soon equipped with their first military weapon!

"Now I could take you through the etiquette of sword-play and make you learn the names of all of the guards, the attacks and the defences..." he demonstrated a range of positions with the wooden handle as the sword blade "...however, the most important rule is this..." (he paused for full effect and lowered his voice to almost a whisper, as if in a confidential meeting where none should overhear). "You must hit and hurt the bugger trying to kill you, without letting him give you as much as a scratch!" He walked up and down the line and continued his advice. "I saw this little game at a country fair when the last man standing would win a barrel of ale. It was no holds barred and the closest thing that I have come to being in battle without the battle raging round you. We will be limited to this yard, no going in the stables and hiding...." (a few chuckles spread through the gunners) "...and you will learn to keep your eyes open, your wits about you and I hope a few useful pointers so as not to get skewered on a Frenchie's sword!"

He walked to the centre of the stable yard and shouted, "On guard!" and then charged at the unsuspecting gunners cracking Bill Bennett a blow to the left arm, George Rogers a slap on the back of his thigh and Noah Hogg a swipe to his left ear before any had moved. "Them Frenchies don't ask if you are ready, they'll just as soon cut off your arm, slice your throat or stick you through your guts!" By the next time, the gunners had spread out and avoided any further blows from their sergeant. "You see that bottle on the mounting block? If you reaches it, you keeps it!"

The game as Sergeant Webber described was a very good exercise in self-preservation with gunners avoiding any swinging blows and the occasional sound of wood hitting wood indicated that they were learning to parry as well. Fin had backed away towards some steps that led up to the hay loft, surveying the scene but realising that anyone wanting the bottle would have to fight across the yard, including passing Sergeant Webber. Fin exchanged blows with Dai Davies. Dai had swung his 'sword' at Fin's head and Fin instinctively raised his arm to protect himself. Dai had swung hard but Fin realised that having taken the power of the swing, he had Dai with his arm well above his head. Fin brought his weapon down and flicked with knuckles up into Dai's ribs. "Go easy Fin, that hurt!"

"And your swing at my head would have split my skull!" Fin enjoyed the advantage and forced Dai backwards, realising that making your opponent react to defend one part of his body always left another open to attack. So quickly was Dai evading the swipes at his body that he caught the heel of his boot on a slightly more raised cobble and fell sprawling, drawing a command from Sergeant Webber: "Davies, you're out. Get up and stand at the stable doors." Fin had no time to relax as a swinging blow aimed at his right arm just missed, as his next attacker – Wee Willie Wilkinson – misjudged the distance and only kept his feet by over lunging, giving Fin the chance to jab the blunted point into Wilky's chest and send him to the ground. "Well done Ross. Wilkinson to the stable door, and you Taylor, Hughes, Campbell, Hogg, Black – You've all hit the floor so you're out!"

Fin was feeling pleased with himself as he glimpsed the next attack scything towards his head; he blocked it as he had done before but this attacker – Donald McConnell – just hacked down again and again, leaving no time for Fin to hit the unguarded ribs. Fin edged back as slowly, meeting every blow with as much force as he could muster but the sudden sound of splintering wood brought a look of surprise to Donald's face as he was left with only a third of the length of his weapon. Fin took the chance to drive Donald back and although he parried the first blow, he couldn't avoid Fin's cut to the leg, and the crack on the knee made him reel back and out of the fight.

"And you Bennett, out you go. Smith join the group at the doorway."

There were only six left. Fin never saw the blow that hit him. George Rogers had cracked him in the lower back and Fin arched his spine in agony turning in a wild swing against whoever had hit him. George was surprised that Fin was still standing, hadn't expected a response and took the blow straight in the mouth, knocking out a tooth and showering blood across the cobbles. George held his face as the pain hit worse and retreated to the safety of the growing gathering at the doors. "Go on Fin go and get it!" it was Elijah Black cheering him on.

"No Thomo, you get it!" shouted Noah Hogg.

"Hey Parky, you can use that stick as well as you say those long words, go on!" encouraged Wilky. Sergeant Webber was pleased that there was no favourite, but all had their supporters.

Fin was smarting from the slap across his back. *That brown paper and vinegar would be in use again tonight!* he thought. He didn't try to move quickly but was aware that the other four were edging closer to the bottle and he looked for a pathway that would cause least resistance, just as he would when out in the woods with his bow at night. The sudden break for the bottle was Arthur Parkin. Whether he thought Fin the weakest, no one knew, but Parky swung at Fin's left side, drew the parry and switched to the right. Fin had trouble keeping up with the multiple attacks and then Parky aimed at Fin's head. Instinctively, Fin threw up his stick to guard himself but then felt a surge of pain that made him drop his 'sword'. Parky hadn't carried through with the blow to his head but had turned his wrist and flicked his fingers to catch Fin on the inside of the elbow. Why anyone called it a funny bone Fin could not imagine, but he was left bent double clutching his right elbow, the pain pulsing down to his fingers. Just to rub it in, Parky slapped him across the backside and went for the bottle.

"You all right Fin, you done well boy.". Elijah meant well rubbing Fin's arm, but that just made it worse. "Who'd you reckon will win the bottle?" Fin looked up to see Dicky Dickinson let Bob Halls come past him glancing a blow off his shoulder, to enable him to trip him over and stand above him point on his chest.

"Alright, Dicky, you win… this time!" Bob got to his feet and took his place with the rest. Parky had noticed Dicky enjoying his moment of victory over Bob and attacked from behind and to the right, scraping his handle down the forearm and into the wicker protector rasping Dicky's knuckles. The scything horizontal response was clumsy. Parky squatted to avoid the attack and within a blink had cracked both of Dicky's knees, rendering him incapable of any movement and open to the final attack that knocked him to the ground as Parky had circled behind and slapped the back of the knees. Dicky folded in on himself and lay clutching his aching joints. Peter Taylor and Thomas Hughes ran over to collect their wounded friend who was able to sit up but was totally bemused as to what had happened and how Parky had hit him so many times. "I think Parky is a bit of a dark horse, he is, been in use of the sword many a time!"

"Only him and Thomo left. Up you get Dicky, come and join us at the door." Peter took one arm and Thomas took the other as they supported a very sore friend to the stables.

Thomo had waited for Parky and had noted the way he had attacked, the change of direction with the merest turn of his wrist, the straightening of his fingers to hit the target. He knew that Parky was a better swordsman, so he would have to use something else.

Parky approached and aimed a blow at Thomo's head, knowing it would draw the instinctive covering, but Thomo hadn't left his elbow stuck out as others had and Parky withdrew and straightened his arm high with the blunted point aimed at Thomo's head. Thomo ignored the intimidating stance, but just circled. "How much d'you want that bottle Parky?"

"Enough to beat you Thomo!" The sudden dip of the blade and change of stance caught Thomo unaware and he had no chance of blocking the stinging blow on his unprotected left arm. As soon as he was hit, there was Parky in front of him again. He could hear the cheers from the other gunners and knew he had to think quickly. He pretended to aim at Parky's head but Parky saw through the feint and was ready for the real attack that Thomo aimed at his right armpit in an upper cut. The attack blocked, Parky slid his blade straight towards Thomo's chest. He could not believe what happened next as Thomo did not try to recover his sword arm but twisted to allow the wooden pole to slip through his shirt, tearing a hole under the armpit. At the same time he grabbed Parky's sword arm in a vice-like grip with his left hand, pulling him so close that their bodies crashed together before he swung his left boot into Parky's heels, upending him onto the cobbles! Thomo casually walked over to the bottle, his own 'sword' raised aloft, whilst Parky's 'sword' hung out of his shirt, the wicker basket bulging underneath his raised arm.

"Well done, Thomson. Unconventional – I wouldn't recommend you try that with a real blade, but well done!" Sergeant Webber passed the bottle to Thomo who went to Parky still bemused on the cobbles.

"Never beat you with a real sword Parky, but I've learned the hard way as you might say!" and with a beaming smile he offered a hand to help him up.

"Not quite what I expected Thomo, but you won fair and square. Expect the unexpected, I suppose."

"Now that is a good lesson you've learned Parky," and with arms around each other's shoulders they walked gingerly back to the rest of the gunners. "Expect the unexpected!"

"Not sure if that's in the rules Thomo?" commented Bob Halls.

"No I don't expect it is… but it won this didn't it? Mind you, I didn't want you to rip my shirt!" and he held the bottle aloft again before lowering it, removing the stopper and offering it to all. Their first weapons training had left all with the need for the best brown paper and vinegar boiled in the pot; it had left some with a closed eye and George Rogers with one less tooth, but Sergeant Webber knew that it had done them all the world of good, let off some steam and created a closer bond between them all. Rivals yes, but ready to help each other as well.

"Now go and get those bumps sorted, we're up early again for riding!"

"Yes sergeant" they all replied and vied for the bottle as it was passed from one hand to another.

Chapter 14

The next morning saw the mist cloaking the valley below Goodwood but the Downs above in clear sunlight. The usual routine of hot tea, bread dipped in the remains of last night's stew, shaving, washing was completed but they spent time getting the wounds ready for the morning ride. As they left the stable yard, they were surprised to have a limber join them. "Hey Parky, what's goin' on here? We never had a limber with us?"

"I don't know Thomas, the sergeant hasn't taken me into his confidence as far as training goes."

"Why can't you just say it as it is, Parky?" Bob Halls was enjoying the opportunity to poke fun again. "Just tell Tom 'ere, you haven't a clue!" and he laughed at his own jest, drawing a chuckle from others within earshot.

"Leave off Bob. That's just the way Parky was brung up, he talks dif'rent to us." Thomas defended, but got a slap on the shoulder from Bob and a reassuring;

"Never you mind Tom, we love his way of speaking and it was only in jest. I'm not pickin' a quarrel with Parky havin' seen how he fights!"

The early morning sun cast sharp shadows across the meadow as they crested the brow of the hill, and to their amazement, the gunners saw another limber already in the field hammering in stakes at different heights. Sergeant Webber lifted his arm and directed them to turn to their left before ordering all to dismount and tie up to the temporary hitching rail created by the drivers of the first limber.

As they made their usual two ranks, the second limber drew to a halt and Sergeant Webber helped open the various boxes and containers. Mouths gaped as they saw what he had taken out – a sword, not their handle and basket, but a real sword. He unsheathed the blade from the scabbard but immediately replaced it. Reaching into a second box, he withdrew a white belt and proceeded to place it over his right shoulder.

"Today we start our real sword drill! Yesterday was fun and taught us all some valuable lessons about the confusion in battle, never standing still and keeping all parts of the body protected..." He paused and could see gunners wincing as they recalled the bruises and cuts that had made sleeping fitful at best. "First of all, we will wear our sword belt across our chest over the right shoulder thus smoothing the belt over his jacket, and these studs push through to fasten the belt together and then both are attached to this cross belt plate so that it won't fall off as you ride – and woe betide any of you who should lose his weapon!" (having secured his belt he turned side-on to display two rings). "The old belts only had one large ring with two straps, but this is the improved version and you will always have the shorter strap at the front. It is fed through the higher loop on the scabbard... thus... and then back through the buckle and loop to keep it flat. The same will be done with the longer strap passing through the lower loop... thus. When you're walking in your finery about town, you will not scrape your scabbard along the floor, but you will adjust your straps accordingly; when riding, you may need to adjust again. Now the first rank will pass along the limber and collect their belt, straps and sword. These will be yours for the rest of your life... however long that may be! Front rank, right face... fall out!"

Within moments the excited gunners had received their newest piece of equipment to be followed by their fellow troopers. When they settled back into their ranks, Sergeant Webber recommenced his instruction: "I will command: Prepare to draw swords... you will move your eyes only to check that you can reach the hilt – that's where you grip it! I will then command: Eyes right – so that you will all check where the next man is – we will not be having anyone returning to camp with one less ear or eye because some clumsy ox is too close! I will then command: Draw, and you will reach your right hand across to grasp your sword and pull six inches out of your scabbard – thus," and he demonstrated slowly just how far he meant, "I will then finish the command... Swords, and you will pull the sword out of the scabbard and have your right arm in front of your eyes with the elbow level with your shoulder – thus – and finally you will bring your sword close to your body to 'Carry Swords'. On foot this will be thus!" He tucked in his right elbow with his arm parallel to the ground and sword vertical. "On horse-back your right hand will be just above your right knee, and not resting on it! The final command in this procedure will be to 'Slope Swords' and you will be able to lean the rear edge of your blade onto your right shoulder." He replaced his sword and stood absolutely still.

The lifting of his chest shown by the movement in his jacket lace alerted every Gunner that a command was coming. "Prepare to draw swords!" As a gunner twitched, he snapped, "Just your eyes Davies, not your head! Eyes right!" All turned to ensure alignment was correct. "Draw…."

At last, Fin thought, *I can get hold of the sword,* and he was surprised by the scraping of metal on metal.

"Swords…" all had remembered to bring their arms in front of their faces, Sergeant Webber fussed around the files readjusting an elbow here, a hand there. "Get it right now gentlemen and we won't have accidents later." By this time he had regained his viewing point in front of the two ranks'. "Carry Swords…" The unaccustomed weight led to a few wavers, but the balance was regained and two rows of proud Gunners displayed their swords, blades glinting in the sunlight. "Slope Swords…" and the blades rested against the shoulder.

"Well done gentlemen, and now we will put them back where they came from!" The audible groan was the sign that they were keen rather than rebellious. "But never you mind. We will be getting them out again! Now copy me…Carry Swords…" All returned to their former position. "Prepare to Put Up Swords… Just your eyes to look down to check where the scabbard is…" All tried to glance but there were plenty of heads bemused as to where and how their scabbard had twisted so far round. "Put Up… take the blade across your body and down to have your arm across your face and put the first six inches in…"

"As the actress said to the bishop!" quipped Halls.

"Enough of your ribaldry, Halls, now put up…" this proved the most difficult manoeuvre so far and many had to use their left hand to steady the scabbard. "Problem is gentlemen, when you is riding, your left hand will be occupied with the reins, so you will be needing a lot of practice! Having 'Put Up' you will finish with 'Swords!' sliding the rest of the blade into the scabbard."

The Gunners repeated and repeated the procedure until their sergeant was satisfied, no one had been injured and the speed of 'Put Up' was improving. After what seemed an endless repetition to Fin, Sergeant Webber paused and withdrew his blade without any orders. "Now we can get the blade out, we'd best learn to use it! First of all, you will always have your hand through the sword knot, this strap with the tassel on, and tighten it with this loop – it isn't just for decoration but if you were to have the sword knocked out of your hand… it will prevent you having to get off and find it in the middle of the fight! You were all holding the grip well but make sure your thumb puts pressure on the top to allow your fingers to take control of the blade. We will not be swinging wildly but cutting precisely. By the time you have taken your arm back to swing at your Frenchie…" he took his sword across his body in the largest arc possible… "your Frenchie will have stuck you already! Keep your sword in front at all times so that you can guard yourself and parry any attacks. This blade is the same the cavalry use. The blade is thirty-two and a half inch long and has this groove called a fuller on each side. Now there will be those that tell you that it is made this way to let the Frenchie blood run out, but well as that may be, it is so that the blade can be made as strong as possible and as light as possible. I daresay that you will already have noticed that it has some weight to it – two pounds nine ounces I was told – and if you have to fight long, your arm will be telling you that it hurts! We will only be sharpening the last six inches of the blade and you will notice that the tip is more of a hatchet shape… we will learn to cut and pierce just in case we ever get too near to their cavalry – we shouldn't need to, as our guns will keep them well out of range, but you never know!" He sheathed his sword and ordered the front rank to collect a sack each from the limbers and then for all gunners to follow him to the poles.

A line of poles had been erected about as tall as a man, but with a nail hammered at an angle into the end. "Tip out them sacks." A shower of vegetables littered the grass.

"They're neeps!" Donald McConnell bent to pick one up.

"You're quite right Donald, they were introduced to Britain quite recently and the word 'neeps' comes from the Latin Napus. When I was given some to eat, I was told they are called 'swede' because they came from Sweden."

"Thank you for enlightening us Parkin, but whether you want to call them neeps, swedes, turnips is all the same, as for us today they is all going to be a Frenchy's head! Mark you, a head is very tough and requires a good cut." He smiled, the gunners unsure of a jest or not. "You will also collect all remnants because these will be your supper tonight!"

Every pole was mounted with a head and the sergeant demonstrated: "You will have drawn swords and be stood one step away from the pole. Our first cut will be from two o'clock to seven o'clock; arm straight, point at the target, push off your left foot, fingers and thumb direct the blade and..." he lunged cut the vegetable and returned to guard, " a nasty scar for our Frenchie! We are not trying to knock his head off, but if you are accurate, 'if' you are accurate, you will have sliced your enemy and he will be..." he paused to think of the expression he wanted, "what is it Parkin... horse der...?"

"Hors de combat," Parkin replied with an impressive accent. "It literally means that your opponent is outside of the fight."

"I'm sure you are correct Parkin. I was told this by an officer who had been scouting in the mountains for General Moore on our retreat to Corunna. The more of the enemy we could get horse der combat, the better chances we had to evacuate... and we did all right."

"Sarge, I understand the cutting and using thumbs and fingers, but what is two o'clock?"

Sergeant Webber was silent for a moment. "Well Campbell, I am glad you asked," he took his watch out of his pocket. "You see this watch? Did I tell you that I was donated it by a Frenchie Colonel during the retreat to Corunna when I was with General Moore himself, God rest his soul? This watch tells me the time; The number at the top is a twelve and then at regular intervals, just like you lining up in ranks, are the numbers one, two, three, four, five..." he pointed to each one tracing the outline of the circle, "so if I says cut from two o'clock to seven o'clock... then..." holding the watch at head height, "you will cut from here... to here!"

"Oh, I never had a watch sergeant."

"I daresay that few of these here have either!"

The afternoon was spent lunging, cutting and returning to guard as they learned cut by cut: two to seven; eleven to four; five to nine; seven to two; three to nine; nine to three... Sergeant Webber would call the time rather than 'cut one' – it felt it was easier to learn, and served the same purpose – and soon there were chippings of vegetables gathered below each pole. Fin had been surprised how much his wrist jarred as the blade made contact with the swede. He wondered whether a real head would be the same. They were delighted when their sergeant called a halt, ordered sheathed swords, after they had cleaned the lumps of vegetable and occasional tuft of grass from the blade, and announced that in the first limber was bread, cheese and a drink.

It soon became obvious that the next stage would be carried out on horseback as the drivers were placing vegetable on taller poles. It didn't seem long before that they had struggled to mount their horses, turn the full circle in the saddle and ride without stirrups or reins, but now they were confident and about to attempt to attack an enemy from the saddle. It was only walking, but it made it so much harder. Countless thrusts and cuts missed the target completely throwing the rider off balance; some over exuberant cuts found their blade impaling the 'head' and lifting it straight off the spike! As before, the remedy was to repeat, and repeat and repeat. Fin found that eleven to four was his most accurate; he was not the only one who had received a rebuke from Sergeant Webber to, "Mind your horse's head, you'll have its ears off you clumsy oaf!" as cut one from two to seven went too far and too close to the horse. Fin was surprised that he had hit the target at all, but cuts away from the horse seemed a little easier. As they collected the fragments of vegetables, each gunner displayed the piece that he had sliced, vying to have sliced the biggest chunk off the head; Noah Hogg was holding the best part of a quarter of a swede when Bob Halls remarked, "It's all that practice in peeling the spuds, Noah!"

Having replenished each pole and remounted, they moved onto the trot but nothing more. The fact that no pole had to have a new 'head' demonstrated that there was still a lot to learn. Walking back slightly disconsolate into the stable yard, Sergeant Webber had caught their mood perfectly: "Never mind gentlemen, you may not be the best cavalry in the world, but you will be the best gunners..." he paused as the cheer subsided, "and you will have a great supper tonight! Black, take the sacks to Mrs Black and then get back here quick to tend to your horse." As Elijah disappeared through the gateway, Thomo reflected, "I think we'll have more than one supper from that lot Sarge."

"You're probably right Thomson, and judging by your exploits on horseback, we will have to have you making some more suppers!" Sergeant Webber led his horse into the stables to the stalls separated for all sergeants, each gunner following in the prescribed order to allow those needing the further stalls to get in first. As Elijah returned to his stall, he announced, "Martha says it will be neeps and tatties for all and some sausages that she got from the Duke's kitchen!"

"Best you get the horses sorted, and remember to see the blacksmith if any shoe isn't right – we are not having anyone... what was it Parkin? Hors de Combat!" in his best French accent, creating a great cheer from 'his' gunners.

Chapter 15

Sergeant Webber had finished his rounds of the stalls checking that all had been completed as ordered and briskly walked out of the stable yard with the intention of washing and getting ready for supper after, what he had reflected on as, a good day's exercise. Seeing Fin staring towards the Grand House, he followed his gaze and could see a group of people on the immaculate lawn of the formal garden. "Wishin' you was there, Ross?"

"No Sarge, just watching them shooting arrows at the targets."

"Didn't I hear that you are a bit of an archer?"

"Not like that Sarge. My grand-father taught me when we was out and about, usually in places where we shouldn't ha' been. No sound with the arrows, Sarge, and cheaper. We made our own arrows, fletchings and all, we found goose feather the best and willow for the straightest arrows."

"What sort of bow did you use, not a long bow from the days of old?"

Fin laughed and faced his sergeant. "No Sarge. Too big for a start: can't get in amongst the trees as easily if you are forever tangling in branches. Had to be able to get away quick if you know what I mean?"

"I can follow what you mean Ross, but what was your bow made from?"

"It was from my grand-father, he had had it a long time. Made from yew it was, the sort of trees you find in church yards so the sheep don't stray over graves – they don't like the berries I was told. My bow was about as tall as me, perhaps a bit shorter. We had animal horn 'nocks' on each end where the string would be attached, but you never leave the string on, ruins the bow and the string, always keep the string wrapped and dry. Twisted fibres of flax my string was."

"That's very interesting Ross, how far could you hit a target?"

"Most of what we hit were no more than a cricket pitch away, but I have hit a deer at fifty paces."

"And you didn't get found out?"

"No Sarge, family at the great House were all away and the game-keeper – Old Spiky we'd call him – knew when to turn a blind eye and claim a wild animal had taken a deer off."

"So if you had to, how far could you shoot?"

"Well just for fun, I used to play a game shooting across the river, then swim over and get the arrows back; that was about as long as the horses would pull a plough before turning, so it must be two hundred paces or so, but my grand-father says that in times of knights when we beat the French, they put arrows through chain mail, plate armour and that was over three hundred paces!"

"That's a lot further than our muskets the foot sloggers use, but I hear the riflemen can get somewhere close. No match for what we'll be firing though, Ross."

He started to walk away but turned abruptly, "Fancy your chances against those down there, a challenge perhaps?"

"Not sure Sarge. Different with another bow, and perhaps what they don't know won't get me into trouble on another day."

"Point taken Ross, but I'll see what I can do to get hold of a bow and some arrows: weapons is weapons whatever the age, and artillery now can learn a lot from trajectory of arrows." Fin was surprised at the interest Sergeant Webber had shown and didn't realise how important archery might be. He stood watching a little while longer, smiling to himself as countless arrows missed the targets, even at the short distance they had set up. As he walked back, he wondered if he could have beaten them with a different bow – with his old bow he was certain: it would be good to shoot again.

Walking back into camp he noticed that his fellow gunners engaged in a new task, cleaning sword blades and whitening the cross belt. "Where you been Fin?" Thomo had looked up from his sword.

"There was some archery in front of the great House, would have liked to have had a go."

"You can shoot arrows Fin?" Martha had been stirring the bubbling pot full of vegetables freshly cut from sword practice!

"My grand-father taught me Martha, came in useful in adding to the pot without anyone hearing!"

"Perhaps you could find something for us then Fin?"

"Haven't got a bow Martha."

"Never mind that Martha, Fin 'ad better get his sword cleaned before Sergeant Webber comes for inspection. Here you are Fin, take some straw to wipe the blade clean of the vegetable bits then use this cloth with oil to wipe it down. And don't cut your hand on the blade!"

Fin settled to the task making sure that all slithers of swede had been removed before wiping the oiled cloth down the length of the blade and replaced it into the scabbard. Undoing the press studs on the belt, he copied the method for whitening the belt, which had become surprisingly grubby after so little time. "Don't get that on your overalls or you'll be cleaning those as well." Fin looked at Bob Halls not sure whether he was making fun of him or giving good advice, but nevertheless he adjusted his position. Each gunner had taken their belt and sword and carefully hung it across the newly erected weapon stand.

The light was fading as the group relaxed eating the prepared meal and drinking their customary beer. Peter Taylor had started tuning his violin with Arthur Parkin as Elijah Black ran his hand loosely over the drum skin creating different rhythms between thumb, fingers and the ball of his hand. It was Sally walking and rocking her young babe who noticed the approach of Sergeant Webber: "You smelled the vegetable stew did you sergeant?" she teased.

"Never know when you might next eat Sal! Take what you can when you can!" and he winked at her as he strolled into camp.

"There's always enough for you, sergeant, here you are." Martha had already served a wooden bowl full of the meal with a spoon stuck in and was offering the sergeant before he had arrived.

"Thanks Martha, but before I join you I have to see Ross. Where is he?"

"Fin!" Martha called out, "Sergeant to see you."

Fin emerged from the tent and walked over, noticing a blanket rolled under the sergeant's arm. "There you are Ross. Saw one of the gardeners responsible for the archery practice and he gave me this. I told him that we were setting up a contest and needed to find a champion; he wants a challenge match so you'd better get some practice." He carefully unwrapped the bow and quiver holding six arrows. "What do you think?"

"Not as old as mine back home but I think it is yew wood and the horn nocks are just about copies of what we had." He took the arrows and examined them for straightness and flexibility. "Fletcher made a good job of these." The sergeant reached into his jacket, and unbuttoned three loops from the neck.

"You'll need this Ross." He handed a small package that Fin opened with a whistle.

"Silk Sarge! I've heard about them, supposed to be the best, but never seen or felt one."

"Not the only thing you can feel in silk!" laughed Sally holding the babe in the crook of her left arm but glancing down at the rising hem of her skirt as she pulled with her right hand, drawing glances and cheers from the men as well as a mocking scold from Martha:

"Behave yourself Sally – can't have our men overheated!" Sergeant Webber noted the reference again to 'our men' pleased that the Troop were continuing to bond.

"Let's see what you can do Fin." Sal continued the mocking.

"Yes, go on Fin, I've never seen arrows fired, how far can it go?" asked Thomas, Sal's husband.

"You see the sheep wandering across the meadow with their shepherd, he's taking them to the pen for the night."

"Yes, they're shifting them tomorrow to the back of the great House I heard… don't know why though?"

"I could hit them."

"But that's miles away Fin." It was Sal who had walked to join them.

"No it's not as far as that, but not far off three hundred paces. I won't be shooting that far – getting dark and I've got to get used to the feel of the bow." Fin strung the bow, carefully tested the power before rolling down the sleeve of his left arm.

"Why d'you do that Fin?" Thomas was taking everything in.

"When you release the string, it can take the skin off the inside of your forearm."

"What you going to aim at Ross?" this time it was Sergeant Webber.

"I'll hit that oak fifty paces away."

"You're confident Fin." Thomo had emerged from the tent to join the group of spectators enjoying a new diversion.

"It's not too far, even with a new bow like this."

"Go on Fin." Thomas was excited as a child receiving a gift.

Fin took an arrow, and fitted it onto the string, resting the shaft against the bow and his fist gripping the leather strip wound around to prevent slipping. It felt familiar to Fin and in the light breeze he was confident. He raised the bow, at the same time pulling the string back to his cheek and breathing in as he did. "Big strong boy you are, Fin!" admired Sal, drawing laughs from the men watching but Fin was only aware of a noise as his focus was fully on the target.

As he released the arrow, several exclamations of admiration followed the flight.

"Did you hit the tree, Fin, I can't see that far?" it was Peter Taylor plucking the strings of his violin.

"Course he did!" Sal had turned mockingly towards Peter: "Never in doubt was it!"

Fin butted in: "It did hit the tree but it glanced and flew to the right, I'll try again." Fin repeated the procedure and with equal admiration the troop watched the arrow fly towards the tree and this time embed itself into the bark, drawing cheers and slaps on the back.

"Well done Ross." Sergeant Webber had finished his food, handed the bowl back to Martha Black and had been just as keen to watch. "You handle that very well."

"Light's going Sarge, better go and find that one that deflected before we lose it, don't want any questions." Fin took the string off the horn nock by partially bending the bow and wound it carefully before placing it inside the leather pouch. "Can I keep the blanket Sarge? It will keep the bow safe?"

"You know better than me, Ross, I didn't want anyone asking questions of me with a bow in hand." Fin walked to his tent, ducked inside and quickly reappeared to start his walk towards the tree.

"I'll give you a hand," Thomo offered as he joined Fin. Out of earshot, Thomo asked, "Could you really hit a rabbit for the pot? A tree fifty paces away is impressive but it wasn't moving."

"It's easier if it's bigger like a deer, but if I get out early enough and find a place where the rabbits usually come, I could catch one off-guard, but only one shot then the others are off!"

"We best go out hunting then!" and Thomo slapped Fin on the back who winced, still aching from the wooden sword fight lesson. "Sorry Fin, still sore?"

"Yes, George gave me a good crack" rubbing the lower spine.

Arriving at the oak Fin placed his left hand against the trunk with the shaft protruding between the thumb and forefinger as a brace to push against as his right hand slid as far down the shaft against the tree to pull the arrow free. Even at fifty paces, the arrow had embedded for over an inch and Thomo raised his eyebrows. "I wouldn't want that hitting me!"

"They say that the old arrows could pierce the armour knights wore. Mind you, the long bows would have been pulling a lot more power than this."

"Well that looks pretty lethal to me! I'll look for the other."

"Should be another ten paces away to the right" directed Fin, as he pushed and pulled harder to finally release the arrow. He turned to see Thomo bending to collect the second arrow, inspecting it as he returned to Fin. "Still a useful weapon Fin."

"Takes time to learn but it can still kill."

They walked back into camp hearing the strains of a quiet song being sung by Sally still holding her babe, admired by the listeners, and not just because of her voice. "We could be in worse places, Fin!" Fin turned and grinned, took the two arrows to the tent to put them in the quiver and then re-joined the group, staring at Sal finishing her song:

"I'll dye my dress, I'll dye it red, And through the streets I'll beg for bread, For the lad that I love from me has fled, Johnny has gone for a soldier."

Chapter 16

The usual morning routine had been followed and they had been accompanied onto the downs by not only a limber but a second limber pulling a six pounder gun. The excitement grew as they tethered their horses to the makeshift hitching line and they repeated the procedure of collecting new equipment from one limber as the drivers set up a target across the pasture.

The new recruits lined up in two ranks, still dressed in their grey overalls but still without jackets and in shirt-sleeve order; on their head they had their fatigue caps, blue cloth edged in yellow. All had been issued with a new weapon and a second belt and had emerged slowly with a fussing over the cartridge boxes, the strap to be comfortable and not letting their pistols fall.

"Get in line gentlemen, you ain't waitin' for a beer!" Sergeant Webber looked at his 'new boys' and knew they had started the process of training well.

The two lines dressed accurately with heads turned to the right. "Right, now what you have in your hand is not a toy, it's a pistol, 'The New Land Service Pistol' to be exact." The sergeant paused to observe the reaction and immediately saw one head turned away. "Who gave you permission to speak, Halls?" The sergeant was not the tallest of men but his upper body was immense from endless working with the guns. He approached the unfortunate gunner and was almost nose to nose when he asked, "What may I ask is so important that you have to be interrupting me, who is your guardian angel and will train you to stay alive as long as possible?"

Bob Halls was rarely short for words but his voice quavered, "I thought we were here to learn to fire the big guns."

"I thought we were learning to fire the big guns, 'Sergeant'!"

"Sorry Sergeant, I thought we were learning to fire the big guns Sergeant?" Bob was looking towards the gun attached to the limber.

"Well my fine fellow, when you have fired those big guns at those massed battalions of the Imperial Guard or at those huge fellas on horses, what might you be doing then?"

The sergeant paused for full effect.

"Well, I'll be telling you. You do not hide under the gun (pointing towards a six-pounder across the meadow), you do not stand still, but you join our brave foot sloggers and help shoot the Frenchies some more. Now you can't be doin' that if you haven't got this!" and he took his own pistol from where he had pushed it into his crimson sash, in piratical fashion, raising it above his head. "And by the way, that gun and team has been brought here to have the new horses get familiar as a team. While we are learning to shoot these," he looked at his raised pistol, "they will be learning to control the weight that they are pulling."

"I don't care if you have fired a gun before or if you have never fired a gun, 'we' (and he stressed this slowly), 'we' will learn together. This (stroking the metal barrel that measured just over nine inches) is a metal tube!" He waited for the men to all look at their weapon. "Now look very closely here." He pointed at the small touch-hole in the right side of the barrel. "Through this hole, a spark will ignite the powder charge in the barrel and the ball will explode out to fly to wherever you are pointing!" The sergeant carelessly waved the barrel at the recruits making some duck and cover.

"But unless we load it correctly, it is useless and we might as well turn it round and hit the Frenchies with the stock like a club! Those clever chappies who invent these things have made life a bit easier for you all. You see this?" The sergeant extracted the ram rod. "You won't be dropping this vital piece of the gun, nor will you be firing it away to the Frenchies, because they have made it fix to a swivel so that, even on horseback, you could load the pistol! Mind you... you will always replace the rod into its correct position before firing...Do not leave it dangling loose!"

"Right, look at your flint." He inspected every man to ensure that they were all looking in the right place. "Without this flint, there is no spark, without the spark, there is no ignition, without the ignition, there is no bullet out of the end, without the bullet there is no dead Frenchie... and that means that they get you!"

He paused again and demonstrated with his own pistol. "You see this screw here?" He waited, but there was no response. He raised his voice, "You see this screw here?"

"Yes Sergeant" chorused the recruits.

"This has to be tight, it ain't no use if your flint falls out. Some people use a patch of leather to fix it tighter in the metal jaws, but you have the tools in your equipment issued this morning, never lose

101

them and always check before you fire… it's too late after you lost it in the dirt."

Fin forced himself to concentrate even though he had fired a musket before, at least this was a lot shorter and easier to handle than his previous experience.

"And for the final piece of this part of the puzzle… the frizzen." The sergeant moved the hinged frizzen plate to show the priming pan. "Now this is where we pour a little powder and don't forget to close the frizzen so that the powder doesn't fall out."

Some of the recruits were a little awkward touching each part of their new weapon to be sure that they knew what to do.

"Now then my brave boys, put your right hand in the cartridge box and take out 'one' cartridge. If you are not sure which is your right, let me know and I will come and mark it for you! These cartridges are specially made for us so don't be taking any other cartridges or you'll have too much powder and blow the gun out of your hand… with some fingers with it! Anyway, the ball won't fit as this pistol is unique," (muttering quietly) "and a fat lot of use except to kill a dying horse." No one dared move, but there were eyes making sideways glances from several gunners.

"Right, now I will be needing a volunteer and you (looking directly at Bob Halls) are it. Out you come Halls!"

"Right Halls, ever fired a pistol before?" The sergeant was inspecting Bob as if he could see through into his mind and what he was thinking.

"No Sergeant, but I have fired a musket."

"Well just take it nice and slow so that all of our new gunners can see. See that target yonder?" The Sergeant pointed but never took his eyes off Bob. Bob turned ninety degrees to the right and saw the outline of a man painted onto a canvas target full of straw pinned to the same poles they had used for sword drill. "Yes Sergeant."

"Well, Halls, when I say so, you will be aiming to hit that. Now, all of you look at the cartridge. If you feel tightly at the top, that's the twisted end, you will feel a ball." All tried to feel for the ball that would be the way that one day they would try to kill a Frenchman. "Ready Halls?" and without waiting for a reply, "When you bite the cartridge, there will be the ball and some powder in your mouth, it doesn't taste nice, it makes your mouth as dry as a desert but don't let me see anyone of you drop that ball! Halls, bite the cartridge." Bob knew it would taste bad but he had to force his teeth shut to prevent himself from spitting out the ball. He kept thinking, "Don't swallow the ball, don't spit it out."

"All of you hold your pistol in your left hand, horizontal to the ground. (He checked all had done this). Don't let go of the cartridge and pull back the hammer with the flint one click. This keeps the mechanism safe and we won't have any accidents shooting each other. Push the frizzen towards the muzzle... the end of the pistol where the bullet comes out. You will pretend to bite the cartridge and pour a little powder into the pan then pull the frizzen back to lock in the powder." All recruits rehearsed well. "Now Halls you will do this for real." Bob was relieved that he could move at last, still gritting his teeth. He quickly levelled his pistol, pulled the hammer to half cocked, pushed the frizzen, poured a little powder into the pan and sealed the frizzen back into place.

"Well done Halls, I'll make a soldier out of you yet!" The recruits smiled, it wasn't the first time Sergeant had seemed a little human but they were growing to like him. "Now as Halls does this for real, you will copy... Ready?" All but Bob shouted "Yes Sergeant!" excited at the prospect of shooting at last. "Remember, you have the ball in your mouth. Lift your pistol to the vertical, butt end to the ground." (He watched Bob at all times but still noticed one gunner get it wrong) "Smith, the butt end is the bit with the wood on!" The embarrassed Gunner quickly corrected his error. "Now pour 'all' of the powder down the barrel. Spit the ball down the barrel." Bob was relieved to have gotten rid of the ball but the taste remained. "Now pull the ramrod out." A scraping and grating sound setting teeth on edge announced that all had succeeded. "Watch Halls as he puts in the cartridge paper and then rams it down the barrel to get as tight and fit as possible. It is important that the ball is tight against the powder to get maximum speed to the ball – we don't want any balls rattling around and falling short." Bob squeezed the cartridge paper into the end of the barrel and then forced it down as far as he could. "Now replace the ramrod. No dangling rods gentlemen, put them in the right place." Every recruit carefully made sure that the ramrod was in place, including Bob. "Now we are almost ready to shoot. Just Halls this time. He will return the pistol to the horizontal and pull the hammer to full cock. He will bring the pistol up to be level with his right shoulder, he will lean forward to have his weight on his front foot, which will be the right. He will look down the barrel to see the target and squeeze the trigger gently, not pull it!" The sergeant waited for effect and then continued, "There will be a big bang, there will be a cloud of smoke, there will be a smell of rotten eggs and if you don't have the weight forward, you will probably fall backwards and the ball will end up in the sky. You ready Halls?"

"Yes Sergeant."

"Go on then, let's see what you're made of." The sergeant stepped two paces to one side, not sure how good his 'volunteer' would be.

Bob went through the routine the sergeant had described. Hammer full-cocked, raise the pistol level with the shoulder, look down the barrel at the silhouette on the target, lean weight forward, squeeze the trigger.

Although he had fired a musket before, the noise, the heat, the smell, the smoke seemed to be all exaggerated.

"Don't just stand there Halls, we haven't got all day, everyone wants a go!"

The gunners cheered Bob on his success. "Enough of that, we all have to do this," (he strode down the line) "and we have to be able to do it as fast as possible to kill the Frenchies. Now make ready." As he passed Bob, the sergeant didn't turn his head but in a low voice meant only for him, "Well done Halls, but don't get carried away, son." With that he was gone, leaving Bob proud to have gained some sort of praise.

The next hour was a series of repeated movements to bite the cartridge, prime, pour, spit, ram and fire at a line of targets the drivers had set up. They got better and by the end had even managed to get three shots in one minute of the sergeant's watch, the one he said he had been donated by a French colonel during the Corunna Campaign with the great Sir John Moore – "God rest his soul, as fine a general as ever you might want to serve under." – but if you looked closely it had been seventy seconds; there was more to this sergeant than was apparent on first meeting. Only one ramrod had been left swinging free in the air and that had been right at the start but the targets, set twenty paces away, had been peppered with many balls.

Faces were dirtied, shirt sleeves scorched, mouths dry, lips swollen and shoulders and wrists aching but the sergeant was pleased with his work: "Well done boys, you'll soon be ready for the big guns! Atten...tion!" (All straightened with pride of a job well done), "Right face. Fall out – let's get home and get cleaned up!"

Mounted and riding in pairs, they now each had a sword, a pistol, tucked into the top of their overalls and cartridge box. Riding through the arched gateway to the stable yard they were greeted by two sergeants with a wagon containing more leather equipment. Having dismounted when ordered, each gunner was given an addition to his saddle, a pistol holder that would be attached at the front on the near-side. As well as this, each horse was to have a saddle cloth to cover the entire saddle, pistol holder included, and a further strap, a surcingle, to keep all in place.

As the gunners cared for their horses, their sergeant was in deep conversation with the two visitors. Having completed their consultations, Sergeant Webber led his own horse into the stable and called the men to attention at the end of each stall. "Tonight we will be supporting Ross in a challenge. An archery contest on the great lawn. We will have the Duke and Duchess in attendance, so it will be best behaviour. Tomorrow, we will be assisting the servants of the Great House to prepare for a great event to end the summer season. The Duchess is famous for her hosting of great social occasions and the ball tomorrow night will be a time for many of the high and mighty to meet, not only to dance but to conclude business contracts and to encourage greater support for the war against the Frenchies." A buzz of excitement flew through the stalls at the prospect of their engagement for tomorrow. "Now let's get the horses seen to, check those shoes and get some food inside you before we see Ross beat the gamekeepers at their own game! Isn't that right Ross?"

"Will do my best Sarge."

Chapter 17

Fin needed no encouragement from his fellow gunners but they exhorted him to do well with slaps on the back and encouraging comments and cheers, as they ambled along the path from their tented home, past the stable and down onto the immaculate grass of the lawn. Sergeant Webber was already there looking the smartest that any of the gunners had seen him, every part of his uniform immaculate right down to his spurs that he had not worn when training the new recruits, even when riding! "Looks like Sarge is trying to impress those other sergeants," whispered Thomas Hughes, "You really think you can do this Fin?"

"I hope so Thomas, though it's been a bit of a while since I used the bow."

"You was fine showing us though?"

"I was aiming at an oak tree! These targets won't be as big."

"Hey Thomas, Fin – what you whispering about?" It was Sally catching up with the group, babe in arms.

"Nothing Sal," Fin was relaxed in her company now. "Thomas was just encouraging me to do well."

"Do well Fin, do well…" Sally pushed through the group. "You ain't just going to do well, you will win it for the troop, isn't that right sergeant?" Sergeant Webber turned stiffly, the collar of his shirt and jacket restricting the movement and he had to pivot on his heels to answer.

"I'm sure Ross will do his best." And deflecting further comment he continued, "Ross, you are to go to the line marked over there," pointing to the centre of the lawn, "but we will support you form this area, marked by poles with bunting of patriotic red, white and blue flags. And before any of you get any ideas, the seats are for the Duke and Duchess!"

"Oh Sarge, I thought you'd specially brought them for me!" and Sal winked at him, drawing the slightest hint of a smile from the sergeant but a broad grin and flash of teeth from Sally as she walked to the designated area.

As Fin approached the firing line, he was greeted by three gamekeepers dressed in their working clothes: tight-fitting dark green jackets with large pockets buttoned flat, dark brown breeches that were met just below the knee by long boots designed to keep feet and legs dry as well as protected from thorns, brambles and anything else that might attack the lower leg. Fin hadn't seen the style of boot before, but was impressed by the design as the sort of thing that would benefit all labourers – he had often returned home with sodden feet and had to put on wet boots next morning, in spite of leaving them in the hearth overnight.

The senior keeper raised his hand to welcome Fin, "Good evening master..?"

"Ross, I'm Fin Ross." He hadn't been called 'Master Ross' for a while and smiled to himself reflecting on how much had changed recently.

"He's Gunner Ross now, Mister Lamb." Sergeant Webber had followed Fin across the lawn.

"No doubt Sergeant Webber, but this evening we are all archers. Isn't that so Ross?" the keeper had turned to face Fin.

"We are, but," he looked at his sergeant, "I have the honour of representing our Troop of Horse Artillery and intend to show you that we can use ancient weapons as well the new."

"Well said lad, well said," responded the keeper. "We will be shooting at these targets." He led Fin and the sergeant across to a stack of three straw circles. "Takes a time to make these darned things. We used to shoot at wooden models of animals, but some fool in London has had the idea that we should all have the same targets. This one," he lifted a target that was two feet across, displaying the back, a coil of straw of about four inches thick, tightly wound to create the circle – "we will be shooting at about sixty paces." He flipped it over to show coloured concentric circles, the outside border as dark and green as his jacket and then painted circles of white, black, white, red and a centre of gold. "They say you score nine for the gold – that's real gold leaf, that is, more money than sense if you ask me but that's what it is, seven for the red, five for the inner white, three for the black and one for the outer white. We keep the scores for each arrow and the winner will be the highest scorer."

Fin looked at the other two targets still on the lawn. "They will be for eighty and a hundred paces Ross, three arrows at each." He passed the target to the second keeper. "Cooper, you set up this target," then turning to the third keeper, "Dyer, you do the middle target and me and Ross will carry the farthest. Sharpish now, I can see the Duke and Duchess coming out of the House."

As they walked the hundred or so paces to a stand that had already been erected, Fin could feel Keeper Lamb trying to assess him as an opponent, glancing at him, trying to see how easily he carried the heavy target, the easy gait even with a burden that he knew would be tightening the muscles in Fin's arms and back. "Ever shot at targets before, Ross?"

"Not like this, Mister Lamb. I did shoot at a country fair, but they had animal targets like you said."

"Done much shooting?"

"My grand-father taught me and we had some fun in the woods."

"I bet you did Ross. Your woods, or did they belong to someone else?" Fin just grinned. "I see where you learned to shoot then. How did you get on with the bow I gave Sergeant Webber?"

"Never had a string like it but it was fine."

"Yes, I was impressed, about fifty paces I'd say?"

Fin was surprised, "I didn't see you Mister Lamb?"

"I was with the sheep in the meadow, herding them into the pen." Fin realised that this competition was a more serious proposition than he had first thought. "Right Ross, we fitted the tripod of staves and have a hook attached to the apex ready for fitting. On three: one, two, three!" They lifted in unison and the straw caught on the hook without any problem. "Best we get back to the shooting line, Ross. Cooper is shooting for us game-keepers and the Duke has a guest who will be joining in as well."

As they walked back to the start, Fin noticed a small group on a converging path, a man and woman ahead, the Duke and Duchess he assumed, and a small group behind carrying wicker baskets. Lamb touched Fin's elbow as they got within ten paces: "Best we stop and let them pass through." Fin knew how to behave when in the presence of titled people, he had had enough practice at home. He stood head bowed, slightly bent at the waist, eyes averted to the ground.

"Good evening Lamb, is this the young man who intends to take the honour tonight?" The Duke was obviously in good humour, dressed in the deepest blue coat and breeches with white stockings and shining black shoes with silver buckles. Fin noticed that the white stockings had already got signs of green stains as grass had brushed from the heel of one shoe against the inner leg as the party had walked across the lawn.

"This is Gunner Ross, new to the Horse Artillery and their 'champion' of archery!"

"Ross, Ross." the repetition of his name made Fin look up to be astonished at who was in front of him, "Ross, weren't you one of the chaps who helped save my lioness?" Fin was a little uncomfortable, not at the question or the Duke speaking to him but who he had seen.

"Yes sir, I helped with the other gunners to retrieve her."

"I hear you did far more than that young man, and greatly am I in your debt. You don't get many lions in England do you Ross?"

"No sir, first I ever saw."

"Quite Ross, quite, now how good are you with the bow?"

Lamb intervened allowing Fin to regain his composure, "I think he will be a tough opponent for us this evening. Cooper is shooting for us and your guest?"

"Ah, yes, Lady Ellen." He turned to introduce his guest, the person that had almost left Fin speechless. She was dressed in the same dark green as the gamekeepers but in a tight fitting jacket and long skirt with laced boots slightly protruding from beneath the hem. At her neck delicate lace from her blouse cascaded over the collar and her hat was almost like Fin's forage cap but pulled to one side and with large feathers – Fin guessed that they were pheasant – trailing behind. The Duke resumed the introduction: "May I introduce our guest, Lady Ellen Banbury-Williams, her husband died serving his country with Sir John Moore. In the Buffs he was, isn't that right Lady Ellen?"

"Yes he was. Like many brave men he died on the terrible retreat to Corunna." She extended her gloved hand which the Duke gently took and brought her to face Fin and the gamekeeper. "This young man wrestled my lioness which had escaped. Saved her life he did. The yokels would have killed her."

"Did he now? My word, that's a tale to tell Robert when he arrives tomorrow." Lady Ellen fixed her gaze on Fin who wondered whether she was warning or threatening him with the news that Robert de Lacy would be coming to Goodwood. "So you are an archer are you?" Fin found it difficult to look Lady Ellen in the eye.

"Yes my lady, my grand-father taught me."

"Do you live far from here?"

Fin was certain that Lady Ellen was deliberately laying a trail to ensure no one knew of their previous meeting.

"I grew up in Dorset my Lady."

"But now you have volunteered to serve your King and Country to rid us of the tyrant across the water?" Fin didn't know what to say but nodded his head in agreement. "I intend to beat you in this challenge, and the gamekeeper!" She turned and went to the footman who had carried her bow.

"Excellent, Ellen, excellent. Your Robert comes from Dorset, don't he?" and without pause for reply, "Come my dear." He turned and held his hand towards the Duchess who wore a light blue cloak that hid the rest of her clothes, to guard against the evening chill, sweeping the ground as she walked. The gamekeeper bent at the waist and Fin copied to allow the Duke and Duchess to take their seats in the viewing area. By the time the hosts had reached the chairs, draped in blankets to further ward against the cold, footmen had set up trestles and laid out an array of delights to eat and drink, much to the appreciation of the gunners and women.

"Time to string your bow Ross," Lamb started to walk to the shooting line. "You met that lady before?"

"Where would I have met a lady like that?"

"She was very talkative, not like ladies I've met before, they don't speak to people like us."

"I've never known ladies taking part in a shooting contest either."

"No... you're right there Ross. Best be on your guard young man, never know what might happen!" and Lamb gave Fin a dig in the ribs with a mischievous chuckle.

Gamekeeper Cooper had already strung his bow, Lady Ellen had dismissed attempts to string her bow to do it herself, and Fin took the leather pouch from his pocket to string his own. Placing one of the loops over the horn nock, he used the ground to brace against the bow to loop the second nock and test the string. Lamb checked all were ready, turned towards the assembled spectators and called: "Contestants ready! The first arrows will be at sixty paces, Dyer will be calling the scores. Lady Ellen will fire first, followed by Gunner Ross and then, representing Goodwood, Cooper!" The Duke waved a hand in acknowledgement and returned to his drink offered by an observant footman.

The first round of arrows all hit the target with Lamb keeping score: "Lady Ellen five, Gunner Ross Five, Keeper Cooper seven." The spectators anticipated each shot, willing the archer to hit the golden centre! The closest target finished with all three archers having totalled seventeen points, several arrows hitting red but none in the gold! The middle target at eighty steps saw Fin raise the loudest cheer as he hit gold with his first arrow, but after three arrows each he was only two points ahead of the other archers, with Cooper hitting inner white every time.

The spectators were gratefully enjoying the refreshments provided by the Duke and Duchess and after several glasses of wine, much to the embarrassment of Thomas, her husband, Sal shouted across the lawn: "Come on Fin you can do it!" Lady Ellen walked behind him and in a low husky whisper asked, "Someone you know?" Without turning Fin responded calmly, "That's Sal, Thomas' wife, she's holding the babe in that shawl, but probably had a few too many drinks of the wine!"

"So you're Fin Ross, the poacher spy!" Fin turned this time ready to defend himself to see the broadest of grins lighting Lady Ellen's face. He returned the smile. "Gunner Ross now, my Lady!"

Lamb announced that the final round of arrows were to commence and Lady Ellen took her place, feet at right angles to the line of fire. She attached the arrow to the string, took a breath as she raised the bow, pulling the bow string to her cheek that was rapidly rising in colour to match the pinking sky as the sun slipped lower to the horizon. Holding her breath for a fleeting moment, she released the string, sending the arrow across the hundred or so paces towards the four-foot straw circle. Dyer's cheer transmitted the score before he had announced it; "Lady Ellen. Gold and nine points!"

"Well done!" encouraged the Duchess. "Good shooting Ellen, good shooting!" was the Duke's response. Fin was next and the groan of disappointment that met the announcement "Black and three points" was easily audible to the contestants.

"Too far for you young'n?" Cooper had remained silent until now and was trying to intimidate Fin. Fin just stared at the gamekeeper knowing better than to respond, but simply watched the arrow fly towards the target and heard the shout of "Red and seven points! Lady Ellen leads with forty-one, Cooper next with thirty-nine and Gunner Ross thirty-seven!"

"In't over yet, still two arrows to score." Sergeant Webber was talking in a low voice but the gunners could hear. "That Lady Ellen puttin' him off, you think Thomo?" Bob Halls had slipped next to Thomo, "He's a bit susceptible to a pretty face Bob."

"He's not the only one, is he? Look at her, she is a beauty!"

The second arrows brought the scores closer: Lady Ellen hit the target but scored only one, Fin resumed his accuracy to score seven but Cooper was two points in the lead with yet another red. "Last arrow and anyone to win!" announced Lamb. Lady Ellen recovered her scoring to achieve a red, Fin matched her, leaving Cooper to score a red or gold to win the match. "Go on Coop"' encouraged his colleague Lamb; "Only need a red!" mentioned Fin just as Cooper had started to raise his bow, causing him to stop and lower his bow. Cooper turned to scowl at Fin and started his last shot again only to be interrupted by Lady Ellen commenting "You are bound to win Mr Cooper," she walked behind him lowering her voice, "you have already scored two reds this round." Cooper didn't stop, perhaps he should have, but as he loosed the arrow all eyes were fixed to the far end of the lawn and waited for the shouted score. The tone of Dyer's voice gave away the result. "Cooper, inner white and five points."

Lamb totalled the final arrows: "Lady Ellen forty-nine, Ross and Cooper tied on fifty-one!" A cheer from the gunners made the Duke turn his head. Lamb had approached the seated Duke and Duchess. "A tie Lamb?"

"We could decide it the old way?"

"How so?"

"Well if we take down the new circular targets and replace it with a wooden model of a bird, first man to hit the target wins."

"Splendid Lamb, splendid. Lady Ellen, come and sit with us." He beckoned to his guest who gracefully walked across the gap to take a seat hastily placed by a footman and covered with another blanket. "Good shooting Ellen, how did you ever learn to shoot so well?"

"With Harry away and living in London, I met a group who had the wonderful name of the Toxopholite Society, they taught many ladies to have the skills of archery. Their meetings attracted many young men as well!" The Duchess raised her eyebrows and dipped her chin as she replied "I am sure that they did!"

A shout from Lamb announced that they were ready to have the shoot-off. "Archers will fire when ready until the bird falls." Fin and Cooper had both stuck their three arrows into the lawn to give greater speed of access. "Ready Ross?" Fin nodded. "Ready Coop?" The gamekeeper nodded. "Good luck to you both. Loose your arrows!"

Both had their first arrows ready on the string and almost in unison they raised and fired! Both arrows hit the poles of the tripod but deflected away from the bird target. "Unlucky boys, try again." Lamb encouraged. Fin fired first, the arrow glancing the bird but not knocking it down and he watched Cooper's sail over the top as he attached his last shot to the string. Breathing out he momentarily paused, looking at the ground, then he slowly breathed in raising the bow, focused his eyes on the bird as he pulled the string to his cheek and released his fingers. He heard Cooper's string loose his arrow a blink after his own. The cheers from the watching gunners announced the success of Fin's arrow making its mark on the wooden bird, toppling it from its perch on the tripod just as Cooper's arrow struck the head.

"My word, good shooting you two!" exclaimed the Duke as the ladies gave a polite round of applause. "Lamb, whose arrow struck?" Dyer had brought all six arrows back to the crowd and met Lamb, handing him the target. "The winner is Gunner Ross, but Cooper cut the target here." He pointed to a slither of wood newly detached from the head of the bird. "A thoroughly entertaining evening but the winner has to be Gunner Ross. Well done young man, come and have some refreshment, I would like to hear more about the capture of my lioness. And you too, Cooper, Dyer, Lamb, come and join us." Dyer handed the arrows back to the finalists, congratulating Fin on his shooting and commiserating with his friend: "You were only a whisker away Coop – he just got there first. If it had been real it would have had two arro's stuck in it!"

"Miss is good as a mile. He won fair and square, taught by a goodun' he was."

"Well done Ross, just in the nick of time or Coop would have got it. Your grand-father taught you well. I daresay it mightn't be the first pheasant you have struck!" Fin grinned and shook hands with each gamekeeper.

"Do you want a hand with the targets?"

"That would be most helpful, got to get them into the stables. I'll collect the cart if you can get them to the road with Coop and Dyer?"

"No problem. Some of the lads will lend a hand, the more that help, the faster the job's done."

Fin walked over to the gunners who cheered his arrival. Having explained the task, there was no problem in getting volunteers: "Least we can do after you won the honours for us!" Elijah Black clapped Fin on the back. "Thought that lady had put you off there Fin. The Duke laid on a good spread for us though."

"It would be nice to have something… if you lot have left anything!"

By the time they had packed the targets, unlashed the poles and hooks and stored them onto the cart, the Duke, Duchess and party had retired across the dampening lawn to the warmth of the House. Fin stared at the group wondering whether Lady Ellen would tell

Master Robert that he was here and he wondered how he would be able to remain invisible. "Too good for you Fin, but you showed you could shoot an arrow!" Bob Halls had crept up beside him and joined his stare. "She's a beauty that one, isn't she?"

"Can't take what's not yours Bob."

"What was that Fin?"

"Nothing. Just somethin' I was told a while back, Bob. Probably good advice though." Fin turned and hurried to join the rest at the remnants of the food and drink, leaving Bob bemused.

"Well done Ross, kept the honour of the Artillery, well done! Mind you, it were closer than I would have liked! I had a bet on with the gamekeepers!" Another cheer rang round the gunners.

"Never in doubt Sarge," Thomas Hughes butted in, "Fin was always in control, weren't you Fin?"

"I was more than a little worried when that Lady hit the gold!"

"You weren't the only one Fin, she was a very good archer… and a lot prettier to watch!" Thomo cuffed Fin round the ear and then hugged him in celebration. Whilst so close, he added in a whisper "How did she know you Fin? That's not the first time you've met is it?"

"She's one part of the reason I had to run, Thomo, and the problem is the other part of the reason will be arriving tomorrow. I'm going to have to keep my head down so that he doesn't recognise me."

"He can't touch you now Fin," Thomo continued the whispered conversation. "You're artillery property now and no one can get you out."

"But he could make life difficult, I'm sure!"

"Come on you two," Elijah Black called over. "Time we was back in camp."

Chapter 18

Fin awoke still worried at the thought of Robert de Lacy discovering his presence – even Thomo's reassurance hadn't given him the night's sleep he had wished for. He had kept waking with a start, expecting angry hands wrenching him from his blankets only to slowly come to, realising he was still with his fellow gunners. Finally with the light from the rising sun seeping its way across the horizon, he had given up hope of any further rest and, as quietly as he could, left the tent. As always Martha was up first, the fire was going and the pot was boiling away with the promise of the first tea of the day. "Up early Fin, somethin' ailin' you, or is it that 'lady' we saw you with last night?"

"No it's not her Martha," and lowering his voice, in spite of no one else being up, "the man she is to marry is coming today and it wouldn't be good for him to know I'm here. He accused me of poaching, which I hadn't been." Martha stopped the kneading that she had been busily involved in, ready for bread rolls to go with a vegetable soup later in the day and turned to look Fin straight in the eyes.

"Listen Fin, we all got things that we'd prefer others not to know. What these men say," jerking a thumb towards the tents behind, "and what really is the reason for being here isn't always the same. But what I do know, Fin, is since we have been together we have grown into a big family that would fight to protect one of their own; none of us will be letting you get taken." Martha returned to her task while Fin took a steaming mug of tea.

"Thanks Martha, I see the House is already busy." Fin was staring towards figures coming and going around the entrance to the grand house.

"They were up before I! And I dare say that you will be busy quite soon enough!"

Martha was proved to be right. Sergeant Webber had collected the gunners and distributed them into three groups. The first group with Fin and Thomo included were allotted to game-keeper Lamb with the task of securing a line of lanterns – glass sided boxes with a hook in the top to be attached to the metal stakes that looked like shepherds' crooks. The two wagons loaded with stakes and lanterns promised a long morning ahead and they set to, first laying out at set intervals along the whole of the drive to the House stipulated by Mister Lamb and then returning to hammer each into the verge. "They arriving late mister Lamb?" asked Bill Bennett.

"The Duchess never has these things start early, always the dramatic with lighted drive and magnificent chandeliers inside. Likes to let everyone know how well she is doing, all new candles tonight."

"Who does the lighting of all these lanterns?"

Lamb simply looked back at Thomo. "Who d'you think?"

"Thought as much."

As they finally reached the House Fin noticed the extra lanterns and stakes in an awaiting wagon. "We got some more work mister Lamb?"

"We're off to the Menagerie now: the Duke likes to show off his animals to the guests so we have to light through the tunnels and around the cages."

The second group selected by Sergeant Webber had included John Smith, Arthur Parkin and the five married men: Noah Hogg, Elijah Hogg, Thomas Hughes, Donald McConnell and George Rogers. They accompanied a footman into the grand House and were given the task of lowering each chandelier from winches set in the ceiling space between the ground and first floors. The first lowering had been undertaken with a great deal of trepidation but they soon gained confidence and working in teams, shouted up to their partners in the void between floors without fear of being told to be quiet. Servants, footmen, maids and man-servants came and went without more than a cursory glance at these shirt-sleeved workers. The entrance hall, the rooms set aside for the refreshments, the large room being decorated with garlands of flowers suspended across windows and colourful broad ribbons in the patriotic colours of red, white and blue ready for the ball, all had to be prepared and cleared. It would be the footmen who would lower the chandeliers again to carry out the lighting.

The third group had been taken to the stables to prepare additional stalls for the guests' horses as well as opening the large double doors to provide space for the expected carriages. Layers of dust had to be washed off both wood and metal-work, brasses polished, floors raked and scraped to prepare for fresh straw, water poured into freshly cleaned basins and the stable-yard made immaculate, just in case a guest may come to check on their horses.

As the different groups returned late afternoon to camp, they shared stories of their 'chores' as Bob Halls called them. "Same as always. If there's labouring to be done, get the army to do it, cheap labour that's what we are and always will be!"

"You're an old cynic," suggested Arthur Parkin, "but I have to agree that you are right."

Bob laughed loud and long. "D'you all hear that, Parky says I'm right!" Sergeant Webber arrived interrupting the jollity.

"Another wagon in the stable-yard, jump to it! All of you to be ready in your lines."

"Sarge, we've only just got back from the stables, we cleared everything." complained Alexander Campbell.

"Well, it's a great big thing, painted grey, two large wheels and two small wheels pulled by four horses…and it's sitting in the middle of the stable-yard now!" The gunners reluctantly trudged to the stables asking the group who had just come back how they had missed the wagon? As they walked through the arch, one of the drivers was standing between both leading horses holding the head piece of each horse.

"Hey Xander!" Bob Halls couldn't resist the opportunity. "You sure you cleared all away? Looks like you missed one!"

"I'm telling you…" but a dig in the ribs from Arthur Parkin prevented Campbell from any further attempt to justify himself.

"Two lines, standing easy," ordered their sergeant.

It had been a long day of tedious tasks, the last thing the gunners wanted was to have to start over. "Now you have helped the duke and duchess prepare for the festivities this evening, you have to prepare for your evening duties." A murmur ran through the gunners. "It is not a matter for discussion. You have to learn to take orders and tonight you will have a further task…" The sergeant went around the end of the front rank and down between the gunners. "You will be representing the Horse Artillery and we cannot have you looking like this! It is about time that we had you kitted up to look like real Gunners and this is why the wagon has been brought in. Quartermaster Kemp," a man, face swathed in fire red whiskers, so long that they almost met at his chin, emerged from behind the back of the wagon carrying a ledger, quill and pot of ink… "will be issuing each one of you with your full kit. Our first task will be to get each of you to sign for it! You will be given your best boots, spurs, stockings, breeches, gloves, jackets and helmets. You will wear this full dress, with swords, for the evening ceremonials at which we will be an honour guard for the guests and guides to ensure that any guests wishing to see the animals can get to the Menagerie and back to the House safely, while the drivers will take care of the carriages as they arrive." The sergeant had reached the front of the line again and was wearing a huge grin, reflected back by every gunner. "You have learned fast, and although you will stop the grumbling, you have the making of a great gun crew. Once we are clear of the festivities tonight, we will move onto the big guns! Now listen for your name. Quartermaster Kemp will call you forward, you will sign the book, collect the uniform and then get back to camp to polish the boots, whiten the belts, shine the helmet, brush your jackets and make the swords and scabbards gleam like a mirror!"

The process took time for the drivers to parcel out the items from the boxes in the wagon but the sergeant had been right, the men all walked back into camp feeling so much more the proper gunner.

Martha's bread rolls and soup had been eaten in a trice as men, as excited as children at Christmas, set about the task of helping each other into stiff and unfamiliar clothing. They couldn't do anything but hold their heads slightly tilted backwards as the new collars didn't bend at all. Their gait was stiff as they desperately tried not to catch their spurs on the ground or on each other, but they were almost unrecognisable, even to each other.

At the appointed time, all were ready on parade as Sergeant Webber strode into camp. "My, Sergeant Webber, don't you look the dandy!" Sal teased as their sergeant, with ruffled shirt cascading out of his collar, inspected his gunners.

"You all look so smart. I'm so proud," called a usually silent Moira McConnell. "Now don't you go and get these uniforms dirty. As soon as you are finished it will take them off and pack them neatly in your bags."

"That's right missus McConnell," reinforced Sergeant Webber. "No need for extra work tomorrow." He inspected each gunner, straightening a collar, hitching a belt higher, smoothing the belt clasp, flattening the helmet straps, but he was ready to issue orders to place them in position. "Ross, Thomson, you two were the lion tamers and so the duke has asked for you to be in position at the Menagerie. Off you go, it will take some time to get there in those new boots and take this," he handed Thomo a long stick which had a lighting splint curled around it, and handed Fin a small box which held a flint, metal striker and dry lint ready for catching a spark to create the flame necessary to light the lighting splint and lanterns.

"No sign of Robert de Lacy?" asked Thomo as they walked the track to their designated duty.

"Well, he didn't appear while we were fixing the lanterns, perhaps he arrived later? I hope he doesn't come our way tonight."

Even as far away from the Great House as they were, Fin and Thomo could hear the music drifting across the fields. "Parky said he saw a pianoforte, harp, two violins and two flautists this morning. Don't recognise the tune though?" Fin turned to face the House.

"I believe that that piece was composed by Beethoven," replied Thomo.

"How do you know that?"

"I don't, but if you say it confidently, you get away with a lot, Fin!" A horseman trotted towards them and they immediately recognised their sergeant.

"Time to light the lanterns. Use that tinder box and then pass the taper to me once you've lit your set."

Fin took the tin and opened it, striking the flint with the metal, seeing a spark and blowing lightly on the dry tinder. "I'm impressed Ross, first time as well. Thomson, get that taper lit." Thomo lit the lanterns at the start of the tunnel, ducked under the arch and lit the pair marking the further end. On his return, he lit the two that each would hold to escort guests through and then handed the taper to the sergeant who turned his horse and made his way back up the track to the next pair of gunners to light their lanterns and further to the House. Meanwhile, the gamekeepers had carried out the same process from the gates at the end of the drive to the House.

Sergeant Webber handed Lamb the lighting splint. "Not much different to a port-fire that we use, waxed taper that will hold an ember."

"Does the job and inside the House they use shorter tapers with guards to stop wax dripping." They both turned to look at the glowing chandeliers flooding light onto the lawn as the darkening sky was illuminated by a myriad of stars gracing the clearest of nights. Sergeant Webber escorted Lamb to the front of the House to inspect the gunners. "Enjoying the music Parkin?"

"Yes Sergeant: Haydn, Beethoven and I understand that there will be music from Michael Turner, a new English composer who has taken a Mozart melody and created a dance especially called the Sussex Waltz. A bit of a scandal Sergeant, dancers holding each other very close, it's come to Britain from Europe, some want it banned! The musicians have planned a wide selection of dances from different composers with country dances, reels, minuets and a polonaise. I always like to hear good musicians play, I've enjoyed our musical evenings in camp."

"High praise indeed Parkin, but don't forget to only speak if spoken to," turning to John Smith, "What about you Smith, what do you think of the music?"

"Like a good tune Sergeant, prefer a good sing-song though."

"Not sure if you will hear much singing tonight, but keep your ears open – never know what you might learn?" Sergeant Webber retraced his steps to mount his horse, returning to the stables as the first guests appeared at the entrance to the drive.

Footmen walked between Parkin and Smith down the steps and prepared to welcome the guests. Glancing through the open double doors, Parkin could see a group ready to receive the new arrivals. The women both wore white shining materials. The older lady he recognised as the duchess had crimson bows at the shoulder, a daringly plunging neckline and a matching sash tied behind in a large bow with trailing ribbons to the floor. Long white gloves covered her arms to the elbow and a beautiful necklace matched a sparkling bracelet. The other lady, the lady that had competed against Fin in the archery, had large shoulder ruffles with very short sleeves tied in emerald green bows, a far more modest neckline and a matching broad ribbon tied at the small of her back accentuating the thinnest part of her waist with an elaborate bow. The two gentlemen contrasted strikingly with the ladies: one was dressed in infantry uniform, scarlet jacket with strikingly green facings, white breeches, stockings and shining black shoes whereas the duke was instantly recognisable by the sash worn across his long tailed coat reminiscent of a naval captain with the same white breeches and stockings as the infantry officer but shoes that were adorned with silver buckles.

The guests arrived at regular intervals as the evening darkened and the House glowed even brighter. The chatter of so many guests mixed with the musical accompaniment but the short musical march announced that the dancing was about to start.

Parkin straightened as a carriage was brought up to the House at the same time as four guests appeared, ladies cloaked against the chill, escorted down the steps to be carried to the Menagerie.

Fin and Thomo had a steady stream of visitors, all inquisitive to discover what the wild beasts looked like, but also to view the men who had tamed the lioness. Fin was polite but short in his response to questions, he didn't want to draw attention any more than necessary and made sure that Thomo received as much of the questioning. The music was still playing quite faint in the distance but it was still possible to make out the changes of instrument as the guests enjoyed their night of dancing. A footman had informed them that there would be one more party to view the beasts and Fin waited with his well-rehearsed story. As the carriage approached, there were four passengers: a man dressed in infantry uniform complete with cocked hat; a lady swathed in a wrap covering all that could be seen of her in the coach; and two smaller figures, children Fin assumed, girls wearing flowered hair ties holding back curled hair, especially fitted for their first ball. Fin also noticed that, with the light of the House behind the carriage, it was very difficult to make out anything of the colours. He knew the officer to be in a bright red jacket but he could not say with any certainty that he could confirm it. Only as the carriage came within the last set of lanterns could he discern, not just the red, but the contrasting pea-green collar and lapels partially buttoned back. "Bugger!"

"What's wrong Fin?" Thomo whispered his reply, the carriage being too close.

"It's him."

Fin went to the far side and Thomo opened the near side doors, offering a hand to the occupants as they stepped down. The two young girls were excited to lead the guests to the animals. "This way Lady Ellen, father has fantastic creatures." "Let us wait for the lanterns." Her voice was instantly recognisable and Thomo and Fin lit the way through the tunnel. They didn't need to conduct the tour, the two young girls literally pulled the guests from cage to cage, giving every detail that they could about the creatures: where they had come from, who had captured them, the names they had given them… Fin and Thomo simply lit the way and Fin dared to hope that his uniform was sufficient disguise to prevent Master Robert recognising him. It was only when the tour was almost over and they were leading back to the tunnel that the girls excitedly pronounced: "These two soldiers rescued the lioness, capturing her in a net. If it wasn't for them, she would have been killed, shot by the innkeeper."

"Well done you two, just the sort of men we need in the army, pity you didn't join a proper regiment like mine, we could do with fearless fighters to beat the Frenchies!" Fin and Thomo stood silent, but as they made a move to light the tunnel, Robert de Lacy continued, "Don't be bashful you two. Can't gunners speak for themselves?" Fin turned from his slightly bent position to stand upright. Perhaps it was the chance lighting of his face as he ducked away from the tunnel but immediately the tone changed. "I know that face, I ordered your arrest. You are Ross, what the hell are you doing here?"

Thomo stepped between Fin and De Lacy, "Artillerymen sir, we volunteered to join the horse artillery, gunners now."

De Lacy eased Thomo aside with his left arm as he went to draw the dress sword with his right, "I'll have you under guard Ross just as I said I would."

A voice from the tunnel warned them of the arrival of Sergeant Webber. In a low voice that only the men would hear, "I wouldn't be drawing that sword sir, making a scene in front of the ladies, not good sir. You know that sworn in and serving men can't be taken out. If they could we'd lose over half the army wouldn't we sir?" The lantern now fully illuminated the faces and the sergeant had deliberately stood close to De Lacy, the light giving the untried officer the view of a face that had been through many battles.

"But this m…"

"This man is a gunner in my troop and he will be serving King and Country with me sir!" He paused to let the impact of what he had said sink in. "Best we get back through the tunnel to the House," and in a louder voice for all to hear, "They have just announced that the last dance, Sir Roger de Cleverley will be starting imminently!"

The two young girls brought further discussion to an end: "Lady Ellen, please can we go, we must dance the last dance." And they reached to take a hand each, almost pulling Lady Ellen through the tunnel.

"Lead the way Thomson. After you sir. Ross, bring up the rear to light our feet." The party retraced their steps and having been helped into the carriage, Sergeant Webber ordered the driver to walk on.

"Thanks Sarge, how did you know?"

"Saw the lady we met last night. Saw the officer and put two and two together."

"Glad you were here. Not sure what we would have done." Thomo added.

"Knowing you two, you probably would have wrestled him to the ground, put him in a net and thrown him in a cage!" All three smiled and watched the carriage disappear back to the House. "Right, job done, bring the lanterns, we have to put them back in the stables for the gamekeepers to sort out."

Fin and Thomo were careful not to allow the lanterns to dirty or snag their new uniforms and were relieved to have placed them down on the table allocated in the gamekeepers' room. As they stepped into the stalls, two figures hurried across the open doorway at the far end and disappeared into a nearby stall. Fin was about to call out when Thomo put a hand on his arm, a finger to his lips and whispered: "Shh, don't know who they are or what they're up to, but we're not letting anyone mess with our horses." He beckoned with his free hand to keep close to the chained entrance to each stall and walked as stealthily as he could towards the entrance. Fin felt his new boots creaking, certain that they would be heard; he desperately tried to prevent his spurs making any sounds and by the time they were half way up the aisle, Thomo raised his hand to halt. A rustling ahead was a sign of feet shuffling in the straw but alongside that were whispers and the muffled sounds of clothing being rearranged. Thomo beckoned Fin to close in and they reached two stalls from the end before he raised his hand for the second time. The whispers were more audible now and they could clearly hear a woman's voice, "Oh Donald, oh Donald, oh Donald!" followed by the whispering low tones of a Scot; "Nay sa loud Moira, softly now."

"Oh Donald, that's the last thing…" Giggling was followed by a final "Oh Donald!"

Thomo turned suddenly, twisting at the waist, surprised at a loud noise from behind them. The single door from the back wall of the stable block had been opened but due to its being little used, it creaked on stiff hinges. "Who's in here?"

"No problem mister Lamb, we've just been returning the lanterns to your store room, all present and correct." Thomo had stepped into the middle of the aisle taking Fin with him so that there was no chance for Lamb to see past them. As the gamekeeper walked towards them, Thomo and Fin closed the gap in as relaxed a fashion as possible.

"You the only two, I thought I heard voices from the other side of that wall?"

"Mr and Mrs McConnell have just been checking the far horses. When we came in, one of the horses were restless, shifting her hooves and swinging her head. McConnell has treated horses before and was best to check her over."

"So that's what you call it is it?"

"That's right mister Lamb, we put the lanterns, as instructed, in that room," pointing beyond Lamb, "and Donald…" turning to face

123

the open doorway to see Donald and Moira unhooking the chain and replacing it as calmly as they could. "All right Donald?"

"She were a bit warm but we gave her a good rub down and replaced the water, bit excitable but she'll be fine." Moira had her hands behind her, secretly trying to smooth the wrinkled folds of her skirts. Lamb took one more look, then turned to walk to his store muttering, "Not the only one who were excited and got a good rub down!"

Fin and Thomo walked to Donald and Moira who mouthed a silent "Thank you," blushing so deeply that it could be seen even under the moonlight breaking through the opening of the door. "How long were you in there, you two?" asked Donald.

"Long enough Donald, long enough!"

"Glad you were there – I wouldn't have wanted Mister Lamb to have found us. Moira couldn't resist me in my finery!" He turned to his wife and pulled her close to his side. "Could you ma sweet thing!"

"Our secret Moira, our secret," reassured Thomo, "No one will know, will they Fin?" Fin was unsure of what he should say, he was not sure that he should have intruded on the intimacy but nodded his assent. "Mind you Moira, best you get that straw out of your skirts before we get to camp!" Thomo chuckled to see her turn, first left then right to see what he had seen, slowly realising the jest.

"Get away with you, Thomo, you wicked man, there's nothin' there." They all laughed, Fin included, finishing another long day. "Best you look after your new clothes, don't want anything spoiling them."

"Will do Moira, that straw gets everywhere!"

Chapter 19

"Right my brave boys, this is what you have all been waiting for."
The sergeant paced the line staring into the eyes of every gunner.
"We will learn to fire the piece in front of you. We have learned to
ride and fight, but how will we fire it? We have come out here onto
the Downs so that we have more space and when we do fire the gun,
we won't be upsetting too many of the neighbours! We have raised
a red flag, warning of our intention to test the guns so we must stay
within those limits," and the sergeant pointed towards distant flag
poles, red flags fluttering gently in the early morning breeze.
"Everyone will have a number and this will correspond to your role
in the sequence. You will all learn the roles of each other in case of
anyone having the misfortune to become injured on account of those
Frenchies trying to kill us, or some of you woebegotten demons
who, having caught something terrible from all your drinkin' an'
whorin' that you are incapacitated." He paused as a chuckle slipped
through some of the men. "And I can tell you this… if any of you
do miss serving my guns because of your uncontrolled urges, the
scratching from the pox will be the least of your worries!"

The gunners faced front, some shuffling uneasily, realising that
their sergeant meant it and no one wanted to incur his wrath.

"Bennett, you will be number one, Smith number two,
Wilkinson number three, Halls number four, McConnell number
five, Davies number six, Dickinson number seven, Rogers number
eight, Thomson number nine, Taylor number ten, Ross number
eleven, Hughes number twelve, Campbell number thirteen, Parkin
number fourteen and Black number fifteen."

Fin wondered how these had been given – it hadn't been a
simple numbering along the ranks but as if a specific role for each
gunner had been selected. His experience of his army life so far
doubted that any thought had gone into any action but this seemed
different.

"Now boys, we have just ridden to where we were ordered.
Bennett!"

"Yes Sergeant."

"You will hold Ross's horse when he dismounts and that of any officer with us. Smith, you will hold the horses for Thomson and Taylor but you will not dismount."

"Yes Sergeant."

"Wilkinson, you likewise will hold the horses for Hughes and Campbell."

"Yes Sergeant."

"Dickinson and Rogers will have ridden on the limber; you will get off and go to the muzzle to bear weight in turning the gun."

"Yes Sergeant," they chorused.

"Ross, your first job will be to unkey. There's a six inch L-shaped key that fits through the key hole, turns and the weight of the handle hangs the L downwards and there it is locked. You unkey the limber so that Hughes and Campbell can raise the trail. We always turn the gun to the right when we unlimber so, while Hughes and Campbell are lifting the trail, Dickinson and Rogers will be at the muzzle." He paused to let that sink in. "Thomson, you will be bracing the right wheel and Taylor the left wheel." Gunners exchanged glances in anticipation of the drill whilst others wondered about their role still to be designated.

"Ross, once the gun is unhooked, you will order the limber to 'Drive On', and we will have the gun clear and we can prepare for action!"

The sergeant made his way around the gun pointing out each part as he spoke, just as he had done with the pistol drill.

"Ross will unhook the elevation locking chain, Taylor will un-strap the traversing lever and give it to Ross who will fit it to the trail. Rogers will un-strap the rammer, Thomson will take the sponge head cover and Dickinson will be given the rammer. Rogers will then unhook the bucket from the axle and remove the lid to check that we have water! Thomson, you will check the vent and make sure you have the vent pins, the quills and your thumb stall from the right axle box or the limber if somebody has forgotten to replace them! Taylor, you will take the slow match from the left axle box, light it and then fit it into the portfire stick that Hughes will have given you!" He paused again to let the instructions sink in. Fin was impressed that the instructions had been given without any reference to notes at all. "Now, Parkin and Black, you haven't been forgotten, nor you Halls and McConnell. Parkin, you will be running from the limber to meet Campbell with the next cartridge and projectile who will run back to the gun to pass onto Hughes, who will pass onto Rogers for loading into the muzzle. Black, you will be stationed at the limber to help Parkin be as quick as possible. Halls and McConnell will be our reserves and will have to step in for any gunner, so you will know the lot! The good news is that you two will be stationed fifteen yards back to avoid getting hit with the rest of us!"

The next hour was spent riding around the Downs and then halting and unlimbering the gun. When Sergeant Webber was satisfied, he called the drill to a halt. "Now what about trying to fire this thing! Remember the pistol drill? Well it is similar because we have to ram the cartridge and projectile down the barrel, 'but'..." and he emphasised once more, "BUT we have a big difference. We have to sponge out the barrel after every firing so that we don't ignite the next cartridge with any embers left in the barrel, 'and'... we have to cover the vent."

"So, we are all in position, the gun is ready, Parkin and Campbell have relayed the cartridge and shell to Hughes from the limber, Hughes is taking them to Rogers... Thomson, you must 'serve the vent', which means keep your thumb sealed over the vent hole and you will be given a special thumb stall to prevent you getting burned! Dickinson, you will put your sponge in the bucket, knock it against the barrel to get rid of any excess water, then ram it hard to the end of the barrel and turn it to extinguish any little embers. Your job is crucial, everyone is crucial, but if you get that wrong, when we put the cartridge in, we will be blown to God knows where – and for you lot, it will be very hot!" Fin thought it was good that Sergeant Webber could be light-hearted over such a monumental mistake. "Then Rogers will have taken the cartridge from Hughes and loaded it into the muzzle. By this time, Dickinson will have swivelled his rammer and can now push the cartridge down the barrel, Thomson, still with his thumb over the vent! Dickinson pulls out the rammer, Hughes puts in the projectile and Dickinson rams it down, tight as he can against the cartridge, removes the rammer and steps away to the front of the right wheel, opposite Hughes at the front of the left wheel. At last Thomson, you can remove your thumb! But you have not finished. You take your pin and insert it down the vent hole to pierce the flannel bag containing the cartridge so that the quill will properly ignite the powder. Thomson, it will be all go now. Remove your pin and insert a quill into the vent covering it with your left hand until the order to fire... we don't want any stray spark setting it off early, do we?

Taylor will have the portfire in his hand and on order to fire, Thomson removes his hand from the quill and steps back. Taylor steps forward, making sure that he is clear of the left wheel which will recoil and crush him if he don't, and applies the burning end to the quill. There will a very short delay before an almighty explosion will deafen you all! The remains of the quill will fly out of the vent, the gun will recoil backwards and the projectile will fly towards the target!"

"Hooray!" the gunners cheered.

"But wait… it's not over… Rogers and Taylor, to the left wheel, Dickinson and Thomson to the right wheel, Ross to the trail and we must get back in line ready for the next firing. Dickinson will dip his sponge in the bucket, tap it on the barrel, swab out, Thomson will have his right thumb over the vent, Parkin, Campbell, Hughes and Rogers will have carried out their relay and we are ready!

Now let's see if we can fire this gun."

Fin knew everyone was nervous but with Sergeant Webber making a non-stop instruction manual, the firing went well, except for Hughes tripping and dropping the shot on his foot and so Jones had to run into position instead. After the fourth round, Fin felt like he was going to drop, he hadn't realised how exhausting it would be. Luckily after the sixth round, Sergeant Webber called the firing drill to a halt, ordered Taylor to cut the portfire and replace it into the bracket on the left axle, Thomo cleared the vent and Dicky swabbed the barrel once more before passing the rammer to Thomo who replaced the sponge cover and secured the rammer in its loop under the trail. Fin was ordered to secure the elevating hand wheel with the locking chain and then unship the traversing lever for Peter to buckle it to the side arm straps at the trail and under the axle. The limber was brought forward, Thomas and Xander replaced the trail, just as they had unlimbered, and the troop were ready to return to barracks, save for Thomas replacing the lid to the bucket and securing it under the gun axle.

"A good start boys, but it will have to be faster and we will all have to be stronger. You might be firing for hours during a battle, not just six rounds, and we have to learn about the different projectiles and when to fire them, but… a good start!"

With blackened faces and hands, uniforms no longer the rich blue from when they had been issued, aching limbs but happy faces and proud of their achievements. As they walked their horses back through the hedgerows towards Goodwood, Sergeant Webber twisted in his saddle and shouted, "Hey McConnell, let's have one of your songs to wend our way home."

McConnell hadn't been engaged in the drill as much as the rest of the troop and Fin knew that the sergeant had done this to keep him as part of the team, essential if they were to succeed when it wouldn't be just a drill. *"I'm lonesome since I crossed the hill, And o'er the moorlands sedgy, Such heavy thoughts my heart do fill, Since parting with my Betsey, I seek for one as fair and gay, But find none to remind me, How sweet the hours I passed away* (McConnell had sung on his own, but as he reached this last word the whole of number six gun roared)*, With the girl I left behind me!"*

The walk was immersed in a gale of laughter, Fin and Thomo sharing a nod and a wink as memories of the previous evening's discovery in the stable flooded back.

Chapter 20

The next morning saw a further ride than usual as they headed for the coast. They passed through villages, even turning the heads of labourers in the fields as the jingle of harnesses, steady sound of shod hooves and rumble of wheels with their heavy burden passed by. Sergeant Webber gave the order to halt and unlimber. Staring out over the mud flats, it was soon apparent why they had ridden to this location: a stranded and rotting hulk was to be the target to allow the new gun team to learn the impact of their shooting.

"Right, today we don't just fire, we hit a target. First…all of you collect a smooth stone and come to the water's edge." The gunners were getting used to their sergeant's strange orders and all searched for a suitable pebble and crunched the gravel as they made their way to the water. "I'm always one to learn from those who have gone before, and the Navy has learned an interesting fact that we can turn to good use. If I drop this stone into the water here, what will happen?" "It'll sink Sarge," Thomas Hughes volunteered.

"Quite right Hughes," and to demonstrate, he carelessly tossed a stone over his shoulder to land – splosh – in the shallows. "However, if I take this smooth stone and throw it thus…" he immediately turned and hurled the stone across the slight swell. Most of the gunners had not seen this before and their eyes widened as the stone pitched onto the surface and then proceeded to pitch again and again and again before sinking below the surface in the slightest of splashes. "Now imagine what a cannon ball would do?"

"Really Sarge? A cannon ball will bounce off the water?"

"Yes Hughes, Navy have been doing it for years. A bit like cricket – pitch the ball in the right place and the batsman doesn't know what to do! Same principle with the cannon ball – pitch it right and it will slam into the target – pitch too early and it will bounce right over, too late and the impact is reduced. Come on then, let's see what you can do. Count the pitches."

The gunners enjoyed throwing their stones, finding another and another to become the record breaker: Fin managed four bounces as did Thomo, Wilky, Parkin and Bob Halls but it was George Rogers who managed to eke out an extra pitch and achieve the greatest success.

"Well done Rogers! I hope you were watching. It all depends on the first pitch whether you will get it to pitch again. Too steep a trajectory and the stone sinks, too flat a trajectory and it will pitch a couple of times. Ross, you're used to having the arrows flight, so you're in charge of the elevation screw. We'll start at five degrees and then slowly lower it so that you will all see the difference. Now back to the gun and be at your stations."

The excitement of the target firing saw everyone rush to their places. "You know what to do, we've done it before, but this time watch the flight of the ball. Thomo, thumb on that vent. Now we will fire three rounds."

The first shot pitched in front of the hulk, clipped the remnants of the rail on the port side and cleared well into the harbour. The second and third crept closer to the target and took a large splinter from the hull, bringing cheers from the gun crew.

"Lower by one degree, Ross!"

Fin managed the elevation screw, turning the four arms of the handle to reduce the elevation as instructed. "Ready Ross?"

"Ready Sarge!"

The three following shots pitched fractionally shorter but pierced the hull with devastating effect as the rotting timbers disintegrated.

"Well done gunners! Now what if the Frenchies get through that storm and are still coming?"

"What about two balls at once, Sarge?"

"Good idea Halls, we could do that…"

"Have we got case shot Sarge?"

"Well, well Thomo, where have you seen that?"

"Living near the dockyard at Chatham, I heard the matelots talking about battles at sea, sounds pretty awful."

"Wait till you're in the midst of it! Campbell…" he shouted back to Xander who had been collecting shells and cartridges and passing onto Arthur Parkin, "Go and get that cartridge I showed you and the case shot… we have just had a new batch of shot, they say it will have a better impact. Used to be a thin metal canister filled with balls but now they fill the canister stacked row upon row – increases the number of balls to hit the Frenchies. If they do get close, we fire this." Parkin had been handed the new cartridge and canister, Thomo was dutifully standing thumb on the vent, and the barrel had been cleared with water ready to ram the cartridge and projectile. Thomo removed his thumb, pricked the canvas bag through the vent and placed the goose quill full of powder ready for firing. All stood clear and the order to fire was given.

The shock of the erupting tin brought the gunners to a standstill; only Thomo reacted with the necessary speed to replace his thumb over the vent. "You don't want to be on the receiving end of that!"

"That's stating the obvious Thomo. Mind you, wouldn't know much about it, would you?" answered Bob Halls.

"You're right there Halls," agreed Sergeant Webber, "no good trying to duck our fate in battle – if the ball is going to get you, not much you can do about it, so back to work and Campbell, bring that other projectile I showed you."

On return, Sergeant Webber took the projectile from Parkin, allowing him to hand the cartridge for placing in the barrel. "Now this, gentlemen, is what is called 'spherical case' designed by a chap called Shrapnel. They always come fitted to a wooden bottom and you will note that there are two tin straps pinned to the wooden frame, which stretch over the ball and meet a circular strap at the top. If by chance, you see a similar shot with only two tin straps, do not use it – that would be a common shell and not for our guns! Notice that Parkin handed me the projectile with his hand covering the opening – we don't want any stray sparks igniting the charge inside too soon. We will put the explosive charge in this hole and ram it immediately down the barrel. On firing it will go beyond the distance of the first shot because Ross will elevate the barrel and, when it gets to the distance set by the fuse, it will explode, raining small balls onto the enemy. In a battle, we will open with these, then turn to the round shot and finally resort to canister... if they are still standing!" The sergeant walked to Parkin, carefully handing the hollow ball back to allow the charge to be placed into the opening and passed onto George Rogers for loading."

The flight of the shot was eerily visible against the cloudless cornflower sky. It cleared the hulk with ease and in a sudden silence shattering storm break, the deadly rain showered the harbour.

"Cease Fire, Ross secure the locking chain on the elevating handle. Thomo, don't you move until Dickinson has swabbed the inside of the barrel and washed down the barrel, then clean the vent, fix the sponge cover and replace the rammer into the loop. Taylor, don't forget to cut the end of the portfire and extinguish the slow match."

The gunners had emerged from raw recruits into a good gun crew' Fin had ordered "Halt, limber up!" as he had detached the traversing lever. Horses were remounted and Sergeant Webber, having surveyed the crew, ordered them to move off, satisfied with another stage of the training.

Chapter 21

Before they had reached the stables, they were met by an excited Captain Ramsey. "How went the target shooting?"

"Common Shot, Canister and Shrapnel sir! Accomplished as planned, plus a lesson in making solid objects float!" Sergeant Webber proudly reported.

"Been skimming stones again have you? A good lesson, couldn't believe it myself when first told." He turned and walked alongside the sergeant's horse, giving instructions but just far enough out of earshot to keep the gunners in the dark. Captain Ramsey suddenly stepped to one side, ordered, "Carry on" and watched the gun and crew pass.

The gun unlimbered, horses stabled, saddles removed, brushed down, hooves checked, fed, watered, straw renewed, all leatherwork cleaned and rubbed with wax, the gunners could return to their tents.

Sergeant Webber was waiting having already spoken to the ladies: "Captain Ramsey has received orders that we are to proceed to London where we will be joining the rest of a newly formed troop to display in front of the Prince of Wales and his guests!" He paused as usual to allow the message to sink in. "So tonight is our last night at the duke's pleasure. We will strike tents at first light and start our journey up over the Downs, onto Richmond and then use the barracks at Hounslow Heath where we rendezvous with the rest of the guns that will make up the next troop to go to Portugal!" He knew that this news would create a stir amongst the men and didn't prevent the gunners turning to each other to share the excitement. "But before we start heading off across the sea, we will exercise with the full Battery of six guns on Hounslow Heath to be ready for our display in Hyde Park in four days' time."

"Why us Sergeant?"

"Now that is a very good question Parkin. I'd like to say it is because the Prince has recognised the Horse Artillery as the most prestigious fighting men in the army, which of course we are," again he paused to allow the expected cheer to quieten, "However, he wants to see the effect of artillery on an attack by infantry and cavalry, and… as you know, we do not have a great deal of surplus guns and we are the nearest thing to a trained unit. So enjoy your meal. The ladies know where to pack the stores in the morning. Make sure you sort the tents and the pegs, we will need them again, I dare say!"

He started to walk away but turned; "And three more things: you will all be issued with a blue shabraque edged red; bearskin fur flounces to cover the pistol holders; a valise to strap behind your saddle; a haversack and a water bottle that you will wear on a shortened strap under your left arm to stop it flapping about and getting in the way! The second thing… Well done! You have learned well and I know some have still got the scars and bruises to prove that it has been hard at times. Tomorrow we start our journey towards a real battle, our chance to impress the Prince will help you understand a little more about what a battle will appear like. Needless to say, we will not be loading projectiles of any sort, just the powder charge! But it will still be like nothing you have experienced before. Finally, Captain Ramsay has orders to leave for Portugal immediately and therefore we will be leaving without him, with me in charge." Mumbles and mutterings spread through the group at this last news, "I know you won't let him down and we will meet up with him when we get to wherever we are sent! Goodnight!"

"Never been to London Thomo." Fin was as excited as any at the prospect of the new twist to his adventures.

"Not really London Fin," butted in Dicky Dickinson, "Hounslow Heath is out west with space for training. When we get to Hyde Park, you will see what London is like, p'raps we could all go to Vauxhall Gardens?"

"I'm not sure we will be gettin' time for jollies Dicky." Thomo slapped Dicky on the back. "Mind you, from what I've heard, it's an interesting place these Vauxhall Gardens!"

"It's a great night out, have to pay to get in mind. There's always lots of food, drink and entertainers. Those that can afford it have pavilions for their meals but there's always plenty to see. If we're lucky we might see a hot air balloon. They burn a fire and the heat goes inside a big colourful bag – red, white and blue, the one I saw. The hot air makes the balloon rise up and then it cools down and the balloon comes back down. I think the Frenchy who flies it is called Monsewer Garnerin?"

"Sounds a bit risky having flames below you," suggested Bob Halls.

"No Bob, the basket for the fliers is below the flames and the heat rise up through the hole into the bag."

"But what if a spark went up into the bag, you'd fall down in flames?"

"Hasn't happened so far."

"From what I hear Dicky, hot air balloons aren't the only attractions on show!" Thomo teased, flouncing around the fire with his hand on his hip.

"Only if you go off the lantern lit pathways, Thomo – never know what or who you might find in the bushes!" Roars of laughter were interrupted by Martha Black.

"Well I never Dicky, and with ladies present too, should be ashamed of yourself all this bawdy talk!"

"Sorry Matha. I didn't mean any…"

"Get away with you Dicky, just teasin', we've 'ad worse round this fire since we met up haven't we…" More laughter met a blushing Dicky. "And in the stables from what I've been hearing!" She rolled her eyes and inclined her head towards Donald and Moira McConnell. "Now what about some food, it's been ready long since and we have to get packin'. Won't be time tomorrow for everythin', so fetch your bowls and mug. We're off to show His Royal Highness the Prince of Wales who the best gunners in the army are!"

Chapter 22

Tents struck, everything stowed, horses saddled, the troop were ready to leave. The trundle of the gun and limber with the drivers slowly commencing the march away from Goodwood was the signal for Sergeant Webber to order all to mount, followed by the order was given to move off at the walk. The sadness of leaving their training ground was mixed with the excitement of what was to come: the journey to London, the first time many would have been in the capital, the meeting with the rest of the battery, the presentation before the Prince of Wales... and onto Portugal. So much would happen but would all return?

The stiff slope up to the Downs brought the horses out in a sweat, none more so than the animals pulling the guns, or as one driver had corrected Fin: "They hint pulling but pushing ag'inst them collars round their necks, more effective then pulling!" The early frost had given way in front of the warmth of the low sun causing animals and men to steam, bringing the variety of aromas that all had got used to. The morning saw villages come and go as they made their way down the easier slope: Singleton, Cocking, Bepton – all pleasant looking settlements at peace with themselves and the troop intruded on this for a fleeting moment before tranquillity returned. It wasn't until Midhurst came into view that Sergeant Webber warned the troop that they would be halting to refresh the horses. "Time for a brew sergeant?" called Martha from the following wagon.

"Yes Mrs Black, time for a brew." Fin noticed that the formality had returned to the sergeant now that Captain Ramsay had left them. They pulled through the village and surprisingly turned east at the cross roads before pulling up alongside a large green with accompanying duck pond. "I thought we's headed for London Sarge?" The question came from Dicky Dickinson. "It's not this way, sun's in our eyes."

"Well spotted Dickinson." Sergeant Webber was holding a map recently provided after the Ordnance Department had carried out a survey mapping as far as they could. "We have an appointment to keep that means we will be taking a slight dog-leg following the line of the downs before striking north later."

The opportunity to stretch legs and backs was welcome relief, but all gunners knew that they had best see to their own horse before they sought refreshment for themselves. All had been used to riding for this sort of distance as they had become acquainted with the south-west of Sussex, but all knew that they were headed further in the saddle than they had ridden for some time, so stretching at any opportunity was essential!

Like bees round the honey pot, the gunners swarmed Martha and the bubbling pot of tea. "Here, Elijah, be taking this to Sergeant Webber and see if he would like a mug?" Having taken the steaming mug across to the sergeant, he waited patiently for him to stop studying the map. "Would you be liking a mug of tea Sarge? Martha says there's plenty in the pot."

"Thank you Black, that would be splendid." Elijah allowed the Sergeant to walk ahead of him, noting how he folded the map before replacing it in the protective case slung from a strap over his right shoulder. "There you go Sergeant Webber." Martha had expected the answer.

"Thank you missus Black, always good to have a mug of tea and you make the best tea!"

"All depends on the leaves we get sir, and never mind the 'missus', I'm Martha to everyone here you know that."

The sergeant thanked her again and turned to address the gunners: "Well done. I'm glad you've included the drivers in our refreshment, we have to be one team. They get the gun there and back while we do the firing!" He paused and then looked up the new road ahead. "We're heading this way because we've been asked to collect some barrels of powder from a factory near Worcester Park. The display in Hyde Park is going to have a few loud bangs to excite the crowd." He knew that he didn't have to say where or why but he wanted the men to know that he trusted them as well as expecting them to follow him without question. "The Prince of Wales likes a show and we will do our best to give him something to remember. We will meet the rest of the battery at Hounslow Heath Barracks and go through some manoeuvres on the heath before parading into London. Tonight we will halt at the Running Horse in Leatherhead after we cut through the Downs at Dorking. It'll make a change to have a roof over our heads rather than canvas!" A cheer went round the group. "However, there will be a need for the provision of pickets to guard our gun and wagons, as well as keep an eye on the horses, so it will be a disturbed night for us all, but one which we need to get used to as we will soon be off to Portugal." Another, louder cheer greeted this news. "So… Martha, thank you for the tea. It's time to put out the fire, pack up and be ready to mount in five minutes – we still have a way to go before night-fall."

Their journey took them between the South and North Downs through patchwork quilt fields bordered by lush hedgerows. The villages came and went, some with strange-sounding names like Petworth and others more obvious like Five Oaks. Fin was always interested in the origin of names whether a settlement or of a person. He had guessed that Beare Green was linked to the village having the large green, but why Beare? Was it a throw-back to bear baiting or was it beer making? Dorking was a much larger settlement obviously used to having military traffic as they had no one turn their heads to watch the gun and wagons travel through the gap in the downs. On they went and the sun was slipping below the horizon as they came to their destination. Pulling into the yard of the Running Horse, it was plain to see that there was not enough stabling for all horses, but a ready supply of hay and oats had been stacked in one corner and, once the gun team had been taken out of their traces and led by the drivers, the gunners created a temporary hitching rail and set about creating as comfortable sleeping quarters as possible, in the loft of the stables. Sergeant Webber had informed them of the routine for the night pickets and settled the men to their routine of caring for horses first, equipment second, weapons third and food last!

Fin had slept well until Dai Davies shook him awake for their turn of duty whispering, "Come on Fin, time for us to relieve Bill and John." Fin pulled his arms through the sleeve of his jacket which felt damp, but soon warmed as he moved down the stairs. He hadn't bothered to take off his trousers knowing that he was on first change; he was surprised that he felt that he had had a reasonable sleep knowing it was only two hours since he had turned in.

"Halt, who goes there?" It was Bill Bennett's voice. They had all been instructed what to do in the event of anyone coming into the yard, from any direction.

"Ross and Davies that's who, who did you expect."

"Evening boys, can't wait to get up into the warm hay loft – there's a chill in the air and the frost has started to form on the roof. Wouldn't be surprised if we didn't have ice by morning."

"Not tonight Bill," pointed out Dai Davies, "it feels chilly 'cause we had a warm day, that's all. Now get off with you both, see you in the morning." The shuffling feet on the darkened steps gave away how dark the courtyard had become, the little light from the moon was obscured by the drifting clouds, and only a lantern hung up at the entrance to the yard gave any illumination.

"If you take that corner Dai, next to the back door of the inn, I'll go to the gateway. You'll catch anyone coming from their drinking, I'll catch anyone from the road."

"OK Fin, you done this afore?"

"No Dai, just been in places that p'raps I shouldn't have been. Have to be on your guard." Dai chuckled to himself as he made his way to the doorway and wedged himself against the wall. The clouds covered the moon again and Fin could not see Dai at all, then he appeared again as the clouds were blown across the ink-black sky. *Way the wind's pickin' up, we're in for a bit of a storm,* Fin thought, *keep any unwanted guests away I hope.*

A creaking door and part-shaded candle sparkled behind the glass of the first floor windows alerting Fin to somebody on the move. A creaking door and muffled voices revealed a couple reunited or a midnight assignation, then the candle disappeared and all returned to the quietness of the night hours, the occasional call and return of owls, loud snores from the loft and a squeal from the inn. Just another night, but it was chilly.

Fin moved from foot to foot, his pistol in his belt and sword in hand, glad that he had his gloves. He wondered whether he should check on Dai but something made him stop as he took his first step. Someone had peered round the wall of the inn, they must have been kneeling so low to the ground. Fin returned to his spot, made sure that the blade of his sword was in shadow and braced himself against the wall, ready to challenge the stranger if they dared come into the yard. The soft steps of the stranger were almost imperceptible. Fin couldn't believe that boots would be so quiet, perhaps it was bare feet? He allowed the intruder to get well into the yard and watched as the figure went to the wagon loaded with the gunners' possessions. The figure was nimble enough and had swung up onto the back of the wagon, searching the nearest haversacks. Fin stepped out aware that his legs were stiff after not moving far for so long; "Halt. Who goes there?" he barked out, aware of a creakiness that embarrassed him.

"What is it Fin?"

"In the wagon Dai. Take a care."

Steps from behind him announced that Sergeant Webber had been alerted, "What is it Ross?"

"Someone in the wagon Sarge. Going through the bags. Hasn't answered the challenge." Sergeant Webber had brought a lantern and raised it above his head, left-handed pointing a long double-barrelled fire-arm at the wagon. "Come out, whoever you are." He ordered and stepped towards the wagon as the intruder launched themselves over the higher front rail, landing cat-like in a crouch, assessing options before making a dash for the shadows against the inn wall. Fin guessed correctly and moved to the gate-way just as the figure bolted for freedom. The intruder crashed into Finn knocking him towards the open gate but Fin had grabbed the jacket and was able to wrap his sword arm right around the body, hearing an exhalation of air as he tightened his grip. As Fin straightened, he took the intruder off their feet and walked back to the lantern light.

"Who we got here Fin?" asked Dai but was interrupted by Sergeant Webber:

"Davies out to the gate, have a look up and down the street – might be others waiting for a signal."

"Yes Sarge." and he crept up the wall to peer around the corner.

The lantern lit the face of a dirty young girl with charcoal black matted hair and piercing blue eyes. "It's a girl Sarge."

"Yes Ross, I can see that. But what is she doing here? Who sent you girl?"

The anger in her response was evident in spite of its brevity. "No one!"

"So what were you hoping to find?"

"Anythin' I could eat or sell!"

"Well, she's honest at least!" Fin was tempted to release his grip but as she struggled against him, she attempted to bite his hand, forcing him to squeeze the air out of her even harder. The wheezing sound wasn't pleasant, but it disabled her – temporarily.

The sergeant continued the interrogation, "Where's your home girl?"

"Ain't got one."

"You must sleep somewhere?"

"Anywhere I can find, or with anyone who'll pay." Fin was shocked. She couldn't have been any older than his tormentor Betsy Smith back home, but he hated to think of a child selling herself.

"What's goin' on down here, can't we have some peace and quiet?" Fin turned his head and could make out the figure of Sally Hughes, babe in the crook of one arm and lantern in the other hand.

In as loud a whisper as he dared Fin called over to her, "Caught someone thievin' Sal." She descended the rest of the steps and crossed the cobbles.

"Had to get up, this one wanted feeding." She nodded towards her babe, warmly swaddled in a blanket. "She's a feisty'n, got your hands full there Fin!" Sal smiled at his embarrassment. "What you goin' to do with'er Sarge?"

"We'll take her into the stable and tie her up till morning, then we can see what the innkeeper wants to do – it's his property we're on." Fin lifted her off of her feet and walked with the sergeant and Sal into the stables where they tied her hands and feet.

"You got a name girl?" asked Sal.

"Becca!" she spat back.

"Is that short for something?"

"Rebecca, but everyone calls me Becca!"

"Why you been here tonight?"

"Saw you lot arrive and knew there'd be somethin' worth havin'. Could be 'nough to keep me goin' for weeks without havin' to go wi'v no men neither!"

"How'd you like to join the army Becca? Come and help us, food every day, can't promise a roof every night though."

"What stay with you and them?" She shot an angry glance at Fin and Sergeant Webber.

"They're not so bad, you just got off on the wrong foot… Mind you, if you steal, you'll get a good thrashing. And… you will have to help out with the chores."

Fin stepped closer to the sergeant, "Can we do that Sarge? Saves a lot of trouble with the town."

"See what she says first."

The girl struggled against her bonds and looked up into Sal's face. "And none of these soldgers will get me?"

"No Becca. I'll say that you are my little sister and had come to meet us here, just got here late. It'll be hard but you're used to that I can see."

"Got any food?"

"Yes if you come with me, I'll find something. What do you say Sarge?"

"Can we trust you Rebecca?"

"You sound like my dad, he's the only one who calls me that. Haven't seen him in weeks, not since the last soldgers came through in their red coats and bright green flag."

"On one condition Sal."

"What's that?"

"Before you take her to get fed and watered, she must have a wash and a change of clothes – a dress or a skirt, make her look like a girl, do something with her hair…"

"Sarge, never knew you cared so! Come on Becca, we'll have you bright and shiny in no time. I've a few old clothes that will have to do. Fin, get those ropes off her." Sal had a power over all of the gunners, the sergeant included. Fin knelt down, untied the ropes and watched the two women disappear into the shadows.

"Hope Sal knows what she's doin' Sarge."

"D'you know Ross, I think it might just have reminded her of someone." He turned to check on Davies, "Well done Ross. Keep alert! Soon be changing of the guard!"

Chapter 23

The Running Horse provided the best breakfast they could have expected: sausage and bacon and egg with bread and hot tea. The sergeant had signed for the inn-keeper to claim recompense and no one had questioned the arrival of Sal's little sister; Dai and Fin knew better but they wouldn't be telling. Sergeant Webber strode to the road outside of the gate to check no other traffic would obstruct their departure, waved them forward and the second half of their journey to meet the Prince of Wales was underway.

The incline onto the northern downs didn't seem to trouble the horses as much as the Trundle of the day before and the clear day gave a first view of the city. "Just make out St Paul's Cathedral," pointed Dicky Dickinson, "never knew you could see it so far off."

"How many miles is that?" asked Fin.

"Well, I reckon that we must be the best part of a dozen miles away."

"We can see that far?" this time it was Bill Bennett questioning.

"When you're up in hills, you can see much further on a clear day. I remember once in north Wales looking across the Isle of Anglesey all the way to Ireland!"

"You sure Dai?" The doubter was Bob Halls.

"Sure as eggs is eggs like what we had this morning! Mind you, most of time it's raining and you wouldn't see one end of the gun team from the other!"

They were soon at their destination, William Taylor's gunpowder factory on Hogsmill River. The pyrotechnics were ready and boxed for collection. Sergeant Webber dutifully signed the receipt and the ladies made extra space in the wagon, not sure whether they were happy to have explosives quite so close, except for Rebecca that is, who perched herself on top of the boxes, letting her new skirt cover the additional baggage, admiring the deep blue colour that Sal had said matched her eyes. Her hair had been washed, brushed and tied back in two long plaits, each with a matching blue ribbon, courtesy of Martha who had taken her under her wing, as with all of the troop. The boots, laced up over her ankles, didn't quite fit as well as Sal hoped but it was better than nothing and an old pair of Thomas's socks, double rolled, made them snug.

The noonday sun was still low in the sky and the wind plucking russet and ochre leaves from branches reluctant to let them go, foretelling the onset of winter, gave a chill to the crisp air. The road undulated through parkland with deer ambling at will and they were soon on a steady descent towards the Thames at Richmond. Crossing the hogs backed bridge, Fin noticed many craft of all shapes and sizes crossing the river as a ferry further upstream, as well as barges and wherries transporting produce and passengers to destinations downstream.

They passed through Isleworth and arrived at their destination on Hounslow Heath early enough for Martha to be able to make camp and the remedy for all aches and pains – the steaming tea. They were soon joined by two riders who in unison dismounted, saluted Sergeant Webber and reported for duty. "Apologies for not having been here to greet you onto the heath, Lieutenant Smythe and this is Sergeant Major Simons."

"Compliments to you Sergeant Webber, gunners look well drilled and have set up camp in an orderly fashion. It will be interesting to see if they're as good when on exercise with the rest of the troop."

"They won't let you down Roger, good to see you again." The Sergeant Major turned and was greeted warmly by Sergeant Webber, an obvious old acquaintance.

"We both came back from Corunna sir, 'bout time we went back hey William?" No one had ever heard their sergeant called by his Christian name, it gave another measure of informality amidst the regimentations of the artillery.

"Sergeant Webber," interrupted Smythe, seemingly put out by the camaraderie, "Officer commanding this troop, Captain Bull, has instructed you to be number six gun on the left of the field and as such, Sergeant Major Simons will be your outside man."

"Understood Lieutenant, been in the troop long?"

"Just out of the new college at Woolwich sergeant. I had trained with the foot artillery but my riding selected me to be here."

"Very well Lieutenant, if you'd like to go over to the lady by the fire, missus Black will, I am sure, provide you with the best tea you're likely to taste in any troop!" turning and pointing to Martha, who had already made acquaintance with Sergeant Major Simons.

"Looks like Simons has beaten you to it!" The lieutenant was a little uncomfortable with the informality of the newly arrived gunners; he had been residing in the artillery college and barracks with the segregation between officers and other ranks far more distinct, but he couldn't argue but that they were a well organised unit.

"Lieutenant is it, we haven't got one of those here. Hey Sal, we'll have more officers than gunners soon!" Martha handed Smythe a mug of tea, aware of his blushing face and followed his gaze towards Sal. "Never you mind with the missus Black, I tell all of you men that I'm Martha and all of us women here are married to a gunner, well, all, that is except for young Rebecca, she's Sal's sister." Lieutenant Smythe was totally lost for words, bowed slightly in thanks for the tea, turned and retraced his steps to the security of his newly met sergeant.

The rest of the troop arrived shortly and the gunners were mounted and ready for inspection in their usual two lines in front of the gun, with the ladies safely returned to their place at the back of the column and their wagon. "Sergeant, how'd the training go? Damned good of the Duke of Richmond to accommodate you." Captain Bull was everything that a commanding officer was expected to be: confident in appearance, manner and voice, he ensured that all knew that he was in command. Sergeant Webber saluted smartly and Captain Bull was invited to inspect the new addition to his troop. As he walked his horse past the first row and turned into the gap dividing the two rows, he called over his shoulder to Sergeant Webber: "These men have no cloaks sergeant."

The response came from the end of the second line, "None issued sir!"

"Sergeant Major, we cannot set off for the Iberian Peninsula without appropriate protection – you know what the weather can do out there!"

This time the response came from in front of the leading line: "Yes sir, I will requisition enough from the Quartermaster, sir!"

Captain Bull complimented the men on their turn-out and continued speaking before riding off toward the rest of the troop. Sergeant Major Simons gave the order to move off and they followed him to the left of the line, riding behind the other five guns and gun teams. As soon as all were in position, Captain Bull ordered the guns to move off and they aimed for a pennant stuck into the heath, a quarter of a mile away. Number six gun team were the fulcrum making the tightest turn, allowing the rest to catch up as they made their wider turns and then returned with number one gun being the fulcrum and number six making the largest turn. In effect the troop had made a figure of eight and as they drew to a halt in the original positions, Captain Bull ordered for guns to make ready to fire. The exercises around Goodwood had given the team the speed necessary to keep up with the rest and in fact they were ready first with all in place. The dummy firing continued as Captain Bull rode the length of the battery, the guns fifteen to twenty paces apart. Having ridden behind all gun teams and satisfied that his troop was ready, he ordered all teams to cease fire and limber the guns.

The route taken to reach the Hounslow Barracks was not the shortest by any means but it soon became apparent why Captain Bull had decided upon the choice. Having moved off in file with gun one leading, leaving Fin and newest team in gun six to wait what seemed an age, the Troop was led west before leaving the heath onto the Great West Road and turning back towards London. The noise from six teams surprised Fin – how would the army ever move about a country without the enemy discovering them? Added to this, the recent dry weather had resulted in horses and gunners being covered in fine dust turning jackets and trousers a pale grey and all knew that a long night of cleaning lay ahead.

The sudden command from Sergeant Webber surprised them: "Gun six, prepare for eyes right... Eyes right!" All turned to see Captain Bull standing at the junction of two roads, but not as a marshal for the correct route. His face was stern and jaw firmly set and he spoke to gun six just as he had to the other five; "Mark this well," and he pointed to a gibbet gently swinging with the body of a criminal, "this man was a highwayman caught and hanged at Tyburn. They exhibit his body at this gibbet to warn all would be criminals of their fate. You may not be Highwaymen but neither will I have any gunner hanging from gallows when we arrive in Portugal. You will follow orders and the gallows will be a welcome relief after any have had to deal with me." He paused but then finished with a flourish: "The Horse Artillery will be the elite of the army, our Troop will be the elite of the elite, and you gun six will want to be the best!" Fin joined all gunners in their cheering and watched their new commanding officer disappear to the front of the column.

"Eyes front!" Sergeant Webber had retaken command. "And before any of you get to Captain Bull, you'll have me to answer to!"

Chapter 24

Hounslow Barracks may have been set aside for any troops exercising on the heath but all of the gunners had spent the larger proportion of the night grooming horses, cleaning harnesses, saddle-cloths and weapons before taking a hasty supper and getting to sleep long after the moon had spread its creamy light over the rooftops.

The sound of a trumpet wakened all gunners. The sun hadn't decided to make an appearance yet but all was busy; gunners in their working clothes were grooming horses, checking shoes and ensuring that their mounts were properly fed and watered. By the time they were finished, the sun had finally decided to show, the merest hint of tangerine and salmon leaking across the horizon. Martha hadn't let them down and all were ready for their breakfast. "Big day boys, not every day you meet a Prince!"

"You coming Martha?" asked Fin.

"Wild horses wouldn't keep me. They say a big crowd will be there in the park but the women with the other guns are all going on the wagon, so we're joining them."

Sergeant Webber had checked all of 'his' gunners, ensured that enough charges had been loaded and Sergeant Major Simons had brought thick grey cloaks for later use. "Bring out your horses when the clock on the tower strikes half six. We'll be in Hyde park before eight."

With the six guns polished especially for the day, six gun teams stood by their mounts waiting for their commander. "Prepare to mount…" All gunners stood ready. "Mount." They left in the same order as they arrived except a wagon driven by a group of engineers had left earlier with the boxes of pyrotechnics. The Great West Road was clear all the way through to the Kensington Gate and the battery set up just as they had on Hounslow Heath with gun six on the left.

They had been waiting a while dismounted when the signal gun announced the arrival of infantry and cavalry. The chimes of nine o'clock were greeted with a further signal gun and orders were given across the park to mount and form up for the march past. Fin wondered why it had been so early as he sat on Gretchen who casually nodded her head as if it were just another day. The chimes of ten and a further signal gun brought cheers from a crowd that could not be seen from the battery end of the park due to the undulations sloping down to the Serpentine Lake. A large group of horse riders in uniforms of dark and light blue, scarlet, green as dark as black at this distance, white and even canary yellow were the reason for the cheers. "Prince of Wales has turned up, he's the one at the front in the scarlet jacket." Lieutenant Smythe was responsible for guns five and six. Talking to the gunners was a good way to break the nervous tension that all carried, but also attempted to help him become part of what had become a unique team within the battery. "His brother, the Duke of York, will be in the second group, probably in scarlet as well, but he might be in the uniform of Admiral! The others will be Princes from across Europe – we fund many armies to fight against Bonaparte."

The audience were joined by a number of carriages which, having delivered their passengers, rode down and behind the artillery. Drums and bugles sounded to alert Captain Bull that the infantry was about to move off followed by the cavalry and it was time to move off to take their turn in line. No marker pennants this time, the whole Serpentine was the marker. Music caught the ear as the battery made its way down the southern edge of the lake before turning and making review in front of the Princes. Fin had noted the infantry to be the familiar red coated, pea-green facings that Robert de Lacy would be leading. At least they shouldn't have to meet. The cavalry were light dragoons in blue coats and yellow facings, black shakos on their heads, the same pattern that the French wore; all had swords drawn ready for general salute. The review went without a hitch, the infantry and cavalry marching past and following the route the artillery had started so that the audience had a prolonged display of marching infantry, trotting cavalry and walking artillery for the best part of an hour.

As the 'eyes right' command was given, Fin was surprised to see the figure of Lady Ellen, dressed in the same green as the facing colour of De Lacy's regiment, sitting only a row behind the Prince of Wales amidst other young ladies who turned out to be the royal Princesses. Fin thought the Prince of Wales to be rather over dressed with radiant blue sash over his left shoulder hiding a number of star shaped honours whilst a further sash, this time gold, was wrapped around a waist that displayed perhaps a little too much over indulgence. More gold cords covered his right shoulder and the cocked hat, bedecked in the finest white over red feathers that Fin had ever seen, finished with a gold tassel at either end of the bicorne. The Prince waved, or rather twirled, a white gloved hand in acknowledgement of the salute, turning his head to share comments with his brother, the Duke of York as well as other onlookers to left and right.

Refreshments were taken by the audience in the stand erected especially for the review, a buffet served by immaculately dressed footmen from Kensington Palace. The massed crowd, in their thousands behind a simple post and rope barrier, made do with street sellers among them offering food and drink.

The battery had unlimbered and awaited the display of fire-power.

The stroke of mid-day was announced by the chimes of the city as well as the signal gun that alerted the infantry to start their attack. Captain Bull paraded in front of the battery: "We will open fire at twelve hundred yards at an elevation of five degrees. You will continue firing until I order cease fire. Each gun will have the number of rounds counted; we are not using a projectile so I expect a slightly higher rate of fire than in a real battle. Do not fire unless you can see the target, blindly firing into the smoke can waste valuable ammunition." He trotted behind guns three and four and ordered all guns to make ready.

The infantry had their Union and Regimental flags flying. They knew that none would be maimed by splintering shells, solid ball or a hail of canister, but on the first salvo they visibly shook as the ground erupted in front of them to the cheers of the crowd: "Seems no one told them about our extra parcels!" Thomo peered through the smoke, thumb glued to the vent. "Engineers did a good job." Fin was helping to manhandle the gun back into place after the recoil.

They had fired twenty rounds before Sergeant Webber ordered Fin to lower the elevation by a degree. Fin could feel the heat of the barrel and he shouted, "Get that sponge down the barrel Dicky, don't want it exploding!"

The park was a drift of smoke, all flowing toward the public crowd; the smell wasn't pleasant but the gunners had become used to the pungent odours of burning powder. Another fifty-five rounds were fired before Fin was instructed to lower the elevation for point blank range. The signal for cease fire was given, the infantry turned about and marched past the dignitaries for one last time.

"How many Sergeant Webber?" called Captain Bull. "Eighty-two cartridges fired sir." "Well done number six, that puts you in second place behind number one gun who managed three more!"

All gunners took a swift drink from canteens to slake the thirst that became more noticeable the longer they had fired. The smoke drifted away from the crowd to clear the park ready for the cavalry. "This time, they will complete their charge and run through the gaps between the guns. Do not step in their way: they seldom have control of their mounts, and on display for the Prince, I am sure that they will be out to impress at their speed," and without further pausing he ordered all to make ready.

The bugles rang out across the park as the cavalry started their walk. Fin, along with all other teams, had raised the elevation back to five degrees and all at gun six were determined to win back the three rounds. "Fire!" As soon as the first sound had left his mouth, the crashing salvo erupted smoke and flame and appropriate pyrotechnics erupted from the ground either side of the horses. Time flashed by much quicker with the onset of the cavalry. They were all brandishing glinting blades and by the time Fin lowered the elevation, thirty cartridges had been used, by the time of the second reduction, a further thirty had been fired, and for the final assault, as the horses increased speed, the crew worked flat out to obliterate would-be enemies. The smoke clearing their end of the line quickest gave them the advantage and as the cavalry thundered past all gunners ensured that they were inside the wheel lines of the gun, staring unimpressed at the screams from the riders. "Wouldn't have even got close if we had been firing with the real thing," muttered Thomo.

"Think they own the place they do," suggested Dicky.

"Wouldn't want any Frenchy cavalry that close!" added George Rogers.

Their reflections were interrupted by Captain Bull: "How many Sergeant?"

"Seventy-one sir."

"Thank you sergeant, that makes a total of… well I never, we have a tie! All guns were over one hundred and forty rounds but guns one and six both score of one hundred and fifty-three!"

The Captain rode in front of the battery praising the blackened and sweating faces of the six gun crews. "I have to attend the Prince of Wales. Sergeant Major, take command and prepare for our return to the barracks. A more leisurely afternoon gentlemen, but don't get too comfortable, we leave for Chatham in the morning to board our transport for Lisbon!" A tremendous cheer turned heads from dignitaries and public crowd alike. "A successful demonstration!" He wheeled his horse and trotted towards the Prince.

Groups of dragoons wandered back through the guns in twos and threes intending to rendezvous at their forming point, but the gunners ignored them, readying themselves for the return to barracks and preparation for battle.

Chapter 25

Red noses, coloured cheeks and breath-filled air marked the start of the journey to Chatham. Horses appeared dragon-like with every step as their exhaling gave evidence of the exertion required to take the guns and gunners on their journey. Everything that was needed had been loaded into the troop wagon last night and the chill of autumn cut through the layers of the uniforms so proudly worn. Following the Great West Road into the city, they crossed the Thames over London Bridge and wound their way through the suburbs rising onto a plateau where they made their first halt, being allowed to dismount and stretch. Looking back across the city, the spires of churches poked eerily above the smoky fog. Fin had warmed as the ride progressed but used his gloves to knock the dust and mud splats from his overalls. "No point Fin, just get covered again when we start," offered Thomo, "problem with being number six gun, the rest throw up a right mess of a cloud."

"Sergeant Webber, what's this place?" Wilky Wilkinson asked.

"Called Blackheath – some say it was where they buried London's dead from the Black Death!"

"That was over four hundred years ago Wilky, no worries now!"

"You're right Parkin, but it is a favourite haunt of highwaymen so that many will use the river ferries rather than risk the road." Sergeant Webber pointed down towards the Thames silver pathway dotted with tiny craft.

"How d'you know that Sarge?" asked Wilky.

"Sergeant Major Simons told me... so it must be true!"

"Quite right Sergeant, never lie to you, would I?" The Sergeant Major had walked from gun five to check that all were ready to proceed. "Sergeant Webber."

"Yes Sergeant Major."

"Did you explain to the ladies the process that we have to go through at Chatham?"

"They aren't happy but we knew they wouldn't be, didn't we. They will all draw lots to see who will come and who will stay. They know they have to be included with the women from the other guns."

Simons lowered his voice, "I hope Martha gets the ticket, we'd all miss her cooking and looking after us!" A simple nod gave Webber's answer.

"Ready to Mount!" Sergeant Major Simons returned to his usual volume preparing all gun teams to make ready.

The road was straight. *Another Roman Road,* Fin thought, confirmed by Parkin as Watling Street, and the miles slipped by passing an occasional coach, announced by blaring horns, advertising services from Dover, Canterbury and Chatham to London. The over-night halt was destined for Gravesend in a simple barracks attached to a fort guarding the Thames and river approach to the capital. Looking across the river, a mile or so to the north, was a more imposing fortification. "Never been there William, but good Queen Bess rallied her troops with a rousing speech before the Spanish Armada attempted their invasion." Sergeant Major Simons was studying the shape of the fort with protruding bastions to allow defenders to fire on any would-be attackers from a variety of directions. "Clever design using water from the Thames, as well as the star shape for enfilading fire."

Sergeant Webber had waited for an opportunity to speak, "Says on the map that it's called Tilbury."

"That's right. The idea being that it links with where we are to catch any ship in a cross-fire. This town had been attacked and burned to the ground before this fort was built. They even heave a boom across the river. If any warning is sounded it acts as a barrier to ships as well." Almost without pause for breath, the Sergeant Major continued. "The men all right William?"

"Yes Roger. Martha, Mrs Black, has the food under control. Quite a favourite she has become, all the women from the other guns look up to her even though we was the last to arrive as part of the troop."

"Yes, I had noticed her, a good woman – no favourites with her, treats all alike. No special privileges for rank, everyone welcome to her tea!"

"We only have two horses needing a new shoe, farrier's sorting it now."

"Good, we'll need extra sets with us, don't know where we might find a smithy."

"From our last experience, we'll need a large village sir. Those hamlets we passed through on our way to Corunna didn't seem to bother, just had to make do until they could get to the nearest blacksmith."

"Let's hope we won't be needing the navy to rescue us this time William. Have you seen the newspapers? They seem to think that our army will be pushed back into the sea again."

"Just Boney's big talking sir. Our new leader knows what he's doing. I hear he learned a few tricks out in India, he won't be afraid of large numbers against us."

"I hope you're right William, masses of native troops aren't the same as the veterans of the French Imperial Army though."

"No sir, but we ain't the same as elephant-pulled artillery and those light pop guns they had out there either."

"Point well made William, we'll be out numbered for sure."

"So we'll have to show that we can load and fire faster than them, won't we! Pretty impressive in front of the Prince of Wales in Hyde Park though?"

"Very proud of gun six, you've made them become a good team."

"Why couldn't we have got the ship from here?" asked Bill Bennett.

"Have to be at a Royal Dockyard to get the supplies for the navy," replied Thomo, "That's why we have to go to Chatham. Could have been worse Bill – we might have been asked to go to Portsmouth or Plymouth, much longer ride."

The early start had been a repeat of the chills of their first day of the journey. The mist across the marshes towards the Thames hid anything moving to their left and the gentle rise to the right was covered in the same quilted field patterns that they had seen before: cows, sheep, ploughed fields, woodland all matched together, as if by some designer from on high, covered the farmland. A quartet of young girls laden with heavy pails suspended from shoulder yokes brought ribald comments from the more awake of the gunners, but they were largely ignored, apart from a blush on the youngest cheek, on their way to Gravesend to sell the results from the early milking. "Don't you worry dearies," Martha's voice was clear as a bell, turning heads from the gunners of number six gun, "They wouldn't know how to treat ladies like you even if you offered!" The roars of laughter brought Sergeant Major Simons back down the line:

"All going well Mrs Black?"

I told you Sergeant Major, it's Martha to everyone here. We just said good morning to four young ladies."

"It won't be long before we get to our billets. Not going to be as long a ride as yesterday."

"Make sure you come and join us for supper then!"

"I think I might very well do so, missus… Martha."

The view from the top of Strood Hill was impressive: the imposing keep of Rochester Castle, side by side with the spire of the Cathedral, and the masts of many boats and ships in the Medway towards Chatham. "Good to be going home, Thomo?" asked Fin.

"Haven't been home for a while, Fin. Don't even know if my family are still living where I left." They crossed the bridge at Rochester, and all eyes turned to the Norman castle. "Fin, you know that story I told the Sergeant and Captain about the tunnel and pigs when we first met them?"

"Yes, they dug under the castle."

"Look closely at that tower in the wall and that tower in the keep." Thomo was pointing along the road through a gateway to the city. "That's the towers they brought down with the tunnel, and when they rebuilt them, they made them round not square!"

Sergeant Webber had ridden back down the line and asked Thomo the exact same question about the towers being round. "Surprised you remembered the story Sarge."

"I always listen well Thomson. An important lesson that might come in useful one day, never know!" Sergeant Webber imperceptibly increased the pressure from his legs and urged his mount forward.

"Did he mean an important lesson about listening, or about undermining a castle?"

"D'you know Fin, I'm not sure. See that building built into the city wall?"

"The one with the tower?"

"That's the one Fin. If you look at the sign on the wall, you'll see a coat of arms: a gold shield with a black chevron and three symbols that look a bit like clover leaves." Fin looked closely and attempted the words; "Sir Jo-seph Will-i-amson's Math-em-at-i-cal Sch-ool."

"Well done Fin, Parky's doing a good job teaching you. That was my school where I had to learn about the measuring and maths for the dockyard."

The troop took the lower road from Rochester to Chatham, following the line of the Medway. The number of masts to be seen increased just as you find as you get deeper into a wood, but instead of heading for the impressive entrance gateway to the dockyard, they continued up onto a grassy heath covered with numerous tents denoting different facets of the army. The troop made its way to the right of the encampment being the closest to a newly built redoubt. Stretching before them were lines of fortified earthworks ready to defend the dockyard from a landward attack; the tents were simply erected to house the numbers of troops about to embark for Portugal.

Having set up camp with the tents they had brought with them, the routine of caring for the horses, equipment, weapons and then finally to settle to have some food for themselves began. The warmth of the sun had dissipated before they had finished the tasks, but each of the gunners was sweating from their exertions and welcomed the hot drink that Martha had ready for them. Sergeant Major Simons joined them as promised, informing them that they would be transported to Portugal on HMS Bellona alongside the Adventure, Philarea and Salus. They would be part of a combined reinforcement of infantry and artillery much needed for the army, but the embarkation would not take place for at least five days as the wind was set to prevent anything leaving the estuary and the sailors wanted to enjoy the Christmas festivities. They would get all of the infantry on board and leave the horses till last, but it meant that they would spend Christmas there and sail as soon as possible thereafter. He added that there would be a full parade and service to bless the expedition in the Cathedral on Christmas morning.

Chapter 26

Fin was keen to go with Thomo to find his family and as soon as the morning routine of grooming, inspection and orders had been read by Sergeant Webber, they both set out in their undress uniform. Walking off the Lines they skirted the impressive redoubt of Fort Amherst and Fin judged that they were headed towards the castle they had passed the previous day. Fin was surprised at the number of buildings of small size, simple wattle and daub lower walls with tiny windows and upper floors clad in timber that had seen better days. "These are worse than my home Thomo, and that is nothing special."

"Overcrowded, dark, dismal, smelly and a great breeding ground for illness and disease. But," he pointed down a dingy alleyway that led to the river, "they pour their pots into the river then wash their clothes on the next tide! If it's a choice of a roof over your head or staying out all night in all weathers, it's at least one step up the ladder." The stench made Fin wince. He had been used to the odours from stables, farms and even the packed tents that had been shelter at night these past months, but the mixture from low tide on the river and these buildings was worse than he had ever experienced. One smell he did recognise from helping his own father and grandfather.

"Thomo, where's the tar from? We used it for the coracle and it's better than the stink from the houses."

"The wind's bringing it from the dockyard. When we get on the ships, you'll see lots of buildings, which all have different functions: they make rope, they make flags for signalling, they make rigging, but in one building they cover rope with tar to protect against the sea water and weather." Thomo led the way out of the main street to a no-man's land and pointed to a flint-walled building. "That's where we're going, that taller building is the chapel, but next to it is the hospital, dedicated to Saint Bartholomew. A priest told me it's been here since Bishop Gundulf in Medieval Times, the oldest hospital in England!"

"Is your family ill then?"

"No Fin, the buildings next to the chapel are leased to people working in the hospital, my mum has worked here ever since she could remember and her mum before that. My dad, if he's still alive, will be at the dockyard till late." They crossed the street and approached the isolated building.

"Why is it on its own? No building close."

"It was built between Rochester and Chatham, neither in one nor t'other. If you are so poor that you get any of our 'popular' diseases or leprosy, no one wants you near. They call this place Chatham Intra. No one wants to take the responsibility for it, that's why the church organises it."

Thomo went towards the front door and tried the latch, "What you want here soldier, hospital's next door." Fin turned to see the wrinkled face of a middle-aged man with hair swept back and tied in a ponytail, dressed in a faded red coat that had the dirtiest looking collar and cuffs, that resembled soot, unbuttoned to reveal a slightly less dishevelled shirt. The crooked crutch under his left arm-pit supported him to compensate for the missing left leg which had its trouser leg folded around the stump.

"Is that you Fred?" Thomo hadn't even turned from the door but took his hand from the latch to face his interrogator.

"Jeremiah…" Fin stared at Thomo who sent a glare which meant no further question would be asked, "is that you looking so dandy? Thought the press had you?"

"It were close but managed to get onto old Matthew's boat and went south."

"Still got caught, though. What's this outfit?"

"Royal Horse Artillery Fred. Is Mum still here?" indicating the front door.

"Will be back soon enough, she's at the hospital this morning. Lift the latch, let's get the kettle on, she will be surprised. And who's this young fella?"

"Name's Fin. We 'volunteered' together, didn't we, Fin?"

"Sure you did Jeremiah. Never volunteer for nothing, that's what I always told you, wasn't it, cost me me leg volunteering!"

"Well, we joined at the same time, that much is true uncle."

"He's your uncle, Thomo?"

"Yes, my mum's brother. Lost his leg at the Battle of Vimeiro a couple of years ago, served with the dirty half hundreds, West Kent regiment."

"Make yourself useful lad, pass that kindling, we need to get the fire restarted." Thomo collected a bundle of sticks and arranged them in the hearth while his uncle scratched at his tinder box to create the spark necessary for the flame to start. "There's a pot of water over there, get yourself out to the pump and fill it up." Thomo followed his uncle's bidding and left Fin alone in the room, standing awkwardly as the one legged veteran struggled to his feet having lit the fire and placed the branches to make it stronger. "So where was it you two got nabbed?"

"Down in Christchurch. Thomo has looked after me ever since."

"Never heard of it, but you're right there – he's a good lad is our Jeremiah. We thought the navy had done for him though: we saw the press gang headed for the Admiral de Ruyter and feared the worst when he didn't come home." Thomo reappeared with the pot and hooked it on the metal frame that held it over the flames. "You 'ere for the transports in the dockyard?"

"Yes uncle. We've been told that we'll be here till after Christmas though. The winds hard off the North Sea and until that shifts, no one will go anywhere, well… except the likes of old Matthew who seems to be able to control the winds and waves!"

"Come on you two gunners, never served with horse artillery, only had footsloggers with me. You must have had some training in cooking, not much here but we can make the best of the fish caught yesterday and have a brew of tea ready for your old mum. You'll be the best Christmas present ever when she comes home." They busied themselves with the meagre meal of carrots, a couple of potatoes and the fish that had hung over the fire since yesterday.

"Just a stew uncle, but it will be enough for you, Mum and Dad. We have to be back on the Lines this evening." The water in the pot had been brought to the boil and Thomo ladled some into a smaller pot before stirring in the prepared ingredients.

"Always time for tea, eh boys?" chuckled Uncle Fred.

Fin was just about to agree when the door opened, making him stand immediately as Thomo greeted the surprised shawl-covered woman in the doorway with a huge hug. "Why Jeremiah, what are you doing here? We saw the troops marching through yesterday but never knew you to be one of them. Look at you," she held him at arms' length, "What they be feeding you on, you're skin and bone!"

"Stop fussing Mum, this here is one of my new friends, Fin."

"Oh, I'm sorry young man, where's my manners? Have they given you a drop of tea yet?"

"Just made Mum, Uncle Fred is getting the mugs. How's Dad, still in the ropery?"

"Oh yes, they need so much cabling for the navy, the work never stops. He won't be home before it's dark though, can you wait that long?"

"Sorry Mum, have to be back up on the Lines. He won't be working all Christmas day, will he?"

"That will depend on the winds and the good Lord. If he decides to keep blowing up the Medway, no one will be going anywhere! Dad might get half a day off."

"We have a parade in the cathedral, 'a proper send-off' our sergeant major called it!"

"Perhaps we could get up to your camp on the Lines?"

The tea was poured and Fin was amused by the stories that his best friend had to endure from both his mum and uncle. Stories of his youth, stories that told a tale of an adventurous boy that got into scrapes and then got out of them, stories of amorous adventures, stories from proud relatives happy to have him home. Before too long, it was time to retrace their steps back to camp, the light being drained from a darkening sky and a simple candle providing the illumination inside this small home. Stepping into the chill of the street, both Fin and Thomo pulled their collars up, trying to prevent the wind from sending its icy fingers over their skin. "So Jeremiah!"

"Not a word to the others Fin, Thomo is good enough for me, only family are given the grace to use that name."

"Why's that then?"

"I spent my younger years fighting off boys who were always making fun of it. I got into more fights over it than any other reason. It's from the Bible. The sermons at church, the lessons at school were constantly reminding us of who Jeremiah was, the great prophet who gave so many warnings but was little heeded till too late. The great prophet who pointed the way... You can guess the rest."

"So you and me both are supposed to be wise and speak with knowledge?"

"If you believe in a name!"

Chapter 27

The order had been given for full dress uniform. Christmas Eve had been spent in washing and cleaning horses and men, harness and clothing. "Happy Christmas Sergeant Webber! You joining us for a Christmas warmer? Special extra in the tea this morning to stop that chill wind gettin' into your bones." Martha was offering the mug which the sergeant always gratefully received. The first flakes of snow had arrived and a strong breeze made them dance across the lines spiralling and swirling, twisting and turning in the same way embers from a fire rise on the heat from flames.

"Happy Christmas Martha, and to all of gun six!"

"Happy Christmas Sarge, here's to next year!" Bob Halls had raised his mug and as the sergeant took a mouthful of hot liquid, he recognised the familiar taste of rum added to the tea.

"Where did you get this from Martha?"

"Ask no questions, but we are near the navy Sergeant, very obligin' they were yesterday! Must be because it's Christmas!"

***

Fin sat squashed between Thomo on one side and Parky on the other, helmets held on their laps, awaiting the start of the service. The announcing of Bishop Walker King, preceded by an elaborate cross borne high with two men holding candles flanking the cross-holder, was the signal for all to stand. Smithy, Wilky and Noah Hogg had been left with the horses in the Vines, the frost still painting the branches white even though it was mid-morning.

The familiar responses were said almost by rote: "O Lord open thou our lips." The bishop's voice carried clearly to all parts of the cathedral.

"And our mouth shall shew forth thy praise."

"O God make speed to help us."

"O Lord, make haste to help us." Fin had often said these words and he took in the surroundings of the biggest church building he had ever set foot in: every arch decorated in its own individual way, each opposite pair of columns matching in masonry but none adjacent matching, the high clerestory windows glimpsing the snow laden sky, coloured glass with saints; shadows dancing from flickering lamps suspended on long chains. Fin could recite the Venite and Te Deum with little attention and it wasn't until the responses from the prayers that it struck him how significant the words were:

"Give peace in our time, O Lord…" led an Archdeacon, "because there is none other that fighteth for us, but only thou, O God." That is why he was there, it was why his new 'family' was with him, they were about to go to fight. Fin felt he would need the Lord fighting with him if the rumours about the French Imperial Army were true. As he listened to the Prayer of Saint Chrysostom, he became keenly aware of the need to have a guardian watching over all of them, they would need something to protect them: "Fulfil now, O Lord, the desires and petitions of thy servants, as may be expedient for them; granting us in this world knowledge of thy truth, and in the world to come life everlasting. Amen."

"Amen!" was the reply.

Bishop Walker King rose from his seat, took his mitre and replaced it on his head with a flourish of trailing ribbons, reached for his crozier and stood in front of the congregation. "On this Christmas morning, we remember the birth of our Saviour. Take him with you on your adventure to Portugal to rid us of the tyrant that leads France. I ask the blessing of Our Father on you all, the wisdom of His Spirit and the protection of His Son born this very morning!" He took three steps forward and raised his left hand in preparation for his final commissioning prayer: "I encourage you all to hold onto the scripture given by our great Saint Paul who in writing to the people of Philippi told them in verse thirteen of chapter four: 'I can do all things through Christ which strengthens me.' You leave for distant shores with right on your side and…" he paused turning his head to take in every member of the congregation and stopping on the soldiers in the Nave, "The Grace of Our Lord Jesus Christ, and the love of God, and the fellowship of the Holy Ghost, be with us all evermore. Amen." "Amen," was the heartfelt reply of many. Then just before he started to process down the aisle, "And lastly… a very happy Christmas to you all!"

"Deep in thought, Fin?" Parky was in step with him.

"I've said those words many times but that bishop, what he said, fighting on the right side and all… we won't all get back here, will we? And I bet the French say that they have right on their side too."

"Quite a philosopher Fin. You hold onto your faith, others will mock and some will scorn but we know that it will be very tough when we get there," he lay a hand on his shoulder as a reassurance, "But today it's Christmas and I know that Martha, Sal and Moira were cooking up a special feast to celebrate!"

The conversation was interrupted by the loud voice of Bob, "Look at you three!" He was laughing at those left to look after the horses, "You thought you were the lucky ones staying here, but you look like you've frozen stiff!" Bob was right – Smithy, Wilky and Noah were covered in a fine white dusting as the frost had descended again, "Proper snowmen!"

"It's been freezing. Thought you were never coming back!"

"Lucky the bishop didn't talk too long then!" Thomo had joined the discussion.

"And by the way," Bob had come up level with the tethered horses, "the bishop wishes you a happy Christmas!"

"I'll be happy when I get round that fire in camp and thaw out!" suggested Noah.

Wilky added, "I don't think I can thaw out, these breeches are solid, how will I sit in the saddle?" They all laughed before being brought to order by Sergeant Major Simons, "It may be Christmas but we do not let the foot sloggers see us un-regimental like. Now prepare to mount!"

As they rode back to the Lines, they passed Thomo's family home at the hospital where a strong voice shouted, "Proud of you Jeremiah, proud of you we are." The merest eye contact between Fin and Thomo told Fin that not a word was to be said, no acknowledgement to be given. Several gunners had turned heads towards the voice, a man standing in the doorway, arm in arm with a woman, a raised hand holding a mug in a toast to the troop. Only the sergeant major acknowledged, riding at the rear of the column, with the simple raising of his hand to the peak of his helmet.

The expected meal was as good as had been hoped for, there was even a steaming pot on the fire which held a boiling pudding of flour and fruits that Martha, Sal and Moira had been able to acquire since their arrival in camp. The toast "Happy Christmas!" was led by Martha's husband Elijah and grateful thanks were given by all of gun team six with their trusted sergeant and sergeant major. "Best

Christmas ever Sarge!" Wilky had successfully defrosted from his morning duties.

"And here's to many more!" responded Sergeant Webber to which Fin whispered, head lowered, "Many more?"

"What about a carol?" chipped in Peter Taylor, raising his violin and bow in one hand whilst keeping his grip on his mug. "I met a composer in Canterbury who taught me a new tune a few years back, Tom Clark was his name, been popular every year though."

"Hey Parky, where do we get carols from?" Bob asked and before he realised it was another jest Arthur had already started.

"Well some people say that carol comes from the Latin word carula whilst others say it comes from the Greek word choraulein…" the roar of laughter stopped him.

"Sorry Parky, couldn't resist it."

"You leave him be Bob, just 'cause you're such an ignoramus, don't mean the rest of us don't like learning." As so often Martha had become the peacemaker: "Go on Arthur, don't you mind Bob, tell us where we got this lovely tradition from." Parky made to move away from the fire.

"No Parky, we want to know." Sal had joined in with Martha to encourage him to stay, putting her arm through the crook of Parky's elbow and turning him back to the warmth of the flames.

"Well…" he stared at Bob who held up his hands as a sign of no further interruption, "well, whether Latin or Greek it is agreed that the origins come from a circle dance which was accompanied by a flute type of instrument. We can thank our enemies, the French…" jeers interrupted the explanation, "No, it was the French who changed the musical accompaniment to a song and they sang them at different times of the year. We have songs that link the events of the first Christmas in Bethlehem and many people have learned through these songs."

"You're right there Parky, until I met you, and you have been teaching me to read and write better, I only had the ideas from the songs or stories told by our minister in the church," Fin had joined in the support for Parky, "So what's this new song Peter?"

"You all know 'While Shepherds watched' I hope?" A chorus of agreement answered Peter's question. "It goes like this." He lifted his violin to his chin and started: *While shepherds watched their flocks by night, flocks by night, All seated on the ground, The Angel of the Lord came,"* and in a slightly lower tone, *"the Angel of the Lord came,"* reverting to the original note, *"The Angel of the Lord came down. And glory shone around, And glory shone around, and glory shone around!"* Cheers and applause greeted the end of Peter's rendition.

"I like that Peter, a catchy tune that we can sing and dance to," suggested Martha. The usual group of musicians gathered around Peter to add extra volume and soon the whole gun team were joyously celebrating their Christmastide, attracting members of other gun teams to wander to their campfire and join with them in a boisterous improvisation of dancing interspersed with drinking.

The night was clear with the myriad of stars watching over them as they finally ended their celebration and retired to the tents. Fin stood with Thomo staring skyward, taking the last warmth from the embers of the fire. "No Angels shining glory all around Fin?"

"No Thomo, and I can't see which star to follow neither."

"Actually Fin, it should be... I can't see which star to follow either." Parky had joined them.

"Well whichever way it should be, it must have been some special star. How do you pick just one out?"

"Some say it was a comet, but whatever it was, started the greatest change to faith in the world. It's not the oldest faith but it's had greater influence than any other."

"And probably more wars from what I hear," responded Thomo.

"You're right Thomo many wars fought over Holy Cities and lands."

"Not our war though?" asked Fin.

"No, not this one, we're fighting the Corsican Tyrant."

"How did one man from so far away come to cause such a stir?" asked Fin.

"Well you could ask how one man from a tiny village thousands of miles away caused so many to still be celebrating his birth thousands of years later?"

"Careful who you let hear that Parky. Some get very touchy about such talk." Thomo had even lowered his voice. Fin looked puzzled.

"You're right again Thomo, people have been burned for less! But it is pretty amazing that a little baby born in a stable, so they say, in a tiny province of the once powerful Roman Empire, has had so much influence."

"Perhaps because he is who they say he is, the Son of God?"

"Don't we all believe that?" Fin asked.

"Far too philosophical for this time of night, let's just wish each other a happy Christmas and may we celebrate many more

166

together!" Thomo stretched his arm to shake hands, Parky taking the hand in both of his.

"Amen to that!" and having exchanged warm hand-shakes, they found their way to their blankets crunching the grass already frosted around the tent.

Chapter 28

The Feast of Stephen dawned with a severe frost, so severe that even in the tent blankets had frozen to the ground causing much merriment as the slowly waking gunners grumbled at each other to roll off their bedding until they realised their error, prising the stiff covers from reluctant grass fingers.

Emerging from the wood-like opening of the tent, Fin stamped his feet and swung his arms across his chest in the attempt to get his circulation rushing to his extremities. He quickly retreated into the tent and grabbed his cloak amidst the various cries to shut the cold out. Martha was wrapped in a shawl, scarf, fingerless gloves and even a pair of Elijah's trousers as she crouched, determined to get the customary kettle of tea boiling. Fin looked across the Lines, where isolated whisps of smoke indicated other early risers, but continuing his gaze around the full circle he could see chimneys emitting their own smoke, homes trying to fight off winter. The tall masts of the ships in Chatham Dockyard stood bare, no sign of sailcloth on any, but a large chimney belched a dirty smoke contaminating the early morning air. The wind was taking the black smudge up the river towards the castle and cathedral in Rochester. Fin guessed that Thomo's family would be breathing in tar smoke again and this would also mean that they were stuck in camp for another day.

The approaching figure, also wrapped up against the cold in cloak and woollen gloves as well as the familiar forage cap pulled well down against the upturned collar of the coat, soon revealed itself to be Sergeant Webber. "Good morning Sarge."

"Morning Ross."

"Here you are Sergeant Webber, this will warm you, not as much as yesterday, I'm sorry to say, but it is Christmas only once a year!"

"Thanks Martha. Anyone else up Ross?"

"Not yet Sarge, should they be?"

"No, no, but you can come with me. Want to check the horses, we have orders to take the guns down to the dockyard today, they'll be taking the barrels and wheels off the carriages so that they can be loaded onto the transport. We're going on the Bellona, an old seventy-four gun ship of the line but past its prime and used for transporting us."

Walking across the frosted ground they both took care with their footing over the ruts transformed into granite like spines. "Wouldn't want to ride Gretschen over this Sarge."

"Never should you do so, in weather like this, we walk and lead our horses, we won't be destroying them before we get started.... mind you, we'll face even worse if we end up in the mountains."

"What's it like over there Sarge? In the war I mean."

"Before you get to a battle, it's marching and riding and walking. Sometimes in the heat of summer, which will suck the air out of your lungs, so hot it gets and the dust covers you so no one can tell the colour of your coat. Then there's the rains which cut through every layer like you're naked and no coats or cloaks will stop it. The wind blows straight off the ocean and can sweep you off your feet, but then, there's other days when you'd give anything for a breeze to ease the soaring temperatures. But it's the winter we'll be facing which can be just like here. If we have to get into the mountains it will test the best man to survive. Just taking a step can feel like a mile as the mud sucks at your boots. Seen plenty with bare feet and lacerated skin crippling them and no use for battle. And if you survive all that, and it's a big if... you come to battle with the smoke and noise and aching limbs. No one knows what anyone else is doing, you do your job and fire as many times as you can at the Frenchies, do your job and fire, do your job and fire, limber up get out of it, unlimber and start again. Not for us a big redoubt but up and move, supporting the Light Division I'd guess. Don't you worry Ross, you'll do fine and I want you to be our bombardier!"

Fin stopped and stared at his sergeant. "Me Sarge, you sure?"

"Had my eye on you and Thomson from the moment we set eyes on you in Christchurch. The way you spoke and Thomo, you wouldn't give in, even if you hadn't been horse riders before!"

"You knew... and Captain Ramsey?"

"Plain as the nose on your face Ross, but he knew you two were good'uns. And you've proved him right. You've a good eye for distance, you learn fast and the others look up to you, you can do things they can't. I'm going to have Thomo as corporal as well – between you two we'll have the best gun crew in the Troop."

"There'll never believe this at home Sarge."

"Don't have to Ross, you're here now and about to go to war. Now let's check these horses."

Bill Bennett and John Smith came to attention as Fin and their sergeant approached: "Any problems?"

"No Sarge, no one daft enough to be out in this cold."

"What about the horses?"

"Munching at the fresh hay and we made sure that they had their blankets strapped on."

"Well done boys, what about the hot oats?"

"On the way Sarge," came a call from the far end of the make-shift stables. "Bubbling nicely, looks good enough to eat!"

"Well I wouldn't try it Halls, you'll give yourself a bad stomach if you've put in all the ingredients that I told you to."

"Every last one Sarge."

"Let's get cracking then, with five of us, we should get all horses fed before breakfast! And you three should know that Ross here is now your bombardier!" Following slaps on Fin's back and ribald comments expected from friends, they all set to the task in hand, ladling out oats with a distinctive tang of herbs rising in the steaming mixture.

"How come you had all these extra herbs this morning?" asked Bob.

"We're about to set sail and these horses won't be getting the exercise they need for weeks on end. An old wives' tale is this mixture; helps animals transported across the sea to keep their condition. I know this chap on the General's staff who swears that it helped his horse be ready in less than twenty-four hours, once landed in Lisbon."

The horses took the mixture, readily pleasing Sergeant Webber that his concoction had been a success. "Here comes Hughes, Parkin and Campbell to relieve your duty, time for our breakfast now the horses are fed. Good to see you on time Campbell!" Alexander dipped his head fully aware of the meaning that he couldn't tell the time until just a few weeks earlier.

"Hey you three, meet Bombardier Ross!" Bob Halls put his arm firmly round Fin's shoulders and ruffled his forage cap so that it slipped over his face. Amid further slaps on the back and laughing, Sergeant Webber walked away back towards camp and the welcome cooking that he knew Martha would have ready, smiling again at the closeness of his gun team. "After you Bombardier!" Bob bent low with a leading arm pointing back to the camp.

"Oh yes Bombardier, lead us on!" joined in Bill. Fin ignored the jibes but was proud to have been chosen and happily led the way with three friends, now subordinate, in file marching stiffly behind with the biggest grins they could muster.

Chapter 29

It was a strange and eerie feeling that passed through Fin's mind as they left the dockyard and made their way back to the camp on the Lines. The morning routine to prepare the horses for the journey to the dockyard went without a hitch and taking the guns through the town turned not a head. But leaving the guns, limbers and wagons in the hands of the organising ordnance officers to be dismantled and loaded as additional ballast... it didn't seem right. Their gun had become part of the 'family' as much as any of the men he had come to know, so parading back through the dockyard gates with horses only just didn't seem comfortable, just didn't seem right. After all, what were horse artillery without the artillery? A bunch of riders in uniform with a sword and pistol that seemed mainly there for show, the little training they had.

"Penny for them Bombardier?" The interruption to his thoughts made Fin jump and he turned to see Thomo smiling at him.

"What Thomo?"

"What were you so deep in thought about that you missed those pretty girls waving their scarves at you?"

"Where were they?" Fin twisted left and right but to no avail.

"Just inside the dock gate. I guess they'd been at the ropery, that huge building we came past – they say it's the biggest brick building in Europe, only ever been in there once with my dad, huge it is. Could fit all of us and the horses inside."

"Nothing really Thomo, just leaving the guns behind doesn't seem right."

"We'll soon be with them. You know what the sarge said, we'll get on with the horses and then sail, no need having them on board longer than needed."

"Suppose not, but you get used to things, don't you?"

"Hark at you! It wasn't a year since that you'd never set eyes on a gun like ours let alone fired one, and now look at you... Bombardier Ross of the Royal Horse Artillery!"

"Strange how one event can change your life. If I hadn't seen what I had, I'd never 'ave been accused, would never have had to escape, would never have met those smugglers, would never have been taken in by that girl... and would never have met you!"

"Not all bad then!"

"D'you know Thomo? I wouldn't want to be anywhere else. I've met a great bunch and we are going to be the best gun crew in the artillery!" Thomo's roar of laughter turned heads from ahead and the street and Fin continued back to camp in a far more settled frame of mind.

"You took your time boys, tea's in the pot." Martha was always ready to cheer the spirits and the crew gathered their mugs to take the warming liquid, with the odd addition from a concealed flask. "Now don't you be letting the fire go out, vegetables are ready for the pot and us women have been summoned to the commander's tent." Various suggestions as to the purpose of the visit brought the usual raucous cheers and laughter, but the married men knew that this was a serious decision. Some women would be allowed to follow their men in the army, it was useful to have a help with camp duties and the like, but not all would be allowed. Some regiments would not allow women with children, others put a limit to women with no more than two children, in all cases it was a lottery as to who would be joining the men and horses to go to war. Only six per hundred men would be allowed and so the six women, so much part of the family of number six gun, knew that there was no way that all would be lucky enough to draw a 'to go' ticket from the hat.

The women had been assembled in front of the commanding officer's tent, being the women for number six gun: Martha with Adam and Joseph gripped firmly by the hand, Moira, Georgia, Sal with baby Jane wrapped in a shawl, Mary and the latest addition, Rebecca, had to wait longest for their turn to place their hand into the hat. The expressions of joy and relief, as well as the tears and heart-rending cries had been all that was needed for the waiting women to learn the outcome of the drawing of the lots. Those 'lucky' in the draw tried to console their friends but there was little comfort in being told that they would be issued with a small cash allowance to return home. They all knew that they might never see their men again and adding to the worry of supporting themselves was almost unbearable. There were heartfelt cheers when a popular woman gained a 'to go' but groans of resentment when a woman felt as less deserving, cantankerous and meddlesome won the same prize. The constant trail of disappointed women became harder and harder to bear but eventually it was Martha's turn and dragging the two boys with her, she whispered, "Wish me luck." She plunged her hand immediately into the bag and withdrew the first ticket she found. She dared not look and handed it to the recording officer:

"Mrs Black…" he unfolded the ticket to see it more clearly, 'to go'." The cheers from her awaiting friends were sincere, no one begrudged her the ticket but as she waited in hope for the others there was no one else as lucky.

The men had been instructed to wait for the return of their women and it was obvious long before they were within hailing distance that disappointment had been dealt to so many. Even Martha was head down and pulling her boys in the midst of the group with tear-stained faces, bodies trembling with sobbing.

"Can't nothing be done Sarge?" Fin had approached Sergeant Webber on behalf of the unsuccessful women.

"Sorry Ross, that's the way it's done, only those with a 'to go' will be allowed, they say it's the fairest way."

"But what will become of them that don't come with us?"

"They have to go to the place that they will live until their men return."

"Do women ever swap their tickets Sarge, couldn't we ask…"

"Never heard of it Ross, those tickets are a strange prize: hard marches, no privacy, they'll see things that no one, let alone a woman, should see, go without food, clothes, shelter and heaven forbid they get caught by the Frenchies. No it's a strange thing Ross, it means so much hardship, but they all want to go so bad." Fin returned downcast to a silent camp fire. Even the warmth of Martha's tea couldn't pierce the frozen hearts so close to breaking. "Fin, you still got enough light to catch us something for supper? We all need cheering up and what we have in the pot ain't going to get close. I've still got a bottle or two and I know we aren't celebrating but a good meal would help."

Sal added, "You're right Martha, I know us women would all swap with you, but a good meal with some fresh meat would help."

"I'd best get out of this uniform then. Thomo, you coming? You know these parts better than most?"

*

Being out of uniform seemed strange. The old leather coats felt stiff through lack of wear and the trousers baggy around the waist but it was the best that could be found at short notice. They did keep their own boots – the last thing they wanted was sore feet impeding their hunting. Thomo led Fin back towards the impressive Fort

Amherst redoubt and slipped down the bank that formed the first obstacle for any would be attacker. "Been up here plenty of times Fin, there'll be lots of traps from the people of Chatham to add to their meagre meals but by going this way round, we should have enough light left in the day to spot rabbits and you never know, a pheasant or two. They often shelter in here after a day in the long grass. You got your bow ready Fin?"

"Just stringing now." Fin used a large stone to brace one end of his bow to create enough bend to allow the loop of his bow string, given by the gamekeepers at Goodwood, over the horn end. He took one arrow from his quiver and placed it across the bow, making sure that the nock was fixed firmly to the string.

"Have a care Fin, locals won't be happy with us interfering on their patch."

They slowly paced forward in a crouch, laying each booted foot as lightly as possible onto close cropped grass. The ditch gave the appearance of the day being much later than it actually was; the light struggled to reach the bank and the remnants of the morning frost still clung stubbornly in patches. A raised hand from Thomo had both men crouching even lower and Fin following the line of his friend's outstretched hand. A small group of three or four rabbits were lapping over the lip of the bank and darting back onto the Lines. "Close enough?" Thomo asked in a hoarse whisper.

"It's not the distance, but how quick they move. I haven't done this for months. Last time was that competition at targets." The rabbits appeared again, dark shapes against the lighter sky. Fin slowly drew the arrow towards his body preparing to stand; he felt certain that the shadow of the slope would hide the danger he posed. Straightening his legs and drawing the string fully to his ear, the arrow was sent on its way. Even the slightest noise of the loosing of the arrow made the rabbits alert, but perhaps it was that momentary glimpsing for danger that cost the rabbit furthest down the slope its life. "Good shooting Fin! That'll do nicely. Let's go and collect it and make our way down the slope of the Lines." The force of the arrow had impaled the creature into the bank and there was no need for any further knocking on the head. Fin retrieved his arrow and pouched the rabbit into his haversack hanging at his left hip alongside the quiver of arrows. They made their way up a simple set of chalk steps, the result of constant use and an easier way to climb the face of the ditch. They lay flat to peer over the lip of the bank, blinking to allow their eyes to adapt to the light. Thomo pointed to the right and they set off, crouching as low as possible down the open slope. They could see the gun emplacements of the fort behind them on the right and the newly built redoubts spaced at regular intervals far up the slope to the left. It struck Fin as unusual that they could be so close without any challenge but then again, what could two men do against these defences? The eruption of a startled pheasant only a pace in front of them brought him back to reality but the opportunity to add to their supper was gone. "Thomo, you go on ten paces and then if a bird goes up I'll have a chance."

"Don't you hit me!"

"Course I won't, don't you trust me?"

Thomo set off brushing the grass with outstretched arms, creating enough of a stir that would set off a bird but nothing more than the effect of the breeze to the casual observer. Walking at the crouch is energy sapping at the best of times, but Fin, trying to hold tension in the bow string, soon found his shoulders stiff and aching, unaccustomed to the strains of an archer. Thomo had been following a zig-zag path ever since they had reached the far end of the Lines. They had covered over a mile since the pheasant had flown, but nothing else had been flushed out. Thomo waited for Fin to catch up: "If I aim diagonally across the slope, we can end up at the place we slid down the bank in the first place."

"One rabbit isn't going to set aside the upset for the women."

"I don't think anything we bring could do that, but let's hope for another offering at least."

Fin watched as Thomo set off again. It was more difficult this time as the light was fading fast and Fin settled to adjust his vision. He noticed the wind coming more into his face so the weather forecasters had been right about the change. Having counted to ten he set off and almost immediately two pheasants flew to his right. He stood and instinctively fired, setting off for the falling bird immediately. "Well done Fin, but it wasn't me who sent them two up. Keep your eyes peeled, we ain't alone." Thomo had drawn his long knife and scanned the grassland for any tell-tale signs as Fin, arrow firmly knocked again, approached the direction of the bird. Retrieving his arrow, he bagged the bird at the same time as a gruff voice accosted him: "What you doin' 'ere? This in't your place." Fin saw a weather-beaten face under a thick green woollen bonnet, the sort that he had often seen fishermen wear at home.

"Findin' food like you, that's all."

"Fancy shooting and quiet too, p'raps you wouldn't mind sharin' summit?" The blade waved in front of Fin's face was meant

176

to be intimidating but Fin could see Thomo standing behind the stranger.

"And p'raps you best be getting off to see your traps!" The man turned surprised to have someone behind him and angry to be caught off guard; "We all shouldn't be here. You have your traps, we have our methods, but what them don't know…" Thomo jerked a thumb towards the Lines, "won't harm 'em, will it?"

"You two are good, caught me proper, now bugger off with the both of yer and let an honest man try to get something for his dinner!" Fin smiled at the thought of the man being honest, checked that he had truly gone and then set off after Thomo.

They had almost reached the ditch when the baying of hounds and the sound of hooves made them freeze. Glancing to the noise they could see three riders with dogs swirling between the horses, bounding their way up the slope whilst behind them at the foot of the slope stood the short figure of a man in a green woollen hat. "We make enemies quick!"

"Not only that Thomo, look at those colours on the collar, cuffs and lapels. I'd know that regiment anywhere and you've met him before remember. He hates me and would delight in finding us out of uniform poaching."

"Best we get out of here. If I'm right, they won't think of this ditch in the dusk and if we can get there fast we'll be safe. Come on." They stayed in the crouch and ran as fast as they could. It was only thirty paces but they could hear the pursuers gaining on them. Thomo took a sudden turn to the left, almost back to the chasing riders and then disappeared. Fin soon realised why the chalk steps were there. Even in the time that they had been away, the steps had become more slippery as the frost bit into them, but at least they could stand upright as they scampered and slid their way to the foot of the ditch.

The whelping of the lead dog, when they were only half way down, signalled that their pursuers had caught up but not realising the severity of the obstacle, the dog had raced straight over the edge, tumbling down the bank into the ditch like a skittle in an alley. The shadow created by the low sun had been dark when they first walked down the ditch but now it was almost impenetrable. Thomo stood by the body of the fallen dog lying winded and whimpering. Fin bent to stroke it and it calmed its breathing. Voices from above were calling: "Major, where are you? Come here, you stupid animal. Can you see anything?"

"Nothing at all Robert, it's too dark and we can't get the horses down this slope in the dark."

A third voice chipped in: "I believe that old fella has had us on a wild goose chase, no one here at all!"

"No I'm sure there was and I'm sure I know who it was, can't be too many archers around today… and especially when I know the very man is camped on the Lines with the Horse Artillery." After a short pause and a final "Major!" bellowed into the darkness, the voices retreated into the fast approaching evening, with mutterings about being late for dinner and losing a good dog.

"Come on then Fin, let's get back, you know which way we have to go," Thomo set off holding a line close to the shadows but whispered abruptly to Fin, "What you doing?"

"Can't just leave it here, we'll let it go soon as we can."

"You're daft as a brush Fin, what if he finds out?"

"He won't though, will he?" They found their way back into camp without any challenge and gave a delighted Martha the two for the pot. "Best we get into uniform again though!"

Chapter 30

The dinner had tasted great. Sergeant Webber was surprised and Sergeant Major Simons amazed at the contents – but very grateful! The morning had dawned with less of a chill as the wind had turned towards the west and the Lines were full of action as men prepared to take the short march to their allotted ships. Little sleep had been gained by those with women to leave behind and no amount of consoling could break through the despair. George and Georgia Rogers held their Charlotte in turns throughout the night, tears streaming down ashen faces. Donald and Moira set off on a long walk through the Lines returning at breakfast. Noah and Mary huddled inside the tent sheltering from the cold, clinging so tight as if they hoped that they could never be prised apart. Sal had tried to keep spirits up with a song but Thomas sat resigned to his fate, staring aimlessly into the embers of the dwindling fire. Even when Sal covered him with a blanket, he didn't move, desperately hoping that he could prevent the dawn bringing the inevitable heart-wrenching parting.

The women had agreed that it was best if they did not accompany the men into the dockyard, but as the men of number six gun mounted for the short journey, it was distressing for even the hardest hearted among them not to be touched by the pleas of Mary and Georgia on their knees, arms raised begging Sergeant Major Simons for another place; Sal and Rebecca clung to each other with the babe between, sharing the grief of parting, just as the sisters they pretended to be would. Only Mary had tried to break the promise, running to cling to Noah's stirrup, desperate for one last chance. It was Martha who slid off the wagon to prise her away from the horse before she was injured and return her shuffling to the arms of Mary and Georgia.

The sobbing could be heard long after they had left the camp site as their route took them in a serpentine pattern and the wind caught the sounds to torment them once again. More than one glanced back towards the Lines, tempted to make a dash and smuggle the women on board, but no one did. They arrived at the main gate to the dockyard as they had before and made their silent procession past the Ropery, Church, Admiral's Offices, Clock Tower and down to the quay. They boarded with little issue: one or two of the horses needed encouraging, perhaps they had sensed the mood amongst their men, but all were safely stowed in their new 'stables', hauled across in slings rigged from the yard-arm high up on the main mast by the time midday came. Each man had been given a blanket and allocated a space to sleep: one blanket space for six men or three married couples. "There's no way we'll fit in that! The tent was bad enough!"

"Don't worry, Halls, you will all be split into three watches so that every four hours a third of you will be able to get on deck, weather permitting." Sergeant Webber had experienced the confines of transport before and knew that it wasn't going to be pleasant. Three weeks if they were lucky but it could easily be over a month if the weather gods were unkind.

Leaving the quayside on the afternoon tide, they all agreed that leaving the women in camp had been better than to see the distressing scenes of women screeching, wailing and pleading with outstretched arms on the quayside. Fin noticed many a red-coated man turn his back and seek the rail on the far side of the ship, trying to shut out the cries amidst the strange whispered conversations of the ship. Thomo tried to distract by pointing out the fortifications along both de Lacy of the Medway: "They don't want another episode like the Dutch Admiral de Ruyter coming up in 1667 with broom on his bowsprit burning and capturing our warships." Fin nodded an acknowledgement that he had heard but was in little mood to discuss the defences built to protect his homeland.

"Won't be the same Thomo."

"No it won't Fin, different landscape, different language, different weather…"

"You know what I mean Thomo!"

"Yes I know Fin."

"It's like when my Gran died. One of the family gone."

"And it's up to us to make the best of it for us all. When we get to Lisbon, we all have to be ready and any one moping will do us no good with them Frenchies all around us."

"You're right Thomo but it will take time for those who have left women behind." Fin didn't wait for an answer but released his grip of the rail and attempted the tricky steps to go below.

"Where you going?" Thomo called.

"Check on the horses!" was the only reply as Fin's head disappeared below deck.

He knew that the horses would be fine, they had only been on board a matter of hours. It would be the days and weeks to come that he would need to be checking, but it gave him some consolation and he spoke softly to Gretschen about the scenes he had seen and heard, smoothing her coat, pulling her ears, running his hands down each leg, lifting the hoof to check that which he had checked as soon as she was on board. It helped distract him but he felt that he would see the haunting images and hear those heart piercing cries every time he closed his eyes. He moved down each horse, checking in the same way, chatting quietly, trying to gain consolation, at least reassured that the horses were starting in good condition.

"Thought I'd find you here." Fin turned to see Sergeant Webber.

"Just checking Sarge."

"That's right Ross, keep checking, but it takes the thought of the women away for a moment at least, don't it?"

"Daren't shut me eyes Sarge, can't stop seeing them... will they get over it?"

"The women will look after each other..."

"No Sarge: Noah, Thomas, Donald and George... will they cope? We have to be ready to fight the Frenchies and we have men so distracted..."

"Don't you worry Ross, we'll get them through it, the first thing we have to do is get ready to be looking after the sick. We'll soon be having our hands full of landlubbers who are puking up with every lurch of the ship. If we can we get the sailors to open the gratings and get air down below, it will help, but be prepared Ross, most of us will be sick. The navy's idea of a latrine is what they call the heads up the front end which means hanging your arse over the side. When you feel that sick, the chances of reaching them will be limited and we will all be living in filth. I'm relying on you to make sure our crew arrive in the best of health, and not just the men – these 'orses as well, they get sick an'all." Sergeant Webber turned to walk away, stopped and turned back, "We'll do fine Ross, you'll see."

By the time Fin got back to the deck the first of the men being sick had started. "Always the same Fin, can happen to anyone. They say even the admirals get sick after a stay on shore. And don't believe any of those daft remedies about drinking sea water or hot fat; fight your way through it and fresh air will help."

"What about the horses Thomo?"

"Never been on ships with horses but if it makes men sick, probably do the same for them though. Don't like the thought of the mess to clear."

"To be honest Thomo, I'm more worried about those who left the women behind."

"That'll be last of our worries, look at this lot..." pointing at men heaving their guts over the side, "we're going to have our hands full! That's Wilky, Dai and Xander, and we haven't got to the estuary yet!"

Chapter 31

Their short convoy inched out of the Medway into the wider reaches of the Thames estuary and more open sea. Fin was in charge of one of the watches from number six gun, Thomo in charge of watch two and Sergeant Webber for watch three. It did give more room below decks but four hours on deck was welcome relief, whatever the weather. Fin noticed that they stayed in sight of land and a sailor would sometimes point out something on land: "Isle of Sheppey there," or, "Reculver, Isle of Thanet, Roman fort there sir!" Fin was pleased to share conversation, he couldn't see the fort but took the word of the young man, well his junior in age but far better dressed in uniform. By the time he was told "Margate there, Ramsgate coming on the starboard bow," bells were sounding and he was ushered below as the watch changed. The stench was grim: vomit mixed with the sweating bodies of crammed and cramped passengers mixed to create a cocktail of stomach churning odours. Fin bypassed the tiny patch set out for him and went to check again on the horses. They seemed settled and he wasn't surprised to find Sergeant Webber already there. "How are you doing Ross? Just coming below?"

"Yes Sarge, the stench is pretty bad already and we've only just started the journey!"

"It won't get better, just hope we can ventilate regularly. Any idea where we've got to?"

"Young chap told me Ramsgate."

"Doing quite well then, soon be Dover and the white cliffs, then into the Channel proper. We'll be stopping at Cowes on the Isle of Wight to collect more ships and other passengers."

"I could see the Isle of Wight from the hills near home Sarge. Get up on Badbury Rings and you could see for miles."

"Tell you what Ross, if we get a clear day, you'll see what we're fighting tomorrow." Fin was confused at the comment.

"We won't be there that quick Sarge?"

"No Ross, we'll be able to see England on our right – starboard – and the coast of France on our port side. Come on, can't stay with the horses, let's go and brave the stink."

Those early hours were misery for many, for some it lasted days but most managed to find their sea legs and eventually tried to eat the rations given. Martha had offered to help the cook, sweating over two huge wood fired vats and an oven churning out a never ending supply of bread. She couldn't accept that the liquid served as the meals for each watch was the best that could be offered. Surely there could be better, but having worked with the cook, she realised that only the commanding officers would be getting anything that resembled the food they were used to and the stew served up in a number of different guises was the best it would be. Ships' biscuits were so hard they had to be soaked and despite the consolation of hardened sailors that the meat crawling through the teeth-shattering provisions were fine to eat, it put many a gunner off his food.

The watches came and went, the wind with them; at times the sails were full and at others hung limp. It had taken two days already but the small convoy anchored at St Helen's overnight before sailing next morning onto Cowes. Salutes were given and received as other shipping came into view. They were to be joined by three more transports: Fortune, Malabar and Laurel as well as a forty-four gun frigate, the Nymph, and the sloop Kangaroo. Anchored and waiting for the new passengers, Fin had come to his turn on deck. Stare as hard as he did, he couldn't make out his Dorset home but the shouts of the sailors rigging the slings to load the new cargo brought his attention to a flat-bottomed boat containing a magnificent-looking chestnut horse, ears flicking nervously, constantly soothed by a man in red jacket and grey trousers, whilst a further red coated man held a bicorne firmly in place as the wind did its best to pluck it from his head. Shouts from the boat saw oars raised and a gentle brushing of the gunwale against the ship's hull. The bare head that appeared over the side was the same man who had been protecting his head-gear which was now stuffed inside his lapel, firmly wedged with no fear of getting a bath in the sea. "Mind my baggage there!" Fin wondered why so many officers took it upon themselves to look down on all others. The young boy who had pointed out landmarks saluted smartly to the new passenger:

"Welcome on board sir, Ensign Howard. Your baggage and horse will be brought on board presently."

"See to it Mister Howard that nothing is lost."

The slings were lowered and the red coated man delicately passed them through the legs of the horse and tied them back on the hook suspended from the yardarm. "Ready!" he bellowed and the sailors took the strain. The horse was skittish, stumbled before regaining its feet and swaying as the roll of the skiff went opposite to the Bellona. The whinnying and flailing legs brought alarm to the newly arrived officer: "Take a care there, that horse is worth more than all of you put together!" Fin watched anxiously watching the slings slip one way and then forward, holding the creature suspended with hind legs in the sea before tipping it backward into the sea. "What the hell are you doing!" The roar from the officer left no one with any doubt of his feelings.

Fin didn't think but took off his jacket and boots before jumping into the sea. The shock of the cold was enough to make every fibre of his body feel numb but he struck out for the horse, clasping the halter collar and smoothing its neck whilst struggling to stay afloat, kicking his legs as hard as he could. "Pass those slings again." Everyone obeyed as if it had been their captain; the ropes were lowered and the slings soon were within reach. Fin knew that he had to fix the wide strap as far forward and backward as possible to prevent the same mistake happening again. Having unhooked the first strap, he whispered to the nostril-flaring horse. Smoothing the neck once more, Fin ducked to the other side, taking a mouthful of salty water, spitting it straight out as he coughed. He took a breath before he submerged, passing the strap between his hands and behind the legs. Resurfacing he fought for the hook to attach the strap to it but could not mistake the warning voice: "Don't just sit there, get my horse out of the water. I'll have your guts for garters if there is any harm done." Some might say thank you for rescuing the horse but here was another typical officer.

Fin could tell that the horse was doing its best to stay afloat and he hoped that the metal ring would sink low enough for him to reach through the hind legs without swimming between the thrashing kicks. Luckily the strap was almost vertical and it took little effort for the strong swimmer that Fin was to reach through and securely attach the strap again. He could feel the slack being taken up and shouted for the sailors to stop: "Wait, same will happen again, I need rope." Fin swam to the skiff where the red coated man searched his bags for some rope.

"Will this do lad?" He held up two lengths that he had previously used, securing straps for his officer's baggage.

"Fine, sir." Fin didn't know why he added the sir, just a habit when talking to military personnel, assuming they out-ranked him.

"What you doing with it?"

"Stop the straps slipping. Loop it round the straps and take it across the chest and then under the tail at the rear."

"Done this before?"

"Never!" Fin succeeded, in spite of further oaths from the officer above, in securing the straps and waved a hand that he was ready.

He swam away on his back watching the bedraggled creature dripping water rise into the sky above him. The cheer that greeted the horse arriving on board was audible even to Fin in the sea, and it was then that it dawned on him that he had to get back onto the ship. The answer appeared in a large hand over the side of the skiff. "Here lad, you did well. Hold on tight." The strength in the arm of the red-coated man surprised Fin – one-handed he had raised Fin out of the water. "Harry Wheeler, lad, and who are you?"

Fin shook the offered hand: "Gunner Ross, Fin Ross." Fin coughed up more sea water and Wheeler slapped him hard on the back.

"Got me out of trouble there Ross. Officer will be livid. His pride and joy that horse."

The uproar had brought all watches up onto deck to see what had been happening. As Fin scampered up the side and over the rail, he was brushed aside by the offended officer: "Wheeler, what the hell were you up to? Can't you even tie a harness?"

"Strap slipped, sorry sir."

"You useless waster, if anything is missing, it'll come from your allowance." Wheeler knew better than to answer and stood eyes fixed ahead as his officer turned and headed for Fin. "What took you so long – you sailors are supposed to be able to tie knots fast, aren't you? You left my horse in the sea while you took a swim."

"Some would say that this man saved your horse, sir." The young ensign had stepped forward.

"I wasn't asking your opinion but wouldn't expect anything more, navy sticking together."

The dismissive tone was interrupted by the arrival of the captain. "This man has taken a risk to save your horse. He is not part of my crew but a passenger like you... sir." The pause was intentional and had its effect. The red coated officer spun and attempted to replace his bicorne, recognising that he was facing a

186

higher ranking authority, making a swift salute and adding a hasty "Sir!"

"I know this man no more than you, but if one of my men had risked what he has just done, I'd show a damn sight more gratitude than you, sir!" Without further hesitation the captain continued. "Captain Hervey of the ship Bellona, welcome on board. Ensign Howard will show you to your quarters…sir." He turned and walked away towards the stern. "Captain Augustus James, sir, promoted to the staff of our commanding officer in Portugal." Captain Hervey continued his walk without looking back, unimpressed by the name dropping, leaving Captain James a lonely figure.

"This way sir, if you please." The Ensign outstretched his arm, indicating the direction for the newly arrived officer.

"Wheeler, please bring my baggage." Fin noticed the request rather than order. He felt the officer retreated as a dog with its tail between his legs.

As soon as the officer ducked his head out of sight, Fin was surrounded by gunners and sailors alike, congratulating him for his rescue. "What is it with you and animals Ross?" a beaming Sergeant Webber was holding the jacket and boots. "What with lion taming and now swimming horses, you could open a show!" The slap on the back confirmed the pride felt by the sergeant. "Now get below and into dry clothes." Fin was almost carried below to the cheers of the crew of number six gun. The warmth of below decks hit Fin harder than the cold of the sea, making him light-headed.

"Steady now Fin," it was the welcome sound of Martha's voice, "Don't you go fainting. Here, Elijah, give me a hand taking these wet clothes off of him, he'll catch a chill." Fin had little that he could do to prevent the wet clothes being stripped from his body, but he was still aware that he stood naked in front of his friends. "Here Fin, wrap yourself in this." Martha raised her eyebrows, wide eyed as she enclosed his body in a great hug, the rough material enclosing his embarrassment, "No need to be shy Fin, you're a fine lookin' boy. Now you sit here while I get your clothes dried out. Soon be dry if I take them to the ovens." Fin was slowly coming to his senses and he was grateful for a mug of warm liquid, even if it wasn't Martha's best tea!

The standing of men all around made Fin aware that something was different. "Officer!" shouted a voice further down the deck. Fin got to his feet, clinging to the coarse material wrapped round his body. "There you are. I owe you an apology. You risked your life before anyone had thought of what to do… 'and' you saved my

187

horse, which is doing well with your artillery mounts." Fin had learned not to say anything, but stared ahead, clinging to his covering and hoping that he could remain covered. "What's your name?"

"Ross sir."

"Well Ross, you did me a great favour and I'd like you to have this." Captain James held out a bottle of wine which Fin gratefully took.

"Thank you sir, hope the horse is all right, I'll take a look when I go to check on ours if you like?"

"Wheeler will help you. Wasn't his fault, never had to haul a horse onto a ship before."

Fin realised that his initial impression was wrong. Captain James may have appeared the pompous stuck-up officer as so many were, but he had been big enough to apologise, and not only to him. Perhaps he would be helpful in the future.

Chapter 32

The signal for sailing came later that evening as the tide turned, and the enlarged convoy set off, Bellona in the lead with transports in her wake, whilst the Nymph and Kangaroo showed their talents as the eyes of the commanding officer to see beyond the horizon.

The new year was seen in at sea and after they had settled into the routine of the watches changing with the bells, squalls further delayed the convoy causing all ships to find safety in the shelter of Plymouth harbour. Several times it seemed to Fin that the wind was set fair but it proved contrary and they were stuck for over a week before the little fleet set sail again. Just when everyone breathed a sigh of relief having been aboard two weeks already, the wind battered them to find the safety of yet another harbour, this time Falmouth. Finally after three more impatient days, the pennant was raised and the convoy set off again. Fin was intrigued to see little boats toing and froing between the convoy. Ensign Howard informed him that different officers were invited to dine with Captain Hervey each day, it was his duty to mind all of his convoy. Fin was also intrigued to be told that far off on the port bow was the hazy coastline of France, this time the coast of Brittany. Fin had never been at sea with no land in sight and he felt reassured that at least there was land in that direction.

The horses were fretting more and more, some had lost weight visibly and the provisions set aside for them alone were getting low. Water was constantly a problem for both man and beast and any rainfall was gratefully caught in canvas sheets funnelling the water into large casks. The sailors' warnings that the Bay of Biscay would bring greater misery than anything before proved to be scare-mongering. The sailors assured the landlubbers that this was a notorious part of the sea and many had suffered crossing this stretch in the past, Sergeant Webber supported them with stories of great distress on a previous voyage, but the 'seasoned' passengers, having been on board for over three weeks, took it as another story like the monsters drawn onto old charts.

Parky, still one of the few who valued the time to read and write, had been keeping a journal and noted that on the thirtieth day aboard, the twenty-fifth of January, land was sighted. The sun glinted across the eastern sky and golden reflections came from what became clear to be windows in a large building. Fin carefully took the steps below decks to find Sergeant Webber. "Sarge, Ensign Howard says that we can see Cabo Priory near Corunna. We're not stopping but passing close by to get to Cape Finisterre."

"Long time since I was here last. I was talking to Wheeler an' he was 'ere with General Moore as well. Came home with a wounded leg but wanted to come back to finish what we started."

"You coming up Sarge?"

"Right behind you Ross." The coast had cliffs with many rocks that had crashed onto the beach below, making an imposing sight in the early morning light. "Sends shivers down your spine just looking. We were up on the cliff tops fightin' for our lives waitin' for the navy to come and take us off. Saw many horses shot on the beach to stop the Frenchies gettin' their hands on 'em. Gunpowder blown up, guns disabled, the local guerillos were given muskets and swords to carry on the fight the best they could. I heard some troops stayed behind to help train them, don't know if it were true though?"

"So, we almost there Sarge?"

"Not far now. That's Spain and we have bit more to go till we get to Lisbon.

"Sail ho!" The shout came from the masthead.

"Where away?"

"Starboard bow, two masts headed sou'west."

The captain was soon on deck consulting the officers and then chasing up the rigging like a sprightly child, before bringing his telescope that had been suspended on his back from a strap across his shoulders, to bear on the sail, still not visible from the deck. Orders were given, more sail was set and Captain Hervey returned to the deck, jumping up onto the rail for a better sight as we closed rapidly on the vessel.

"Can't be a Frenchie or they'd be running as fast as the wind could carry them!" Sergeant Webber was right, they had been allowed to stay on deck because, as Captain Hervey had rightly surmised, the ship turned out to be a Spanish vessel taking her cargo to the more lucrative markets in Lisbon. The captain hailed the ship in what Fin thought was very good Spanish and had the grateful reply that the ship would join the little convoy.

The improving weather saw evening entertainment on deck: sailors had fiddles and fifes and with the addition of a variety of instruments from the soldiers and gunners, including the musicians of gun six, singing and dancing whiled away a happier time, a welcome relief to the fetid atmosphere of below decks. Sailors enjoyed teaching hornpipes and soldiers enjoyed singing their favourite songs. The women took advantage of the light and fresh air to catch up on washing and darning clothes. As the sun set casting a long shadow of the ship across the sea, the estuary of a large river was passed. Fin, having got to know Ensign Howard well during the journey, asked what it was. "That's the Douro River, we could sail a long way up if we wanted, but we have to go further south."

On the twenty-seventh of January, according to Parky's journal, two vessels approached the Bellona from the coast at speed. Thomo had been on deck but called for Fin to see the race. "Who are they Thomo?"

"Not sure. I think that one on the left is that little one that joined us at Cowes."

"You're right. It's the Kangaroo, lot of flags flying."

Ensign Howard overheard the discussion. "Kangaroo is letting us know that she's leaving to return to England, protocol for them to salute Captain Hervey. He'll order the answer signal." As soon as he had said it, flags flew into the breeze giving their response.

"Remember how we saw those signal stations Thomo?"

"Yes, on a clear day a message from Portsmouth to London in fifteen minutes they said!"

"You've been to a signalling station?"

"Yes, when we first... enlisted," Fin grinned at Thomo, "we saw the telegraph system in operation, paddles opening and shutting."

"Flags do the same at sea."

"Needs a good eye, Ensign."

"And a code book."

"So what's the other ship?"

"Not quite a ship Fin," smiled the Ensign. "It's a Portuguese pilot coming aboard to take us through the Berlengas. Saves us time but a tricky channel through rocky islands. You'll see a battery sited as protection for the coast."

As the ensign had predicted, the Kangaroo shot away, signalling to each in the convoy in turn, and a squat Portuguese man scrambled up the side, judging the roll of the ship and rise and fall of the waves

191

perfectly. He took off his hat, a common shape to all navies it seemed, as a salute to the ship and was welcomed aboard by the ensign, with a file of marines at attention, who took him to the Captain for formal introduction. Fin didn't know whether Captain Hervey appreciated the stranger in command of his ship, he doubted it, but he also recognised a professional man who would work with anyone to complete his mission as well as he could.

The winds dropped and it was dawn on the last day of January that saw the convoy slowly enter the Tagus estuary. The Rock of Lisbon appeared sombre and imposing overhanging the sea as the sun slowly spread its fingers over the ground lighting what appeared to be a charming city. The convoy anchored close to Lisbon and almost immediately numerous boats started from the quayside to begin the process of disembarking and unloading. Men gladly took to the nets provided over the sides to allow them to get into the transport below. Only one unfortunate red-coat missed his footing and landed in the harbour, fortunately missing the swell as the two hulls came together and able to clamber into the boat, bedraggled and the subject of much sarcastic comment. Fin and Thomo had stayed on board to organise the horses lifting from the hold to flat-bottomed barges. Previous experience had taught Fin to attach the additional strap to prevent slipping and avoid any further swimming adventures. Each horse was taken to the beach rather than the quay to be given the opportunity to exercise at the walk. They included Captain James' horse accompanied by Wheeler, delighted to have reached dry land safely. Fin had more than one concern about the horses, he wasn't convinced that they would be able to seat a rider, let alone haul a gun into battle. Thomo soothed each horse from the hold, dodging the contents of emptying bowels as frightened creatures were lifted skyward. "Not cut out to be Pegasus!"

"Who's that Thomo?"

"The flying horse Fin, never heard the story?"

"Don't think so."

"We'll have to get Parky to educate you better!"

"How many more to go Thomo?"

"Just our two and that's it."

They may have arrived at dawn, but it was dusk as Fin finally set foot onto dry land, into Portuguese sand. "That's better!"

"Know what you mean Fin, good to have solid ground under your feet again!" chipped in Bob Halls.

"I still feel wobbly like I'm on the ship!" added Dai. "Thought I'd never survive when we started, sick as a dog I was."

"Never noticed!" and Bob added a dig into Dai's ribs. "Come on, you lot, let's make sure every horse has had a good walk, no trotting mind, and no one to try to saddle yet."

"Yes Bombardier." Fin's sharp turning of the head made all of the team realise that it was neither the time nor the place for frivolity.

"Bill, John set up a temporary picket line up by those trees, seems to be a track off the beach."

"Judging by the small craft, that's the way the fishermen get their catch off to market." Thomo was pointing at a line of nets and pots he recognised as those that would catch crabs and lobsters. Fin turned and led Gretschen along the beach to join the long line of horses from the newly arrived transports.

"So this is Portugal."

Chapter 33

"Where we headed Sarge?" Wilky was asking what all wanted to know.

"Prince's Park in the suburb of Belem, Sergeant Major told me."

"How far we walking…" The look from Sergeant Webber cut short the question, they had only just arrived and no one knew their way round.

"Here's a nice place Sarge!" Bob Halls had regained his sense of humour, now back on terra firma and was indicating a larger building with a glorious sign of a Golden Lion.

"Too expensive for you Halls, we're off to the cheaper end of town!"

Fin stared up each side street. To him Lisbon had promised so much from the ship, with its brilliant white buildings hugging the contours of the northern bank of the river Tagus. Fin had thought the city to be planned around the harbour as every street and alleyway seemed to sweep in varying degrees of curve down to the quaysides. Beautiful plants of vibrant colours and fragrances, unfamiliar to the newly arrived reinforcements adorned balconies and terraces, and orange groves squeezed into the sides of the hill at every opportunity contrasted with the packs of dogs yelping and scavenging the gutters and dung heaps, bringing many a shout and boot from the crew of number six gun to clear the path for horses still recovering from weeks below decks. "Never seen so many monks Thomo." Fin was looking towards a group of men in different coloured habits indicating their particular Order.

"A glass of what their having wouldn't go amiss either,"

"Probably lemonade Corp'," the suggestion had come from Bill Bennett, "Seen plenty of peddlers walking the streets in hope of custom."

"How d'you know it's lemonade Bill?"

"I seed the sign on the skin container – limonada!"

"Didn't know you were fluent in Port'ogeeze Bill"

"Never you mind Bob, sure you'll make yerself understood!" Cheers and laughs turned the heads of locals: men of dark brown skins, bare arms and legs, thick set with flashing white teeth and eyes that almost spoke so expressive their movement, short pantaloon style trousers amazingly white in the filth of the gutters and always tied by a scarlet waist sash and armless jackets open to the chest, evidence of hard manual labour.

"Good to see them returning to good spirits."

"Plenty of hard work ahead Ross. They'll need to be fightin' fit before we leave Lisbon." Before Fin could reply, Sergeant Webber had stopped and was turning a piece of paper left and right and peering up and down the streets; "Can't be that way, it's going back to the quayside. Can't be this way, we've just come from the Golden Lion…" A group of young boys crossed the street and the sergeant did his best to ask the way: "Onde… Esta… Principes Park?" The boys stopped, having heard something different from the chattering foreign languages and stared at the sweating man holding a horse… but said nothing. "Onde… Esta… Principes Park?"

"Pera cima a colina, vire a esquerda e depois a diverta para o grande predo da colina." Then they disappeared.

"Stone me. Haven't got a clue what they said…" Turning back to the gunners: "Any of you got any ideas… Parky you're good at the languages, any idea?"

"Only caught one or two words at the end, went a bit fast but I think they said a big building on a hill."

"Well there's plenty of them up there." The sergeant had returned his stare towards the road ahead. A voice interrupted his thoughts:

"I could help you." All eyes looked skyward to see the owner of the voice, a young woman in a white blouse hooked over the shoulders leaning over a balcony adorned by vines and flowers trailing and acting as a screen to hide whatever she was wearing below the waist. Her long black hair flowed loose in curls, and her sparkling eyes and bright smile welcoming to men who had little contact with any new females for so long.

"Thank you miss, very welcome to hear English. Did you hear what the boys said?"

"They told you to walk to the top of the hill, turn left and then right and to aim for the big building on the hill." Many hearts had been given in this brief encounter and a simple wave of her hand as they left turned this band of liberators into pining Romeos, hoping for future meetings. Several stumbles brought a familiar rebuke from their sergeant: "Eyes front, don't want anyone falling in this muck, nor can we afford a horse injurin' itself!"

Eventually, they found their temporary homes in Prince's Park; dilapidated buildings, once homes and shops had been set aside for each newly arrived regiment. Fin noticed that his allocation was shared by those of the teams of gun team four and five. "See to the horses first." The expected order was no surprise and they all set to, employing the well learned techniques from what seemed a lifetime ago. Martha had set off with the two children to search out wood for the fire and by the time the men walked through the front door, the smell of wood smoke filled the house, escaping through the gaps between broken roof tiles. It may have been a different aroma to home but it was a welcome change to the stench of below decks and the open sewers of the gutters. "We'll have some bread for everyone, the ladies from the other guns have found some flour, bit gritty but it will do. Not much of a stew, more of a soup. Fin... would be handy for you to go and do a bit of silent hunting!" They all knew that nothing could be stolen but the park backed onto a rocky slope, where perhaps a few creatures would be venturing out or returning home at dusk.

"I'm with you Fin." Everyone knew it would be Thomo. "See what you can make up for furnishings – there's a broken door out back and a few casks. Might be somethin' hidden away, I expect everythin' has been found that is worth findin' but you never know. Get sniffing out and take those lazy gunners lounging outside with you! And we'll be needing more firewood!"

**

"We're not going to find much out here Thomo." Fin was staring into bare fields edged with silver-white trees, the bark so thick and gnarled that you could fit your hand inside. The leaves had long gone but judging by the litter on the ground beneath Fin thought that it had to be some kind of oak. "Best we come down to the harbour to see what fish are left."

Passing a group of white friars clustered around a table, glass in hand and ignoring yet more soldiers passing by, they had more effect on a similar huddle of nuns a little further on. The bowing of heads towards them at least acknowledged them and they both touched their hands to their forage caps in return. Continuing their walk downhill they passed beneath the ancient aqueduct, over three hundred feet high and two hundred feet wide, stopping even the hungriest of men to stare and admire the skill of ancient craftsmen. "Amazing Thomo."

"Shows how valuable water is, must get very hot in summer. Best we crack on to get something to take back." Their eyes tried to take in as much of the streets as they could, memorising their way around an unfamiliar city – streets of shops selling jewellery, a theatre in the Rua das Condes, hotels or inns, open squares with fountains refreshing the air as people took their ease at cafe tables, public gardens offering pleasant walks under shaded trees – until by accident they reached the Commercial Square.

In the centre an imposing bronze statue of a man riding a horse celebrated John the Great, meaning nothing to Fin and Thomo who turned full circle admiring the buildings with so many well-dressed men discussing what they were reading, in what looked like newspapers spread across tables held down against the increasing breeze by small cups full of coffee. Three roads led away from this square with numerous signs indicating the opportunity to buy from the interior but on the fourth side of the square steps led down to the river and it was here that Fin had spotted baskets with fish.

Walking down towards a man tying a small boat to a large ring bolted into the stone, Fin took a couple of coins that he had in his haversack: "Sen-your." The man had the same familiar red sash tied around his waist that they had seen so often in their short time in the city, but this time he had dark green pantaloons hanging loose to the knees and bare legged to feet simply shod in laced shoes that looked more like dancing shoes than working footwear. The dark skin and wrinkled features were framed by long thick locks of black hair the colour of charcoal, pulled together to the nape of his neck and tied with a matching red ribbon. The face indicated the man had seen many years but his eyes opened wide and the white teeth became a wide grin as he spied the coins. "Fish?" Fin made a sign with his hands that to him indicated a fish swimming in the river and then offered a coin in his right hand as he held up three fingers of his left. Whether the fisherman understood, he stood blankly, unmoved at the attempt to communicate. Fin tried again: he held three fingers up and pointed at the fish in the basket and spoke a bit louder: "Fish?" offering a coin.

"Ah, peixe!" Responded the man picking up the basket and stepping towards them.

"Peixe is fish?" continued Fin.

"Sim, sim, peixe" and heaving the basket under one arm, he mimicked the fish sign Fin had used. Fin, worrying that he was about to lose the opportunity to get any fish, stepped in front of the man and offered coins again. Immediately the man shook his head and raised his open hand: "Cinco."

"I think he wants five coins Fin, you got enough?" Fin reached into his haversack and brought out more coins, again offering the money to the fisherman. The wide smile meant success and he gratefully took the coins, passed the basket to Fin and headed for an open-sided hostelry full of similarly clad local men cheering the arrival of a friend.

"I think we may have been conned Thomo!"

"Just the same in London for any yokel arriving green like us. Main thing is Fin, we have got something for the pot and we have paid just like we were told to."

They started their return journey by taking the road that they thought they had arrived in the square by, but it was soon evident that it wasn't. "How the hell did we get that wrong, Thomo? Only three roads and we've taken the wrong one!"

"Here, this way, has to be up the hill, doesn't it?" The smell had attracted a family of cats expectant of a reward. "Don't encourage them Fin or we'll have all the cats of Lisbon after us. What is it with you and animals?" Thomo laughed as they took a road past the Golden Lion. "Haven't we seen this before?"

"Came this way with Sergeant Webber, just got to keep up this hill."

"Wasn't that the house the young lady shouted to help us from?"

"She'll stay away from you smelling like a fishmonger Fin!"

"Never know Thomo, she might be the daughter of the fisherman we bought it from!" They continued like two without a care in the world taking an evening stroll, but the sudden mewing of the cats stopped them in their tracks. "They complaining about not getting any fish?" The cats had pressed down onto the cobbles, ears flat against their fur, tales erect and a whining coming from them as if ready for a fight.

"Look there Fin," Thomo was pointing down a narrow alley that erupted with a pack of dogs yelping, snarling and barking, "Who's after them?" Heads had appeared from first floor windows, including the young lady from earlier in the day, searching for an answer to the noise.

"Quieto!"

"Ficor longe de aqui!"

Fin looked up straight into the eyes of the same young lady. The long black hair cascaded over the balcony but Fin noticed more of the sparkling eyes as brown as the chestnuts of home and the glowing smile; "They are telling the dogs to get away from here. You have a good catch there!"

"We paid for them miss – five coins we gave." The laugh she gave was captivating and even more so as she threw her head back displaying such beautiful skin from her chin, disappearing lower and lower below the balcony rail without any apparent covering.

"Told you we were conned Fin."

"I don't mind if this is our reward, she's beautiful."

"Senhors, you should have paid no more than two or three; dois ou tres." And with that she was gone again.

"Come on Fin, let's get back."

More dogs ran across their path, birds screeched as they flew to who knows where, cats whined and then a tile landed in front of them, smashing to pieces just a pace ahead. At first Fin thought that they had been attacked but a second and then a third tile followed by pots of flowers crashing to the ground alerted them to something different. "Get in the middle of the street Fin, get away from the walls. Quick, up the hill to the square by the white monks and nuns…this way." Fin didn't need telling twice, but their way became blocked by more and more inhabitants flooding onto the street. A tile crashed onto the head of a man, dressed in a light blue cavalry jacket adorned in lace, knocking him off his feet and blood streamed from the wound that had opened across his nose and cheek. "Don't stop Fin!"

"Are the French attacking?"

"We can't stay here, too many things could fall on us."

Cries from the owners of houses that were being ripped apart; "Tremor de terra, tremor de terra!"

"What are they shouting?"

"Haven't a clue. Come on almost there." The final twenty steps led them away from the risk of falling debris but looking back was a distressing sight: injured men and women with open wounds lay in the street as others bent over trying to shade their loved one against further injury. Some were dragging the injured up to the square and the monks and nuns were emptying their buildings, hurrying across the square to offer help. A cloud of dust was rising above the city but mixed with smoke from fires started by shutters and shades falling onto street ovens that they had seen in so many cafes baking the bread all day. "Come on Fin, we've got to check on the others. The building we had been billeted in was falling down before the start of this, so goodness knows what we'll find.

Fin kept the basket but hurried as fast as he could into Prince's Park. Horses had bolted with men trying to recapture them but they headed for their temporary home. Lumps of masonry, statuettes, tiles, wooden shutters and glass still crashed to the ground as they found their friends well away from the buildings. "Everyone all right?" asked Fin.

"There you are Ross, Thomson. Where've you been?"

"We went for some extras for the pot. Is it the French attacking?"

"No not this, no cannonade did this."

Parky butted in. "It's an earthquake. I heard some of the locals shouting tremor, tremor."

"There's a lot injured down in the street Sarge, shouldn't we do somethin'?"

"Now you two are safe, we're all present so let's get back down there. Ready, two files, fall in."

"Here Fin, give me that basket, I'll rescue the stew when it's safe to get back inside."

"Thanks Martha, glad to get rid of the smell."

"It'll take more than that Fin!" laughed Thomo.

The devastation that met them was a sad introduction to future scenes of horror, but all set about taking care of wounded locals: broken limbs were plenty and all needed careful lifting up to the relative safety of the open square. Walls leaned precariously and many buildings would need total demolition but it was at least safe to walk in the street again. Alternate cries of "Me ajude!" and "Help me!" drew the men of gun six to what had been a two storey building but was now barely one level. A cloud of dust hung heavy over the rubble and the men followed Sergeant Webber into the rubble. The cries grew louder: "Me ajude! Help me"

"All stop!" was his command. "Listen, where's that shout from?" Roof beams had fallen onto the upper story creating such stress that the floor had collapsed bringing walls in on themselves.

"Over here Sarge." Bob Halls was pointing to a heap of rafters and tiles.

"Form a chain, men, careful now, can't have any more come down on us." The men lifted beams and passed them to a point that the rubble could be piled safely in the backyard. Tile after tile, floorboard after floorboard the pile grew. "Quiet men..." Sergeant Weber waited for the work to pause, "Can you hear us miss?"

"Help me, help me!"

"We will miss, we're trying as fast as we can."

To the amazement of all the men, the voice replied: "Is that you Sergeant Webber, is my Thomas with you?"

"Sal, is that you?" Thomas had heard the question.

"It will be as soon as you get me and the baby out of here!"

"How did you get here?"

"Never mind that Hughes, we've got to get her out, come on set to!" The pile slowly lowered as the darkness brought a deep chill to the air. Heat from sweating bodies rose in the moonlight but eventually the rubble was removed to reveal a large dresser. "Sal, you under the dresser?"

"Just as well as I was or I would be a gonna!"

"Right men, three each side. On three... one, two, three!" The straining limbs lifted the heavy piece of furniture to allow Sal to crawl her way out of her prison, clutching the baby. Sergeant Webber didn't stand on ceremony as husband and wife clasped each other. Suddenly Sal broke away from the embrace.

"Where's Rebecca? She was with me." They overturned furniture, lifted plaster and tiles, but it was Thomas who discovered the crushed body of Sal's 'sister'.

"She's over here!"

They stood aghast at the crushed limbs of the girl they had become so used to being with.

"Can't just leave her, Sarge."

"No Sal. Let's pick her up and get her a proper burial." Thomo picked up the lifeless body and followed the group back to Prince's Park.

"How did you get here Sal?"

"Well, that's a long story..."

Chapter 34

The grave had been dug in the graveyard adjoining the monastery, it wasn't the only one that the monks were supervising. The first death for the 'family' was a salutary lesson for them all. No one wanted to think of their own mortality but this brought to mind deep-rooted fears that all tried to suppress. Sergeant Webber asked if any could say some words.

John Smith offered: "I don't know the words exact Sarge but…" he bent to pick up a handful of dirt, "We brought nothing into this world and it is certain that we can take nothing out. The Lord gave, and the Lord hath taken away. Blessed be the name of the Lord. Amen" They all echoed 'Amen', bent to take a handful of soil and copied John, tossing it onto the blanket wrapped body.

"Well said John." Fin tried to encourage the bashful gunner.

"It's not all the right words but all I could remember."

"You did fine John, good words for Rebecca."

Martha had prepared the stew which all gratefully received but it was Sal who became the centre of attention as the men listened to her story of arriving well before they had because she had attached herself to the wife of an officer who needed a maid to go with her on the voyage. "Where's the lady now Sal?" Martha was stirring the pot as Parky fed the fire with more branches.

"Her hubby had to go up to the Lines of Torres Vedras with his regiment and she was off after him. She was comin' back though, that's why she left me here to look after the house with Becca."

"What was she like Sal? Look after you did she, or one of those snooty women treating you like a slave?"

"No Martha, you seen her when we was training. It was that lady that 'Master' Ross knows, you know, the one who had that husband angry after him."

"Hear that Fin, your lady friend has come out here, must love that husband of hers!" Fin hadn't been paying a great deal of attention but had heard the tone that meant he was at the end of a joke again.

"Sorry Martha, who's come out?"

"Sal was looking after your lady friend, the one who had that husband angry after you."

"Lady Ellen, here, in that house that collapsed?"

"No worrying Fin," Sal reassured, "she went off a week or more back. That's why I can speak a bit of the local – starve otherwise."

"Did you feel safe on your own?"

"No fretting Thomas, there was the old owner of the house with his wife. They rented the rooms to us and protected their property."

"Were they in the building with you?"

"No, they had gone to a theatre show. They'll have a shock when they get home though!"

The next week was spent in the city doing the best they could to repair homes devastated by the earthquake. The daily ritual of buying fish from the steps to the river and collecting local wine became a pleasant diversion, all gunners happy to volunteer, certainly less strenuous than the exercising of the horses, which were very slowly regaining their condition after the sea voyage. More troops arrived onto Prince's Park from England, but many also arrived in the city on the back of noisy squealing ox-carts, bound for the hospitals set up to deal with injuries from the front.

The last week of February at last brought news of their moving to their allotted division; Sergeant Major Simons had a document in his hand as he strode towards their temporary home. "Sergeant Webber."

"Yes Sarn't Major!"

"Good news William. Just had this arrive from Captain Bull, we're to make ready to leave to join the Light Division under Crauford."

"When do we leave?"

"First thing tomorrow. Line of march is included but we have to get a map from the quartermaster."

"Very well. I'll supervise the horses and gun-carriages, I'll send Thomson and Ross."

Fin and Thomo had been around the city often enough to recognise familiar landmarks and knew that their short trip to the offices of the quartermaster shouldn't take long. They found the Convent d'Estrella and the large building adjoining, still minus a few roof tiles, housed the object of their search. They walked through the front doors held open by a pink-faced red-coated man – obviously newly arrived in Lisbon – the red dye still held in the fabric. "Take a seat sir, you'll be seen presently." The smile across

Fin's face matched that of Thomo. "Not often been called sir!" whispered Fin. The shade held a slight chill, even if the winter air hadn't been as severe as some they had experienced at home, and both edged towards the glowing fire. A door opening from the far end of the lobby brought both gunners to attention, as a civilian in black frock coat, grey breeches, white stockings and shiny black shoes, reversed away from his meeting, talking in Portuguese and closed the door behind him. Turning towards the waiting men, he bowed and walked to the already open door without another word. "Cloth merchant sir, come to offer his material for uniforms sir."

"How do you know that?"

"Came with a wad of cloth under one arm and book of designs under the other, left with neither."

"Very observant, who you with?"

"Twenty-fourth sir."

"In this light your facings looked like the local regiment in Dorset that I have often seen."

"No sir, Warwickshire."

"Not long been in Lisbon?"

"No sir, just a couple of days, arrived just after the earthquake. Made a mess, hasn't it?"

"That it did, we saw plenty of injuries and buildings ruined."

The opening of the door a second time interrupted the conversation and a voice called the two gunners into the office. Walking into a large room, Fin was surprised to see a view down to the harbour from a large double-doored window that led out into a well laid out walled garden with statues and a small fountain in the centre. "Good morning sir." Offered Thomo, but no reply was returned. Finishing the writing in a ledger, the man looked up. A weather beaten face, wrinkled many times over, betrayed the concern and anxiety created by the need to provide for an army constantly growing.

"Over there, over there…" he pushed the chair back at the same time as waving a hand vaguely to the left. Fin and Thomo turned to see a pile of rolls on a large table. They allowed him to overtake them and he searched the rolls opening and closing until he found the one he wanted. "There you are, map up to the Lines and onto Spain, best we got, not much but all you can have." Thomo reached out a hand, expecting to receive the roll but was surprised to see the man return to his desk. "You can have your map, but you will take this message to your commanding officer, whoever that may be. The man who preceded you has informed me of alarming news and we have to act quickly to avoid any embarrassment." He sifted some sheets, folded the corners of one to form a square, melted wax over the centre meeting point and impressed a seal. "Take this and your map, and make sure that your officer knows of the urgency of this order."

"Yes sir." Thomo took both documents and turned to leave the room.

"I'll know whether you delivered the message if I meet you later. If I don't, you'll answer to a higher authority!"

Walking back into the sunlight, Fin paused to replace his helmet. "What's going on Thomo?"

"Haven't a clue Fin, best we get back quick!" They almost trotted their way back through the streets to Prince's Park and were greeted by a display of gun teams and limbers exercising while all gunners attached their tools to their pride and joy.

"And no one will arrive without any tools, fix them firmly!" Sergeant Major Simons left no one with any doubts. Thomo approached the Sergeant Major, offering map and letter at the same time.

"Well done, you were quick," and looking at the two gunners added, "been running?"

"Quartermaster was quite insistent Sarn't Major, important orders."

"What orders, already have ours?"

"In the letter sir." Sergeant Major Simons broke the seal and as he read through the page mouthed the words silently.

Without looking up, "Sergeant Webber!" he roared, a distant "Sir" in response was followed by a single figure striding towards the trio of men. "William." The Sergeant Major hadn't waited until the Sergeant had arrived, "Limber the guns, we've a job to do."

"Thought we were off tomorrow Roger."

"We are, but something has cropped up and we are going to be like a cork in the bottle, stopping any contents escaping!"

Orders were given, all gunners mounted and a column of march set up. All sergeants had been ordered to meet the sergeant major and street maps were drawn, but the first movement made was as if they were at a review in Hyde Park – a long column circuit around the edge of the park and then the six guns fell into line. Silent signals indicated the guns splitting into pairs and with dusk settling over Lisbon, the sound of hooves on street cobbles was the only sound from the gun troop. As number six gun they followed their predecessors into narrowing streets, streets that Fin recognised as heading towards the Commercial Square and their fish seller's steps. A raised hand was followed by all stopping and the guns were unlimbered as horses were led into the nearest courtyard that would fit. "Load with canister." Was the whispered order passed through the gunners, causing surprise to all. The two guns were side by side, filling the space that led onto the square aimed fair and square at the bronze horseman at the centre. Shouting from the cafes, opening onto the square alerted the gunners to a large group of armed men erupting from the interior followed by blue coated soldiers with impressively crested brass Greek-style helmets.

"Provost Marshals," whispered Sergeant Webber.

"What's going on Sarge?" asked Thomo, thumb stuck firmly over the vent.

"We're stopping a coup, that's what we're doing!"

"A what Sarge?"

"Some Frenchies have got into the city from across the river and have whipped up a storm. They've planned to kill all the officers they can find, as well as the wounded in hospital, and imprison as many men as they can lay hands on."

Further shouts and a solitary shot from the centre of the square was followed by a commanding English voice: "Look around you…" He pointed to the cannon at the entrance to each street. "There is nowhere to run. These Frenchmen here…" indicating three men tied with hands behind their back being led by further blue jacketed soldiers, "These Frenchmen have misled you and they will be punished. Your only escape from the tyranny of Napoleon Bonaparte is the army protecting this city! Put down your weapons and you will be treated fairly." Some lay down their guns immediately but a dozen turned and fled for the steps, hoping to escape to the river. Their surprise in seeing a line of red-coated men with willow green facings, pointing their muskets at them, bayonets fixed, standing less than twenty paces ahead had the desired effect and all weapons clattered to the ground. The small red line of men advanced, herding the group around the statue. A long rope attached all prisoners together by passing the rope through the legs of the man in front, and a sorry line of revolutionaries headed for the prison.

As the provost marshal passed Sergeant Webber, he saluted. "Much obliged to you Sergeant. Could you do me the favour of firing across the square to show that we meant it!" As he rode on, he added, "Don't hit the statue, important figure for them hereabouts."

"You heard the man. Let's give them a show so that no one tries it on again!" The guns were manhandled into position to avoid the statue, and they awaited the command to fire. The noise erupting from the narrow streets was deafening. Birds flew into the air from their roosts, dogs barked and shutters closed with a loud bang, "That should do the trick! Ready to limber…"

Chapter 35

After the excitement of the previous evening, they were greeted with the sobering sight of three bodies hanging from the gallows as they left Lisbon. "Swift justice Sarge." Bob Halls pointed towards the dead Frenchmen.

"Frenchies trying to get the locals against us, has to be dealt with, can't have an enemy in behind us."

The first part of the journey led them parallel to the river Tagus, still wide as it made its way into the country. "There's typical Sarge." Dai Davies was pointing towards the river where a line of boats with sails filled were crammed with red-coated men. "They must have liked the journey out so much they thought they'd join the navy!"

"Keeps the roads clearer and using the tide they should get there faster." The villages all looked similar with a church and its statue, an open space, probably a market area and small homes clustered together, but on the hillside there were more impressive buildings almost hidden amongst trees. "Those trees must be some kind of fruit, wouldn't bother setting so regular otherwise."

"Quite the farmer you are Bill!"

"Spent so much time hiding from 'em I got used to knowing what the fields were, Bob."

"Could be orange groves though, plenty of fruit next summer, I'd guess."

"Those lines up the hillside are vines Bill, that's where they get the grapes for all of the wine we've had."

"You sure Parky? Looks a tangle of branches."

"They're low enough to harvest from the ground and easy to access up and down the rows."

"Wouldn't be a good place to fight through, never get the guns along those narrow lines." John Smith had joined the discussion.

"Don't you go worrying about fightin' John: where we're going is a massive wall of forts and gun emplacements, no Frenchy is coming this way!"

"Where d'you hear that Dai?"

"When we was oiling the gun and sorting the tools, a fancy looking cavalryman was leading his horse back into Lisbon, just come from these Lines of Torres Vedras or somethin'." The early morning amble was interrupted by the order to dismount and walk the horses – they needed looking after was what Sergeant Webber told them.

At the break for lunch, all guns were pulled to the side of an open square in a village and each team were allowed to see if they could find any food or drink to buy. Being on such a busy route to Lisbon, the locals had become well practised in providing for groups of soldiers stopping off and many a gunner paid far more than they should have. The wide smiles and simple beckoning of a hand following the usual "Mister Ingles, que como o vinho?" took in many a new arrival and the proud owner of a skin of wine became a red-faced gunner as he realised how much he had spent. Martha and Sal had more success, the pace being so slow, even their wagon had kept up. Sergeant Major Simons had checked all gun teams and was staring down towards the river with Sergeant Webber, chewing on a chunk of bread and holding a tin of liquid, supposed to be the finest wine. "They've done a good job William," pointing across the valley, "cleared all buildings from the banks so that if the Frenchies got across, they'd have hell to pay getting to here."

"Artillery would have a field day."

They turned as a horse arrived in the square from the direction of Lisbon. The rider was dressed in the same blue as their own jacket but his headgear denoted a foot artillery officer. "May I join you gentlemen? I'm just going up to the Lines."

"Yes sir." Simons recognised the protocol necessary. "Just admiring the preparations made clearing the ground to the river."

"Colonel Fletcher and the team have been busy men. Wait till you get to the Lines, fortifications like you've never seen. I'm posted in Torres Vedras itself, the front line of redoubts and forts that stretches best part of twenty-nine miles from river to coast, but…" and he didn't wait for comment, "the first set you'll see is not too far yonder and that is a line of twenty-five miles!"

"Two sets of lines sir, continuous from river to coast?" Simons' disbelief was obvious in his tone.

"Quite right Sergeant Major. Not quite continuous: there are mountains between some forts that are impassable with no need to build on, but there isn't a gap anywhere."

"And the Frenchies knew nothing of it till they saw them?"

"Right again Sergeant Major, best kept secret of the war. I hear that our commander didn't even tell London the full extent! Didn't trust them to keep it quiet, would have been in the papers and Boney would have been wise to it!"

Sergeant Webber offered a cup of wine, "Much obliged Sergeant. Where're you posted?"

"Attached to the Light Division, sir."

"Oh you'll have no trouble finding them – they're looking after the eastern end for us, right up to the French, mind. Been out long? I hear there was a to-do in Lisbon with the earthquake."

"Yes sir, arrived earlier this month, helped the locals with the clearing of rubble and the like, gave more time for the horses to recover from the journey though."

"Quite right, some of the men, I dare say, as well. Now I must be off, good to meet you. Captain Webber by the way." The offered hand was left hanging mid-air as Simons stared smiling at his friend.

"Well that's a coincidence sir, this is Sergeant Webber, and I'm Sergeant Major Simons." They shook hands laughing at the chances of meeting someone in the same profession of the same name, then the new acquaintance mounted and took his leave adding, "Well I never, another Webber, I'm William…" The laughter erupted again.

"No… so am I sir, good luck!"

"Good job you joined the horse artillery or there'd be no end of confusion." He turned his horse to lead away from the village but twisted in the saddle to add a warning: "Take care up ahead – a group of officers have set up a day at the races, cross country and the like, stop for nothing!"

"What's the chances of that William?" slapping his friend on the back, "Don't know what you lot are gawping at. Get ready to mount!" The welcome interlude over, Simons took his position at the head of the column and they set off again.

Just as their guest had warned, it wasn't long before they came across a most unexpected scene with crowds in the fields, down to the river. Riders were dressed in all colours and shades, just as if it had been at home. The gunners had seen the Duke of Richmond's new racecourse and the flag markers gave a clear indication of the course, fairly level but with a few undulations and obstacles. The cheers erupting from the fields announced the start of the next race and a small group of riders headed towards the road; red, blue, yellow, green and white-shirted riders raced their mounts up the slight incline before turning left and galloping for the river. The artillery column continued their march but kept a view of the race.

"I'll wager the red will win!" shouted Dicky.

"I'll take your wager, but it'll be the blue, look at him biding his time." Was the response from Peter Taylor.

"No you're both wrong. I was watchin' that white rider, calm as anything coming up the hill, he's holdin' back for the final sprint."

"Here's you sounding so knowledgeable George, but it won't be any of those, the green will have it!" Bob Halls joined the debate: "So it's red for Dicky, blue for Peter, white for Georgie and green for Xander! Well looks like we will have a winner anyway!" Laughter rolled along the line. "What about you Sarge, which colour will win?"

"Don't be wasting your money."

"No Sarge. No money, just saying like."

Sergeant Webber scanned the field and after some thought, he announced, "The yellow rider!" Even greater laughter followed as Bob announced that every horse was going to be a winner! The noise from the spectators in the field grew as the horses approached the finish line, the race was far closer than the gunners had predicted and the whole group crossed within a blanket of each other. It wasn't until a flag was raised with yellow at the top, followed by red and green that a cheer went up from the gunners. "Told you boys, just you listen to your sergeant and you won't go too far wrong."

Fin turned to Thomo. "Thought we was going to war, seems more like a country fair."

"Have to keep occupied before the fightin' starts again."

The crowds were swarming back towards the road, the day's races having finished. Sergeant Major Simons ordered the trot and all were passed before the obvious blockage occurred as carriages, carts, horses being led as well as ridden tried to return to wherever they needed. The fortifications soon came into view, every hill-top bristling with earthworks, ditches, fascines and the promise of death to any attacker as guns poked from emplacements. The final part of their journey brought them into an area of clustered villages, farms dotted between and roads connecting each, running ahead towards a substantial bridge on the far side of the plain. The order to halt in the square of the first village was altered to moving off to the right as Sergeant Major Simons was greeted by an officer clothed in dark green with an embroidered jacket slung over his shoulder like a hussar. Fin couldn't hear what was said but the pointing of arms indicated that they were to be on the far edge of the village, closest to the bridge. "See that Fin?" Thomo was pointing ahead across the valley. "See the glinting?" Fin stood up in his stirrups to see what Thomo had seen.

"What is it?"

"That's the French…" (he was pointing ahead across the valley) "…sun going down catching on metal. Could be a musket, bayonet, helmet or one of those big cavalrymen with the armoured chest plate!"

"A bit different from the fun of horse racing then!"

The raising of hands and nods of the head were all that welcomed the gun crews, men who had long been in the field, uniforms patched and darned, dye almost run from the material, simply got on with their routines almost ignoring the new arrivals.

Chapter 36

"How close?" Fin was almost incredulous. He had walked from their allotted billet, simple cottages, much like all the others they had seen on their journey from Lisbon, down towards the river to collect a bucket of water with Bob Halls, Parky, Thomas, Elijah and Noah. Two green-coated figures, cradling their rifles in the crook of their right elbow had approached and halted them; Fin had noticed one wore brown trousers and the other grey, both had patches across their jackets and their boots were not the standard issue.

"Just across the bridge there." He lazily raised his left arm and the figure at the far end of the bridge responded. "We take it in turns to use the river, sometimes share rations, they've got nothing' mind, been stuck here so long that there isn't anythin' left to find, whereas we get regular supplies up from Lisbon. God bless the navy eh!"

Fin just stared in disbelief, the enemy was that close and no one seemed worried.

"Very friendly they are." The rifleman extended his hand as he switched his rifle to his left arm. "King, Johnny King. Good to have some extra fire-power with us rifles, you'll have to keep up though!"

"We'll do our best," Fin extended his own hand. "Fin Ross, we're number six gun under Captain Ramsay."

"This here is Rifleman Hopwood, Harry to everyone though. If you want to go down to the river you'll not be bothered."

The new arrivals edged their way cautiously down to the water, Fin kept his eyes across the river as they filled the buckets and was greeted by a shout and a wave from two Frenchmen playing the same role as the riflemen they had just met. Fin had no idea what was said but waved back. They made their way back towards the rest of the team passing others going to the river. "Funny way of fightin' a war Fin."

"Know what you mean Thomas. Come all this way and we just smile and wave at each other."

"Better than being shot at!" Bob chipped in his usual two penny-worth.

"It's expedient for our commander."

"It's what Parky?"

Arthur Parkinson had grown accustomed to the ignorance of his fellows. "If the French army is situated over there long enough, we won't be fighting any battles because they will starve. All of the food has been taken away, the mills were destroyed so that any grain found has to be ground by hand and the locals have come in behind the fortified lines."

"How do you know all of that Parky?" Elijah asked.

"While we were in Lisbon helping the victims of the earthquake, I spoke to several who had come in from villages where the French are now."

They took the water to the horses and were delighted to see Martha fussing around a pot over a fire, "Here you are boys." She held the lid in a cloth and stirred the contents.

"Thanks Martha, just what we needed."

"See anythin' of the Frenchies?"

"You'll not believe it Martha."

"Not from you Elijah, you're full of stories!"

"No, wait till you hear woman!"

"Just teasin' Eli, you know."

"We were down by the water, met a couple of riflemen, and there they were, waving at us, bold as brass."

"What did you do?"

"We waved back, what d'you expect!" Laughter rang round, a common occurrence amongst the happy crew.

The blur of a creature fleeing from the noise of chasing hounds disturbed their meal, followed by a group of horsemen in red and blue jackets with a variety of facing colours: blue, buff, yellow, white and pea-green. "Haven't they got anythin' better to do?" Sergeant Webber had arrived with Sergeant Major Simons.

"Been here a long time, need a bit of a diversion before the campaign starts for real, William." Sergeant Webber continued his approach. "All doing well Thomson?"

"Yes Sarge, Fin went to the river, horses are settled and Martha has the pot boiling!"

"As soon as we finish this drink, thanks Martha, we have to be saddled and ready to go."

"Where we going Sarge, we've only just got here?"

"Nowhere yet Hogg, but every evening we will be ready to go at a moment's notice. We'll only unsaddle when given the signal in the morning." The return of the horsemen from the river drew everyone to turn and look.

"No dogs Sarge."

"Frenchies probably have them over the fire by now!"

"No Halls, I expect they'll be through and away the speed they were going."

"What was they chasin' Sarge?" Thomas Hughes asked.

"I expect it was a rabbit or hare the way it zig-zagged away."

"Anythin' for me to have a pot at Sarge?"

"I'm sure they'll be somethin' for your silent killers Ross!"

As ordered, they were all fully equipped before they tried to sleep, but all found it difficult to do so on their first night so close to the enemy. A single shot shocked everyone to jump to their feet but no further noise allowed them to return to their blankets.

The chill of the night was melted by the orange glow seeping across the eastern horizon. Fin stretched his legs and shoulders, welcoming each member of the team to a new day. Thomo was returning from the river alongside a rifleman followed by four dogs on rope leads. "Never believe it Fin! The Frenchies came across the bridge with these dogs. The same as went chasing after the hare last night! They said the hare escaped but they brought back these dogs and apologised for the shot last night. A nervous sentry, 'a stupid fellow' they called him, thought that he had seen us advancing towards him. This is Sergeant Tom Knight. The ball hit the log on the fire he had been sittin' round with his friends."

"Knocked our pot over an'all. We knew it weren't aimed – they can't hit nothin' from that range, no rifles see!"

"What you going to do with them?" Martha was looking at the four animals tamely sitting at the feet of the rifleman.

"Find the fool who couldn't look after them himself!"

"Have you time for a cuppa?"

"Always time for that, never know when you might get your next one!"

He gratefully took the mug. "I'll camp near you again!"

"You make sure you keep our men safe then you'll always be welcome."

The signal came from a rider on a grey horse patrolling the villages. The horses could be unsaddled, belts and weapons taken off and a more relaxed atmosphere spread through the village. Riflemen came and went: the news of a woman cooking had obviously spread quickly, and gun six was a popular and happy camp to be with.

215

Fin got his opportunity to try out his poaching skills. Making his way back towards the Lisbon road with Thomo, they headed for the best alternative for an English meadow. "If there's going be some game it'll be here or into those woods." Thomo hadn't the experience of his younger friend and trusted him to lead him on. "There Thomo, see that?" Fin whispered, as he pointed towards a bird almost still in the air, "If that bird has seen somethin' worth stoppin' for then we might be in luck." They kept to the edge of the field, the soil strewn with rocks but grass was growing and the odd flower had invaded as well. "Surprised it's so mild, I was expecting cold and ice."

"Same at home Fin, some winters are frozen solid and snow for weeks, others just a chill."

"Might mean we have a few more targets." The bird fell to the ground and arose triumphant, a small rodent in its claws, making its way to the nearest branches of the woodland. "Might have to wait till dusk Thomo. Let's try to get to the edge of the wood." They waited in the hope that they could supplement the rations issued in Lisbon; the trees had littered the ground with an acorn like nut but they both agreed that you would have to be more than desperate to try these, or be a pig.

"What's that Fin?" Thomo was pointing across the field towards the river, something was casting a shadow from the sun, slipping behind the fortified hillside.

"Rabbit or hare like those hounds were chasing." Fin carefully stuck arrows into the moss at the base of the tree and then attached one to the string and waited.

"How you going to hit that, never stays straight for more than four or five strides?"

"That's enough Thomo. Just watch the pattern, and then you predict the change of direction." Fin had been right, the hare had a regular pattern even though it looked random and it was its regularity that was its undoing!

"One arrow Sarge, that's all it took! I wouldn't have believed it if I hadn't seen it. Dartin' this way and that, thirty paces away at least and then the arrow's gone and the hare is dead!"

"We'll be the envy of the army with your poachin' Ross, just make sure that you never take anythin' from a local, or if you do, pay for it."

The groaning chorus "Yes Sarge!" indicated a certain irritation from the repetition of the order given many times already. "I'm not havin' any of you hung for stealin' that's all. Now I have to report in, I'll be back in half an hour and all of you will be saddled and kitted ready." As he went to mount his horse, Fin noticed that Sergeant Webber had the weapon Fin had only seen briefly once before – the first time they had met Becca. "Sarge, what's that pistol? Not what we were given."

"No Ross." He slid the strap from the gun and pulled it from the holster. "This is one of the few items I brought back when I was with General Moore at Corunna. Twin barrels, the left one is rifled with nine grooves for greater accuracy and a folding sight. The right barrel is a smooth bore just as your pistols are. Mister Nock made these for the horse artillery but they weren't too popular because the stock is quite short and this makes it too difficult for most to use. That mister Nock was an ingenious man, same rifle maker we see the green-jackets use. He had a detachable stock made that you could add to fit into your shoulder, but can't have it fitted and still use the holster. Two triggers, front one for the smooth bore, back one for the rifle. You load it just the same as any pistol but the rifled barrel gives you a surprise factor for the enemy who think they can take liberties and get too close! Might let you have a go Ross... if you're lucky!" He turned his horse and walked away, leaving the crew to anticipate what promised to be a substantial meal.

Chapter 37

"Ross!" The hand shaking his shoulder belonged to Sergeant Webber, "Ross!" Fin slowly came out of deep sleep, the result of a hearty meal and local wine.

"Are we leavin'?"

"Come with me, and bring your bow." Fin realised that it was still dark and only the merest hint of light had broken the eastern sky. "Somethin's not right Ross. Rifleman came up and gave the warning." They made their way down to the river bank, the lights of the glowing fires across seemed welcoming as Fin shivered.

"Over there Sergeant, see at the edge of the trees, sentries posted at alternate trees. They ain't movin' and if you wave, they don't wave back." The rifleman demonstrated. "We had a chat with those on the bridge last night, swapped some wine for bread, but seen nothin' of 'em since."

"What d'you think Ross? Hopwood here is their best shot but he daren't shoot." Fin stared intently, trying to let his eyes adjust to the shapes at the edge of the trees, silhouetted against glowing campfires that occasionally shot sparks skyward.

"Can't see anyone round the fire Sarge, just men at attention."

"Could be the old trick of stoking fires and leaving a few men to scarper as late as possible."

"Been done before, and we've done it Sergeant."

"You're right there Hopwood. We did the same through the mountains, stopping for a short while to take a breather and get any food we could and then sneak off to get a head-start. We used to leave straw dummies."

"Like a scare-crow Sarge?"

"Exactly."

Fin didn't need any further explanation but had taken an arrow and loosed it across the thin mist rising from the water. The second arrow had followed before the rifleman had a chance to comment.

"Crikey, you're good Ross."

The third and fourth arrows thudded into the next two figures, the fifth took the next – all sentries still stood to attention.

"That's enough Ross, let's go and have a look." Hopwood signalled to other riflemen on watch and they made their way slowly across the bridge rifles cocked and Fin with his last arrow ready on the bow. As they reached the far side, Hopwood beckoned Fin forward. "Just to make sure, see that figure there? I'm sure it moved." Fin half-closed his eyes to focus on a crouching figure laying wood on the fire slowly stand up. The arrow hit him with such a force that the man spun round and clattered to the ground.

"Quick, let's go and see." The small group rushed through the campfires, Fin following his sergeant to the edge of the trees to find his arrows embedded into posts holding the straw filled uniforms upright, 'muskets' being simple straight branches tied against the body with rope. The riflemen bent down to a prostrate figure clutching his shoulder. "Where are the others?" The Frenchman looked blank.

A second rifleman bent down, "Ou sont les soldats?"

"Ils ont disparu, recul." The Frenchman struggled to speak, the pain of the arrow was not the only wound he had. His feet were badly lacerated wearing no boots or socks.

"Well done Harris, handy you speaking Frenchy so well. Ask him how long?"

"Il y a combien de temps ont-ils quitte?"

The Frenchman held up three fingers. "Trois heures ou quatre."

"He says three or four hours Hoppy."

"Right, best we get back to report. We'll have to take him," and turning towards the returning Sergeant Webber and Fin, arrows in hand, "D'you see anything there?"

"No they've gone. Left this poor soul to stoke the fires I'd guess. He weren't going to be marchin' anywhere far with those feet. Here Ross, shove the bow under his legs, he can hold onto our shoulders."

The riflemen, having sent a runner to their commanding officer, split into pairs edging their way forward through the remnants of the French camp as Sergeant Webber and Fin carried their casualty back to camp. "What you got there?" Martha was up and about as usual.

"Frenchman Martha, been left by the rest of their army."

"They've scarpered Martha, so get packing, we'll be on the move soon. We're taking this chap up to the surgeon."

"Time for the tea Sergeant?"

"Oh yes, we'll drink it and leave. Do me a favour. While we take this poor fella up the road, pop your head into the rooms to get the men up." Martha busied herself with the pot on the fire and once satisfied, she turned to the task of rousing slumbering gunners.

"Where the devil did you get this Frenchman?"

"From their camp sir. Went into it with some of your riflemen sir." Trying to stand to attention whilst carrying the wounded Frenchman proved impossible.

"Well, who are you and why has he got an arrow in his shoulder?"

"Sergeant Webber of Captain Ramsay's Royal Horse Artillery sir. This is Bombardier Ross. It was him who put the arrow into this Frenchman. We discovered they had stuffed sentries with straw and left at least three hours ago. We didn't want to alert any Frenchies nearby – he's deadly with his bow sir."

"That may be so, but why wasn't I told sooner?" The officer had turned to his staff.

"Sir William, this rifleman has just reported the same to you five minutes since."

"Has he by God. Well you best report it to Sir Arthur and we'd better find how far they have got – three hours, you say?" turning back to Sergeant Webber and Fin.

"This fellow says three or four hours sir."

"Very well, get him off and then get to your guns Sergeant, we'll need you with us."

"Yes sir, we'll be there directly!"

They surprised the surgeon having his breakfast, unaware that casualties would be brought in. "My word, an arrow! Never had to deal with one of these."

"Begging you pardon sir," Fin tentatively suggested, "I only used a needle head so it should come out easy."

"Quite right young man, but what are you doing with a bow and arrow anyway?"

"Good for the pot sir."

"If you don't mind sir, we have to get the guns ready to support the rifles." As an afterthought, Sergeant Webber added, "Sir William's orders." Now the sergeant did not know who Sir William was, but judging by the way the group of officers deferred their places by a couple of horse lengths, he realised that Sir William had to be of importance.

"I'll be glad when we get 'Black Bob' back in charge, someone who knows what he's doing. Mark my words Sergeant, if you are supporting Sir William, you'd best be on your guard, blunders around getting into all sorts of scrapes." A sudden screech was the signal that the arrow had been pulled from the Frenchman's shoulder. The surgeon wiped the blood from the arrow head and returned it to Fin, "Problem with the wound isn't always the bullet, bayonet, sword... or the arrow.... but what is taken into the wound. Keep it clean and this chappy will survive, but if some of his dirty clothing has got in there, he'll get an infection and die! We'll do our best for him, probably a better chance than the rest of his army. Now I'll finish that breakfast. Good luck Sergeant and good shooting, archer!"

There was just time to grab the mug of tea offered by Martha, mount up and retell the tale of their early morning mission, before Captain Ramsay arrived. "Well done Sergeant Webber, well done Ross, talk of the staff you know, archers in the army! Talk of the staff! Right, Sergeant Major?"

"Yes Captain."

"We are crossing the bridge in support of the Light Division. We are to expect some cavalry to join us but our guns must be ready at any time – you never know what Sir William might do!"

"Yes Captain. On your word sir."

The captain rode the length of the troop to take station alongside the senior officer Captain Bull. "All guns ready Captain?"

"All ready."

"Royal Horse Artillery will advance." A slight squeezing of each gunner's legs urged their horse forward and they walked forward to find the French.

Chapter 38

Following the French army needed no specialism in tracking – the remnants of an army long without supplies were shed at the side of the road: hats, jackets, muskets, back-packs, blankets, pots, canteens… everything a soldier would need had been discarded but what Fin saw as they passed through village after village made his emotions tumble and churn. "Thank God that the French have never come to Dorset." Every item of furniture had been strewn across the roads to such an extent that some roads were impassable to horses and had to be cleared; no house had a roof left worth its name, doors and shutters had been smashed and the people left were more skeleton than alive. Bodies of dogs, mules and even men and women had been left to rot in the streets, the stench making the air vile to smell. The gunners had to wait in a village, unnamed on the simple map they had been given in Lisbon, known as Pernes to the locals, whilst the engineers repaired the bridge destroyed by the retreating French. Captain Ramsay had asked whether there was the possibility of a ford but the engineers assured him that it would take no more than one hour. The opportunity to dismount allowed the gunners to explore inside the village, but many wished they hadn't as they returned with stories of atrocities seen; dead bodies of whole families: husband, wife and children left in heaps in front of smashed cupboards, killed by soldiers in search of any form of loot, revenge for having given so little food to the French. Fin and Thomo entered a side street and found a back entrance door-less. Sliding their swords as quietly from the scabbard as possible, they took a wall each sliding down the corridor towards sounds emitting from inside. Peering inside Thomo held up his hand for Fin to stop. "Check ahead Fin, I'll go in here." Thomo sprang forward and froze as he saw the body of an elderly woman crushed beneath an upturned table and loaded with every weighty implement that the murderers could find. Blood leaked from her ears, eyes, mouth and nose creating pools under greying hair that had come loose from a lace edged scarf. Fin nervously moved towards the stairs. The noise was still audible and when Thomo shouted, the noise increased. At the top of the stairs Fin could not help his stomach contorting and he did everything possible not to vomit. Two young girls huddled on a straw mattress, their clothes, or what was left of them, held across their bodies, trying to preserve some form of modesty, had been shredded and the cuts visible to Fin were witness of a brutal attack. It didn't take any imagination to understand what had happened and in spite of Fin putting his sword into its scabbard, the girls wriggled further and further into the corner, sobbing and scrabbling to cover themselves. "Thomo, don't know what you found but two young girls are up here terrified." The sound of footsteps announced Thomo and further torment spread across the girl's faces. "How do soldiers behave so Thomo?"

"It ain't soldierin' Fin, it's animals doing anything to gain revenge."

They tried to offer a hand to help the girls but they battered them away. Fin found some scraps of biscuit he had kept in his haversack and he held them out in an open palm as if coaxing a timid bird. The snatching and eating so fast indicated a way forward. "Got any more Thomo?" A bit of bread and the offer of a canteen encouraged a less fearful response, but the girls couldn't stand, their bloodstained legs too weak from previous torment. Looking round the room there was nothing to act as a cover for the girls' nakedness. "We can't leave them Thomo."

"What we going to do with them Fin? Martha and Sal are well back."

"What if we take them to the square, might be some locals to look after them." With a little coaxing and after a few weak punches landed on both Fin and Thomo, the girls allowed themselves to be lifted and carried out of the building. The comments and cheers greeting the sight of two girls, more naked than clothed, being carried by the gunners brought an anger in Fin that he seldom showed.

"Be quiet the lot of you. What we discovered is shameful to all soldiers and the Frenchies will get what they deserve when the locals catch them. Now find something to cover them!"

Sergeant Webber walked across to meet them and lowered his voice. "Can't take them with us Ross, we'll see worse yet."

"There's an old woman back in the house crushed under a table loaded with everything weighty they could find."

"I know it's a shock, but store this anger for the battles ahead and when you have any doubts, bring these pictures to mind and you might just survive."

"Well done Parky, where d'you find these, they're just like dresses."

"I went into their church, statues smashed, coloured windows shot out and they even killed the priest on the altar, bayoneted him into the wood of the table. Found these behind the altar, must have been the priest's surplices. It'll do for a start." The girls embarrassment was still evident in spite of what had happened to them before, they only dropped the shreds of material that had been their clothes as the full length of the surplice covered them.

"Look proper angels now, don't they Fin?"

"You're right Smithy. Anyone found anyone alive to look after them?"

George Rogers walked into the square carrying the limp body of a child, a black-haired girl bleeding from wounds across her face. "She was thrown against the wall while they attacked her mother." He turned to indicate a woman hobbling behind him clinging desperately to a shawl, all that was left of her clothes.

"Did she tell you that?" asked Smithy

"Course she didn't, I don't speak Portuguese do I. Just used my eyes. She's just like my Charlotte."

The trailing woman started shrieking: "Diablo, Diablo, Assassino, bastardo!" The two girls, newly clothed reached out with their arms, incapable of more than one step, and the three females hugged, tears streaming down tanned and dirty faces.

"Is she alive George?"

"Only just, have we any water to clean her up?" Parky brought a canteen and cloth, poured water onto the child's lips and then dampened the cloth to clean away the blood to examine the wounds.

"These will heal George, superficial. I don't think there is anything broken but the bang on the head must have knocked her out." As Parky brushed the hair away from the lacerations seeping blood, the child moaned drawing the attention of the mother.

"Maria, Maria." She clung to her awaking daughter, kissing her face. The eyelids slowly opened to reveal chestnut brown eyes causing the mother to grasp George and Parky; "Obrigado, obrigado, saude"

"What she saying Parky?"

"She says thank you and bless you."

Captain Ramsay returned from the bridge and announced that they could move on. The bridge repairs were not permanent but each gun could navigate a reduced width roadway and increase their pace once across. Sounds of popping could clearly be heard above the hooves and wheels of each gun team. The order to unlimber brought the opportunity to pay back the French violators and vandals as the rear guard had set itself across the road into a further village. "Let's stop them blowing another bridge, clear the road of them, you've seen what crimes they've committed, let's drive them out of Portugal!" The anger created a determination to serve the enemy with as great destruction as possible and all six guns were soon pouring devastation into the ranks of Frenchmen. Fin counted only four rounds before the order to limber and follow was given. The aftermath of their short introduction to fighting the French was evident in the bodies of dead and dying bodies strewn across the road. "No stopping!" boomed Captain Ramsay, "If they can't be bothered to care for their own, we can't wait either!" The horses trampled and wheels crushed those unfortunate enough to have been left in the road. Some struggled to get to the sides, to prop themselves against any possible support, but the arrival of skeletal villagers may have made them wish that they had been left under the hooves and gun carriages. Even before gun six had arrived at the scene, local peasants had started their torment of the unfortunate French wounded. Not only were bodies stripped of anything valuable, especially clothing, but mutilations slashed body parts in retaliation for the brutality used against every village and town that the French had passed through. The screams were audible above the noise of the artillery chasing the enemy.

"What they deserve!" Bob Halls spat on the bodies of the enemy as he passed. "They'll regret what they done when the locals get their hands on them."

They secured the river crossing and, supported on either side by the green-jacketed rifles and brown-clothed Portuguese riflemen, settled for the night. Riflemen were sent on to keep in touch with the enemy and assess the direction for the morning. As with all villages passed through so far, little was left of use and certainly nothing to eat, but enough wood was found to provide something warm to drink and a simple stew to be boiled. "Can't get those girls out of my mind, every time I shut my eyes I see them."

"I know Fin, but you've seen what the peasants will do. It's like another regiment for our army, any group of Frenchies who leave the army or fall by the wayside will suffer a horrible death."

225

"I said it before Thomo, thank God for living on an island and having the navy to stop the Frenchies invading. It's not worth thinking about what would have happened if they had got across the Channel. That could have been our families."

"But it wasn't Fin and we've started on a course that we have to finish: drive them out of Portugal, drive them out of Spain and get them back to Paris!"

"Sounds easy Thomo."

"I daresay a certain Corsican may have other ideas!"

Chapter 39

Sergeant Webber had everyone up early and the chase was on again. The bodies of Frenchmen littered the roadside. No visible wounds but with faces discoloured by disease, they were lying next to mules and donkeys, ribcages protruding through mangy skins, sores running puss as much as hair covering the hides. The routine of the chase, stopping to unlimber, fire, limber and chase followed hour by hour. Captain Ramsay was keen to press the enemy as hard as possible and alongside the Light Dragoons harassed the rearguard; the dragoons in their French-styled uniform, blue jackets and scarlet facings harried the French infantry. The infantry formed the tightest square that they could as protection against the horsemen, but this only opened the way for the guns to unlimber and plough furrows through the packed lines. The security of walled streets allowed the French greater speed as the cavalry couldn't get around the sides, but each of the six guns redoubled their efforts to catch the massed infantry and cavalry as they passed through. Incidental damage to buildings brought falling masonry, much in the same way as the Lisbon earthquake, tumbling onto the heads of unfortunate men below. The column of retreat was clearly visible as the French tumbled out of the streets and the order was passed to finish with Round Shot. Sweat was running down the faces, arms and backs of every gunner as they strove to fire as many projectiles into the French; Xander and Parky had been back and forth to the limber safely out of range of any French artillery, which had not responded one shot. George and Thomas had maintained the steady provision of cartridge and projectile for Dicky to ram home, Thomo had kept his thumb firmly over the vent until the moment that a quill could be inserted into the vent, Fin was constantly reassessing the elevation and Peter set the portfire to the fuse, making sure the recoil did not hit him. Gun six was first to fire closely, followed by the other five guns and there immediately followed an enormous explosion that seemed to shake the air where they stood. "Was that us Sarge?" shouted Thomo.

"Don't think so Thomson. The Frenchies are probably trying to get away so fast that they have exploded any ammunition to stop us getting it."

Sergeant Webber was right. They passed the remnants of what had been French tumbrils loaded with ammunition, wagons with spare parts for limbers and carriages as well as ropes, tackle and chains. Sergeant Major Simons rode down the line encouraging each crew; "Got them in a hurry boys, keep it up, but watch out, they will stop to shoot at us, we've been lucky so far!"

"A good way to get used to working in battle conditions Roger."

"You're right there William. A step up from a review in Hyde Park, but you and I both know, it will get hotter!"

Having taken the town, half of the rifles were ordered to bivouac in a pine wood while Captain Bull issued orders for the six guns to take strategic places across the front of the buildings in case of French attack. The brown jackets of the Portuguese rifles had been sent on and were just over the brow of the hill. A group of riders came down the road, blue cavalry with red facings followed by a gun with light blue jacketed riders. Sergeant Major Simons bellowed: "King's German Legion, not French, let them pass!" Fin and Thomo turned to watch the cavalry pass at a slow walk with French prisoners riding between the outside files. As the horse artillery drew to a halt behind the cavalry, Fin noticed a familiar face.

"Ludwig!" He started walking across the gap. "Thomo, remember him? Ludwig, he gave us the horses." Thomo followed Fin and as the rider dismounted stiffly they offered hands to shake in welcome. "Ludwig, remember us?" The blank faced response indicated that perhaps he didn't, so Fin persisted, "You gave me Gretschen and you gave Thomo Jager."

The tired face brightened "Ah yees, Vin and Tom-mo, how are the horses?"

"Didn't like the sea journey, but doing well so far, what's going on here Ludwig?" Fin was looking towards the prisoners being made to kneel and cavalry troopers had drawn their sabres.

"They took two off hower men and killed them – they will pay for that."

"That's murder Ludwig, you can't let them."

A red-coated officer shouted for the execution to stop: "I am Colonel Gilmore and you will not murder prisoners."

"They killed two of our men Colonel and now they will pay."

"I cannot let you do this…" He paused, not sure the rank of the officer he was addressing.

"Lieutenant Verden, Colonel."

"We cannot lower ourselves to the level of the enemy Lieutenant. You must hand the prisoners over to the Provosts who will take them back to an appropriate place of keeping."

"And if your men were sabered in cold blood Colonel?"

"You have my sympathies, but I cannot allow this. Now release the prisoners into the keeping of these gentlemen," indicating a trio of riders approaching along the main street, "and find your billet for the night."

"Colonel…"

"There is no further discussion. If you do not hand them over, I will have them taken from you." At this, a line of riflemen lifted their weapons to their shoulders. "They don't miss Lieutenant."

The lieutenant spoke in German resulting in many riders spitting onto the ground, mounting and riding off, jostling the prisoners still awaiting their fate on their knees – knocking several to the ground. "Seems I haf to go Vin. Gut luck."

Colonel Gilmore walked towards the riflemen. "Thank you Sergeant Knight," and without breaking stride, "Provost, get those men out of here before the Germans change their minds!"

Chapter 40

Chasing the French army seemed to follow a similar pattern to Fin: the early bugle call to bring everyone to arms, a hasty breakfast of whatever was to be had, usually remnants of the previous evening without Martha's care, linking with the Light Dragoons to chase along the road and find the rear guard, threaten and maybe fire a couple of rounds but wait for the green and brown-jacketed rifles to come up and dislodge them. The French didn't always need dislodging as Fin discovered. Village after village was passed in the same desolate state with nothing left that could be used again, as well as further bodies littering the streets, but eventually they turned and this time there was an ancient castle behind them, a remnant of the days when the Moors had invaded the country.

Signals from Captain Ramsay directed the guns to allotted positions in a ploughed field, limbers and horses were taken to the rear, and alongside the cavalry they waited. As soon as the rifles arrived they spurred on to attack far greater numbers than they had and it was then that the artillery came into action; they started with shot and changed to shell but at a distance that they could only imagine the havoc they wreaked. The return of fire from the ageing walls did little harm to the guns but a steady stream of wounded men, some hobbling, some carried by friends, alerted all to the perils of the fight ahead. More and more infantry arrived in support for the attack but light was fading and the decision to cease fire and wait for the morning was announced.

"Check your guns, count the cartridges and projectiles, get to your horses – we're here for the night!" Sergeant Major Simons knew that the last announcement would bring a miserable time for all as it had started to rain and a ploughed field would give no respite to falling temperatures either. Each knew their role and although they had been in contact with the French such a little time, it seemed as if they had been there forever; only the deeper shade of their blue jackets made it clear to all that passed that they were newcomers.

The horses – brushed, combed, brushed again, hooves checked – were fed and watered before anyone could relax to their own needs but the welcome sight of a fire with kettle boiling and Martha and Sal warmed the dampened spirits. "How did you get here?" Elijah was clasping his wife in a crushing hug.

"Me and Sal have our ways, you know us. Couldn't leave you wet, cold and hungry boys, could we?" The crew of gun six cheered their private angels, gratefully taking the offered hot drinks and biscuit. "Be useful Elijah, fetch those empty crates and boxes, can't be doin' with sittin' on the wet furrows." Fin noticed the hem of Martha's skirt had been hitched up to avoid trailing through the increasing mud and she had found a pair of wooden clogs stuffed with straw.

"Martha, I haven't seen clogs for many a year, my grand-father used to have a pair for the yard."

"One of the villages we passed through, don't know where, terrible things we seen, but we found them lying near some dead Frenchmen – horrible things done to their bodies, not a sight a lady should see, I can tell you."

"Not a sight anyone should see Martha. We tried to help some of the local people, the French have behaved badly to them and they will be repaid many times over if they get caught by any local."

Martha changed the course of the conversation, "So where we all sleeping tonight?"

"Could try to rig something of a shelter under the gun or the limber but most of us will be under the stars and in the rain!"

"Elijah, just as long as you is by my side, we'll be dandy!"

The evening settled to familiar story telling while some made use of the lull to smoke a pipe brought in their knapsacks and some even tried a local cigar. Sal had managed to find a bottle of wine along the way and all were smiling as they attempted to wrap a blanket around them and sleep with their knapsack for a pillow. No one had tried to change clothes and what they wore through the day they slept in, waking to scratch and stretch stiff limbs. Fin had only woken once when a lizard scuttled across his face but the bugle woke all before dawn and guns were limbered ready to move. Martha and Sal hugged every one of the team before they left, not knowing when they would catch up, even Sergeant Webber wasn't exempt. "You look after our boys, Sergeant."

A cheery wave added to the "They can look after me Martha, gettin' too old for these damp nights."

"Go on with you Sarge, you're just in your prime, a man like you!" Sal was always ready for a saucy suggestion, but even the sergeant smiled.

The French had drawn their rear guard in force and the rifles were soon pushing through a thick wood of fir trees. Single shots indicated the skirmishing of advance and rear guards but the sudden eruption of a volley signalled that the main force had been met with. Green jackets emerged at the edge of the wood using the tree trunks as shelter, still returning fire. A line of red-coated men with bright cross-belts and pea-green facings headed for the wood. Even at the distance from which Fin sat on his horse, the red jackets were clearly visible as they ventured further into the trees. "Thomo," the corporal turned his head, "you can see why the rifles turned to green, look at them," pointing to the trees. "See them targets as clear as anything." The crash of a volley and cheer prevented Thomo's response from being heard and the order to advance took the attention away from the trees. The guns had to stick to the road, the gaps between trees being too narrow on the one flank and the incline too great on the other, but Fin could see line after line of red coated men advancing on and on.

The noise was growing more and more intense, the screech of the French shot and shells flew left and right, more than one splintered trees impaling any nearby. The view below was unlike any Fin had seen before; the French rear guard were desperately defending a bridge over which as many men were passing as could be squeezed like grain through a funnel. Artillery on the far side of the bridge was doing its best to deter the attack but it was plain to Fin that they would never be able to all cross with the red, green, blue and brown coated attackers catching them so quickly. Flames flickered from the roofs of first one, then two, then three buildings near the bridge and it seemed to Fin that it was the result of the French artillery. Many blue-coated figures rushed from the flames, clothing on fire to roll on the ground, weapon-less, and surrender to the nearest attacker they could find, but some tried for the river in a desperate attempt to escape. It was as if he was watching as a spectator at a show rather than as a soldier in battle; green jackets followed to the water's edge and some plunged in to drag Frenchmen back to the bank.

The infantry pushed through the stragglers over the bridge and continued the chase out of the town; a short night's rest inside roofless buildings gave some shelter but before the sun rose the chase was on again. Every village bore the marks of the same barbarity as before. Passing through one more village in flames, Sergeant Major Simons ordered gun six to dismount and help rescue anything not burned from a larger house. Dicky and Thomas found a rake and brush which they used to drag out burning straw that had been stuffed under the stairs; Bob and Parky tore down curtains that had been deliberately set on fire; the rest set to clearing as much as they could from the ground floor. The owners were elderly and could hardly lift their family portraits let alone furniture and although much was lost to the flames, the team helped serve them with a good deed and they were able to return to their home with tables, chairs, cabinets and paintings. The tears and smiles of the elderly couple bid them on their way and by the time they had caught up with the rest of the troop, the French had moved on again, realising that they were going to be caught if they stayed longer. The single shots indicated that the French hadn't all left. The cat and mouse game between advance and rear guard skirmishers had been re-joined.

Sergeant Webber walked his horse past gun six. "Well done in the village, now be on your guard, that's Sir Arthur Wellesley himself on the brow of the hill." All heads turned to see their commander-in-chief for the first time.

"Which one Sarge?" John Smith whispered.

"No need to whisper Smith, he won't hear you from here, he's the one in the plain blue coat."

"Thought it might be the one in the red jacket with all that gold lace Sarge."

"No, he doesn't go in for a lot of that…" and as an afterthought, "except on ceremonial occasions, then it's the full regalia with all of his ribbons and honours!" A noise from the right attracted their attention.

"Ain't they Frenchies Sarge?"

"I think you're right Halls. Too close by half, let's go and see. Right face, at the walk."

The hours of repeated turning and turning, halting and walking, walking and trotting came into their own and the seamless transition from standing still on the road to trotting to the crest of the hill would have made cavalry proud. It didn't stop one or two shots being sent at the group of staff officers but none were hit and the French chased off into the wood. "Shall we be after them Sarge?" urged Dai Davies.

233

"No not for us to be chasin' through trees, look there," he was pointing to a group of green jackets running with rifles at the trail towards the trees.

"Thanks Sergeant, bit embarrassing them getting close enough to shoot at Sir Arthur there. Good job they're useless shots."

"Good hunting to you rifles."

They re-joined the gun and passed a smiling Sir Arthur who raised his hat to them, "Much obliged, can't have me being shot at. What would the army do then?" Laughter from the group of staff officers and a cheer from the gun team brought the action of the day to an end, only the occasional pop of a gun far to the right indicated that any combat continued.

The next morning promised more chasing but the pursuit was delayed by a misty fog that had settled in the valley. "The winter has been quite mild," Parky informed everyone willing to listen. "The moisture from the recent rain has been evaporated by the warmth of the sun, however, as it rose it has hit colder air condensing the droplets into this cloud."

"There was I thinking it was just a foggy day." The chuckles at Bob's remark did not deter Parky.

"It will probably stay like this until mid-morning, at least when the sun will have time to heat the air and disperse this cover."

"Chance of a hot drink, don't you think Sarge?"

"I think you are right there Bennett. There's a stream to the left and some trees, let's see what we can do."

Long after the fire had boiled the water for a hot drink, the order came to tell them that the attack had been delayed. A few remaining biscuits that Martha and Sal had brought were eaten and horses attended.

Finally the cloud cover lifted and the advance began, soldiers scrambling up rocky hillsides and over into the next valley. The guns stuck to the road but by mid-afternoon, orders arrived for them to clear the way ahead. Each gun found a clear platform to unlimber and waited for the order to fire. Musket balls flew overhead, one or two sent ringing notes as they hit the barrel of the guns and a scream of pain signalled their first casualty. "George, where you hit?" Fin had seen George Rogers fall but couldn't see any obvious wound.

"I can't breathe Fin, it's my ribs." Fin turned George onto his side, the groan rumbling from him was enough to tell Fin that was the problem. Sergeant Webber arrived and crouched beside them.

"Where's he hit Ross?"

"He says it's his ribs, but can't see no blood."

"Could be a spent ball. Seen it before. When it gets to the end of its trajectory, it's slowing down, still break a rib though." Without pausing for any further comment, the sergeant shouted to Bob Halls and Donald MacDonald to carry George back to the limber and for Noah Hogg to stand in at the gun.

Captain Ramsay arrived and ordered spherical case to be used. They had been trained to take care with the transport of cartridge and projectiles but extra care was taken by Parky and Xander as they transferred the projectile to Noah, nervous at being thrust into the fray. Keeping his hand firmly over the fuse hole until the last moment the fuse was inserted and loaded into the barrel. Dicky rammed the shot firmly to the base of the barrel, Fin turned the elevating screw until the required trajectory was set, Thomo inserted the quill and Peter set all in motion touching the portfire. Without looking for the effect, Dicky swabbed the barrel, rammed the cartridge and the same procedure followed. Sergeant Webber confirmed the elevation was correct and after three rounds from each of the six guns, the French had disappeared, and the advance was on again.

The winding route of the road gave evidence of the devastating effect of their fire; execution had been dealt on the French battalions, and scores of bodies littered the rocks that had seemed to offer so much protection. The wounds were frightening to the sight of the gunners: faces smashed into unrecognisable lumps of flesh, bodies torn apart, limbs missing or hanging by tendons; the wounded seemed in even worse states, suffering where they lay waiting for a worse fate when the local peasants arrived. Arms outstretched imploring help were ignored. "After what we seen in the villages, they'll get what they deserved." Elijah was in an unforgiving mood.

"Good shooting gunners, saved us many wounds." A cheery rifleman had raised his battered hat in one hand as he looked at some round discs in the other.

"What d'you get?" shouted Bob Halls.

"Took some buttons from the Frenchies' coats, guess what regiment they are?" and without waiting for an answer, "Ninety-fifth, same as us!" He chuckled to himself as other green jackets joined him sharing the same joke and buttons.

The slow advance was interspersed with leading the horses and riding at the walk. "Is this the usual Sarge?" Fin asked.

"Expected them to put up a bigger stand than they have so far. Won't be as easy all of the time. Retreating armies have to slow down the chasing army at some time. We had the same through the mountains to Corunna: contest bridges, passes through the mountains, anywhere that a small compact rearguard can cause damage. Look either side of this road for instance; could have set up guns, used the rocks to create bigger redoubts, then we would have had to make a proper assault and not just fire a few shells as we have."

"D'you think George'll be all right?"

"Sure of it, sore ribs, sore head but he'll be back. Probably having a tea with Martha and Sal!" Fin smiled and wondered how many others would be casualties, or if he would survive to return home.

The shelter of buildings throughout the next village was welcome, the locals even ventured some wine. "Salvador, Salvador!" was their greeting.

"Oi Parky, what they saying?"

"They call us saviours and no wonder after what we've seen. I helped Xander clear next door of an old man, bayoneted through both thighs, sabre cut across his chest, punched in the face and hands stamped on under boots. Left him to die, as if his starving body wasn't enough. When we offered him the few crumbs of biscuit and bread we had, he begged us to give it to the children. Doubt if he will survive."

"D'you see what the peasants did to those wounded Frenchies in the square? They wo're stripped, stabbed, manhood cut off and stuffed in their mouths – they won't be raping anymore!"

"Don't know how the Frenchies behave like we seen?" added Dai Davies.

"You'd be surprised what soldiers of any army get up to after battle, British soldiers have done just as bad."

"No Sarge, surely not."

"When you've been through a bit more than we have, you'll soon see."

The chase was extended next morning as the retreating army had stolen a march and either not halted for the night or halted for a very short time. The Light Dragoons fanned out across different roads searching for the enemy, finding more and more the detritus of a fleeing army: dead and wounded bodies, wagons, carriages, ammunition loosely buried, lame animals useless for their task of carrying the heavier loads, even back-packs and muskets. "Must be getting desperate Thomo, even throwing away weapons. Not expecting to fight then." The guns were split into pairs and followed the cavalry with the intention of slowing the rearguard.

"If it's surviving by running away or dying in a last-man stand, you can see why they get rid of these weapons."

"But that's a gun-carriage, they'll need those in a battle."

"Better to do this than slowing them down even more, then we don't get their gun. We'd do the same, never want our gun to fall into their hands." The halting cavalry brought the pursuit to a standstill.

"What is it Sarge?"

"Now how would I know Davies – we can't see past the horses can we?" A returning dragoon passed on the message that they had found the French and he was going back to get the infantry to follow our road.

Captain Ramsay, who had been allocated number five and six guns, allowed his horse to crop some green shoots at the side of the road as he studied the map unfolded from the sabretache at his side. "Sergeant Webber!"

"Yes sir." He walked his horse to the side of the captain.

"See this river?" pointing to a blue line winding its way across the map. "Only way to cross the river easily is this bridge, Foz de Aronce I think it says." An explosion followed by a rising line of dirty smoke indicated the destruction of the bridge.

"Sounds like the Frenchies are of the same opinion sir."

"Let's have a look." Taking up the reins, he urged his horse along the side of the road followed by his sergeant.

"Good heavens." The captain sat open mouthed, not believing what he saw. "They've left a good part of their army on the wrong side of the bridge."

"Engineers panicked sir?"

"Yes Sergeant I believe you are right." Looking across to the officer commanding the Light Dragoons, the captain asked, "Shall you press those trying to get across?"

"Yes Captain, I believe we shall, might encourage some to throw down their weapons." "I'll bring up the guns and give extra encouragement!" The cavalry spurred into a walk and then trotted towards the bridge. As the two guns unlimbered, safe in the knowledge that they were not going to be shot at, each gunner took in the sight of the funnel neck breaking down the sides of the steep river banks and being swept downstream.

"They in't going to swim that." Elijah was leaning against the left wheel. "What d'you do though? Bridge has gone, you've been

237

left by your countrymen, do you stand and die, surrender or swim for it?"

"Sarge!" Fin called. "Look down there, it is possible to get across – the explosion only destroyed part of the stonework, a man could get across if careful."

"You're right Ross, I'll tell Captain Ramsay." Sergeant Webber returned with orders to fire across the bridge, in the hope that it would deter would be escapees. They steadily worked their gun, throwing shell after shell into the fleeing French, alternating with gun five so that there was no respite.

"Good work, keep it up and be ready to limber at a moment's notice."

"Thank you Captain." Thomo responded. The tramping of feet announced the arrival of the rifles. They passed straight through the guns and headed for the buildings at the near end of the bridge. Dusk fell fast and there was little chance of bringing the French into anything more than an exchange of shots between the skirmishers. Riflemen returned laden with all they could carry; the French had left so quickly that kitchen fires were still burning, soup boiling, wine bottles were unopened and back packs deserted. So much was carried that they even threw the gunners some warm bread, most gratefully received.

The sleep much needed was interrupted by another loud explosion, the French attempting to finish the demolition attempted the day before. "We under attack Fin"

"Don't know Bob, something exploded though, get everyone to the gun." Not having taken their clothes off, it was little time for the team to be ready. Bill Bennett and John Smith came back from their watch duty to report that a bright flash and huge noise came from the bridge but it was too dark to see what had happened. They tried to return to sleep but it was bleary eyed team that stood to arms before dawn. The spreading light across the valley illuminated what had been expected: a better demolition of the central arches, but it also brought the sight of bodies floating in the river. Fin started counting but was interrupted by Thomo, "What d'you reckon Fin, how many?"

"Just counted two hundred bodies trapped by the arches and I haven't got anywhere near across the river."

"How we going to cross the river now?"

"Not on the bridge for a start! But look down there."

Fin was pointing towards a group of green jackets wading into the river. "They're standing!" Fin was stunned. "Thomo, look, they're standing and over halfway across."

"Looks like they're going to get some company." Thomo had noticed a line of French skirmishers making their way down the road towards the bridge. The sudden popping of guns brought them to a halt and Fin searched for the source of the noise. It took him a while but tell-tale puffs of smoke gave away the position of the riflemen protecting their colleagues.

"Without them firing, I couldn't see them Thomo."

"Stopped the Frenchies anyways. Looks like they're coming back across the river."

"So why did so many drown? How come the French didn't know of the ford?"

"Panic I'd guess."

The approach of Sergeant Webber brought the hope of further information. "See they found a ford Sarge, will we be getting down there?"

"Have to be patient Ross – can't get the guns down that slope to the water; engineers will have to help us out."

The waiting took up most of the day and it was only as the sun was casting long shadows through the streets of the town, with the French long gone, that orders to move down to the river were given. They didn't cross till first light, but following the Light Dragoons, the chase resumed. Red-coated troops with white and buff facings followed behind, the trusted green and brown jackets on ahead sandwiched the artillery. The cruellest sight greeted their morning as they came across pack mule after pack mule cut through the hind legs, incapable of movement and suffering greatly. "Would have been better to kill them, poor creatures," the strong accent of the Scot, Donald, muttered, but all agreed. Finding another bridge destroyed, another wait allowed time for searching buildings. Little was found but Bob brought in a French back-pack, displaying a spare shirt, razor, soap, comb, brush but best of all, a stocking full of biscuits and animal skin full of wine.

The noise of larger guns announced the start of the assault; nine pounders from the foot artillery had caught up and began pounding the massed ranks opposite. The explosion of a limber taking a direct hit from the newly arrived guns encouraged the French to vacate the town faster than they might have wished, but the infantry rushed across the pontoons to take possession of the buildings. Sergeant Webber ordered the horses to be led across, as did the cavalry, but as soon as they could, they remounted. A night in a pine forest was followed by a hungry start of the day as no wagons had been allowed to cross the river for fear of slowing the advance. "These generals want to try fightin' on an empty stomach. I bet they have their food provided."

"Yeah, and what about the horses?"

"Stop your grumbling Halls and Campbell! Get ready to move off, there'll be worse than a couple of days without food. Keep your eyes peeled for anything dropped by the Frenchies." Sergeant Webber had withstood worse, but getting across the hunger wasn't easy for man or horse. The tightening of girths and saddle straps took the attention, but day followed day without supplies arriving. Fir woods, oak woods, burned village after burned village presented a sorrowful sight, but at least provided a sack of grain to be ground to flour and baked for bread.

For five days they marched and bivouacked, marched and bivouacked before they were finally given orders to halt and wait for the wagons to catch up. Sergeant Webber instructed Fin and Thomo with a long list of tasks to keep the men occupied. "Don't let them sit and worry about the lack of supplies, keep them busy." The horse furniture was never looking better; leather straps and saddles were spotless, uniforms had been rinsed rather than washed in a swiftly flowing stream and hung out to dry, faces were shaved in hot water freshly boiled and the gun carriage was clean of the mud and grime of previous weeks traversing Portugal. Captain Ramsay was pleased to see the pride in the work and complimented the crew.

As he was doing so, a long line of French prisoners straggled through the town guarded by the Light Dragoons. In the midst two figures stood out: a man wearing a black bicorne, red jacket, green breeches and black calf length boots, all adorned with gold lace was accompanied by a hussar in the usual shako, sky blue dolman and pelisse covered with an abundance of braiding plus white skin tight breeches and boots. Like a candle in a darkened room, all eyes turned on them. "Who are they Captain?" Fin was curious at the perfection of the uniform when all around were covered in dust, dirt and mud.

"Cavalry overran their rearguard and captured the Aide-de-Camp for General Loison. He is a Portuguese and seen to be a traitor; they'll put him on trial and his sentence will be death, no doubt, but that will be the best he gets – if he were to be left in the street at the mercy of the locals, they'd make him suffer. His Hussar attendant, however, now that's a different matter. Take a good look men, notice anything?"

"Ain't been in battle sir!"

"I'd guess you are right gunner?"

"Halls sir."

"Bit small for the cavalry, in't he?" Thomas Hughes added.

"Yes, right again. Now look at the fit of those clothes."

The smile spreading across the captain's face gave a further clue which Thomo solved first: "It's a woman sir!"

"Well done Corporal?"

"Thomson, sir"

"Very observant. Yes that's his woman, a Spanish lady he found."

"What'll happen to her then?"

"I'm sure she'll find her way into another officer's care: British, Portuguese, Spanish... who knows?"

Here, what you lot gawping at?" The dulcet tones of Sal announced the arrival of the long awaited supplies.

"Hey Sal, see that Hoozar over there," pointing at the prisoners. "It's a woman!"

"You been drinking Thomas?" she teased.

"No honest Sal, Captain Ramsay told us."

"Must be true then. P'raps I should get a uniform so I can be close to you!" The swift turn and scolding look from their Captain brought a swifter response from Sal: "Only kiddin' Captain, this ain't no place for a lady!" and she laughed as she got down from the wagon, helping Martha to do likewise.

"Right then, got a fire going, have we?"

"Yes Martha. It's over here, away from the limber and in the shelter of this wall. You're a sight for sore eyes, I can tell you, we haven't received any food for five days!" Elijah led his wife to the fireside and they all set to unloading the wagon with the other gun teams. As the evening darkened, the welcome food seemed the best feast they had ever had.

"Strange how a meat stew can taste so good Thomo."

"You're right there Fin, good company as well though, especially with George back." Thomo raised his voice and lifted his mug in the direction of George Rogers: "Here's to everyone healing as quickly!"

"Amen to that!" was the chorused reply.

Chapter 41

Staying in the same place for a couple of days was a godsend to all; the chance to recuperate, replace the shoes for three horses and enjoy a greater quantity of food lifted spirits before the inevitable pursuit resumed. The same sights greeted them whatever the village names were: houses devastated, roofs gone, set on fire, men and women left dying where they were attacked, even children killed. But then it rained. The cold wind cut through the protection of the cloaks and Fin felt weighed down as they slithered through roads turned to sludge. Once contact was made, the cavalry threatened the flanks, the rifles went forward, chasing the skirmishers from the rearguard, back onto the main body of their army, the guns were brought forward and unlimbered, but more often than not, the French retired before them, destroying bridges where possible, anything to delay the inevitable battle that would come. Trying to sleep was not easy in the open fields, arriving soaking wet, wrapping themselves in blankets that were just as sodden, finding a less wet spot to lie down was the best they could hope for and being on picket duty brought one more tiresome task to lower spirits.

"Where they running to Sarge?"

"Captain Ramsay says it looks like they are headed for Cuidad Rodreigo, guards the way into Spain, or Almeida, fortress town where they can get new supplies and the security of the walls."

"And a dry roof over their heads Sarge!"

"Yes Ross, would be nice on a night like this."

"Or like last night, or the night before or the night before…"

"Yes Ross, but we have to keep the spirits up, can't have the heads dropping. We'll have a fight soon and no use to anyone, a man moping and groaning."

"Not easy when you're soakin' wet, nothing we have keeps you dry," and as an afterthought, "an' the 'orses aren't doing so well neither."

"P'raps tomorrow will be better, was red sky this evening, you know what they say Ross!"

"Yes Sarge, shepherd's delight an' all. Well, I best be off to get Wilky and relieve Bob and Parky."

As they approached the allotted places for duty, Fin soon found Parky. "Where's Bob?"

"He'll be here soon, won't be doing extra time, will he!"

"Not Bob," laughed Wilky, but he didn't appear.

"Right you two, stay here," Fin instructed. "I'll set off this way and return." He walked off into the darkness, counting his steps, he had reached forty-eight when he was challenged by an unfamiliar voice: "Halt, who goes there?"

Fin approached with caution. "Ross, Royal Horse Artillery." He still couldn't make out the face, but recognised the dark green jacket of a rifleman swathed under a blanket hiding a rifle with protective cover wrapped around the firing mechanism.

"Password, Ross of the Artillery."

"Green before red."

"As always Ross, advance friend. What you doing over here...sir?" as he noticed the chevron on the sleeve, indicating that Fin was a Bombardier.

"Lost one of my men, on picket like you."

"Done a runner like 'as he?"

"No not this man, you haven't had trouble from the Frenchies 'ave you?"

"Would you be out 'ere if you didn't have to?"

"Element of surprise?"

"Not likely, too busy running they are."

"Right, I'm going back to my other man. If you find a lost gunner, his name is Bob Halls."

"Right you are sir."

Fin retraced his steps and soon found Wilky and Parky. "Any sign Fin?"

"No. I found a rifleman and he hadn't seen him either. Where the hell is he?" Fin tried to pierce the darkness but the rain obscured anything more than ten paces ahead. "Parky, stay here. Wilky, you come with me."

"Where we goin' Fin?"

"Goin' to find Bob, come on." Fin stepped forward but stopped as Wilky asked another question, "Ain't the Frenchies this way?"

"Course they are, but if he hasn't gone that way and Parky was that way, he has to be this way." They slowly edged forward five paces apart. Fin called in a whisper at regular intervals "Bob"... "Halls"... but no response returned.

243

"Fin, we've come thirty paces."

"Glad you're counting as well Wilky. He has to be nearby surely, Bob wouldn't do a runner." A shot passing overhead had them both crouch and take their pistols from the security of their oiled wrappings. A voice shouted "Halt who goes there?"

"You daft bugger Bob what you shootin' at us for, its Fin and me, where've you been?"

"Password?" came the reply.

"Don't be daft…"

"No Wilky, he's right. Green before red."

"Advance friend." The figure appearing from the gloom was a bedraggled sight. "Where's Parky, haven't seen him for ages? Thought you two creepin' round might have been Frenchies."

"You walked yourself straight to the Frenchies and shot back at our lines, good job you're such a useless shot, went miles over our heads."

"Just a warning shot that was."

"Yeah, likely Bob, and what would you shoot with next, it's only got one barrel?"

"Got me sword."

"Come on you two," interrupted Fin. "Let's get back to Parky your shot will have alarmed him."

As they retraced their steps they were met by Sergeant Major Simons and Sergeant Webber, "What's going on Ross?"

"Halls thought he saw somethin' and gave a warning shot, we were just changing the duties."

"Halls, as admirable as it is to give a warning, what Frenchy is going to be out on a night like this, and if you do fire a warning, why did the bullet come in this direction – landed right next to Sergeant Webber and myself!"

"Bit disorientated sir."

"Next time keep facing the same direction and then you won't put us at risk!" The two senior men laughed and even Bob could see the funny side. As Simons and Webber walked back into camp, Fin took a few steps to one side, "What happened Bob?"

"I don't know Fin, I walked the steps, counting as I went, saw Parky and went back just as we trained but then I missed him so went back and tried again and still missed him."

"You must have been takin' a slightly different angle each time and it took you further and further apart. This mud gives no indication of footprints and the rain covers all signs of landmarks, can't even see the lanterns of the camp." Fin turned, "See, they've disappeared already."

"Ain't goin' to live this down in a hurry am I?"

"We knew you hadn't deserted Bob."

"What, is that what you thought?"

"No, knew you'd be around somewhere. Now get off with Parky. Hope you get some sleep." A slap on a sodden back closed the excitement for the night as Fin and Wilky took their turn on duty.

The rain eased as they set off, only to return with a vengeance by mid-morning. Following the ridge of hills it seemed like a case of follow the horse in front to avoid going off track. Messages passed back from the skirmishers indicated a large formation of French had been found defending yet another bridge. The rifles were sent off to cross at a ford and the cavalry sent to the left, in the hope that they could find their way round the flank. The rain increased, reducing the visibility even more; the sound of rifles could be heard but no French could be seen. An order to prepare to cross the river was received and each gun took its turn to use the same ford as the rifles. Getting into the water proved little problem, but slithering up the far bank created more of a challenge; Dicky and Elijah jumped from the limber to add their weight to the gun wheels, Fin and Thomo took the harness of the lead horses to find a firmer footing. A runner from the direction of the attack requested that the guns prepare to support the right flank as French artillery had been captured; The wheels slithered on the soft surface gouging arcs of mud as the gun was turned in the direction of the, as yet invisible, threat.

"Load with canister!"

"Canister it is, Sarge."

"Who we aiming at Sarge, can't see a thing?"

"Look to the right, messenger said that they were in that direction." The sudden appearance of red-coated infantry walking backwards made all jump to. The red line funnelled through the guns and reformed, followed by pairs of riflemen, including an officer riding a horse with a brown and white spaniel, chasing in and out of the men sniffing the ground here and there. "Cavalry approaching, clear them off and we'll take the gun back from them, howitzer." The sudden thud further to the left announced the arrival of a shell submerged in the sodden ground. The spaniel ran to the fizzing shell, yapping and barking, jumping alarmed as it exploded.

"Daft dog." Muttered Thomo, "How did it survive that?"

"Shell must have been sunk deep into the mud…" started Fin.

"Cavalry!" the shout had come from Dicky, pointing to the emerging horsemen.

"Prepare to fire… Fire!" All six guns erupted, adding to the lack of visibility and within fifteen seconds a second belching of death convinced the remaining cavalry to retreat and saw the infantry advance back into the rain. The dog followed its master back into the fray and the battle was over for the artillery. The rain had increased to torrents but at least they had the compliment of spending the night in the nearby town.

"No rest for the wicked!"

"Who you calling wicked Johnny?"

"No offence Bob, just a manner of speaking! Almost got dry last night in that house. Slept on the floor mind, not a stick of furniture left. And now we're back to this." He raised his eyes heavenwards to send a stream of water down his back.

"April showers boys, tha's what this is!"

"We in April then Sarge?"

"Yeah, five days since."

"And we're the fools for being here!"

"But where else would you be Halls, in trouble at home?"

"Not me Sarge, never get caught!"

"Glad to see you're still in good spirits."

The road was passable but the horses were sinking further and further into the hoof-sucking mess, plenty of boots had been discarded, plucked from the feet of infantrymen fleeing to safety in the French rearguard.

At last the rain ceased and the skies brightened. Orders were given to dismount, a break for both horse and riders. Captain Ramsay approached Sergeant Major Simons and Sergeant Webber; "Into Spain, once we cross this bridge!" He indicated a point on a map neatly folded to provide a view of the immediate surroundings.

"Driven the Frenchies out of Portugal sir?"

"In this part of the country, but don't be too sure, we could be back to the Lines if needed, Sergeant Major."

Sergeant Webber asked, "Is the bridge still there or are we wading across?"

"Cavalry and the Rifles went across earlier so we should keep our feet dry, well less wet!" The captain smiled at his own jest, but swiftly returned to more serious matters: "Orders say that we should be set for a few days in a village not far ahead, chance to dry everything out, and we hope to get the wagons to catch up and have a decent meal again. How are the men faring? How are the injuries mending?"

"Been lucky so far sir, bruises and a few cuts but we've lost no one from gun six. Rogers is back in action, ready to take his place at the gun."

"Good news, Sergeant. The rest of the troop have had similar, only lost a handful to battle wounds, almost all fully manned guns and just as well – not much chance of replacements out here." As he walked away he called back to the two friends, "Keep up the good work Sergeant Major. Sergeant, leave in five minutes."

The change in the billets allocated was a welcome one. "What's this Parky?"

"I do believe it's called a bed Xander."

"Hear that, Parky's cracked a joke!" Bob slapped him on the back, "Got sheets and a pillow an' all!"

"Best we get ourselves cleaned before we use it then."

"Good suggestion Dai, I saw a well and there was a good fire – we could have hot water to shave and wash for a change! Come on Bill, let's get the fire going and we can have a hot drink as well as a wash!" Before they got to the kitchen they could smell the smoke from the fire.

"Gracias señors, es para vos." The lady, head covered in a dark blue scarf, spread her arms towards the fire crackling beneath a pot of bubbling liquid.

"Smells good Bill, what about water, haven't got a clue what she said, need Parky here." Dai turned and shouted for their most educated gunner to come and help. He soon worked out what the lady had offered and arranged for each man to have hot water.

The opportunity to get out of wet clothes at last saw the cottage resembling a laundry. Shirts washed in the same hot water used for shaving hung out on a make-shift line outside, jackets stretched across any available piece of furniture inside, steam was soon rising as the moisture left sodden cloth. Spirits were raised further after they had gratefully eaten the soup and even the routine of tending to the horses seemed less arduous without rain streaming down on them. Fin was brushing down the hind quarters of his Gretschen as Sergeant Webber came to inspect, "Got two admirers Ross." Fin stopped momentarily before realising who the sergeant had indicated.

"Daughters of the house – looks like they were dressed specially to welcome us in their best dress and sky blue ribbons. Don't think they've seen horses so close up Sarge."

"Probably seen a lot they shouldn't have seen though, Frenchies cut a bad path on their retreat. Mind you this village seems to have come off not too bad, roofs still on and not a dead body in the street!" He paused momentarily before continuing, "Real reason I came across was to let you know that the Commissary has got its act together and we should have our wagons arrive later tonight or at least first thing in the morning."

"Will be good to get a better meal than crushed biscuits; mind you lady of the house gave us all a good soup. Go and see if there's any left Sarge."

"I think I'll do just that Ross, could do with something!"

They could hear the wagons squealing down the road before they reached the village and the welcome for Martha and Sal wasn't anything less than expected. The wagon was swiftly unloaded and combining dry clothes with the prospect of bread and meat, the crew soon regained its voice and songs echoed through the buildings. Elijah set the beat, Peter fiddled the lead with Fin and Dicky accompanying on recorder and flute as Sal sang...

"And here's a health to the bird in the bush, Here's a health to the jolly dragoon, For we've tarried all day to drink down the sun, Let us tarry here and drink down the moon."

"We'll drink to that!" cheered Thomas clasping his wife around the waist.

"We would if we had any drink!" chipped in Bob in inimitable fashion.

"Well just look what Sal and I brought you boys!" Martha reached into a box and pulled out four skins sagging under the weight of their contents, "Don't know what it'll taste like but we was assured it was the finest wine!"

"Likely Martha!" "

Well you don't have to have none Elijah." The cheers echoed again as they filled their mugs and even included the host and hostess into the party, oblivious to the words, but empathising with the sentiment, so different from previous soldiers.

Fin took a turn and retraced his step towards Parky whom he met in twenty paces, "All clear your way Parky?"

"Nothing moving, but I thought I heard the hoot of an owl."

"Yeah I heard that too, reminded me of other nights back home."

"Poaching nights?"

"Well, you could say I was in places that I shouldn't have been. Funny thing Parky, during the day I had to work hard on the same land and was for it if I weren't there, then at night when I was there, I was for it for being there!"

"Time and place Fin, time and place. Bit like us training surgeons. We are wanted to cut off limbs and open people up to cure them and then when you try practising on a dead body, there is hell to pay, but how can you operate on some internal organ if you don't know what it looks like in the first place?"

"You weren't one of them grave robbers though Parky?"

"No, not involved in that, but I knew people who used the dead bodies to advance our medicine. This war will take surgery to another level."

"What, because of the injuries."

"Yes Fin, so many get hit by musket balls, cannon balls, swords, lances… and the rest, so surgeons have begun to understand the way the body work so much better."

"A bit different from your best brown paper and vinegar oil then."

"No Fin there's a place for that as well, minor injuries you see, but the major injuries have to be treated in a different way or we will see so many die when they could have been saved."

"That why you're out here Parky?"

"No, no, that's a different reason, private matter Fin."

"We all have our reasons Parky. Right let's be on our way again, see you soon." Fin turned and walked his set course, listening intently for anything untoward but only hearing an occasional grunt, snore or cough. On his return to Parky, they were joined by Sergeant Major Simons checking the pickets.

"All quiet Ross?"

"Yes Sergeant Major."

"You been given a password?"

"No Sergeant Major, we were told there is a line further out, we're just looking after the horses and guns." As Simons began to turn, Fin asked, "How come we get to stay here for a few days? The French aren't anywhere to be seen?"

"Well the rifles tell me that they have been to the walls of Almeida, been taking pot shots at the shepherds herding the cows bold as brass in front of the town. They keep them there as they've no feed in town. More importantly, our great leader, Sir Arthur, has been off to another part of the army near Badajos and so we get to have a bit of a rest before we get going again. Won't be long, that's for sure, can't let the Frenchies get too comfortable can we!"

249

Life had just begun to set itself into a camp-like routine when Captain Ramsay ordered all to be mounted and ready to move again. Martha, Sal and the wagons went south as the guns went further east. Not a Frenchman in sight. Fin tried to take in the surrounding landscape, quite flat, rocky outcrops, one or two attempts to make dry stone walls but in poor repair, occasional trees and the roads in better repair than before. Stopping in one village, the men immediately set about a search for bread and a drink, wine preferably but the lemonade if not, no chance of a tea here. Thomo and Fin were called to meet with all sergeants in front of Captain Bull. "This is Villar del Puerco and we are heading further east and then turning south to the village of Gallegos, only two or three miles hence. We are covering the crossings of the River Agueda. Sir Arthur has returned to the army and so we expect an action soon." He paused to allow the murmur flicker through the group. "Cavalry are up ahead as are the Rifles, they have been as far as Almeida but are falling back on us for support. So far we have acquitted ourselves well but sterner tests are ahead and we have few guns compared to the French. We must conserve our guns, horses and men, we have no replacements nearby. Captains Ross and Ramsay will be designated as responsible for guns three and four, five and six respectively, I will lead guns one and two. We are a troop but may be required to split into smaller units as Sir Arthur demands. This will give you an indication of how short he is for this weapon. Get to your gun teams, we leave when the cavalry escort arrives."

Thomo and Fin relayed what was needed to their team and as the dragoons entered the village square, all gunners mounted as if on review, in unison. Gallegos was slightly larger than previous villages. They encountered infantry and cavalry already established and their billets were cramped compared with previous nights. The mix of red, blue, green, brown and black jackets brought colour to the white-washed buildings and many a local was trying to sell their wares to the gathering throng of soldiers.

Chapter 42

No sooner had the sun started to cast its first shadows of the day than Fin was in the saddle, heading towards the river. All guns unlimbered alongside red coated infantry; one regiment he was told were the 'Guards' regiment. More infantry and cavalry arrived – red jackets with buff facings for the foot sloggers, whereas the cavalry had all blue jackets with bicorne hats alongside those with orange facings and French style shakos – and more green jackets, but they were still the only artillery. A rider came from the direction of the river, wearing an unconventional uniform: green jacket like the rifles but black breeches and boots, bicorne on his head with a waxed cover and long brown coat split at the back to allow cover whilst riding.

A short discussion was followed by orders to limber. Fin, Elijah and Dicky straining to hold the gun as the limber was put into place and Fin could gratefully secure the key to keep the gun attached. The retiring troops were in no hurry to evacuate the field, they took a slow walk across a plain strewn with rocks and isolated trees, and where it reached a stream, becoming more sodden and bog like. Staying to the road, they passed through narrow streets of stone-built buildings, the same stone as seen littering the plain, and approached a large area of woodland to create as comfortable a bivouac as they could. Fires were lit as soon as horses were tethered, but none were permitted to unsaddle. Kettles were soon boiling and the view over the last village passed, directly below them, gave a clear view of the approaching French.

A group of riders reached the crest of the hill, and those who possessed one used telescopes to inspect the enemy. "Thomo!" Fin walked across to the bubbling pot that his friend crouched next to. "That's Sir Arthur up there again, but isn't that the Duke of Richmond, the one we met when we were training?"

Thomo stood and looked up the hill. "I think you're right Fin, and that one with the top hat and umbrella is Picton, real stickler for discipline. Looks a bit shabby against that cavalry officer in his bright jacket and lace all over it."

"Setting up for battle d'you think?"

"Looking at what we have around here," Thomo waved a hand lazily towards the trees, "we need a lot more men to take on the French."

The knot of riders split up and the black coated, top hat wearing figure waved his umbrella, resulting in red coated men with dark green, bright green, yellow, blue and white facings marching down into the narrow streets and disappearing from view. Sergeant Webber approached and ordered the men to bring the guns into positions, ready to open fire over the village. "Where are we Sarge?" asked Bob Halls as he strained with Parky on one wheel while Dicky and Elijah levered the other and Fin, assisted by Thomas and Xander, swivelled the trail.

"Captain Ramsay says it's called Fuentes, looks like we in for a tough day tomorrow, we are stretched very thin at the moment."

"We ain't all the army are we?"

"No Halls, if you could get up that slope, which you can't, you'd see more men spread across the ridge of the countryside, and if you can make out those buildings over there," he twisted to point in the opposite direction, "we have our irregular allies, the guerrillas, looking after our flank."

"Sorry to seem impertinent Sarge, but aren't there a lot of gaps through which the French could simply march?"

"That you are right Parkin, and that's why we have been placed here with the Light Division so we can be called to go anywhere quickly!" The last push of the trail brought the gun into position, buckets with water were set down ready. All tools were unfastened and Dicky had cleared the barrel, ready for the first charge to be rammed home. "What about that tea?"

"Good idea Sarge, the Frenchies ain't that close yet!"

Each morning saw the gun loaded and every gunner ready to fire, each of the following three mornings was welcomed with the same waiting game. They ate their breakfast around the gun, watched the plain ahead, saw French battalions threaten to attack and then attempt to push their way into the granite streets. It was only then that the guns started their devastating fire. Clearing the buildings they bounced ball after ball into the massed ranks, flinging bodies left and right, smashing limbs, crushing heads but still they marched on. Even once they had reached the streets, Fin was busy elevating the gun to create greatest effect. Sergeant Webber viewed the plain through his telescope, relaying information to Fin and other bombardiers correcting the elevation as necessary with a turn of the screw. The French came on, and the noise from the streets below rose to warn of impending attack, but further infantry pushed their way into the streets and evicted the French again and again. Behind the guns, camped in the woods, the green and brown jackets were itching to get to grips with the enemy again but had to await their orders. As evening came and the sunlight reflected from the metal muskets, bayonets and swords of the French across the plain a sudden cheering broke out, turning the heads of all around as brown-jacketed men were raising their shakos on rifles and waving at a rider making his way into the trees. "Long live General Crauford, who takes care of our bellies!" A simple lifting of a hand to his hat and lifting it from his head indicated that the new arrival was pleased with the reception from the Cacadores. The green jackets stood stock still presenting arms as he passed them, their form of salute to a returning hero.

"So that's 'Black Bob' is it?" Thomo and Fin had watched from the edge of the yard set up as their stabling. "Seems those Portuguese love him. Look at them jumping up and down."

"Well he's driven the Frenchies out of Portugal and by all accounts, he has made sure that his division are well looked after."

"So why is he 'Black Bob' Thomo?"

"You don't want to get on his wrong side – caught an officer taking a ride on the back of a private through a river – made them both go back and the officer had to carry the private. He has officers, but they do everythin' any other soldier does: if it's mud, water, scorching heat, freezing snow, the officers lead by example."

"The way it should be isn't it. Can't have some doin' all the work while others pick up the glory."

"Now that's the sort of talk that'll get you into trouble at home, Fin. People like to have structure and knowing your place – if not, you wouldn't be here would you?"

"Too right Thomo, I'll meet him again and have to scurry away won't I."

"It will be different one day. For a start, there won't be so many men left to work back home once the fightin's over!" A slap on the shoulder indicated to Fin that it was more jest than serious but it was true nevertheless.

Sergeant Webber joined them. "Black Bob's here so we'll be in the thick of things tomorrow, he doesn't stay in reserve!"

Chapter 43

"You were right Sarge, looks like they're off already." Fin was pointing to the woodland behind the guns, watching the green, red and brown jacketed infantry making their way through the trees southwards. Sergeant Webber was still scanning the plain with his telescope, resting his elbow on the gun barrel. "Looks like the Frenchies have been busy and changed their attack to the south east. We haven't got too much down that way. The guerrillas are in that village we can see now that the sun has risen, but I don't know who else is in between." His thoughts were interrupted by Captain Ramsay arriving.

"Sergeant Webber, limber up number five and six guns, we're supporting Crauford and the Light Division across the plain. Frenchies have humbugged Sir Arthur and we will not let them break through this part of the line."

"Yes sir!" Webber snapped his telescope shut and turned, proud to see that even before the order was given, the gun teams had started to prepare their gun for limbering.

The noise from the far side of the ridge gave notice that this was no skirmish action. Captain Ramsay raised his hand and ordered the guns to halt. "What the devil are they playing at?"

"Problem sir?" Sergeant Webber had joined the captain at the head of the two guns.

"This fellow has taken his men straight across our path."

An officer in red coat, with the bright green facings buttoned half open, rode down the length of the guns muttering at the men to get out of his way. When he saw Fin, he reined in. "Might have known it would be you skulking in the woods, no use here."

Sergeant Webber had retraced his steps. "Everythin' all right Bombardier?"

"Bombardier my arse, wouldn't give him any responsibility. This man is a useless criminal and would do anything to stay out of harm's way."

"We are following General Crauford to the south sir, Sir Arthur's orders."

"To the sound of those guns," pointing his riding crop towards the crest of the hill, "the sound of battle, that's where you should be headed, not hiding in the woods with those green jackets. I'll show you how to go to war. Line them up and speed of shot, that'll drive these Frenchies back." With a turn of his horse he swept forward, cracking his crop on the nearest redcoat with the same pea-green collar and cuffs demanding that they march faster.

"He don't like you Ross, does he? Get the idea it won't be the last we see of him either!"

"Pity his men though!"

"Fools like that can get you killed quick as a flash."

Their interrupted march continued, quickening the pace to catch the infantry ahead. Shouts were heard before they saw riders ahead: grey-clad men with wide-brimmed hats and long poles ending in glinting points with a red pennant streaming behind. "What are they Fin?"

"Look like knights of old with their lances but no armour."

"That's what they are Ross, Lancers." Sergeant Webber had joined the conversation, "Seen 'em before, Spanish guerrillas, do nasty things to the French if they catch any. They're the same as them that gave the captured orders to Wellington."

A tall rider in a bicorne worn at an angle across his head, jacket adorned in black fur and lace swept past with the riders who were shouting the alarm: "Los franceses, cabellera."

"What's he say Parky?" Dicky shouted from the seat on the limber.

"French cavalry."

"Well, there must be a lot of them to make this many turn and run."

Elijah interrupted from the other seat. "Don't be daft Dicky, listen to that sound…" he cocked an ear up the slope. "In't cavalry, that in't, guns, and plenty of them, must be infantry." The guns were ordered to follow a road that took the incline and as they emerged over the crest, the view was daunting: lines of red-coated infantry were being pushed back by massive blocks of blue coated Frenchman. They had managed to stay out of range, but away to the south, the cavalry they had been warned of, had started their approach.

"There's so many of 'em Thomo."

"And that's why we're here Fin, even up the odds a little."

Captain Ramsay's approach cut their conversation short. "Time to prove that we can be the force that was envisioned when they created flying artillery. We will be supporting the retreat of those infantry with the rifles and cacadores across the plain to our front. It will not be easy as the infantry will have to form square when those cavalry get near but General Crauford has a plan. Anyone play chess?"

"Didn't bring my set with me sir!" the laugh broke the tension, "Halls isn't it?"

"Yes sir." Bob was amazed that the captain had remembered after such their brief meeting days before.

"Ah yes Halls, met you before with that lady hussar, what is a chess board?"

"Set of black and white squares that alternate colours."

"Excellent description. Sergeant Webber, remind me to play a game against Halls after we see off these Frenchies." Sergeant Webber nodded and Fin felt a calm reassurance that in the midst of what was going to be a fight for their lives, his captain had time for the ordinary. "Well, imagine the infantry go onto the white squares, we will be on the black firing as fast as we can until the infantry retire directly across the black onto the next white square, and then we retire to the next black square. We have to buy time to allow the infantry squares to retire and we will have to cut it fine to avoid the Frenchies catching us, but we will not, 'we will not', leave the plain without our guns" They all cheered, eager to follow their captain. "Now see that large outcrop of rocks between the chaps with the buff flag and green flag? That's our first spot to open fire. Without us, the battle will be lost." He turned his horse and galloped to the leading horse, ordering the guns forward as he went.

The descent to the plain was simple enough. Swarms of green and brown jackets had spread themselves ahead using any rocky lump for protection and the French masses were already feeling the effect as officers were tumbled out of their saddles. The horses swung in an arc as the drivers' pressured, one leg and the order to dismount was given. Well drilled, Fin took out the locking key, Thomas and Xander lifted the trail with him as Dicky and Elijah spun the wheels to face the oncoming onslaught. The tools were unstrapped, and the traversing pin was given to Fin to lock in place. Dicky had the sponge and rammer, a water bucket had been placed at the muzzle, Thomo was in place thumb-stall over the vent and Peter was ready with the portfire.

Fin glanced over to Sergeant Webber who had ordered shot and canister to be ready. "This ever been done before Sarge?"

"Plenty of times Ross. In every officer's training manual: 'Retire in open country in square against cavalry.' All foot sloggers train for square."

"No Sarge, have you ever done this jumping from square to square with the Frenchies at you heels."

"Been in plenty of scrapes Ross, but no, never tried this before, but General Craufurd over there is confident." They glanced for an instant towards the general who was encouraging the squares to proceed as quickly as they could.

"He ain't goin' to be stuck out here on his own like us Sarge!"

"And he ain't got a big gun to scare the life out of them Frenchies. Now let's start paying them back!"

The first blast of the gun sent a shower of sparks onto the plain as the gun recoiled. Thomo held his thumb fast to the vent as the wheels were pushed back into place, and Fin traversed slightly to the left at the same time as the barrel was reloaded. The smoke had just cleared as the order to fire came again and Peter touched the quill to ignite the charge. Smoke and flame again belched from the muzzle. Dicky went straight to work with the sponge, banging it once on the side of the piece before thrusting it as far down the barrel as he could. Thomo could feel the increase in pressure as the sponge reached the end of the barrel. Thomas and Xander had been joined by George in relaying the charge and projectiles to the muzzle. Sweat was already trickling clean paths through smoke-dirtied faces. The approaching infantry had momentarily halted as they replaced the gaps blasted through by the shot. Captain Ramsay alone was still on horseback and he bellowed, "Cavalry approaching, shot and canister, then canister alone. Two rounds only, then we'll get out of here." The vibration from the ground warned them of the mass of horses approaching. They fired and the enemy disappeared from view. They fired the canister, a different sound that ricocheted from the stone on the plain. Even at this distance, the screams of men cut through by the scattered balls, horses felled and thrashing to regain their feet could be clearly heard. The limber arrived. Xander and Thomas held the trail as Fin replaced the key. Bob, Bill and John had ridden the horses, leading those for the gunners on foot and all were mounted and away, skirting the side of the red coated square with the buff flag proudly held aloft by a fresh faced boy waving his sword as an encouragement to his men.

The second pair of guns were firing just as before, covering the infantry as they inched their way back to the ridge to the north. As they unlimbered for the second time, Fin called to Thomo, "Going to be a long afternoon!"

"What's that Fin?"

"Going to be a long afternoon with the foot sloggers in squares."

"Can't just leave 'em." There was no time for further discussion as the first ball was loaded and fired, replaced by a second and then doubled with canister, and finally canister alone before they limbered and scooted behind a larger rock to reappear alongside the same infantry who cheered every time the gun spat out its threat of maiming and death to the advancing French. It was only as they mounted and raced back across the plain that they had a chance to see the effect of their work. Bodies of men and horses littered the plain to the south, some had regained their feet and were walking back, most were lying where they had been struck. But still the cavalry came on, only swerving to the side as the guns threatened their advance. Fin wondered how men could continue to attack when so many had already fallen in front of them, but still they did.

Captain Ramsay constantly switched from gun to gun, urging and encouraging the men to redouble their efforts and fire as fast as they could. As he reined in behind Sergeant Webber, he uttered a despairing cry, "Good God man, what the hell are you doing?" Sergeant Webber had never heard his officer so angry; he knew instantly that something was seriously wrong. Following the stare of his captain, he could see a line of redcoats, a line.

"That's the officer who slowed us down earlier, thinks he can take on the French in line, sir."

"He's had them fire a volley but they should have retreated, the other guns aren't in position to cover them." They watched in despair as the line tried to reform into square. "They'll never make it, look!" Captain Ramsay turned to look where his sergeant had spotted French cavalry about to crash into the red coats. As desperately as the men tried to position themselves in their allotted place, as much as the mounted figure screamed his wrath at the men, it was too late, the cavalry were amongst them and red coats were carpeting the ground.

"What the hell was he thinking of? He's just lost over half of his men for no cause! We're getting back across the plain and he has to demonstrate his ineptitude. Just look at them!" Occasional figures had struggled to their feet, blood streaming from their wounds as they tried to close the gap to the now fully formed square, but over a hundred bodies lay where they fell, their shakos little protection against the razor sharp sabres.

Sergeant Webber knew better than to reply but turned to see his own cavalry sweeping the exultant French back the way they came, taking prisoners. "Not a moment too soon. Now don't get carried away, retire for the next charge – we're not home yet." Captain Ramsay realised he had been talking to himself, turned to order both guns to be ready to fire as soon as their own cavalry retired.

Fin had been joined by a pair of riflemen. "Sergeant Knight, isn't it? We met on picket."

"It is... Ross, isn't it?"

"Come to join our game of chess?"

"Don't know about chess Ross, but it's difficult work leap-frogging between rocks, scarpering into a square, coming back to shoot their gaudy officers. You're doing good work with your guns, and even the cavalry have put in a good stint chasing them Hoozars away from that damned fool over there." He looked across at the remnants of the square and spat on the floor. "Just to prove 'e knows best, which he don't! If he'd stayed in square, they wouldn't have been cut up."

Fin interrupted the ranting rifleman, "Here we go again. What about that chap with the white plume, he seems to be the boss." The rifleman took careful aim, resting his rifle on the left wheel.

"That do you?" The rider was no longer in the saddle, but the horse continued to lead the charge.

"Now, it's our turn. Best step to one side, gun has a bit of a kick!"

"Will do."

The shot erupted again and before the rifleman had fired again, the second blast had filled the air with the pungent smell of powder burning. The cavalry veered away to the left sooner than before to reveal the French had been busy bringing their own artillery.

"Those poor buggers are going to have to take more pounding." Sergeant Webber was checking all gunners. "Ross, it's the cavalry and infantry we hit. Don't change aim for the guns. They'll have to make the best of it, can't expect them to take all of our punishment without gettin' some back." A cheer from behind announced the cavalry starting another attack to chase the guns away. Fin peered through the smoke to see frantic gunners limbering their guns to get out of harm's way. He knew just how they felt.

"Buying the footsloggers valuable time, cavalry doing better than usual."

"You not a fan of the cavalry, Sarge?"

"Not that Ross, we all have our value, but they usually charge off and never come back. If they do that today, those guns will play havoc with the squares. So many men, they can't miss!"

"Like us with their masses of cavalry and infantry."

"Just the same and talking of which, here come their cavalry, traverse to the right Ross. Ready to fire." They managed three more rounds before limbering up and retiring yet again. Clothes stuck to sweating bodies, ears rang with the constant battering of explosions. They all needed a drink, but there was no time for that. Tools were unfastened, buckets in place, charge and shot rammed home and they were ready again. "Keep it going, we've got the seventh division home and dry. Now it's just Crauford's men, the cavalry and us!" Seven squares inched further and further across the plain. The cavalry charged the French guns time and again to prevent their access to the easy pickings of the infantry, while the guns kept up a withering fire holding back the tide of French horsemen.

A group of riders led by a man in plain blue had halted on the ridge overlooking the plain. "A masterly manoeuvre sir." A young staff officer was addressing Sir Arthur.

"Masterly indeed. It will be a near run thing, but if anyone can do it, Crauford can. If only all regiments had the same discipline, we'd have the French out of Spain in no time." Glancing through his telescope, he turned to the closest rider. "Whose artillery are they?"

Flicking through the pad of papers, he lifted his head, "Bull's Troop; by divisions, Captain Ramsay has taken his guns to support the manoeuvre."

"Those cavalry in red and green are getting mighty close, we can't afford to lose those guns. If anything delays the limbering, they'll be taken." The matter of fact tone alarmed all who heard, all knew the gravity of the situation. "The battle will hang on Crauford getting back to Fuentes with as many men as possible. The French outnumber us and only this ridge will negate their advantage." He paused, took one more look through his telescope. "The next hour gentlemen will give us the result, if Crauford can pull it off…" An infantry colonel commented, "It will be a desperate hour for England sir."

"Indeed sir!"

Fin continued to work the elevating screw, adjusting minutely to get the maximum effect from each discharge. "Ready, Thomson?"

"Ready Sarge, he we go again."

"Fire!" The ground had become more and more rock strewn, making the gun jump as it recoiled.

"Clear those rocks, don't want a spoke sprung out here!"

Fin traversed the gun as Elijah, Thomas and Xander kicked the rocks to one side. The next cartridge and canister shell were loaded, rammed and quill inserted into the vent. "Fire!"

"One more round Sergeant, double shot."

"Yes Captain."

The cavalry were within musket range, the squares were even firing, very extreme range but made them feel better shooting back!

"Fire!" and within a blink of an eye, "Limber!"

The riders arrived as every time before, horses turned, the trail was raised and Fin took the key.

Horror-struck, he blinked at what should have been six inches of specially shaped metal. "Sarge, key's bent, won't fit and if we can't lock it the gun will bounce free."

Captain Ramsay rode across to the huddle of figures. "Get mounted, French are almost on us."

"Can't lock the gun in place sir, key's bent."

"How the hell did that happen?"

"Must have crushed on the granite beneath."

"Sarge," Fin interrupted, "we can do it. Wait here."

"Ross, where are you going?" All watched as Fin sprinted towards a fallen red coat. He roughly pulled and pushed the lifeless corpse and dashed back. "What were you after Ross? Not anything of value on his body."

"Could be the most valuable piece of metal sir." Fin jammed the bayonet that he had just taken from the dead man through the lock until it jammed, then using the belt that the infantry wore to hold the same, lashed the temporary lock in place as if holding two poles together at home. "Sure this'll work Ross?" Sergeant Webber had bent low enough for only Fin to hear.

"Has to Sarge."

"Mount up!" Captain Ramsay had been watching the horde of green and red jackets racing to capture their prize. "We are not losing this gun. Draw sabres, we'll fight our way out."

Fin bent low over the neck of Gretschen, at the same time pulling the lead horse as fast as he could and urging the team to get to top speed before letting go and drawing his sword. Dicky and Elijah had drawn their pistols and took as careful aim as they could, holding onto the limber one-handed, and being lifted into the air as the wheels struck rock after rock. Fin fended a slashing blow from a Frenchman, much bigger than himself with an enormous brown moustache stretching across a grinning mouth. The force of the blow pushed the hilt down, allowing Fin to swing backwards and create a gap as the Frenchman pulled slightly on the reins. The second attack was more from the rear. Fin twisted as far as he could, trusting that Gretschen would take him to safety. He knew he was only fending the Chasseur off, he was no swordsman compared to his assailant, but he was still alive.

Thomo had mounted on the opposite side of the team and had his own battle as he held his sword across his body, fending off a hussar in light blue jacket trimmed with brown fur. The point of the sword had cut through his left arm and he could feel blood over his wrist. Thomo squeezed his right leg to force Jagger into the Frenchman. The look of surprise on his face confirmed that it was the last thing he had expected. This wasn't how cavalry fought, nor was the hilt smashing his nose, teeth and jaw, unseating him and giving Thomo respite to spur on ahead to help out Bill and Wilky surrounded by five horsemen. Thomo crashed into the back of two hussars in dark blue pelisses, knocking one horse and rider to the floor to be crushed by the following gun while spearing a second through the lower back erupting from the stomach wrenching the sword out of Thomo's hand. Only the sword knot saved the sword, releasing the blade as the body fell under the hooves of other Frenchmen.

Bill had taken a cut across his back, opening his skin to the air, the red stain already spreading. He vainly fended with his sword but a swinging cut left the arm held in the sleeve all but useless. "Wilky!" Thomo screamed. "Take his reins and get the hell out of here, I'll sort these." He swung his sword horizontally making the remaining enemy sway out of range but straight onto the swords of Sergeant Webber and Bob Halls. "Come on!" he roared.

Fin was battling with another green-coated Chasseur trading blows, but this time the Chasseur was reaching across his body allowing Fin to slash down into the left thigh before lifting straight under the left armpit, causing the man to break off the attack. Fin raced low over the neck of his horse, sabre pointing forward at the back of another enemy. He saw the enemy's sabre hit Dai and blood fountain from the wound in his neck. The gunner fell to the ground as the Frenchman turned his attack onto Donald. The two large men slammed swords together with such force that they snapped, Donald let the shortened blade dangle from his wrist and lifted his opponent from the saddle throttling the life from him as he squeezed the throat more and more. He simply dumped the body, lifeless as a rag doll, swaying and then falling from the saddle.

Musket balls started piercing the charging bodies, both French cavalrymen and gunners taking wounds.

Fin suddenly emerged into the open, a few strides to the side of his gun and a cricket pitch away from Captain Ramsay. The loudest cheer of his life greeted the triumphant gunners; every one of the seven squares greeted them as heroes firing at the retiring French cavalry. The gun swung round the rocks and Fin rushed to unlimber. Xander and Thomas lifted the trail as Fin tried to lever out the bayonet, much bent under the pressure of the race against the cavalry. Sergeant Webber brought George to replace Elijah who had lost the use of his right arm. "That was close Sarge."

"Too close, but well done! Now get that barrel cleaned Dickinson, we have to kill some more Frenchmen!"

Different men but same result. Shot and canister poured into the enemy cavalry as the seven squares inched the final stretch to safety, scrambling up a rocky slope to form up facing the valley of the River Turonne. The final shot over, the ride up the road to the ridge allowed gunners to scan their teams for missing friends.

A rider in red jacket and wearing a bicorne arrived alongside Captain Ramsay who took the note and unfolded it: 'A magnificent example of triumphant discipline! Retake your former position and dig in, we retire no further... Wellesley.'

It may have been a lull in firing for them, but the battle still raged in Fuentes. Hordes of blue-coated French infantry pushed their way across the knee deep ford and into the streets, expelling red-coated men from the far side and up the ridge towards Fin and the guns. Fresh battalions of red-coats marched back, down the road and evicted the same blue-coated enemy. Only darkness brought a close to the firing but, all still stood at their posts.

Stragglers from the plain limped up the rocky slope and onto the ridge, searching for their battalion, but no gunners returned. A French officer, taken prisoner in the town, came to Fin's gun: "This place is called the Fountain of Honour in your English; God knows how many friends on both sides have drunk deep from its waters, and with tomorrow's dawn, most likely many more will do so."

"I don't know where God was in this battle, so many friends and enemies dead or wounded." replied Fin. "How d'you come to speak English so well?"

"My father was an Englishman, but my mother was French. I grew up in Bayeux, so fight for the French."

"Is your father alive?"

"No he died many years ago. Were you the crazy men who fight cavalry by pulling guns?"

"Couldn't let you have our guns could we!"

"Perhaps God was on the side of the crazy men today." The officer turned and walked back up the road, leaving Fin to wonder how men could be at each other's throats one moment and then give their parole to amble among those they had been trying to kill.

Sitting round the fire with a plate-full of stew and biscuits was a solemn experience the first time that they had friends missing; even the wine sent from Captain Ramsay did little to ease the loss. "What you doin' here Martha, you should be with Elijah."

"Don't be daft Thomo, he's all right. Got him out of those filthy clothes, washed the slice in his arm and stitched him up meself. Found a nice new shirt in one of those Frenchy back packs and he'll be here in a minute or two. Give him no sympathy mind, he's lucky to have all you fightin' for him. Heroes you are, the lot of you… including those not coming back."

"I hear Bill will lose his arm if he survives the blood loss; terrible slash he got, saw it happen."

"You're right there Thomo, best you go to get that wound seen to, still bleeding by the looks of it."

"I'll be all right."

"Come you over 'ere and get that jacket off, can't have your arm going bad, need every man of you, we do."

Reluctantly, Thomo took his arm out of the blood-stained jacket sleeve to reveal a gash across the elbow joint. "And the shirt Thomo, mustn't let anything get stuck in there. We'll find you a spare." Martha turned the arm to look at the wound. "Not too deep, don't think you'll be needin' stitches – just a good clean wrapping should do the job. Now you sit there while I find some hot water and cloth." She lifted the lid on the pot and ladled the steaming water into a vacant mug rummaging in her own knapsack, slung over her left shoulder, for a strip of cloth. "This'll have you right as rain in no time. Got these strips from helping the surgeons up the road yonder – been busy all day they have." She bent down to start the meticulous process of taking all dirt away from the wound. Sal draped a spare shirt over Thomo's shoulders making him turn his head.

"Better than the one I had Sal."

"Well the previous owner won't be wantin' it anymore – took it from another of those back packs littering the roadsides."

Sergeant Webber with Sergeant Major Simons joined them round the fire. "Well done lads, you paid them back double for the trouble they've caused." He paused to accept a mug offered to him. "Sir Arthur himself has sent his thanks to Captain Ramsay. What was it he said Roger?"

"He said that it was triumph of discipline. We are all proud of what you did. By all accounts none of us should be here!" He stepped across to Fin. "I hear it was your quick thinking that saved the gun Ross."

"Didn't save all of us Sarn't Major!"

"Now listen Ross, what you did today was never done before. Black Bob himself was amazed how few men were lost. If it hadn't been for that fool with the thirty-ninth it would have been a lot less – as green as his facings, that fool."

"He's right Fin, we've all lost someone we cared for, but you saved us to fight another day."

The Sergeant Major raised his mug. "Lived to fight another day – let's drink to Dai and drink to that."

They all stood to look out over the plain littered with bodies. "To Dai, and to live to fight another day!"

Sal, toddler under one arm, her free arm gratefully hugging husband Thomas, began to sing softly:

"Here's a health to the bird in the bush, Here's a health to the bird in the bush, For all birds of a feather, They should always lie together, Let the people say little or much."

Historical Note

Although based on different incidents that really happened, the main characters are all fictitious. There may be coincidences of names but only the Captains Ramsay, Bull, Ross and Webber were officers in the artillery and I have tried to stay as close to their locations as possible. Sir Arthur Wellesley was destined to become the Duke of Wellington, Black Bob, Picton and the Duke of Richmond were all in the Peninsular but Fin, Thomo, Sergeant Webber and the rest are all simply used to tell the story of the amazing dash made by the Royal Horse Artillery at the Battle of Fuentes d'Onoro in May 1811.

There were Menageries in England at the time, some situated in parks, as with the Duke of Richmond and others that travelled the country to amaze the public. Records show that a lion did escape and attack a coach but not quite where it happened in the story.

You can still visit Christchurch in Dorset and hear the story of the 'miraculous beam' as well as taking a tour around the priory, but bear baiting has long since stopped! The Ship is still there as are the buildings mentioned in Fin's escape down river: St Stephen's church (rebuilt), Wimborne Minster, the water mills, bridges... all part of the Dorset landscape that helped Fin evade capture.

There is a 'Great House' not far from Wimborne Minster, a beautiful property that the national trust now cares for. Kingston Lacy is its name and Master Robert (Sir Robert de Lacy) and Lady Ellen could easily have lived there but they didn't!

Both will feature again, an integral part of the stories with many other characters that will reappear as Fin and Thomo take on further adventures in their part to rid Europe of the Corsican Tyrant – Napoleon!

Some of the books I have found useful in researching the story:

British Napoleonic Field Artillery, C E Franklin
Artillery of the Napoleonic Wars, 1792–1815, Kevin F Kiley
Peninsular Eyewitness, Charles Esdaile
The Peninsular Journal, 1808–1817, Sir Charles D'Urban
Following the Drum, F C G Page
The Peninsular War, Andrew Rawson
The Napoleonic Sourcebook, Philip J Haythornthwaite
The Greenhill Napoleonic Wars Data Book, Digby Smith
A British Rifleman, George Simmons
Wellington at War in the Peninsular, Ian C Robertson
A Dorset Soldier, 1790–1869, Eileen Hathaway
The Subaltern, Ian C Robertson
Marching with Wellington, Martin Cassidy
Life in Wellington's Army, Antony Brett-James
Rough Notes of Seven Campaigns, John Spencer Cooper
Inside the Regiment, Carole Divall
Wellington's Army, Sir Charles Oman
An Ensign in the Peninsular War, W F K Thompson
Sea Life in Nelson's Time, John Masefield
Life in Nelson's Navy, Dudley Pope
Uniforms of the Peninsular War, Philip Haythornthwaite, Michael Chappel
The Peninsular War Atlas, Nick Lipscombe